PROCESS
of *Elimination*

PROCESS
of *Elimination*

A THRILLER

Arthur T. Bradley, PhD

SKYHORSE PUBLISHING

PROCESS
of *Elimination*

Skyhorse Publishing books may be purchased in bulk at special discounts for sales promotion, corporate gifts, fund-raising, or educational purposes. Special editions can also be created to specifications. For details, contact the Special Sales Department, Skyhorse Publishing, 307 West 36th Street, 11th Floor, New York, NY 10018 or info@skyhorsepublishing.com.

Skyhorse® and Skyhorse Publishing® are registered trademarks of Skyhorse Publishing, Inc.®, a Delaware corporation.

www.skyhorsepublishing.com

10 9 8 7 6 5 4 3 2 1

Library of Congress Cataloging-in-Publication Data

Bradley, Arthur T.
Process of elimination : a novel/Arthur T. Bradley, Ph.D.
p. cm.
ISBN 978-1-62087-311-3 (hardcover : alk. paper)
1. Presidential candidates–Fiction. 2. Sharpshooters–Fiction.
3. Martial artists–Fiction. 4. Murder–Fiction. 5. United States–Fiction.
I. Title.
PS3602.R342635P76 2012
813'.6–dc23

Printed in the United States of America

For my father, who taught me to fight, and
my mother, who taught me to forgive

Chapter 1

The mouse pointer slid to a bright purple button labeled *Chat Rooms*.

Click.

"Select an existing room, or press the NEW button to create your own," the computer directed.

A long scrolling list of well over one hundred chat rooms appeared across the right half of the screen. To the left were prompts for creating a new cyber room. The cursor moved past a variety of names, including *Popcorn Daddy, XXX Peepshow,* and *Fussy Feminists,* before finally settling on a room titled *Pecos Bill's Bunkhouse.*

Click.

"Enter a personal identity," the voice prompted.

Letters slowly materialized on screen, *Bulls-eye.*

The laptop whirred again for a moment, and then a soft white bulletin board filled the screen. To the right of the board was a register of participants currently in the chat session. Only two names were listed: *Bulls-eye* and *Pecos Bill.* An icon of a small black padlock flashed in the corner of the screen indicating the room was now secure.

    Pecos Bill: Nice to see you, Bulls-eye. How's the roping going?

    Bulls-eye: We have a problem.

    Pecos Bill: 'Course we do. Why else would you be resting your feet in the bunkhouse?

    Bulls-eye: This one requires immediate attention.

Pecos Bill: What's got your drawers in a wad? One of your heifers get free?

Bulls-eye: No. The targets are unaffected, but . . . the map is loose.

There was no response for several seconds.

Pecos Bill: That's as serious as rattlers in the outhouse.

Bulls-eye: It was personal but can still be contained.

Pecos Bill: Sounds like you're losing your edge. Maybe we got the wrong gunslinger for this here rodeo.

Bulls-eye: A bit late for that now.

Pecos Bill: Never too late.

Bulls-eye: I am not replaceable.

Pecos Bill: That a threat?

Bulls-eye: If you try to remove me, this will not end well.

More silence.

Pecos Bill: Perhaps we're going down the wrong path. We've been kemosabes for a long time, you and me. Seen some things that would make lesser men shake in their boots.

Bulls-eye: Yes, we have.

Pecos Bill: What's the varmint's name?

The cursor blinked for a very long time.

Bulls-eye: Maria Sativa.

Pecos Bill: Ah, now the dust is clearing. But why haven't you just ridden out after the dangerous outlaw?

Bulls-eye: I believe she has hidden it. I will need assistance convincing her to reveal its location.

Pecos Bill: Lucky for you, convincing is what I do best. Rest your heels, partner. Pecos Bill's hot on the trail.

Chapter 2

The men moved in unison with the cautious gait of two feudal samurai locked in mortal combat. Each held onto the other's lapel and extended sleeve, connected as if their hands had been sewn into the reinforced cotton uniforms. Their heavy calloused feet scraped across a spongy white canvas mat covering the entire floor of the large open room.

The taller man stood well over six feet, sported an overweight but muscular physique, and looked to be in his late twenties. A crew cut of sandy blond hair topped his head, and his face was perfectly shaven to the point of shining with a glossy cleanness. The large man's opponent, and teacher, was his senior by a handful of years. Thick black hair hung in small sweat-soaked clumps, and a trace of stubble shadowed his chin. The instructor's physique was athletic but dwarfed by comparison.

As with each of his advanced self-defense classes, the teacher followed basic stretching and throwing warm-up exercises with short extemporaneous matches of *randori*, the Japanese term for sparring contests. Victory could be achieved either through voluntary submission, indicated by slapping the mat in resignation, or when an opponent was physically unable to continue because of injury or unconsciousness.

Each match typically lasted only a single minute or two, and the intensity could vary from the slow, careful execution of techniques to a chaotic, vicious competition. For students, the exercise provided a real-world opportunity to test new ideas and develop skills against the master. For the teacher, *randori* allowed him to get an honest measure of each student's ability and progress.

Both men involved in the competition wore traditional judo *gis*, although the mixture of black pants and white tops was considered unconventional by many martial artists and even sacrilegious by a few old-timers. The only difference between the two combatants' uniforms was the belts they wore around their waists. The burly student wore a neat brown cotton belt tied below his belly and hanging low in front of him. The instructor's was black with tattered white stitching fraying the edges, betraying the hundreds of times it had been tied and untied.

Eleven men and three women, all in identical uniforms, surrounded them in a makeshift circle. Kneeling with legs tucked neatly beneath them, each observer sat absolutely still. Only their eyes moved, following the two interlocked figures grappling in the center.

Adam Reece felt his student press the offensive forward and then back, forward and back. The sequence of steps moved them both slowly in a wide clockwise circle. With each movement forward, he felt a firm push, and with each retreat, a controlling tug. Adam was not surprised that Jim Hatchet was using his advantageous size and strength to control their movement. He was also certain that the rough treatment was meant to hide Jim's reluctance to attempt an attack. What a less experienced practitioner might have taken as danger, Adam saw only as a lack of confidence. Without an attack, control alone could not hold.

Forward and back. Adam continued to move with a practiced grace, feeling the flow of the other man's weight and momentum, never resisting, never completely yielding. The careful surrendering of motion kept Jim from finding an opening. Both men understood that without resistance or some form of excessive motion, it was impossible to correctly execute a judo throw. Jim had not yet fully mastered the ability to dislodge a skilled judoka like Adam. Not finding a definitive opportunity, Jim chose instead to be cautious and control their movement, waiting for a pressure, a resistance that he could use to affect his attack. Forward and—

Adam shot ahead. His shoulder struck firmly into Jim's chest, executing *kuzushi*, the breaking of an opponent's balance. He lifted his leg high in front and sliced back with tremendous power, reaping both of Jim's legs out from under him. As he swept backward, Adam screamed a sharp *kia*. The *kia*, a single high-pitched syllable sounding vaguely like the bark of an angry hyena, served three purposes. First and foremost, it helped to focus Adam's energy. It also tightened his abdomen, making him less vulnerable to having the wind knocked out of him. And finally, the guttural shriek could unnerve an opponent, forcing a critical hesitation.

Both men released the other's lapel as Jim was lifted high into the air. After a brief moment of weightless flight, gravity reasserted itself, slamming him back to the padded mat. Jim's free hand struck out in *ukemi*, hitting the mat with a powerful slap and effectively breaking his fall. Adam further helped to minimize the fall by maintaining a supporting grip on Jim's sleeve.

After the throw, Adam stepped back and waited quietly. With a younger student, he would have immediately dropped to the mat and fought for a submissive choke, but with Jim it was unnecessary. Jim was already quite aware of the disadvantage of being thrown on his back. Besides, Jim was skilled on the ground, and Adam was already weary from his previous matches.

In little more than an instant, Jim was back on his feet and facing his teacher. Both men bowed, their hands glued tightly to their sides.

"Thank you, sensei," Jim said, trying to hide a grin.

Adam nodded.

Jim took his cue to return to the surrounding circle of students.

As with every class, Adam had started their instruction by sparring with the students one by one, with Jim being his last fight. He'd managed to win every bout, but the task was getting harder as his students improved. He knew the day would come when one of them would cause him to tap out. Until then, however, he was going to enjoy the title.

"Still the champ," he said, slowly turning around so his students could see just how badly they'd worn him out.

They replied with smiles and supportive nods.

"I remember the good old days when I barely broke a sweat. Either I'm getting older, or you're getting better." Adam pulled at his sweat-soaked *gi* to emphasize the point.

His students sat up straighter, pride stiffening their spines.

"Jim, what was that last throw?"

"*Osoto gari.*" Jim's voice was loud and confident.

"*Osoto gari,*" Adam repeated, the resonant pronunciation betraying his study in Japan, "is recognized as the most dangerous of all judo throws. Imagine what would happen if you threw someone like this on concrete."

He stopped for a moment to survey the students staring up at him. He had worked with them for a long time, most over two years, and now counted each as a friend. "It'd be ugly is all I can say."

His students laughed and looked to one another sharing their satisfaction.

Adam smiled too. He would often mix humor with his training. Such lightness was not to soften the intensity but rather to help the students feel comfortable enough to perform their best. Adam also held to the belief that a friendly environment helped establish a lasting camaraderie—something that gave him great personal satisfaction. He vehemently disagreed with the traditional self-defense teaching methods in which instruction often resembled military drills.

"The other advantage of the throw," he continued, "is that it actually works. Don't ever forget to make that assessment of any technique before trying something on the street. All of you know that Jim is quite capable. I'll bet he's driven everyone here into the mat a few times. Yet even a skilled practitioner can be thrown cleanly with this attack. Other throws might not be as effective against such a capable opponent. This is why we practice *randori*. It allows us to test the effectiveness of our techniques, reminding us that some are purely for sport, others for flashy demonstration, and a few for dropping three-hundred-pound bikers on hot pavement."

Adam could see Jim staring doggedly at him as he spoke. Adam found Jim to be serenely humble at times and yet aggressively certain at others. For a time, the apparent discontinuity had confused him. But as he grew to know the young man, Adam came to realize that Jim valued honesty above all else. When Jim was paid a compliment he felt he didn't deserve, he would likely stare at the ground or otherwise indicate his discomfort with the praise.

In this instance, however, Jim apparently agreed with Adam's assessment of his prowess, and thus held his head high as if to challenge any who might doubt his instructor's words. When Adam had thrown him a moment earlier, Jim had been strangely elated at his pronounced defeat. Adam believed it was the honesty of the defeat that Jim found so exhilarating. Jim was not the commercialized martial artist who liked to wear hats or T-shirts that openly declared his study. Rather, he'd made it known that he was much more comfortable grappling in a pair of old sweats, executing chokes, arm bars, and pressure points. Simply put, he liked to put things to the test. When they worked, he was the first one to stay after class to get it right. And when they didn't, he was the first to lose interest.

Jim Hatchet was Adam's most senior student and had been studying diligently with him for over three years. During their time together, Adam had seen him change from a lumbering, uncoordinated brawler to an agile and dangerous grappler. In addition to possessing a genuine knack for physical combat, Jim also worked as a bouncer at Tiny Titties, a local dance club with a reputation for attracting blue-collar workers who played hard. The daily routine of ejecting obnoxious diesel mechanics had helped him hone his martial skills.

Soon you will be ready for Shodan, *your black belt*, thought Adam.

Jim and the other brown belts were tangible examples of what the training offered. For Adam, they were his "tigers of the dojo." To measure any studio's effectiveness, he believed one had only to observe the brown belts. The senior students served as a measure of the training. Adam was very proud of his advanced students and would have been confident putting them in competition against any group of similarly experienced practitioners.

As with many martial arts studios, several of the diligent students were law enforcement officers. Of his advanced class, seven were peace officers ranging from county deputies to city police. He'd discovered on more than one occasion that his close contact with the community's law enforcement personnel had its benefits, whether it be a friendly slap on the wrist when caught speeding or the occasional release of investigative information.

"Let's work *osoto gari* for a bit, along with the front sacrifice throw *uki waza*," he directed. "This should keep your partner guessing." With Adam's command, the students came alive as they began pairing up with opponents they considered to be their equals.

A soft ring chimed from a small office to the side of the practice area. The dojo was in reality a dilapidated YMCA center that Adam rented weekly for his martial arts club. He suspected the call was likely someone inquiring about the various recreations the center offered. Adam considered letting it ring, but experience told him callers looking for a free dip in the pool could be relentless.

He moved quickly to the edge of the thick practice mat, bowed slightly, and turned to enter a small, carpeted office. The room smelled of mold, undoubtedly due to a persistent leak in the ceiling that the caretakers had never been motivated to correctly fix.

"Kenju-ryu Dojo," Adam said, announcing the school's name as he put the receiver to his ear. He had founded the studio on a combination of *kenpo* karate and judo, hence the name *Kenju*, which translated only as *ten fists*. The careful blend of two dissimilar styles provided a unique study of vicious strikes along with grappling and throwing techniques. Mixed martial arts of this type were quickly growing in popularity after having demonstrated their effectiveness in sports competitions, including the Ultimate Fighting Championship and Pride.

The voice on the other end was familiar but sounded far away. "Hello, I need to speak with Adam Reece." Without pausing, the voice continued, "Will you get him for me? It's important."

"This is Adam. How are you, Elliot?" He wondered why his only sibling would call him at the dojo, especially now after not having heard from him in over a year.

"Oh . . . Adam. I, . . . uh . . ., I didn't realize it was you," Elliot stammered, obviously uncomfortable at not having recognized his brother's voice. "How's everything going? Life treating you okay?"

"Everything's peachy here," Adam answered, knowing the meat of the call would not be long in coming. Elliot rarely wasted time.

"Good, good. Hey, I'm calling for a favor. You know, brother to brother."

"A favor?" Adam was stunned. "What's wrong?" If Elliot was nervous and asking him for a favor, it meant he was in some sort of trouble. Trouble the likes of which a rich hotshot lawyer couldn't easily escape through litigation or payoff. He couldn't recall the last time his brother had asked anyone for anything. Certainly not a favor. Favors implied debt that might later have to be repaid, and Elliot hated the compromising position that indebtedness carried with it.

"Nothing's wrong. I mean, there might be. I'm not sure." Elliot was struggling to strike the right tone. "It's . . . well, you see, I've found myself in sort of a difficult situation. One that I thought a man with your skills might be able to help with."

A man with my skills? Adam grinned, choking back a laugh. Now that was an expression he hadn't heard before. Certainly not from his older brother who had repeatedly told him there was no future in working as a private investigator or a part-time martial arts instructor.

In truth, they both knew Elliot was right. Investigation was a difficult profession as far as money went. Even with occasional security protection services, it left little at the end of the month. This fact, however, never worried Adam. He had enough to eat and pay the rent on time. More than that was gravy. Sure, it tasted good, but if you worried about it too much, you'd forget about the potatoes.

More troubling for Adam was that unlike the ever-dramatic adventures of Hollywood detectives, real-life investigations generally consisted of gathering evidence of adultery for divorce cases or catching an ex-boyfriend in the act of vandalizing his once "true love's" Camaro.

"What's going on?" Adam asked.

"It's a missing person sort of thing." His brother paused for a moment, apparently trying to decide just how much detail to get into on the phone. "Something I offered to do for a friend of a friend."

"You always were the Good Samaritan." Adam made no attempt to hide his sarcasm. Ever since Elliot had returned from Harvard Law School ten years ago, Adam had found his brother to be completely absorbed with his reputation, lucrative law firm, and a close-knit circle of powerful friends. Family trailed a distant fourth and was only there long enough for the Christmas goose to be carved. Elliot hadn't been like that when they were young boys trying to survive in gang-ridden public housing projects, and it hurt Adam to feel so distant from him now. He'd consciously tried a few times to reach out to his older brother, but on every occasion it was not reciprocated.

"I probably had that coming," Elliot winced. "But it's been a while you know."

Adam immediately regretted his words. The phone sat silent for a few seconds while they both considered a great deal more than what had just been said. Never too proud to retreat for the right reasons, he said, "Sorry, bro. What do you need? A little digging around or something?"

"That's *exactly* what I need," his brother said with relief. "Can you come out and do that for me?"

"You need me to come to Denver for this?"

"Yes, I need you here. Phone calls and that sort of thing won't be enough. I need some footwork and maybe a bit of handholding done. You were always good at that sort of thing."

Adam wasn't sure if it was the footwork or the handholding that Elliot was referring to him being good at, but either way it didn't really matter. He said only, "How soon?"

"I booked you a flight from the Knoxville airport, if you want to call that little puddle-jumping hub an airport. First-class, of course." Elliot paused. "Tonight at nine."

From his brother's hesitation, it was obvious that he expected Adam to balk at the short notice. Undoubtedly, Elliot had some well-prepared argument scribbled on a legal pad in front of him. One that likely involved stressing the importance of family helping family when the chips were down. Elliot never went into a negotiation unprepared.

Adam glanced at the wall clock in the office, 6:20 p.m. It was possible to make a nine o'clock flight, but not easy. He looked out through the large office window at his students practicing. It would mean scrubbing class for the night. He hated doing that. His students had come from all over town to study, and he only rented the building one night a week. Losing the week's practice would disappoint everyone.

On the other hand, Elliot wouldn't have asked unless he thought it was important.

"Give me the flight info."

"Great. I really appreciate this. Such short notice and all. You're on a direct flight." He quickly rattled off the flight numbers. "I booked you a room at the Hotel Mona. I'll have a cab waiting for you at the airport."

Adam was not surprised to hear everything had already been arranged. His brother knew him, and that had been Adam's weakness since they were very young. Elliot had always understood, if not shared, Adam's value of family, but had never been above using it to manipulate him for personal gain.

"I'll swing by my place to clean up and then hit the airport," Adam said. "See you in the morning?"

"Great. I'll send my personal assistant for you around nine if that isn't too early. He's a big fellow named John."

"Fine."

"Okay, see you then. And Adam?"

"Yeah."

"Thanks again."

Adam hung up the phone still wondering what exactly Elliot meant by "a missing person sort of thing." Why was his brother going to so much trouble to get him involved? As far as Adam knew, Elliot had never put any stock in his ability as an investigator. Now, words like "a man of your skills" were being tossed about.

Beads of sweat trickled down Adam's face and neck, reminding him just how much had to be done before the flight. He'd have to grab a shower, pack a few clothes, gather a little spending money, and get to the airport all in a little over two hours. Adam stood and moved toward the door to inform his class of the unfortunate change in plans.

Chapter 3

Eight Years Earlier—Eastern Japan

Adam stood at the bottom of a wide set of white granite stairs, hundreds of passengers filing past him in both directions. A bilingual green sign declared that the Shinkansen, or Bullet Train, lay directly ahead. Glancing down at instructions scribbled on a slip of paper, he nodded. After sixteen hours of flying and another two riding the train from the Narita airport, he was nearing the final leg of his journey. He adjusted his shoulder bag and began to ascend.

Japanese men and women moved past him like a school of silver fish, the collective crowd parting and then recombining without thought or effort. A few glanced his way, curiosity in their eyes, but no one gestured or offered greeting. Americans in Tokyo weren't uncommon enough to draw much attention.

At the top of the stairs, a labyrinth of enclosed tunnels spread out before him. Following the signs, Adam navigated his way to Track 22. A large red sign confirmed that the Hayate25 train was next to arrive. He advanced along the landing to where his particular passenger car was to stop. Several Japanese businessmen stood waiting in a tight line, cigarettes hanging lazily from their mouths.

The scene at the train station was unlike anything Adam had ever witnessed. Along the tracks, vendors had set up small markets selling a wide assortment of beautifully packaged foods, newspapers, drinks, and cigarettes. The scene, alive with activity, struck him as a strange subterranean flea market. The Japanese were living up to their reputation for never missing an opportunity for business.

A long white train advanced into the station, looking more like a futuristic ride at Disney World than practical transportation. Passengers spilled out, students and professionals mostly, very few families.

Even with the cars emptied, the line of passengers ahead of Adam did not advance. Within seconds, a team of uniformed women and men politely worked their way through the crowd, pulling behind them a large cart teeming with bottled water, metal canisters, and food. With the precision of a NASCAR team, the group split, half moving into the Shinkansen with small vacuums and cleaning sprays, the other half beginning to replace spent packaging with fresh supplies from the cart. In less than three minutes, the cleaning team stepped from the train and motioned for the passengers to enter.

Riding Green Class in the Shinkansen was the Japanese equivalent of first-class mass transportation. In reality, it offered little more than clean seats and adequate space to lay out one's feet. Normally, Adam wouldn't have spent the extra money to buy Green Class tickets, but he'd been told that finding a seat in the general section could be difficult without reservations. The extra few thousand yen were worth ensuring he would get to his destination without being stuck at the Tokyo train station for countless hours.

Reaching peak speeds of up to 300 kilometers per hour, the ride from Tokyo to Sendai took less than two hours, with the only interruption being an occasional concession cart brought down the aisle by a bright-eyed attendant. Free green tea and wet wipes for refreshing oneself were provided to Green Class passengers. Adam was thankful for both as they helped to erase the fatigue from a few of the miles he'd traveled, albeit only temporarily.

Once the train reached Sendai, he exited and again found himself in a sprawling complex bustling with travelers returning from work. Having moved away from the paths frequented by foreigners, most of the signs were now only in Japanese. He'd studied the language for nearly a year in preparation but could make out only a few kanji characters—restrooms, lockers, information.

The masses were headed down several escalators, so he entered the stream and followed along. At the bottom were dozens of food stands offering an assortment of sweet cakes, fresh fruit, and prepackaged meats. Bright overhead lighting and even brighter young girls' faces helped vendors push their goods. Adam moved past the stands toward several large doors exiting the train station.

As he passed through the automatic doors, he found himself standing on an elevated, concrete walkway above the busy street. The air was cold, and as he'd just stepped from the bright station, the night seemed unusually dark. To his left was a towering hotel, the Metropolitan Sendai, and to his right were several multilevel department stores already closed up for the evening.

The most prominent light came from a huge electronic billboard hanging high on the face of an adjacent building. On its screen was an immense close-up image of a young housewife dancing playfully around her house dusting, seemingly free of life's worries. Adam stood watching the strange scene with fascination until he realized that the show was nothing more than an advertisement for a new, more comfortable tampon. He sighed and turned his attention to the people around him.

He was to meet his teacher, Matsumoto-sensei, at the entrance to Sendai Station, though at the moment no one stood waiting by the doors. Even though they had never met, Adam felt reasonably confident that he'd recognize Matsumoto from photographs he'd pulled off the Web. Matsumoto's judo team had won many awards over the years, and it hadn't been difficult to find newspaper articles featuring the respected master.

His admission to Matsumoto's school was an honor, if not a bit of a mystery. A foreigner might find an avenue to learn judo through the large Kodokan Institute in Tokyo but not through a small, exclusive club like Matsumoto's. Adam had approached Matsumoto through the mail with a single letter detailing his many years of study in Kenpo karate and his desire to learn traditional Japanese judo. He'd been surprised when Matsumoto had extended an offer for him to study in his school. Now, eleven months after their initial exchange, he stood in Japan, searching a crowd of faces for his soon-to-be teacher.

Adam did not possess a supernatural "spidey sense." He did, however, pride himself on having enough situational awareness to know when trouble was nearby. And the three young men huddled in a shadow to one side of Sendai Station's entrance seemed to fit the bill. Unlike the young couples cuddling on stone benches or the masses of businessmen and women coming home from work, these three stood coiled like an angry cobra. Worse yet, they seemed to quickly draw together, readying themselves as he exited the station.

Adam reminded himself that Japan was one of the safest countries in the world, certainly much safer than the United States. Still, they were watching him. For several minutes, he remained in the protective light that spilled out from the station. Nothing happened, and the young men appeared to go back to their business of lurking.

Rationalizing that the uneasy feelings were nothing more than exhaustion mixed with a bit of travel anxiety, Adam finally ventured away from the station to walk among the many benches overlooking a large bus depot. Most were empty, but on a few sat young couples talking quietly. Matsumoto, however, was not among them.

Adam turned, intending to return to their agreed-upon meeting point at the station, when he found himself facing the three hooligans. They had left their shadow and were now blocking his path. Their body language was aggressive, fists clenched, torsos leaning forward. The lead man said something to Adam in Japanese, but the words came too fast for him to understand.

"*Sumimasen, nihongo ga wakarimasen,*" Adam offered an apology, explaining that he didn't understand Japanese.

"I say go back home, *gaijin*," the man said in broken English.

Adam understood Japanese well enough to know that although *gaijin* translated simply as "outside person," it was often used as a racial slur much like how some Americans used *honky* or *cracker.* In a society where being polite was a way of life, insults of this type were not accidental. Preparing for the worst, he lowered his bag to the ground.

"I'm not the one you're looking for," Adam said, feeling a bit like Obi-Wan Kenobi attempting to influence the minds of the less astute Stormtroopers.

The young man seemed surprised. He turned to his two friends, but they offered only shrugs and grins.

Adam adjusted his stance, turning slightly to one side to protect his centerline. *Kenpo* taught that nearly all targets of unarmed combat resided within a few inches of the body's centerline, including the throat, solar plexus, heart, and groin.

"Here's the way I see it," he said. "You three are out for a bit of rough-and-tumble fun. That's cool. But me, I'm not the guy you want to have fun with."

"Why not? You afraid?" the man asked.

Adam gave him a toothy predator's smile. He was tired, perhaps a bit chafed, but fear hadn't set up shop. If he lived for anything, it was for a good fight. "Let me tell you a little story."

"You going to tell us a bedtime story?" the lead punk snickered, gesturing to his buddies.

"Humor me," Adam said. "See, there was this little boy who got a new kitten for his birthday. Each day, he'd pull on the kitten's tail until it screamed and ran away. After watching this, his parents knew they had to make him understand that his actions were cruel. So they took him to the zoo, hoping he would come to appreciate animals. While there, he saw a tremendous Bengal tiger pacing back and forth in an open-air pen. Foolish as he was, the boy climbed over the rail, thinking that he would pull the big cat's tail. What do you suppose happened to him?"

"Tiger ate him," the lead punk replied, some amusement registering on his face.

"Oh yeah," Adam said, straightening himself to appear as large as possible. "You see, you're the horrible little boy, and I'm that hungry tiger. I'd advise that you give it some thought before you decide to pull my tail."

Adam's confidence took the man aback, and for a moment he thought his attempt at avoiding a fight through a little intimidation might have worked. That hope faded, however, when the young man took a step forward. Following his lead, his two cohorts fanned out to encircle their American prey.

Adam brought his hands to the ready, waiting for their attack. Had he been on the streets of Los Angeles confronting a gang of Crips, he would have taken the fight to them. But given that he was in a foreign country where the legalities of who struck first might make the difference, he decided to surrender the advantage of first strike to his enemies.

The three were ill-coordinated, the lead man coming in alone with a short, shuffling sidekick at abdomen level. Adam blocked it aside and stepped forward with a powerful hammer strike to the man's nose. Dark blood splashed out across his face, and he immediately withdrew.

Detecting the second man advancing to his right, Adam pivoted on the ball of his lead foot and sliced out with a spinning backfist. Knuckles hardened from years of hitting *makiwara* boards made contact with the man's temple. The impact was brief but devastating, sending him spiraling to the pavement like a tranquilized animal.

The third man grabbed Adam from behind, pulling hard at his shoulders.

Adam cross-stepped away and dropped down with a slicing elbow over the top of his opponent's grip. With his entire body weight behind the strike, it was easy enough to tear free. He immediately shuffled forward and caught his opponent under the chin with an upward elbow strike, followed by an eagle claw to his eyes. The rapid succession of strikes sent the young man stumbling backward where he finally tripped over a stone bench and fell to his butt. He made a halfhearted effort to stand but quickly decided against it.

Adam turned back to face the lead man. Surprisingly, he had chosen not to reengage and instead was standing several yards away nursing his mangled nose. Adam considered advancing and finishing him, but decided against it. He lowered his guard and stood straight.

"We done?" he asked, a little disappointed at how easy it had been. These boys hadn't been serious.

The lead punk said nothing, choosing instead to look past him.

Adam whirled, fearing that one of the others might have managed to slip in behind him. Instead, he saw a squat middle-aged man approaching. He wore the same dark suit as countless other Japanese businessmen but walked with a distinctive gait—hips forward, shoulders broad and square. For a moment, Adam thought he might attack, but the man walked past without paying him any attention. He moved to the young assailants, helping each to his feet, dusting them off affectionately like a father might do for his son after losing a baseball game.

"Friends of yours?" Adam asked.

The stranger did not answer.

The three young men straightened and offered a deep bow to the older man. He returned the bow, although it was not as pronounced as theirs. Apparently dismissed, the three moved off into the darkness, mumbling complaints to one another.

"Matsumoto-sensei, I presume." Adam said, finally making the connection.

The man turned to face him. "*Hai*," he confirmed.

"So, did I pass your test? I'm assuming that's what this was."

Matsumoto moved very close to Adam, his breath ripe with the smell of sushi. "No, Cowboy, you failed."

* * *

Adam jerked awake. The airplane's cabin was dark, save for a few overhead lights used for thumbing through the glossy pages of duty-free magazines. He turned to the window and slid up the plastic shade, looking out at a broad wing and flashing marker lights. The dream was already fading, but Adam could still hear his teacher's first words, "No, Cowboy, you failed."

He wondered why the dream had come to him after all this time. Had it been about anything else, he might have dismissed it as simple reminder—the new trip stirring up memories of a previous journey. But Adam watched as his hands began to tremble, unforgettable images manifesting themselves irrespective of their owner's wishes.

Nothing about Matsumoto-sensei was to be taken without proper consideration. He was a man of great power and even greater mystery. There was more to his sudden reappearance in a dream than simple coincidence. Adam's teacher had come to him for a reason. A reason he had yet to understand.

Chapter 4

Charles Benedict Morgan straightened a large stack of yellow billing receipts. Looking about the empty hotel lobby and reception desk, he shook his head with disgust.

Every time I am away for a day or two, this place falls into disarray, he thought.

Grabbing an already-damp dust rag, he went through a long established ritual of first polishing the counter, then the computer, and finally the surface of a large high-backed leather swivel chair. Once satisfied with his straightening, he pulled a carpet brush from under the counter and rolled it slowly across the dense green carpet covering the area behind the check-in counter.

This is what it's come to. My entire life has led up to this. Chasing lint across the carpet. He stopped, self-pity suddenly swimming through his belly like a giant tapeworm. The creature was always hungry, but at night, it was particularly insatiable.

He let go of the brush and looked at his hands. They were soft and starting to show their age. "The hands of a surgeon. That's what my mother used to say." She'd had high hopes, God rest her soul.

He closed his eyes and sighed again. His depression had awoken with the urgency of a bear pulling itself from hibernation. It was feeding on him. Feeding on any modicum of self-worth he had left.

So do something . . . anything. Walk out the door of this prison that's held you for nearly twenty years. Start a new life. Chase the sun and surf at some faraway paradise.

But he wouldn't do it, and he didn't know why. It wasn't the money. Frugality had been passed down from his father like an old stopwatch. He had enough savings to live out his days sipping mai tais and watching suntanned cabana boys. *Why then? What am I waiting for?* He didn't have an answer. Could it be that he actually enjoyed serving as an unimportant backdrop in life? That thought frightened him more than any other.

The chime on the outer set of doors sounded, indicating the arrival of a guest. The concierge quickly slipped the brush back away, smoothed his pencil thin mustache, and straightened his nearly twenty-year-old red insignia jacket.

It is important to present oneself as neat and professional when providing service to our patrons. He shook his head. *The hands of a surgeon . . . that's what my mother used to say.*

* * *

Adam felt uneasy as he pushed through the heavy glass doors of the Hotel Mona. The lobby was much more lavish than the roadside motels that he was accustomed to. Large squares of spotless pale green tile covered the floor, with intermittent black tiles inlaid to create what he took to be a suggestively erotic pattern. Small, wall-mounted flood lamps cast soft shadows across the orange-, green-, and yellow-painted walls. An assortment of neo-deco paintings lined the lobby, most with barely distinguishable splashes of colorful paint. Several antique couches and coordinated chairs were collected around a long glass reading table. A small, complimentary wine bar and a roaring gas-powered fireplace completed the yacht-club ambiance.

"Might I help you, sir?" a sharply dressed attendant asked, his chin slightly tilted up with a stiff stateliness.

The clerk looked to be nearing sixty, although he still appeared quite alert and attentive, if not a bit gaunt. Adam was pleasantly surprised by the man's respectful tone, since he was certain the late-night plane ride had left him more than a bit disheveled. He wouldn't have admitted it to anyone else, but he always felt a bit uncomfortable in places of money.

"I believe I have a reservation," Adam replied, smiling as he approached the counter.

"Your name, sir?" The clerk moved to stand in front of a computer keyboard still wet from having been recently wiped down.

"Reece. Adam Reece."

The man clicked at the terminal for a moment before looking up. "Yes, Mr. Reece, I have it here. And I see the arrangements have already been taken care of. It says you will be staying with us for exactly one week."

A week? Could the circumstances Elliot hinted at really require a full week? Probably not, Adam concluded. His brother was likely playing it safe by reserving the room just in case. Hotels such as the Mona could fill up suddenly with the arrival of a convention or business meeting.

"A week sounds about right, although I may be leaving sooner."

"Very good, sir." The man removed a plastic key card from a large stack and swiped it through a programmer on the counter. A green light flashed on the device, and he handed the card to Adam. "Here you go. You're in one of our finest suites. I hope you find it to your liking," the clerk said with a practiced smile. "Oh, and I have a package for you, sir."

"Oh?"

The clerk handed Adam a sealed manila envelope with his name printed neatly on the front. There was no return address.

"Who left it?"

"I'm sorry. I wouldn't know, sir."

Adam nodded, picked up his large black duffel bag, and moved farther into the lobby.

As he neared the elevators, Adam stopped and turned back to study the hotel clerk. The man was already busy sorting a stack of receipts and didn't appear to notice the sudden scrutiny. The Mona was going to be Adam's home for a week, and during that time, who knew what could happen. Experience had taught that it was often prudent to have a friend, or better yet, a sentry. Adam slowly returned to the check-in counter.

The attendant looked up surprised. "Sir?"

Adam relaxed his posture, leaning lightly on the counter. He sized up the clerk as one might a bartender when deciding if he was worthy of drunken soul spilling. "Would you indulge me for a minute, Charles?" he asked, noting the man's nametag.

"Certainly, sir."

"You see, when I come to a new place, I find I'm always better off if I have a point man. You know, someone who really understands a guest's needs and can handle the challenge of all my little nuances."

He had the clerk's undivided attention.

"This can include anything from reminding the maid not to fold down the bed, to keeping me informed of any arriving messages or inquiries, to dropping a morning paper outside the door. Now I know what you're thinking," Adam said with surrendering hands. "All this sounds like pretty trivial stuff. But trivial or not, it would make my stay so much more remarkable. Do you know where I'm coming from, Charles?"

"Oh, I do. I do," Charles emphatically agreed.

"I couldn't be more delighted," Adam said, patting him on the shoulder. "I know people, and I understood right away you were just the sort of person who enjoys this sort of challenge. Am I right?" he asked with a rich man's smile.

The clerk straightened. "Consider me at your service, Mr. Reece."

"Thank you, Charles. I'll do just that."

* * *

A few minutes later, Adam flopped down on a yellow leather sofa in a small meeting area of his three-room suite. The conference area was suited to business travelers, consisting of four chairs, a handsome oak table, a speakerphone, and the sofa on which he now rested.

From where he sat, he could see the tall wood pillars of a king-size rice bed, an antique bedside table, and a tremendous armoire that looked older than he was, all peeking out of the adjacent bedroom. He felt sure that if he peered into the bathroom, he would find a spotless, ornate commode, white porcelain claw-foot tub, and matching pedestal sink.

"Not that different from a Motel 6," he said, leaning back into the soft leather and closing his eyes. A turbulent flight that offered more white knuckles than peanuts had left Adam tired and sluggish. It felt refreshing just to be motionless.

After a brief moment of calming silence, he turned his attention to the envelope. He carefully tore the flap open and tipped out its contents. A small note, a newspaper clipping, and a wallet-sized photo fell into his lap. He double-checked the envelope, but that was all there was. He was surprised to see that his brother had handwritten the note himself. The situation was evidently sensitive enough that involving a gossiping secretary had not been an option.

Adam,

I thought this article might give you a little insight into what I need help with. Maria was an acquaintance (more than that at one time), and I am concerned for her safety. Her sister came to me a couple of days ago asking for help.

Looking forward to seeing you,

Elliot Reece

Adam was amused that his brother had signed his last name. In the past few years, Elliot had become increasingly formal. Impersonal, really.

He looked next at the newspaper clipping, which was no more than a couple of inches in size.

Police Report No Foul Play in Missing Person's Case

Maria Elizabeth Sativa, age 28, was reported missing several weeks ago. Police reports indicate that her 1998 Buick LeSabre and Wilkeshire apartment on East Broadway were both searched with no signs of foul play discovered. Ms. Sativa 'worked as the founder of a small Denver-based company, Professional Services. Anyone with knowledge of her whereabouts is asked to call Detective Carter of the Denver Police Department. A reward is being offered by an anonymous party for information leading to the discovery of her whereabouts.

He turned his attention to the photo. It was only a head shot, but from it, he could see that Maria was quite striking. Long, curly black hair, rich olive skin, and dark, alluring eyes all worked together to give her a refined sensuality. The photo was professional, the kind you couldn't get at a Sears one-hour photo shoot. Which meant Maria either had entirely too much spare change lying around, or more likely, that she had done some modeling in her past.

Adam glanced back at his brother's note. He wondered at the words "an acquaintance (more than that at one time)." Were they lovers? After all, his brother was single, and it was possible that a successful man like Elliot might attract a woman as beautiful as Maria.

But she just didn't strike Adam as his brother's type. Maria was glitzy, sexy in an experienced way. He envisioned his brother being drawn to a more intelligent, articulate woman, one that might offer nights filled with stimulating conversations about the latest biography they were reading in their book of the month club. This woman was something else altogether. She radiated sex, and from the way she held herself, Adam believed she did so intentionally.

"Maybe I don't know you as well as I thought, big brother."

He looked at the article again. "Professional Services," he read aloud. That sounded like either a headhunter agency or an escort service.

"Let's assume the more interesting of the two," he began. "Why has my brother spent his time and money bringing me out here to find a missing high-class hooker? Someone whom he was evidently involved with some time ago. What are the possibilities? Does she have something on him? Hmm . . ." Could Maria have been trying to blackmail Elliot? But blackmail to whom? Elliot had never been married. His partners then? Perhaps, but doubtful. As Adam understood it, Elliot was the undisputed top dog at his firm. A woman as attractive as Maria would probably bring more congratulatory pats on the back than calls for him to go to confession.

For now, it seemed more likely that Elliot held some genuine concern for Maria. Does he love her? Had she scorned him and then disappeared? Perhaps to escape him? Even as tired as he was, Adam had difficulty envisioning Elliot as a stalker. Stalking took way too much emotional commitment.

There weren't enough facts to narrow in on the truth, and Adam was tiring of the guesswork. Only his brother could shed light on the specifics of why he was here. Curiosity having been peaked, he considered calling Elliot. A quick check of his watch revealed that it was just past midnight.

Too late to bother with tonight, he concluded.

After another moment of studying Maria Sativa's photo, he put everything back into the envelope and began preparing for some much-needed rest.

* * *

Elliot Reece shifted nervously on the handmade Italian leather recliner. A call from the front lobby had just informed him that Adam and John were on their way up. For a reason he couldn't fully understand, or possibly just didn't want to admit, the thought of his brother coming to his office disturbed him.

Perhaps it was his uncertainty about what to tell Adam. The situation with Maria was after all a delicate one. It might not be necessary to reveal their relationship in all its sordid detail. Adam could be judgmental at times, and with Maria, he might well go into full self-righteousness mode. And if that happened, it would quickly spin into something destructive. For Elliot, confrontation was to be avoided at all costs.

Though the circumstances surrounding Maria could easily be blamed for his discomfort, Elliot was candid enough to admit that it was more than his brother's probable condemnation that weighed on him. There was the residual tension from when they had last parted. Words had been said on both sides that couldn't be unsaid.

What was it he'd called Adam? An *underachiever*. Ah yes, there it was. The question of success, the chink in his brother's otherwise impregnable armor. Elliot consoled himself that his criticism wasn't meant to be personal, that it was simply the lawyer in him talking. Always searching for his opponent's weakness; always willing to expose it.

Since then, he'd felt a pressing need to apologize to his brother, to right the wrong. Ego, or perhaps simple shame, prevented the apology from ever materializing. For a time after their fight, Elliot held to the belief that he'd said only the truth, and one should never be ashamed or have to offer recompense for truth. But after many months without contact from Adam, the guilt from causing their estrangement had grown as weighty as a morning hangover.

Elliot was the first to admit that there were already too many demons in his psyche. Demons that each contributed their own little torturous pain. All for the purpose of robbing him of rest. To allow another fiend to set root was insufferable. Elliot had to fix things. But how? He waited, sure that an opportunity would eventually present itself.

Then, as if a godsend, it had. The appearance of Maria's sister, Lara, had set things in motion. It was simply too perfect to pass up. By putting the two together, he could empower his brother, and perhaps even find favor in the eyes of a beautiful woman—something that might lead to its own interesting rewards.

Even with the newfound plan to make things right now underway, however, guilt still weighed in his gut like a pound of shot. Undeniable, soul-haunting shame that couldn't be righted by simple fortuitous opportunity. He knew full well the cause but wouldn't allow it to enter his mind.

Only as he subconsciously acknowledged a dingy, yellowed scarf hanging from a small statue near his desk did a single uninvited name claw its way through. *Jiro Tanaka.* The walls had heard the whisper of his sin many times, the very evil now soaked into their plaster. And with the name came a profound understanding of his discomfort at having Adam in his office. His brother possessed an unnatural sense at times. Surely not logic, something else. A supernatural empathy. An ability to discover emotional secrets. Deep in his belly, Elliot feared that

Adam had only to place a single hand on anything in the room, and all would be known. Every unscrupulous deal. Every tearful plea. Even *it*, his unforgivable sin.

"He's here for Maria," Elliot said aloud, his voice breaking with the words. "Stop it, damn it. Just stop it." He found it strange that words of control always sounded as if someone else were saying them. Some alter ego who was unencumbered by his dark past.

He took a deep breath and forced himself to focus on the issue at hand. "What do I tell him about Maria? If I tell him too much, he will try to shame me. Shame I may well deserve but cannot tolerate. And if I tell him too little, he will resent my lack of candor. Besides, without enough information he might not find her." *But then again, would that be so bad? Do I really even want Maria found?* He sat quietly for a moment, mulling over the question.

Elliot had understood for some time that his mental health was unusually sensitive to the levels of stress he encountered. He admitted the weakness to absolutely no one, certainly not to his law partners. Popular sentiment about lawyers' unethical attitudes might be characterized with worn out clichés, but that didn't make them any less true. His partners were as bloodthirsty as Ahab hunting his leviathan.

To combat his self-acknowledged weakness, Elliot worked diligently to keep his life carefully organized and free of stress. He hired excellent assistants who could resolve issues competently and with only minor intervention required on his part. This left him free to pursue more intellectual pursuits, including the study of history and language. Following the advice of a therapist he'd visited for a short time after college, he also practiced breathing exercises when he found himself becoming irrationally anxious. He was nearing that point now.

"What I tell Adam is obvious," he said, taking in a deep, calming breath. "I must tell him everything that will help him in the investigation but offer nothing additional. I will give facts scrubbed of details."

Secrets would remain unspoken. Like the complete control that Maria had slowly taken over him. Or the disturbing discovery that sex, which had been at times unquestionably perverse, was enough to keep him satisfied in a relationship. Worst of all was the realization that, with her departure, he had become emotionally dead. He closed his eyes, seeking comfort in the dark, but instead saw a bruised and bloody body lying on a wet road. *No!* Jolts of panic surged through his veins.

Elliot opened his eyes and quickly scanned the room, concentrating on artifacts and baubles. Forcing darker images from his mind. With a few deep breaths he was back in control. He nodded tiredly. There was no relief from his suffering. Not today, not ever.

Some things are unsolvable. That same thought had played in his mind a thousand times before. *Some things are unsolvable . . . even for me.* It was particularly humbling because he had always prided himself on possessing the ability to solve problems. Analyzing and strategizing were as much his forte today as they had been when he was a child studying the chessboard. He could quickly push aside useless pieces of information and map a pathway to success.

He leaned forward and swung a suspended stainless steel ball that was part of a small office novelty on his desk. The ball clacked lightly against another, passing along the momentum until it forced a final ball to move away from the symmetric group. The ball swung in a returning pendulum arc, and the process continued in the other direction. He watched the balls clack back and forth as they moved from side to side. Oddly, he found solace in the rhythm.

Life is much like this simple toy, he thought. *Once a motion has begun, a countless string of reactions will follow. The only way to stop the motion is to wait until all the ripples have dampened themselves out.*

He suspected that by now Adam was nearing his floor, perhaps even exiting the elevator. *My brother, do I even know him anymore? Have I ever really known him?*

All his life, Elliot had felt a unique kinship with his only brother. This affinity was not to say they were alike. Little could be further from the truth. They were brothers in every sense of the word, but no less than Cain and Abel, they had been created from two dissimilar molds. Such differences had become apparent when they had been barely old enough to walk. Throughout the years, those distinctions had grown more acute.

Adam was a tough guy, someone always looking to right the wrongs of the world. Street-smart but not educated beyond high school. Elliot, on the other hand, was the brilliant chess player who had read historical biographies at age six, graduated summa cum laude from Harvard, and founded one of Denver's most lucrative law firms.

But they were different beyond just the intellectual. His brother was confident and at times sanctimonious. While Elliot was a calm, retrospective man who considered options and approaches before rushing headlong into something. And though he felt certain that Adam believed him to be arrogant, such was not truly the case. Elliot admitted that it was a persona he often put forward when they were together, but in this moment of self-reflection, he also knew that it stemmed from his own lack of self-esteem. Despite his words or condescending attitude to the contrary, he had a profound measure of respect for his brother. Not for his intelligence or success but for his raw strength. A strength he had felt completely devoid of for a very long time.

Elliot closed his eyes and remembered the first time he had seen his brother in such a light. They were only eight and seven respectively, a very young age for an older brother to realize his sibling was "more of a man" than he could ever be.

It all began when Elliot had committed the unforgivable childhood crime of noticing Patty Kemp. Her golden curls and button nose were irresistible, and he'd made the mistake of mentioning to Patty that she had the shiniest hair of any girl in the entire school. She'd accepted the compliment with appreciative giggles, giving Elliot a smile he would forever treasure.

Little did Elliot know that Martin Barber had overheard his words and promptly reported them to their elementary school gang leader, Jerry Bacha. Ah, Jerry Bacha, now he was a piece of work. Having flunked third grade two years in a row, he was larger and meaner than anyone else in the grade, maybe anyone in the entire school. People got out of Jerry Bacha's way. The fact that he regularly gathered with other degenerates behind the school building to inhale gold flake paint further enhanced his notoriety. Rumor had it he'd even tried to rob a local gas station with a kitchen knife.

Later that infamous afternoon, as Elliot and Adam walked home from school along their normal alley-weaving route, they heard shouting behind them. Looking back, they saw Jerry Bacha, Martin Barber, and two other prepubescent henchmen running their way.

Elliot stood paralyzed somewhere between shock and denial, unsure of what he or Adam had done to bring on the wrath of the Bacha clan. It took only an instant for him to recall his comment about Patty's curls. Everyone knew that Bacha had laid claim to Patty. No matter that she hadn't yet been swept away by his many charms. But when did details matter in love? No other boy in her class would pay her the slightest attention due to the ever-present danger Bacha and his bullies posed.

Quickly turning to Adam, Elliot yelled, "Run home as fast as you can!" There was no way that both could possibly escape the crowd that was quickly approaching. Elliot would have to take a beating, but instinctively, he wanted his younger brother to get to safety.

Adam stood confused, looking to Elliot and then back at the bullies who were quickly approaching. Fear struck at him and he bolted ahead.

After only a few steps, however, he stopped and turned back to face his brother. His jaw was set, his eyes narrow with determination.

Elliot grew angry. "Go on!" he said, frantically stabbing toward the direction of their house with his finger. "What are you waiting for? Go!"

Adam frowned at his brother's words, but said nothing, only shaking his head as resolutely as any seven-year old could.

Confused, Elliot dropped into silence, and then in a moment of understanding, understood why Adam had stopped. Their father, a masculine Vietnam-era marine, had recently shared with his sons some very relevant parental words of warning. He'd told them "never come home alone." He went on to explain how a family has nothing if it doesn't have loyalty. Regardless of how bad the situation, he expected Elliot and Adam to stick up for each other. Though both brothers had nodded their solemn pledge, Elliot had interpreted his father's words as mere bravado. Adam, on the other hand, had apparently taken his oath as a heartfelt pledge.

Elliot shook the memory of his father's words out of his head. There was no more time to convince Adam to run away. He turned to face Jerry Bacha, sure that this was going to be a most humiliating and painful experience.

The boys quickly circled Elliot and Adam like a pack of bloodthirsty wolves. Bacha held an old broomstick in both hands. "Elliot, I heard you been messing with my girl," he said, spinning the stick menacingly.

Elliot tried to talk his way out of a situation he felt sure was not open to negotiation. "I haven't done anything to Patty. We're just friends."

"He's lying, Jerry," Martin Barber said. "I even heard him bragging about how he was going to kick your ass."

"That's not true!" Elliot said, glaring at Martin.

It was what happened next that Elliot would never forget. Adam approached Bacha and stared up at the boy who stood a head taller than him.

"You got something to say, pip-squeak?" Bacha asked.

"Nope," Adam answered, a strange calmness in his voice. "You're wanting to fight. So let's fight." He dove forward, grabbing Bacha's legs and dragging him down to the ground.

The other boys stood stunned as Adam and Bacha rolled around on the gravel roadway, fists flying, the broomstick rolling away harmlessly. When Martin realized things weren't going as well as they should have been for their fearless leader, he moved in to help. Instinctively, Elliot stepped between them. Martin threw the first punch, but it did little more than turn the fight into a raucous brawl. Before long, all six boys were thrashing about, kicking and screaming.

In the end, it was Adam who had determined the outcome. He fought with surprising ferocity, gouging eyes, biting, choking, showing absolutely no restraint. For those few minutes, he'd become a vicious pit bull driven only by the taste of blood. The older boys, although larger and stronger, quickly found themselves unable to mentally cope with his willingness, almost eagerness, to inflict pain.

Between the two of them, Elliot and Adam had managed to send Jerry Bacha, Martin Barber, and the other two browbeats home crying, their hands cupping bloody lips and swollen eyes. Both brothers had taken a few shots, but neither of them had given ground. And though they were both very proud of their accomplishment, Elliot's heart weighed heavy with a profound understanding.

As sickening as it made him feel, Elliot knew that if he'd been in his brother's shoes, he would never have looked back.

* * *

John Murphy, the driver sent to pick up Adam from the hotel, now ushered him out of the elevator as it opened onto the eleventh floor of the Denver Financial Services building. Adam had noticed that a sign in the lobby proclaimed the law offices of Reece, Weismann, and Garner occupied floors nine through eleven.

He found it particularly amusing that John looked more like the right-hand man of a powerful mafioso than the assistant to a corporate lawyer. His high-priced tweed suit bunched at both arms around obvious biceps, and the back of the jacket had the familiar bodybuilder wrinkle indicating the immense sprawl of his latissimus dorsi. Adam wondered if John might in fact be more than just Elliot's "personal assistant." If such were the case, it begged a very basic question: Why would his brother need muscle like big John? He filed away the inconsistency.

"He's just ahead through the glass doors," John said, gesturing with a meaty finger twice the size of Adam's big toe.

Adam saw that the floor was centrally divided by two crossing corridors. A brass plate on the wall informed him that Weismann's office was to the right, Garner's to the left, and his brother's directly ahead. Several small offices, all alive with activity, were to the immediate left of the elevator, and the men's and women's lavatories could be seen slightly down the hallway.

The walls were brightly lit with contemporary track lighting set to carefully predetermined angles, the floor covered in an expensive mahogany hardwood veneer. As John and Adam moved beyond the central intersection, they came to a strip of bone white carpet centered between rows of small potted trees.

They continued past two offices, one on each side of the corridor. Adam saw the offices were subdivided internally into small cubicles, although he couldn't see the inhabitants. Ahead, he made out two frosted glass doors. Just outside, a woman sat behind a sprawling L-shaped desk.

As they approached, the secretary turned her attention from the computer terminal. She was comely in a professional way, maybe forty years of age. Her light brown hair was pulled back in a tight bun, and her face was smooth with a very light layer of makeup. She wore a fitted gray pinstripe suit, with the cut of the skirt just short enough to show her knee.

"Mr. Reece said for you to go right in," she said with a thin smile.

Adam felt her eyes studying him with curiosity. She had apparently been part of the firm long enough to care about who came and went, and he surely didn't fit the mold of their clients.

"Thanks, Betty," John said. He pulled open one of the glass doors and held it open for Adam.

As he stepped into his brother's office, Adam paused a moment to take in the elegant surroundings. Along the right wall was a bright red sofa with a pile of yellow throw pillows. A long rectangular matching footstool sat in front of the couch, with beautiful ebony tables to the sides. On the opposite side of the room was a speckled-green granite counter, above which were several well-lit glass liquor cabinets.

A small, carpeted putting green sat to one side of a massive alder wood desk that looked grand enough to have belonged to Henry VIII. The desk itself was centered between two large windows that looked out over the Denver skyline.

Adam recalled that Elliot had a very expensive hobby of collecting rare items. True to his taste, scattered about the room on pedestals and wall shelves was a large collection of carved figurines that included a milky jade swordsman, a black onyx elephant, and an ancient temple made of soapstone. All were beautiful, and many looked old enough to date back several thousand years.

The walls were covered with a collection of antique maps and paintings, none of which he recognized. Not that Adam was any kind of art connoisseur, and maybe it was just a bit of brotherly pride, but he wouldn't have been surprised to see the works of Renoir or Leonardo da Vinci hanging about as casually as an old Humphrey Bogart movie poster.

A gaunt man, looking closer to fifty than his actual thirty-five, sat dwarfed behind the immense desk. He wore a perfectly tailored gray pin-striped suit along with a bright yellow silk tie. His thinning brown hair was cut short and neatly parted on one side. Seeing the two men enter his office, he stood and quickly moved around the desk toward them.

"Adam, so nice to see you," Elliot said with what sounded like genuine warmth. "How long has it been? A year?"

"Longer, I think," Adam replied, quite sure they both remembered the circumstances of their last encounter all too well.

Elliot hesitated for a moment and then reached out to hug him.

Adam hugged him back but found his brother's frame stiff and frail. He was disturbed by how emaciated Elliot felt. Not much more than a skeleton really. Elliot patted him twice on the back with an awkward mechanical rhythm before finally stepping away.

"You look fit," Elliot said with what sounded like a note of admiration.

"You look like you work too much," Adam replied, noting the circles under his brother's eyes.

"I do at that. And I haven't been able to sleep well for the past few years. Someday it's going to catch up with me." His face suddenly grew long as if he were fighting some hidden sadness.

Adam now felt awkward, regretting his observation. "I know of a good tea if you ever feel like trying something different. Ancient Japanese remedy."

Elliot replied with raised eyebrows. "I don't know if I'm that far gone. Besides, it's nothing that a glass of scotch won't cure." He turned to face his assistant and said, "Thanks, John."

John took his words for the dismissal they were and quietly lumbered out of the office.

"This is quite a spread," Adam said, surveying the room again. "Beautiful."

"It's home," Elliot said, returning to his desk. "And I mean that literally. I spend more time here than anywhere else." He gestured for Adam to take a seat on a red patent leather chair sitting close to the desk.

"Fortunately, my work gets me out of the office," Adam replied.

Elliot seemed unsure of how to respond. He gave an awkward smile. "So, how are things in . . . your business?"

"We're doing well enough. I have a secretary now. I'll know my ship's come in when she starts to dress as nice as yours."

Adam did have a part-time secretary, which he considered quite an accomplishment. Elizabeth, or Libby, as he knew her, was a graduate student in psychology at the University of Tennessee. He thought for a moment before realizing that he couldn't even remember Libby's last name. Ever since they'd met at a women's self-defense course he'd put on at the university a few months before, she'd just been Libby. Now she took care of a host of things for him. Everything from running credit checks to getting photos developed. She had a knack for getting things done, and Adam found himself, and his investigative business, much more productive since her arrival.

"Good, I'm glad to hear it. I know for a while you were struggling with finding the right kind of work and all." Obviously worried his brother might be offended by his words, Elliot immediately added, "But I'm glad to hear that everything's going well now."

"So, what's up?" Adam asked, ending the "I'm okay, you're okay" dance. "I read the newspaper article you left but wasn't clear if I'm here to find this girl or what exactly."

"Well, it's complicated. I guess more than anything I was hoping to get your feel on this whole affair. As I said on the phone, I've always thought you have a way with things like this."

Adam shrugged. "Fair enough. Tell me what's going on, and I'll give you my read on it."

Elliot pushed his chair away from the desk, leaned back, and folded his arms in front of him. "It started a couple of weeks ago. No, that's not exactly true. I guess you could say it began last year." He stopped talking to collect the right words.

"You met the girl last year?" Adam asked, figuring he'd help things along.

"That's right. I met Maria at a party last June. You know, one of those high-society parties. Lots of important people kissing the asses of even more important people. At first, I thought she was a corporate attorney herself. She seemed both interested and knowledgeable in legal matters."

"I see. And when did you figure out she was something else?" Adam was already beginning to see the picture.

"Ah yes, we . . . uh . . . we spent the night together, and it became clear then. She was . . . remarkable. Professional."

"Did she ask you for money?"

"Oh God, no. She wasn't like that at all." Elliot grew flushed. "Maria wasn't into one-night stands for a few bucks. She was looking for a long-term commitment. Not marriage, mind you, just commitment. More of a courtesan sort of arrangement with lots of gifts attached. She even started a little business through which she could write off the expenses. I guess you could say she was resourceful."

Adam was thinking of a different label, but only said, "So, did you take her up on the offer?"

For a moment, Elliot sat silent. Then almost inaudibly he answered, "Yes, yes, I did."

Adam felt sorry for his brother. Even a man as self-absorbed as Elliot apparently felt the drive for love and sex. It was a shame that he'd allowed himself to settle for only one of the two.

"Sounds bad, huh?" Elliot said.

Adam shrugged. It didn't seem like the time to lecture. "The two of you had an arrangement. It wasn't like you were subjecting her to the dangers of being on the street. She wanted to be kept, and you kept her."

Elliot smiled, thankful for his brother's restraint. "I guess so. Still, as you can probably imagine, I feel terribly embarrassed about the whole affair."

Adam was certain there was much more at work than just embarrassment. Elliot had never been one to let a little depravity climb all over his back the way this was. He thought it might become clearer as the extent of their relationship was revealed.

"When did you call it off?" he asked.

"How do you know it was me?" But Elliot didn't wait for an answer. "You're right, of course. It took about three months before the arrangement got to me enough that I brought it to a head. I honestly thought if I explained my feelings for her, she would understand, and somehow we could migrate to a more normal relationship. One that offered a real future together." Elliot closed his eyes, but his face remained pained with the memory.

"Only in *Pretty Woman*, brother. Working girls are working girls."

Elliot nodded slowly, studying his brother. "Right you are. She left the very next day while I was at work. I thought that was the last I would ever see of her. I have to admit that it hurt . . . a lot." He swallowed uncomfortably. "As crazy as it may sound, I think I loved her. She didn't leave a note or anything, just gone. Like, I mean absolutely nothing."

There really wasn't anything Adam could say to relieve the pain, so he sat quietly waiting for his brother to continue.

"Anyway, as I said, that was the last I thought I would see of her. Then about two weeks ago, she showed up here at my office. Just like that, out of the blue."

"What did she want? To see if you might have seen the error of your ways?"

"No. Although, if she had asked, I might have said yes all over again. But that wasn't why she was here at all. She came with a business proposition."

"Oh?"

"She said she knew someone who possessed a valuable map and wanted to know if I might be interested in purchasing it. I suppose she understood from our time together that I have a passion for maps and other collectibles. This was her chance for a big score."

"A map?" Adam's curiosity was peaked.

"Yes, and apparently not just any map. Maria believed it to be very valuable. Like a million bucks valuable. But she was going to let me have it for a mere two hundred grand."

"What a sweetheart."

Elliot grinned. "As you can imagine, I had serious doubts about the whole thing, telling myself she was just a hooker trying to scam a wealthy client. But she seemed sincere and didn't ask for money. Instead, she promised to get the map and bring it to me to inspect. If I was interested after that, she said we could work out some kind of purchase."

"Did she say what was on the map?" Adam wondered what type of map could be worth a million dollars.

"No, and the funny thing is I don't think she even knew. She just said it was valuable and hoped I might be interested. We agreed that she'd bring the map in about a week for me to see for myself. I'll admit that my underlying motivation was to see her again. I really had very little interest in any relic she had come across."

"But she never showed up?"

"No," he replied. "I haven't heard from her since."

"She probably either couldn't get the map or maybe found a better scam somewhere else."

"I thought so too until a couple days ago when her sister showed up."

"Here?"

"Yeah," Elliot said. "I recall Maria mentioning a sister once or twice but never had an opportunity to meet her. Maria didn't talk much about her life outside what we shared directly."

"Introducing family must be like kissing on the lips."

"Too personal?"

"Too risky."

"I see," Elliot said, shifting about uncomfortably. "Anyway, her sister, Lara, came by and asked me a lot of questions about when was the last time I'd seen Maria. She seemed worried. Apparently, she hadn't heard from her in an unusually long time."

"It's curious that she knew where to find you."

"I wondered about that too. I can only guess that Maria kept her informed in case something went awry."

"Sounds reasonable," Adam agreed. "It's a dangerous profession."

"I told Lara that I hadn't seen Maria in a couple of weeks but that she'd promised to bring me a map to look at. Lara said she didn't know anything about the map and didn't particularly seem to care about it either. She just wanted to find her sister. She'd already gone by Maria's apartment, but no one had answered. She also said that Maria's car had been sitting idle in the parking lot for several days."

"Did she report it to the police?"

"Yes, but the police apparently found nothing to indicate foul play and have written the case off as very low-priority. Not knowing where else to turn, she came to me. And this obviously led me to you."

"Okay, but why me? Why bring me a thousand miles to find a missing girl. There are lots of good investigators here in Denver. Surely—"

"Trust," Elliot interrupted. "You and I have had our differences over the years, but I've always trusted you. We're brothers. Simple as that."

Adam looked at his brother, and for the first time in a long time, he remembered why he loved him. They were so different, yet still so much alike. Trust, the kind that can only be found with family, was priceless to them both. It didn't change the fact that Elliot had become an arrogant prick, but it did offer hope that he was a prick who hadn't completely forgotten their childhood bond.

"As you can imagine," Elliot continued, "this is a delicate matter for me. Maria was after all a special kind of girl. I wouldn't want some hot-shot investigator coming across compromising information about me. Who knows, he might try to blackmail me with it."

Adam smiled, imagining sordid photos showing up on the Internet of his brother handcuffed to a bedpost while a half-naked woman teased him with the wrong end of a whip. Admittedly it was cruel, but it was also particularly gratifying. After a moment of enjoying the colorful image, he said, "The first place to start is with her sister. Find out what she knows."

"My thoughts exactly," Elliot said, turning his attention to a gold Rolex that rolled lazily around his bony wrist. "I've arranged for us to have an early lunch with Lara this morning. If we're to be there on time, we'll need to head out in a few minutes. If you want, I can give you a brief tour of the firm on our way out."

"Sure, that would be nice," Adam said. A desire to make amends kept him from telling his brother how little interest he had in seeing more expensive suits and potted plants. "But one thing first."

"What's that?" Elliot asked, already getting to his feet.

"It's important for you to realize this may not end well. These things often don't. Maria was a woman who used her body to gain favor, and that may well have led to a situation she didn't anticipate. An ex-lover or jealous wife might be behind her disappearance. Are you sure you want to go down this path? It might be painful."

Elliot leveled his gaze at Adam before answering. "I understand. The way I see it is that this thing won't go away. Someone's got to find out what happened to Maria. If it's bad, it's bad."

Chapter 5

Elliot had asked Lara Sativa to meet him at the Green Jeans restaurant at eleven o'clock. She now sat on an oversized vinyl sofa in the dimly lit restaurant lobby waiting for her would-be host.

Green Jeans was one of many downtown restaurants that catered to a lunchtime crowd of bankers and lawyers. Its particular motif was that of gardening. Nailed to the walls were rusted antique farming tools, including plows, tillers, shovels, and more than a few items that a city girl like Lara had no hope of recognizing.

Just inside the entrance sat stacks of crates filled with dusty plastic replicas of acorn squash, carrots, and potatoes. The floors were covered in a hardwood intentionally weathered, and the lighting combined filtered sunlight with small oil-burning lanterns strategically placed around the restaurant. A dying fern potted in a wrought iron basket hung above Lara's head, occasionally dropping small dried sprigs onto her shoulder. The ambiance of a rural farmhouse was completed with a petite, yet functional, waterwheel. With each rotation, the painted green wheel splashed murky water onto a bed of worn stones, only to be recirculated to repeat the process again and again.

Lara glanced at her watch, 10:47 a.m. She'd arrived fifteen minutes earlier, and time was crawling. She hated waiting, always had. In her profession, she'd done plenty of it, and it had never sat well with her. She reminded herself that a concerned sister would arrive early. If Mr. Reece had chosen to arrive early himself, it was important that she already be waiting.

Her previous meeting with Elliot had allowed Lara the opportunity to size him up. And in her eyes, there was little to be liked. He was pathetically frail, about as charming as a dead tuna, and interested only in the pursuit of a new piece of ass or his next hundred dollar bill.

Probably most offensive was the irrational certainty he'd demonstrated when discussing Maria's disappearance. He'd played the part of overlord for so long he now genuinely believed that his self-acknowledged superior intellect and wealth could solve any problem. Especially those that lowly womenfolk might have.

Regrettably, Lara felt compelled to play the part of a sweet, helpless girl hunting for a lost sister. So, she'd smiled, laughed at his moronic jokes, and forced herself not to bite his ears off when he tossed around sexually suggestive comments.

"God, Maria," she mumbled, "how could you have gotten in with such an asshole?" But Lara already knew the answer. She knew all too well what Maria did for a living.

It wasn't the conjecture of a disapproving sister. Maria had never been shy about confessing her motivations. She showed more pride than shame when discussing her lifestyle. It was all about getting ahead, regardless of price. Maria Sativa was driven.

She would rarely stay with a client for longer than three months. By then, she had extracted most of what she could and given him most of what she had. Then she'd be off to find another prospect. No hard feelings. Hell, no feelings at all.

She was careful to ensure that there was always another wealthy schmuck in waiting. Maria was a sexual creature that walked the Earth with great prowess. Anyone who didn't recognize that would quickly find himself dangling helplessly from the jaws of a hungry lioness. Truth be told, a bit of Lara felt sorry for Mr. Reece. After all, he probably thought he was something special to Maria.

"Ah, screw him," she spit out in a whisper.

She instinctively hated the men Maria had told her about. They had no problem banging a young lady for a buck but always seemed to get their feelings hurt when things went south. If Maria's clients were too stupid to realize that their money couldn't buy her love, they deserved everything they got. The only difference between Elliot Reece and the others was that he had more money than most. Not all, just most.

She glanced at her watch again. "Shit, this is taking forever." Her leg bounced up and down nervously, the heel of her shoe making a rhythmic *click-click-click* against the antique wood floor.

The restaurant door swung inward and two men entered. The first was impeccably dressed—expensive tailored suit, black Gucci dress shoes, and a yellow power tie that screamed, "I'm rich, so get the hell out of my way." Lara recognized him immediately as Elliot Reece, a.k.a. the scumbag.

The other man was a couple inches shorter but significantly meatier. He wore black jeans, a lightweight cotton jacket, and a faded red knit shirt that looked as if it had been washed a hundred times in cheap detergent. His features were sharp, and he carried an unmistakable air of confidence. Not arrogance like the first man, more of an internal strength easily recognized from any distance.

Lara had an uncanny knack for identifying people who could be trouble for her. And as she watched the stranger approach, she understood that he was dangerous, someone who might unravel the charade. Hell, maybe even the entire game. He was someone to handle with care.

"Guess he uses a different tailor," she snickered, trying to soften the uneasy feeling. Mr. Reece hadn't said anything about someone else coming along, and Lara disliked surprises. Finding no rational reason to worry, she comforted herself by translating concern into disdain. She didn't have to hate him for any specific reason, just for scumbag association if nothing else.

Elliot and the unexpected stranger approached. She watched as both men sized her up, their eyes flashing to her face before moving down her graceful figure. Lara wore loose-fitting red slacks and a navy short-sleeve sweater. She understood that by most anyone's standards, she was drop-dead gorgeous.

The recognition wasn't vanity, only simple truth. She had silky blonde hair with just a few curls, crystal blue eyes, full, soft pink lips, and a trim athletic body with tight curves in places where men liked to find them. Lara breathed deeply, finding a renewed confidence. She could handle these two and get what she needed.

"Good to see you again," Elliot began, reaching out and taking her hand with both of his own. "I hope you haven't been waiting long."

"Just got here myself," she lied. She needed to know what Mr. Reece knew, and now was not the time to piss him off by telling him what she really thought of him. No, now was the time to play it just as Maria would have. Manipulate the hormone-driven jackass for maximum gain. Find out what he knows without giving up anything in return. Then dump him like a pail of soiled diapers.

"Good, good. Let me introduce my brother, Adam," Elliot said, gesturing to the stranger.

"Brother?" Her eyes lit up. "Ah yes, I thought I saw some resemblance," she lied again. *Play them both,* she told herself. "Nice to meet you," she continued, extending her hand and offering the "I've noticed you and think you're special," smile. It was foolproof in that it had never failed her before.

Adam gently took her hand, replying, "Nice to meet you too, Lara."

And there it was. With the stranger's very first words, he'd managed to find her Achilles' heel. Had he kissed her hand or offered a wink, she wouldn't have broken step. But instead he had repeated her name. Telling her in a most flattering way that he considered everything about her important enough to remember. She now found herself blushing, confidence replaced by an unwanted nervous attraction.

Men were easy enough to understand. They liked pretty faces, shaven bikini lines, and breasts that would stand up and pay attention. But Lara had discovered that women were irrational, unpredictable creatures. Each had her own special weakness, perhaps the desire to be occasionally groped in public by her partner or to feel the tickling caress of a man who made his living playing the piano. Once revealed, the weakness would serve as the tool by which a woman could be snared.

It was such unspoken desire that led a minister's daughter to chase around tattooed rock stars in the hope of being haphazardly spread across the drums, or an educated executive to spend her life washing elephant-sized underwear for a disgusting beer-slamming redneck of a husband. Women had strange needs, and often it was the unlikeliest of men who met them.

Adam's simple recital of her name had Lara's heart pounding against her chest. He was trouble all right.

"Let's get a table, shall we?" Elliot said. "We have a lot to discuss." He gave Lara a big white-toothed smile that caused her to lose the small appetite she'd been working on all morning.

With Elliot ushering Adam and Lara ahead like a flamboyant director at an exclusive Hollywood cast party, they all moved further into the restaurant for what was sure to be a fun-filled lunch.

* * *

Adam speculated that the honesty of a man can be measured by how able he is to recognize when a beautiful woman wants to spit in his eye.

If there was anything to that self-imposed metric, Elliot was as dishonest as a stripper come tax day.

Within seconds of their meeting, it was clear to Adam that Lara thoroughly despised his brother. It wasn't anything she did or didn't do. It was just there like the face of an old friend—easily recognized but hard to describe. She smiled politely, listened with feigned interest, and spoke in soft, pleasant tones. But even during their initial introduction, her eyes flashed menacingly with bottled-up resentment.

She was putting on an act of some sort. That much was clear. Adam suspected her indignation probably stemmed from having to rely on help from a man who used to screw her sister for money. It sure as hell sounded like a bitter pill to swallow.

He also recognized that on a very basic level, Lara wasn't what she appeared to be. She carried herself with the natural grace of a soft, sophisticated Persian, but Adam suspected that under the surface lay a scraggly alley cat. He felt certain that before lunch was through, her true feline persona would reveal itself through a *hiss* rather than a *purr*.

"Lara, if I remember correctly, you mentioned that you're a paralegal," Elliot said, leaning in a bit too close as he spoke.

"That's right. I'm currently between jobs, though. My last employer was Judge Carden at the district courthouse. Maybe you knew him?"

"Ah yes, good old Judge Carden," Elliot said with an exaggerated smile that looked more like he was remembering his first date than an old professional acquaintance. "Poor guy passed away last month. A heart attack, wasn't it?"

Lara answered only with a nod and tightly pressed lips.

"Did you work for him long?" Elliot asked.

"Less than a year. But I liked him. He was an honest man with real character. Hard to find nowadays."

Adam grinned, certain she was taking a subtle poke at his brother. Elliot, however, seemed unaware of the jab. Attractive women had always been his weakness. Oddly, he seemed unable to use his intellect when it came to anything even remotely connected to the opposite sex. It was as if his penis was capable of emitting a mind-disabling hormone at the slightest whiff of a sweet perfume.

"Sweetie, if you ever find yourself in need of a job, just let me know. We can always use a good paralegal at R.W.G."

"R.W.G.?" she asked.

"Reece, Weismann, and Garner," he said with a conceited smile.

There was a brief flash in Lara's eyes, and for a moment, Adam thought she might leap across the table to choke the life out of his scrawny brother.

Instead, she replied politely, "I'm taking a bit of a breather right now, but thank you. Your firm has a very good reputation."

As she finished speaking, a tall waiter approached the table. Matching the other servers, his dress included a black knee-length smock and matching white shirt and trousers. He had long red hair pulled back in a bushy pony tail.

"Excuse me, ladies and gents," he said with an Australian accent. "Might I get you something from the watering hole?" The young man pulled a pencil from behind his ear.

Elliot turned to Adam and Lara. "If you two don't mind, I'll order for us. I've been here a time or two, and I know what's good."

They both nodded, closing their menus in unison and exchanging a quick glance. This was Elliot's gig, and he didn't want them to forget it.

After he placed the order, the conversation continued.

"Not to seem ungrateful for what I'm sure is going to be a delicious lunch," Lara said, "but do you mind if I ask what you've found out about my sister?"

Once again, Elliot leaned in close. This time he placed his hand over hers. "I made a few calls to see if any of my associates might have seen her at the nightly cocktail scene." His voice was soft and reassuring, as if he was asking a woman to go away with him for the weekend. "Unfortunately, no one has."

Lara sighed.

Seeing her dismay, he quickly continued, "But I've gone one step further. I've brought my brother in on this. He does this sort of thing for a living. You know, find people and all."

Elliot may not have meant to be condescending, but it sure sounded to Adam like he was trying to win Lara's favor by placing the two of them in a category above a brother who had to get dirty for a living. If this was his intention, he could excuse it. Gorgeous women can make men do lots of crazy things, some of them a lot worse than just denigrating a brother. Unfortunately for Elliot, Adam didn't believe the approach was going to be very effective with the likes of Lara. If he read her correctly, this was a girl who had danced in a few mud puddles herself.

She turned to look at Adam as if just noticing him. "Is that right?" Her voice was colored with a hint of cynicism that made the words come out more like "Isn't that convenient."

"That's me, just a blue collar guy who pokes around in people's closets for a living." Adam met her gaze full on. She was testing him, and he had to admit that he liked it. Maybe it was just that she had a fresh look of uncertainty in her eyes. She hadn't made up her mind about him yet.

"Do you find much?" she asked. "In their closets, I mean."

Adam rubbed his freshly shaven chin. "Sure, if you count old golf clubs and smelly sneakers. I got into this profession thinking it would be like *Magnum P.I.* . . . . beaches, babes, and gunfire. Unfortunately, reality has now set in."

Both of them laughed. Elliot joined in late.

"Ever uncover anything dark and terrible? Maybe a secret your client didn't tell you about?"

Adam had indeed found his fair share of disturbing secrets during his years as an investigator. None of which were appropriate for lunchtime conversation. He thought he saw a way to tie the question to her deception. "Everyone has secrets . . . me, Elliot, even you, I bet."

"Hmm," she said, allowing his words to soak in. "I suppose you're right. And you think you can find Maria with these special skills of yours?"

He shrugged. "If we're lucky."

Lara's face drew long with concern. "That doesn't sound very promising."

Elliot quickly piped in, "My brother is very good at what he does. He'll find her." He said it partly because he wanted to be reassuring, but more than that, he wanted her attention back on him.

Adam felt the need to question Elliot's prediction but not at the expense of bringing additional worry to Lara. Investigation was no place for optimism or pessimism. Maintaining objectivity and not forgetting to get paid at the end of the day were the hallmarks of a good private investigator.

Before he could voice the necessary disclaimer on what he could or couldn't do, Lara forced Elliot's hand. "I want to believe you, Mr. Reece—really, I do. But how can you be so sure?"

Elliot started to answer but then fell silent and turned to Adam. "You're the expert. You tell us how hard it's going to be."

It was Adam's turn to set the stage of expectation. He'd given the speech more than once, and it never went over well. It was a necessary evil. "Finding people is either very easy or nearly impossible," he began.

"How's that determined?" she asked.

He thought about watering down his answer but decided against it. "Missing people can be divided into two groups. The first are those who generally don't mind being found. The second are those who are either hiding, abducted, or dead. The first are easy to find; the second are hard as hell. Given that it's looking as if Maria is in the second group, I'd say we're going to need a bit of luck."

"My sister is not dead," Lara said with complete conviction, looking first to Adam then to Elliot.

"Of course she's not," Elliot consoled, patting her hand. "I'm sure he didn't mean it that way."

Adam took a sip of the tart red wine his brother had insisted they all try. It tasted like grape juice spiked with cat piss. "I didn't mean it any way at all," he said. "I'm just saying that we shouldn't deny the facts. There are several good reasons to suspect that Maria may have met some sort of foul play."

"Like what?" Lara's tone had turned disparaging.

"First, your sister is in a dangerous line of work," he answered. He waited to see if she would counter his unspoken assertion. She didn't.

He continued. "Second, she approached my brother about a questionable financial deal just before her disappearance. And finally, she's vanished without letting you, her only sibling, know where she was going. I'm not saying that something terrible *has* happened to her, only that we should go into this with our eyes open."

Lara looked as if she might initiate an argument but instead bit nervously at her lower lip.

Adam decided to take press things further. "Finding Maria is likely to be difficult work. Our best chance will come from all of us being open and direct. For that reason, I think it's best if we clear the air."

Adam hoped that his sudden change in direction would catch Lara off guard enough to elicit her true feelings and motivations. A part of him hated to become the aggressor, but experience had shown the value of understanding a client's agenda.

His words brought obvious consternation to Lara. She appeared uncertain as to whether she was under attack or just misreading his intentions. "Of course," she replied.

"Good. I know my brother feels the same way. Right, Elliot?"

"Absolutely," he replied, openly curious about where Adam was headed.

"If we're all going to play nice together, we have to get the hard feelings out in the open. If we don't, we'll never trust each other, and in the end someone's going to get screwed."

Elliot looked bewildered. "Huh?"

Adam turned to Lara. "You know what I'm talking about. Don't you, Lara?"

Her gaze turned as stony as that of a basilisk. "You're wondering if I have a hidden agenda. Perhaps revenge or retribution."

He nodded. "Something like that."

Elliot looked back and forth from Adam to Lara, thoroughly dumbfounded.

"The answer is no," she answered. "Rest assured I have no intention of screwing either of you."

Her double entendre was not lost on him, and Adam found himself smiling. Even seeing her pissed off was rather enticing.

"Adam, what exactly are you trying to do here?" Elliot asked.

Lara turned to him. "He's worried that I might want to cut your dick off because you were banging my sister for money. Is that clear enough for you?"

Elliot fell back in his chair, mouth wide open. He looked as if a dog had just wet on the leg of his trousers.

"I just wanted my brother to recognize the resentment," Adam said. "Thank you for presenting it in full color." The masquerade was now over.

"Anything else?" she asked.

Adam stared into her eyes. They were now flickering with blue anger and something else. Maybe a hint of relief. Relief from the charade being over? Apparently, she didn't like pretending either. He liked her already.

"Bottom line," he said. "He and your sister had a thing going. It may not have been the type of thing you see on reruns of *Father Knows Best*, but it was between him and Maria. Maybe you don't agree and blame him for it, or maybe you just hate him for being a rich bastard. Either way, you'll need to put it aside if we're going to have half a chance of finding her."

Even though they had ordered their food only a few minutes earlier, the waiter suddenly materialized with three plates on a large oval carrying tray. The group sat in silence as he carefully served identical plates of chicken marsala with grilled zucchini. He then placed a large loaf of oatmeal pecan bread in the center of the table and bid everyone "bon appétit."

"Okay, so what now?" Lara asked, not touching the food in front of her.

"You said it," Elliot agreed, casting an annoyed glance at Adam. "I'd hoped we could have a nice lunch, laughter all around. I don't see that coming to be."

"How about we all take a deep breath and enjoy the meal," Adam said, fearing that if they didn't eat now, someone would surely get up from the table in anger. Besides, he was hungry.

The three ate in relative silence, with Elliot trying unsuccessfully at one point to lighten the mood with a story of how his broker had recently advised him to buy shares in a start-up Internet business.

"I can't understand the irrational investment in some of these companies," he continued. "Little one-room start-up companies becoming billion dollar valuations just because they offer services related to the Internet. Can you believe that nonsense? It's nuts if you ask me."

After a moment, it became clear that in fact no one had asked him, and worse yet, no one could give a rat's ass. He ate the rest of the meal in mimicked silence.

As Adam finished his lunch, he pushed the plate away and waited for Lara to do the same. Seeing him finish, she tossed an embroidered white napkin on the plate she'd barely touched. Elliot, although not quite finished, looked around awkwardly then put his fork down.

Before Adam could speak, Lara said, "Maybe you're right about the importance of clearing the air, but I want to make something clear to you both." Her eyes shifted to Elliot then back to Adam. "Finding my sister is all that matters to me. I'm not here to cause either of you difficulty, but I'm also not going to kiss your ass. If you're going to help me, do it for Maria's sake. I don't need any sunshine blown up my skirt."

"We're all here for Maria," Elliot began. "No one expects you to—"

"And another thing," she interrupted. "I absolutely insist on being involved in everything. I know it's hard to believe, but you don't have to have a willy swinging between your legs to make a difference."

Elliot's mouth dangled open as he unsuccessfully hunted for words that would somehow neutralize the destructive forces circulating around the table.

Adam took the conversation ahead without him. "Fair enough. I'll make sure you know everything I know." Cannons had been fired, prisoners taken. Now was the time to push ahead.

Adam and Lara both looked to Elliot, who still seemed a bit tongue-tied. "Right," was all he managed to get out.

"Fine. Then let's get started," Adam said. "When was the last time you saw your sister?"

After a slight hesitation, she answered, "Quite a while, maybe two or three months."

The answer didn't make sense. "Then why did you become so concerned? My brother said Maria had been to see him only the week before."

"You asked when I last *saw* her. We didn't often see one another, but we spoke on the phone every Wednesday afternoon without exception. She missed the Wednesday before last and then this past one too. I knew something was wrong." Her gaze turned down to the buried plate of chicken. "I tried to make contact but couldn't find her anywhere. No note, no answering machine message, nothing. That wasn't like Maria. Not when it came to me." Lara fell silent for a moment, obviously struggling with emotion.

Elliot placed a comforting hand on her back but quickly pulled it away when he saw her stiffen under his touch.

"Go on," Adam said, softening the tone of his interrogation.

"I called the police. They did a quick search of her place but said everything looked in order. Can you believe they asked me to wait a few weeks to see if she showed up?"

"And you approached my brother because . . ."

"Because the last time I spoke with Maria, she said something about going to see him. I didn't know the specifics but figured it was the usual thing."

Adam looked to her for more, so she added, "I don't think you want me to spell it out. We all know what she did for grocery money."

"I want you to know something, Lara," Elliot interjected, suddenly coming out of the shadows like a needy beggar.

"What's that?" Her voice was laced with cynicism she no longer attempted to hide.

"I loved your sister," he squeaked.

Lara's eyes rolled back in her head, and she spit out a breath of air.

"Don't believe it if you don't want to. But I did. I'd never done that sort of thing before, and I grew to love her. She eventually left me when I told her so." He delivered the words with more feeling than Adam thought possible of his brother.

Lara's eyes softened a little, and her mouth closed tightly.

She believes him, Adam thought. *Good. Her hatred won't help things.* He, however, wasn't entirely sure that he believed his brother. Elliot was not beyond using the "L" word if it suited his needs.

"Nevertheless, it's now become apparent that you don't think much of me," Elliot continued, "and that, of course, is your prerogative. I can only conclude that perhaps you would be more comfortable pursuing your sister without my interference." He straightened his tie as if about to stand.

Adam sat silent waiting to see what would happen. Elliot had thrown down the gauntlet. It was up to Lara to either pick it up for a fight or take a step back. And though he sensed her to be a fighter by nature, he appreciated that she was in a difficult situation. It could go either way.

Lara glared at Elliot for a moment before reluctantly lowering her gaze. "No, you wouldn't be interfering. You know that I need your help. I wouldn't have come to you otherwise. I have nowhere else to turn." She looked back to him. "But since we're all being so honest here, I want you to know something. I can't forgive you. I don't hate you, and I might even understand your falling in love with my sister. But I can't forgive you. You were all too willing to take advantage of a young lady just to satisfy your desires, and frankly, I find that disgusting. For that, if for no other reason, you owe it to Maria to do what you can. You owe her."

Elliot swallowed deeply, not arguing the point.

"Back to the questions," Adam said, figuring the showdown was at least temporarily over. "Assuming Maria isn't just off with a new sugar daddy on a sunny Virgin Islands vacation, do you know of anyone who might have reason to hurt her?"

Lara's eyes narrowed angrily at his slight of her sister. "It's true that my sister had lots of friends, special friends who did nice things for her. Unfortunately, she was also a bit flippant when moving from one to another. I'm sure she's broken a few hearts along the way, so one of them turning psycho and nabbing her is certainly a possibility. However, my instincts tell me it's more than that."

"What makes you say that?" Adam asked.

"Your brother said she approached him with a big financial deal over some map. My sister doesn't know squat about maps, so I figure she must have been into something new."

"You think the map might have something to do with her disappearance?" Elliot asked.

"Maria getting her hands on a valuable map just before mysteriously disappearing sounds like more than coincidence," she answered. "This isn't a lover gone awry. It's something more sinister, a conspiracy of some sort."

Adam found her use of the word "conspiracy" disconcerting. Did Lara know something she wasn't telling? Who exactly would be conspiring against whom?

"What do you mean by 'conspiracy'?" he asked.

Lara sat up straight as if finding renewed confidence in the single word. "I'm talking about powerful people working together to pursue nasty agendas. These things are all around us. I figured in your line of work you would have come across a few."

"Conspiracies, like who killed JFK and that kind of nonsense?" Elliot asked with a nervous chuckle.

Lara turned to him, her eyes alive with energy. He'd hit a nerve. "Precisely that kind of nonsense." After a moment, apparently unable to stomach his critique, she pressed him. "I can only assume you are a most educated man. A Harvard man, I'd guess. Sure of all things, even the identity of President Kennedy's assassin."

Elliot answered with a glare.

She pressed on. "Perhaps you'd be kind enough to share some of your infinite wisdom. I'm sure the world would appreciate a definitive answer." Her fingers tapped on the table to what Adam could swear was the theme song from *Jeopardy*.

Elliot's face turned angry, and for a moment, Adam thought he might get up and walk out. That was the last thing Adam wanted to have happen since he would have gotten stuck with a hundred-dollar lunch tab. Lara was pushing dangerously close to Elliot's very small threshold of tolerating insult. If it weren't for her having a nice set of knockers and a tight tush, he felt sure his brother would already have been half-way to the door.

Adam was about to intervene, when Elliot held up a hand. "It's okay," he said. "I'll play along." He turned his attention to Lara. "From all credible accounts, Lee Harvey Oswald shot President Kennedy. All that grassy knoll stuff was unsubstantiated speculation by people unwilling to accept a simple truth. The same sort of people who report seeing Elvis eating grits and eggs at the hillbilly diner they stopped in at on their way to see the world's largest ball of twine. Frankly, I find anyone who believes that sort of drivel a bit irrational."

Adam grinned. It was good to see Elliot stand his ground, but to call a woman "irrational," now that was below the belt. He rubbed his temples. The sparring match wasn't over just yet.

"Oh really?" Lara retorted, never losing step. "We'll tackle Elvis another day, but it's refreshing to know things are so clear regarding JFK. Maybe you could explain some of the 'drivel,' like how Deputy Sheriff Buddy Walthers found a .45 slug in the Dealy Plaza grass immediately after the shooting? And why the slug was immediately confiscated by an FBI agent, never to be seen again? And why after continuing to talk about the missing slug, Walthers was subsequently killed in a police shootout by friendly fire?"

Both Elliot and Adam sat back in their seats, puzzled at her rattling of revelations.

"Where are you getting all that?" Elliot's voice had lost the condescending tone.

"Oh, it's all true. Look into it if you like. There's a lot more to it than that. Dozens of people related to the JFK assassination died in mysterious ways. Most of them when they wouldn't keep their mouths shut or just before they were being called to testify before the Warren Commission."

"Where . . . where did you hear that?" Elliot stammered.

Adam concealed a smile with his hand. Elliot had graduated from the best law school in the country, was a master at extemporaneous argument, had a decade of law practice under his belt, and yet had absolutely no chance of winning this argument. For some perverse reason, that tickled him. Elliot might categorize Lara as an irrational conspiracy theorist, and perhaps he'd be right, but he'd have to admit she was a nut who did her homework.

"I can name a dozen sources, from newspapers, to television documentaries, to first-person biographies. It's all true," she answered, sitting back in her seat and crossing her arms in an unspoken declaration of victory.

Before Elliot whipped out a sheet of legal paper and a Cross pen to take down her sources, Adam thought he better get things back on track. "Have you been inside her apartment since she disappeared?"

"What?" Lara said with obvious annoyance, her cold stare never leaving Elliot.

"Your sister's apartment," Adam said again. "Have you been inside since she went missing?"

She turned to him. "No. I went there and banged on the door, but she didn't answer. Like I said, the police checked it out and didn't find anything. The incompetent pricks."

Adam smiled again. Lara was real. Crude as hell, yes. Filled with farfetched ideas, sure. But real nonetheless. Finding someone that hated pretense and refused to straddle the opinion fence on anything was invigorating.

"That's where we'll start then," he said.

"We?" Elliot asked.

"I'm assuming that we're all in this together," Adam answered.

"Uh . . ., yes, of course," Elliot stammered. "It's just that I'm very busy today."

Lara leaned in close to Adam and whispered, "We don't need him." Her voice was easily loud enough for Elliot to overhear.

Adam closed his eyes, hoping the comment wouldn't cause the fight to flare up again.

It didn't. Elliot said only, "She's right, you know. You're the investigator, so you've got to go. And Lara needs to be there since she knows her sister and will surely have a better chance of finding something out of the way than I would."

"You don't want to go then?" Adam said, not the least bit surprised.

"It isn't that I don't *want* to. It's just that I'd probably just get in the way. Besides, I really do need to get back to the office." He glanced at his watch. "Call me if you find anything. Really, call me, okay?"

Adam found his brother pitiful at times. Always wanting to be part of an adventure but never taking the time to skip down the yellow brick road in search of a wizard.

"I'll come back by your office whether we find something or not," Adam replied. Turning to Lara he asked, "Do you have a car?"

"I like to ride the bus."

Adam looked at her, unsure if she was pulling his leg.

She laughed. "Of course, I've got a car. Are we going in it?" Her voice was now more eager than snappy.

"If it's okay with you."

"Fine," she answered, getting to her feet. "Let's get rolling."

Adam and Elliot immediately followed her lead and stood up. Despite the issue of who shot JFK still hanging, lunch was officially over.

Chapter 6

Lara sped her second-generation neon green Volkswagen Beetle past an unmanned guard booth and into the visitor parking area of the Wilkeshire Apartments. The complex consisted of a dozen identical yellow and white stucco buildings radiating the beachfront property look rampant throughout Florida.

At its center was a commons area consisting of a large tennis court, outdoor pool, and clubhouse. A long corridor of blooming Yoshino cherry trees served as a beautiful invitation to visitors or, perhaps more important, those in search of temporary upscale residence.

In front of each of the two-story buildings were meticulously trimmed shrubs and small plots of grass that had recently been mowed. The Wilkeshire had the well-manicured appearance expected of an expensive and professionally maintained community.

"Hey, this is nice," Adam offered as they came to a stop. "Your sister must be doing all right."

Lara cut her eyes at him, unsure if he was offering a simple observation or something more derogatory. After a moment, she said, "She may have been a whore, but she wasn't poor. I know that as well as anyone."

Adam wondered at her last words. "Call her what you will. I was just commenting on her taste in housing," he said with a smile. Before she could retort back, he said, "Something's been bothering me since we met."

"What's that?"

"Why don't you and Maria look anything alike? With a name like Sativa I'd expect to see some Hispanic features. Come on, you have blonde hair and blue eyes. Besides, I saw her photo, and you two aren't exactly twins."

"Aren't you the observant detective," she smarted.

"Years of training, my dear" he said, grinning.

"Well, Sherlock, I'm adopted. Simple as that. My mother and father didn't think they could have children, so they adopted me. I don't know from whom, just that I was adopted. My dad always had a way of making deals with people. Hell, for all I know, I might have been a prize in a Friday night poker match. Anyway, a couple years later along came my sister, natural and all."

"How old were you when you were adopted?"

"Two," she answered. "I've seen the papers myself, and it was all legit. I don't remember life before my adopted parents. Nor do I particularly care to."

"You didn't ever attempt to find your biological parents? I've heard people tend to do that sort of thing."

"Nope. The way I see it is anyone willing to give up a child as adorable as I was doesn't need finding." She winked at him.

Adam wondered if the humor was to help hide feelings he couldn't fully appreciate, not having been adopted himself. Or maybe all that hidden longing stuff was just Hollywood crap. "Do you have any other brothers or sisters?"

"No. It's always just been me and Maria. And we're tight. Through thick and thin."

"I know what you mean," Adam said, opening his door.

"I doubt that," she mumbled under her breath, climbing out of the car.

Looking over the top of the Volkswagen, he stuck his tongue out at her. She returned the gesture and went so far as to put fingers in her ears.

He laughed. Smart ass or not, she was beginning to grow on him.

As they started down the walkway toward Maria's building, he said, "You're only partially right, you know."

"About?"

"My brother and me. You're right in that we aren't really close in a way most people would recognize. He and I have always been different. Elliot's a quicker study when it comes to book stuff, and I have a knack for the more physical pursuits. But even different as we are, we're still brothers. Neither of us ever loses sight of that."

"Being rich doesn't make him smarter than you."

She was still picking at him, but he ignored the slur. "No, it doesn't. But it doesn't hurt me to acknowledge that he's more intelligent than

I am. Ever since we were children, he was considered exceptional, maybe even gifted. Looking back, I can see why. He did all the normal prodigy-type things, reading very early, becoming involved in national chess tournaments, graduating top of his class from Harvard. I couldn't have done those things. Nor would I have even tried."

"You seem comfortable in this role of being second-string," she said. "I just don't get that. Especially not to the likes of him."

"Second-string? Not at all. I have strengths Elliot could never achieve. He recognizes mine, just as I see his. I sense his respect for me, and that's enough. He's often patronizing, but that's just his nature. I can forgive him for it. Most of the time anyway."

Adam was silent for a moment then chuckled aloud.

"What's so funny?"

"Nothing. It just got me thinking about something that happened when we were kids."

Lara turned to him. "Tell me . . . please."

Debating over whether to continue, he finally said, "Understand I was only five. Elliot was six. I doubt he even remembers it anymore." Correcting himself, he said, "No, of course he remembers it. He remembers nearly everything. We were traveling across the country with my father. He and my mother had just separated, and he had the wild idea to drive from California to Maine. I'm not sure why, but I think my dad was just trying to escape the daily drudgery of life for a few weeks.

"Along the road trip, we slept at small rest stops and makeshift campsites. One night after eating the typical grub of macaroni and corn, my father told us to go down to a nearby stream and wash out the pots. Elliot and I gathered up the pans and utensils and proceeded to what looked like more of a raging river than a stream.

"We climbed down a particularly steep and slippery embankment to reach the water, where we used dishrags and a bit of elbow grease to get the pans reasonably clean. As we headed back toward camp, though, we found ourselves in a bit of a dilemma. To get to camp, we had to climb back up the steep bank. Each time we tried, we slipped and fell, thereby muddying the pots once again. We tried it several times, but the bank was just too slippery to navigate with our hands full. I was ready to give up and call for help when Elliot finally figured out a solution."

Adam walked on in silence wondering if Lara was curious enough to ask the question.

After a moment she did. "Okay, I'm hanging here. What in the hell did some six-year-old brainiac do to get the pots up the muddy bank?"

Adam stopped and turned to face her. "Simple. He climbed up the bank and left the pots with me at the river. Then he had me toss them up to him one at a time."

"That's it?"

"That's it, Sure, it's obvious. Simple, really. But I didn't think of it. Like I said, he and I are different."

"Hmph," Lara snorted.

* * *

A few minutes later, Adam and Lara stood in front of a yellow door with the number 254 engraved on an antique brass doorplate. He knocked on the door. To no one's surprise, Maria didn't answer. He tried the knob, but it didn't budge.

"Should I try to get the key from the manager?" Lara asked. "He knows me."

"Sounds like a plan. I'll wait here."

"Be right back," she said, wheeling around and heading briskly toward the stairwell.

Adam didn't like misleading Lara, but he thought it best if he stuck his head inside Maria's apartment before she did. She'd told him that the police had searched the residence, but it wouldn't hurt to make sure Maria wasn't lying dead on the living room floor. Stranger things had happened.

As soon as Lara rounded the corner, he withdrew a small rolled-up pouch from his jacket pocket. Unfolding it, he removed two lock picks: an L-shaped torsion wrench and a small grooved rake pick. He inserted the short end of the delicate torsion wrench into the bottom of the lock, applied very light torque, and then pushed the rake pick into the center of the mechanism. Pressing the grooved tip up, he exercised the tumblers. Within a few seconds, he felt the L-pick turn slightly as he found the correct position of the furthest tumbler. He slid the rake pick forward, exercising the next one. It took less than a minute for him to successfully work the lock.

Adam stepped into Maria's apartment, leaving the door slightly ajar behind him. What he saw surprised him. Adam wasn't sure what he'd expected, perhaps something metropolitan with streamlined furniture and questionable splashes of paint posing as artwork. Instead, what he found was a room with a comfortable, classy feel to it.

A pastel blue-and-yellow checkerboard couch sat on the polished hardwood floor, two of the couch's feet resting on a large white rug that sprawled across much of the room. Opposite the couch was an antique chair with a pinstriped cushion and a mahogany coffee table. A matching entertainment center lined one wall, and three waist-high bookshelves pressed against the other. The room was lit by soft rays that filtered through droopy lavender curtains and the sudden burst of sunlight that now poured in through the open door. The subdued stillness of Maria's living room was disturbed only by several vibrant oil paintings of wildflowers hanging neatly on the walls.

"Very nice," he said, giving her a soft clap of his hands.

He stood very still, closed his eyes, and took a deep sniff of the room. He detected only the usual odors of food, sweat, perfume, and some sort of pine cleaner—thankfully, no hint of a decaying body hidden in a closet or bathtub.

He moved to the entertainment center and opened it. Inside were shelves containing an assortment of popular movies and music CDs, a bookshelf stereo system, and a high-definition LCD television. A remote control sat neatly on top of the TV set. Everything, including the television screen, was free of dust.

On top of the entertainment center were two pictures. The first was of an older couple, probably Maria's parents. The man had a distinct Hispanic look to him with rich skin and thinning black hair. The woman appeared to be Caucasian with maybe a bit of American Indian, but he couldn't be sure.

The next photo was of Maria and Lara. Maria was holding a large stuffed Pink Panther and leaning her head against Lara, a big smile across her face. Lara looked happy too but not giddy like her younger sister. In the photo's backdrop, he saw a Ferris wheel and crowds of people moving about, some holding snow cones, popcorn, or cotton candy. The Sativa sisters were at a fair or carnival of some kind.

Adam studied Maria's features. She was in her late twenties, and there was no question as to her beauty. Morality aside, he felt a fresh understanding for Elliot's indiscretion. Maria was a woman who would be hard to say no to.

Thinking that it might come in handy, he removed the photo through the top of the frame and put in into his jacket pocket.

"Hey, how did you get in here?" a familiar voice sounded from behind him.

Adam turned to see Lara standing just inside the door, hands on her hips.

"I wiggled the knob and it opened," he replied with a sly grin.

"My ass," she said. "Well, it's a good thing you got in, because I couldn't find the manager. The fat bastard always takes long lunches."

Adam stared at her for a long time without speaking.

"What?" she asked, looking first to her clothes and then feeling her hair. "Is something hanging from me that shouldn't be?"

"No," he answered. "You are a pretty lady, Lara, but you should watch your mouth a bit. It compromises you."

"Compromises?" She sounded genuinely hurt. "Fu—" she started, but stopped in mid-expletive. Her upper lip twitched as she considered her response. Finally she said, "I'll make you a deal. I'll watch my mouth if you stop jerking me around. No more sending me on wild goose chases while you play Mr. Detective."

Adam considered her words as he met her gaze. "Fair enough. Let's start over." He walked to her and extended his hand. "Hi, I'm Adam."

She stood stunned for a moment, not expecting her words to be so well received. She suddenly felt the warmth of his hand on her own, and it made her hand go limp. "I'm . . .," she started, but her voice cracked a little. "I'm Lara, nice to meet you." She did a short curtsy, both legs bending gracefully in a pose that reminded him of Shirley Temple.

Both of them laughed, and a big smile remained on his face. "I like you, Lara Sativa."

She paused, letting her confidence slowly return before answering. "I like you too, Adam Reece." They looked at each other for another brief moment. "Now, shall we get to work or just stand here holding each other's hand all day?"

He released her and turned back to face the room. "Your sister has excellent taste."

"That she does. Strange though . . ."

"What's that?"

"It's just so clean. I've never seen my sister's place this neat. Usually there are three or four half-empty beer bottles or a slice of day-old pizza lying on the table, not to mention a pair of panties or a bra slung across the back of the couch. She sure didn't leave her place as tidy as a Marine Corps barracks."

Adam nodded. "Then someone cleaned up."

"But who? Why?"

"To hide something. Maybe signs of a struggle. As for who, that's a more difficult question."

"A struggle? Here? You think she was grabbed out of her apartment?" Her voice was filled with concern.

"We're jumping to conclusions. Maybe she knew she'd be away and just cleaned up before leaving town. Who knows for sure. Let's just take a good look around, okay?"

She exhaled heavily and nodded. "Right."

Not sure of what they were looking for, they moved slowly around the room, Lara never leaving Adam's side. After coming up empty in the living room, he said, "You take a look in the bedroom, and I'll check the bathroom. Then we'll swap. That way everything gets two sets of eyes."

She looked a little reluctant but eventually nodded and headed into the bedroom. As she entered, Lara exclaimed, "Oh God!"

Adam spun and pushed past her into the room, half expecting to see Maria's bloody body draped across the bed. All he saw was more posh furniture and fine decor.

"What is it?" he asked. "What did you see?"

"Sorry," she said a bit embarrassed. "I've just never seen this place so damn tidy."

"Do me a favor?" Adam said, shaking his head.

"What's that?"

"Save the 'Oh Gods' for when you really need them." With that, he turned and left the bedroom. He could hear Lara snickering behind him.

As Adam entered the bathroom, the scent of pine cleaner grew much stronger. Everything about the bathroom was just as immaculate as the rest of the house. He knelt and ran his fingers along the corner of the baseboard and the floor. No hair, no dust. Entirely too clean for anyone's house. Whoever had cleaned the place up had made that mistake if no other.

He opened the drawers of the vanity. Typical bathroom junk sloshed around, including brushes, combs, tweezers, dental floss, and a few hair clasps. Adam swung open the mirrored cabinet. Inside, he saw a collection of small, amber prescription bottles. He read a few: Valium, Prozac, Zoloft.

"Looks like your nerves might have been getting to you, Maria." He removed the Valium and checked the contents. Twenty or more pills. As he worked to secure the cap, it twisted out of his hands, scattering the pills into the basin.

"Damn it," he mumbled, carefully collecting and depositing each back into the vial. As he reached for one near the drain, he noticed something unusual. There was a small object several inches down inside the drain at the metal grating meant to catch hair and wedding rings. A pill? He didn't think so.

Adam stuck his index finger into the drain hoping to wedge the item against the side but couldn't quite reach it. Remembering his earlier find, he slid the vanity drawer open and removed the tweezers.

He lowered the tips into the drain, spreading them apart so he could clamp on the mysterious object. As he pulled it free, his stomach turned, and he let out a heavy sigh.

It was a human tooth coated in dried blood.

Not removing it from the tweezers, he studied it. Definitely an adult molar. Along both sides of the tooth were deep vertical scratches. *Grooves where pliers were used to tear it from her mouth,* he thought.

"In this world, there is good, and there is evil. Of this, I am sure." His words were soft like that of a quiet prayer. And like many prayers, they had originated from a teacher long ago.

"I didn't find much in the bedroom. Are you ready to swap?" Lara said as she moved into the open bathroom doorway behind him.

Adam quickly stuck the tweezers and tooth inside his breast pocket. When he turned, she was at the door peering in. "You find anything?"

He looked at her for a moment saying nothing. He couldn't bring himself to tell her. But he didn't really need to. She stared at him, the playful expression on her face slowly melting. He could see tears welling up in her eyes. Still, he couldn't speak.

"What . . . what is it?" Her voice had risen to that of a frightened, young girl. "What did you find?"

Adam moved close to her and put a stabilizing hand on her upper arm. "You asked me to be straight, so I'm not going to lie. I believe your sister's in real trouble."

Unable to speak, she stared at him, tears starting down her cheek.

"I found a tooth in the sink," he said. Then added unnecessarily, "It has blood on it."

"Oh my God!" she screamed, tearing her arm away from him. "No!" She shook her head. "No!" She began crying, her hands pressed tightly against her face. After a moment she looked up at him, her cheeks covered with streaked mascara. "You don't know it's hers. You don't know that!"

"No, Lara, I don't know."

The anger vanished as quickly as it had appeared. She stepped closer and fell against him, hands still clutching her face. "How could anyone do that to my baby sister?" she cried, her body shaking. "How could they?"

Adam held her, laying his cheek against her soft golden hair. He wondered if she really understood that the worst was yet to come.

* * *

Adam led Lara out of the apartment without further investigation. He doubted that anything significant would be found given the obvious cleanup. Besides, she clearly wasn't up to the task at the moment. As they walked down a long brick path leading away from the main complex of buildings, he saw a small, private post office. Deciding that Maria's recent mail might yield additional information, he excused himself. She nodded, still tearful, saying she would wait for him in the car.

The post office was little more than a collection of drop boxes, the room measuring no larger than fifteen feet on a side. Shiny aluminum doors covered one wall in long rows and columns.

The small room was empty except for a single well-dressed man who was struggling to open his mailbox. He looked to be a typical executive, matching gray jacket and trousers, red striped tie, and white long-sleeve shirt. The stranger looked up at Adam, smiled, and offered a neighborly nod.

Adam returned the gesture as he began to search for Maria's box.

The businessman continued to fumble with a large ring of thirty or more identical keys, trying each in his mailbox lock. With each key that didn't work, he would shake his head and give a carefree laugh.

As Adam got closer, he looked up and saw the number on the box that the man was trying to open. Box 254. Maria's mailbox.

Not wanting to give away any potential advantage, Adam pretended to continue looking for another box while he sized up the stranger. The man stood at about six feet and weighed maybe two hundred pounds. After only a moment of indecision, Adam moved in close as if reaching to open a nearby mailbox.

"You sure you've got the right box?" Adam asked, wondering if it could all be a simple mistake.

"Oh yeah," the man replied with the same calm smile. "This is it." He worked another key into the lock.

"That's strange," Adam said, straightening to face him.

"What's that?" he asked, a note of caution creeping into his voice.

"It's just odd that you're opening 254, and here I thought my good friend Maria Sativa had that box."

The man's frame stiffened, and his face quickly lost the smile. "You must be mistaken." His tone was no longer that of a neighbor who might stop by to borrow a cup of sugar.

"No, I don't think so," he said, watching the man carefully.

"Look, bub," the man growled, "this would be a good time to mind your own business." He pulled aside his jacket to reveal a holstered hand-gun in his waistband. It was a Smith and Wesson revolver hanging in a straight-draw brown leather holster. The restraining strap on the holster was still fastened. Depending on his training, it would take only a second or two for the man to have the gun in hand.

Adam moved a few inches closer. He'd never been one to wet his pants at the sight of a firearm. "I'm afraid I can't do that."

Just then, the stranger's key opened the lock, and the mailbox swung open. Neither of them turned to look at what was inside. Both men were now completely fixed on one another.

"Okay, hero," the stranger threatened, "but you're making one hell of a mistake."

"Maybe. But you've made one too."

"Yeah, and what's that?"

"You let me get way too close."

Adam seized the man's right sleeve and left lapel, driving him backwards. Instinctively, the stranger leaned forward pushing hard against his attacker, his other hand striking out ineffectively against Adam's shoulder. For an instant, the two men pressed tightly against one another with just enough force to prevent the other from moving.

Soften the target, Adam thought. The man looked like he was about to speak when Adam suddenly released his lapel and slapped him hard across the face. Before he could react, Adam had once again found his grip on the man's lapel.

The blow didn't inflict serious injury, but it did cause the man to growl angrily in a fit of rage. He attempted to advance by leaning forward and putting all his weight behind him.

Adam resisted until he felt the pressure grow strong and then suddenly gave into it, twisting his hip in tight against the man's abdomen. Taking advantage of the forward momentum, Adam flipped him high over his hip, executing the sweeping loin throw, *haria goshi*. The man's legs smashed against a small panel of windows along one wall, and his head and back slammed into the concrete floor, sounding like a slab of beef hitting the butcher's table.

The man let out an agonizing groan, and one of his legs began to twitch involuntarily. Adam saw that the handgun had fallen from its holster and now lay a couple of feet away. He kicked the pistol into the corner and dropped to one knee, sliding in behind his stunned opponent.

As the stranger tried to sit up, Adam reached around his neck while simultaneously bracing the back of his head with the other hand. With a powerful jerking motion, he set the choke. He was careful to apply the choke only to the sides of the neck, pinching both carotid arteries without introducing the danger of suffocation.

The man struggled to free himself, grabbing at Adam's arm and pulling with what strength he had left. His fingernails gouged into Adam's forearm, drawing several thin streams of blood, but the added pressure served only to further cut off what little blood his brain was receiving. In less than twenty seconds, he lost consciousness and dangled limply from Adam's grip.

Still maintaining a light choke using one arm and his body as a brace, Adam patted the man down for identification. He found a small black leather wallet, which he immediately flipped open. The man's name was Stephen Dorny, but it wasn't his name that made Adam's heart skip a beat. It was who had issued the ID—the Central Intelligence Agency. Uncertain of exactly what that implied, he stuck the wallet into his jacket pocket for later consideration. Searching further, he found only a set of car keys. He tossed them into a nearby waste can.

"Now what?" he asked himself.

A clear answer didn't immediately come to mind. He wanted to ask the man why he'd been breaking into Maria's mailbox, but it was a little hard to do that now.

As if in answer to his question, a woman suddenly appeared in the mailroom doorway. She looked to be in her fifties and was wearing a red-and-blue fleece jogging suit. As she focused on Adam hunched behind the unconscious man, she covered her mouth in obvious fright.

"Please help me," Adam said quickly. "I'm trying to revive him." He began lifting the man's arms up and down along his sides in flamboyant flapping motions, simulating what he thought could pass as a resuscitation attempt. "He grabbed his chest and fell to the floor a minute ago. I think he may have had a heart attack." It was a reach, but he hoped she bought it.

"Oh . . . okay." the woman said, her face shifting from terror to one of bystander concern. "What can I do? Should I run call someone? The paramedics, maybe?"

"Yes, please. I'd hate for him to . . . well, you know. I think it would be best if he had some professional attention." Adam continued the flapping.

"Okay, I'll go. Just keep . . ." She seemed at a loss for his peculiar form of resuscitation. "Keep doing whatever you're doing. I'll be right back." Then she turned and sprinted away.

Given that he'd just assaulted a government agent, it seemed like a good idea to vacate the premises before emergency services arrived. Adam laid the man over on his side and quickly went to Maria's now-open mailbox. Inside, he saw two standard white envelopes and a small, poly bubble envelope. He grabbed all three before closing the box. Next, he removed and pocketed the small brass key that fit Maria's mail-box, tossing the crowded key ring into the garbage can. He then quickly retrieved the revolver from the corner of the post office, dumped the bullets in the trash, and placed the gun back in agent's holster.

Time to go. On his way out, he took one last look at the subdued man's face. The stranger was still far away in dreamland. Adam grinned as he hustled towards Lara's waiting car. He'd always loved a good fight.

* * *

By four that afternoon, Adam once again sat in the red leather chair opposite his brother's desk. Elliot stared wide-eyed at the bloody tooth and three opened envelopes lying on his desk. His face had lost what little color daytime usually supplied.

Lara had returned home at Adam's insistence and with a promise that he would call her later with a complete update on anything he and Elliot discussed. Before they had separated, Adam had described his encounter with the man in the mailroom. Together they had opened Maria's mail and found an unexpected surprise.

"I didn't think it was going to turn out like this," Elliot said, touching the tooth gently with an expensive designer pen. "I had a bad feeling . . . but not like this. This is barbaric."

"Never underestimate the cruelty of man," Adam answered.

Elliot swallowed with an audible gulp. "What now? I mean it may be too late to help her. She could be . . ."

Adam could hear a squeak of pain in his brother's voice. His feelings for Maria had been brought to the surface with the sudden realization that she was very likely injured. Or worse, rotting alongside a remote hiking trail somewhere. "This is your show. You get to decide when it's over. I'll stay as long as you need me."

After a moment of consideration, Elliot seemed to find a glimmer of hope, "I'm not ready to give up. Maria's clearly in trouble, but it doesn't necessarily mean that she's dead."

"No, it doesn't."

"But what can we do from here?"

"I guess the first thing to do is verify that the tooth is Maria's. In this business, you can't take anything for granted. Her dentist should be able to do that for us. Lara gave me the name of one they both used several months ago." Adam tossed a yellow slip of paper onto the edge of the desk. "He should have records that can positively identify the tooth as Maria's."

Elliot retrieved the note. "I'll get John to check on this right away." He glanced at his watch. "Crap, it'll have to wait until tomorrow morning. The dentist is probably getting ready to head home."

"I don't know about you, but I don't want to wait. Call the dentist's office, and tell them it's a medical emergency. Insist that you need to see him right away, but don't answer any questions. Just tell them you'll be right over. My guess is he'll wait for you." Being a private investigator required being pushy at times.

"Okay, right. That should work." Elliot quickly called the dentist's office and did as instructed. After a brief conversation, he hung up the phone.

"They said the dentist could stay until five-thirty. I think John can make it if he leaves now." He hit a button on his phone, and a few seconds later the oversized assistant lumbered in. Elliot gave him the tooth and instructions. John seemed neither surprised nor overly interested in being handed a human tooth. Moments later, the steroid-slurping legal assistant was en route with a mission.

"After the trip to the dentist, you might want to have him make a few calls to the local hospitals and city morgue," Adam suggested. "Just in case she's being treated, or worse, about to be buried as a Jane Doe."

"Right," Elliot agreed, his face betraying his discomfort. "What else?"

"Take a look at the rest of the mail."

Elliot turned his attention to the contents of the three envelopes. The first was a monthly statement from First American National Bank. It showed a balance of $2,314 and some change in her checking account, and another $30,850 in savings. The statement offered little else since the transaction log ended a week before Maria's disappearance and showed no signs of any emergency withdrawals.

The second piece of mail was an electric bill. He set the bank statement and bill aside, as they didn't seem to warrant further study.

Next, Elliot turned his attention to the small, poly bubble envelope. Inside, he found a note and an orange plastic-topped key with the identifier T1276 imprinted in the plastic. He unfolded the handwritten note and read silently.

Dear Lara,

I'm sure you're going to find this amusing, but I'm in trouble again and am sending you this key for safekeeping. Please don't ask what it goes to or why I feel the need to hide it. Just park it somewhere safe for me. I'll get it from you next week when things cool down a bit. If anyone asks whether you've heard from me, say you haven't. Whatever you do, don't mention the key to anyone. I'm onto something big, really big.

Love your sis,

Maria

"I don't get it. Why was this in Maria's box?" Elliot asked, holding up the note.

"Look at the envelope," Adam prompted.

Elliot turned over the envelope and saw it was stamped *Return to Sender, Insufficient Postage* in bright red ink.

"Best I can figure," Adam said, "her precious package sent out for safekeeping has been floating around in the hands of our postal workers for the last two weeks."

"So it would seem," Elliot agreed, turning the key over slowly. "I don't suppose you have any idea what this fits?"

"It looks like a locker key to me. One of those rental types. The locker could be anywhere, though. I didn't see any identifying marks on the key other than the number."

Elliot nodded. "I'll wager that Maria has hidden that map that she discussed with me. Given the desperate tone of her note, it also seems likely her disappearance is related to it."

Adam nodded. "It does seem like a hell of a coincidence."

Elliot stood and moved to the small bar, saying, "This is getting more and more complicated. A map, a key, a missing girl." Without asking, he popped caps on two cold beers and handed one to his brother.

Adam nodded his appreciation and took a long swig. As he set the bottle down, he said, "Something's not right about this."

"Of course, something's not right," Elliot said, clearly agitated. "Maria's had a tooth ripped out and God knows what else done to her."

"No, you don't get what I mean. This wasn't the work of an ex-boyfriend or a ripped-off businessman. This was the work of several people, at least one of whom was a professional."

Elliot looked at Adam, his expression changing from frustration to curiosity. "Go on."

"First, consider the tooth. Why would someone do that to her?"

"Could be the sadistic work of a scorned lover who didn't want her quite as beautiful anymore."

"Doubtful, but possible, I guess. Consider another motive. Information."

Elliot rubbed thoughtfully at his chin. "To reveal where she'd hidden the map."

"Exactly."

"It just seems so . . . so heavy-handed. Surely there would have been a better way to get her to return the map. Pulling her teeth . . . come on. That's too much for anyone."

Adam shrugged. "Some people threaten. Others do worse. Also, consider that it would have taken more than one person. It would be hard as hell to yank a grown woman's tooth out while she was conscious and lacking the desired effect if she was knocked out. That means there were at least two people in on it. One to hold; one to work the tools."

"Couldn't he have just tied her up?" Elliot countered.

"Even tied up, do you think you could force a person's jaw open while using a pair of pliers in the other hand?"

"I . . . I wouldn't know," Elliot said, his voice shaking. "But no, I guess not. And that leads you to think it was a professional, someone specifically hired to interrogate her."

"That's part of it, along with the unnatural condition of her apartment. Whoever did this cleaned the place up real nice. They'd done this sort of thing before and were careful not to leave any evidence of what went down. If it wasn't for some of that dumb luck I told Lara about, we'd never have found the tooth."

Elliot took a sip of beer, collecting his thoughts. "Okay, so let's recap. What are our clues?" he said, thinking out loud. This was a game not so different from his legal profession, a game of putting pieces together into a cohesive case, and he was beginning to get into character. "We have a tooth removed by force. We have an apartment that has been sanitized to cover up the struggle. And we have a key. Not just any key, but one that we're guessing leads to a map she considered very valuable. If it wasn't all so utterly horrible, it would be . . . fascinating."

Adam nodded, deciding it was time to let Elliot know just how "fascinating" it really was. "We have one more thing."

"Oh?"

"When I went to get Maria's mail, there was a man trying to get into her mailbox."

"What?" Elliot asked, his eyes widening. "Who was he? Did you talk to him?"

"We didn't have a chance to talk." Adam couldn't help but smile. The powerful adrenaline from the fight was still swimming in his veins.

"What are you saying? You . . . you beat him up?"

Adam laughed. It wouldn't have surprised him to learn that Elliot hadn't been in a physical competition of any sort since early childhood. "Yeah, Elliot, I beat him up."

"But why? Couldn't you have just called the police?"

That struck Adam as a reasonable question. One that he didn't have a great answer to. "It all went down rather fast. Before I knew it, we were pushing and shoving." He didn't bother adding the fact that he'd initiated the fight.

"Why—" Elliot stopped himself.

Adam looked at him. "Go ahead. Say what's on your mind."

Elliot took a breath. "I'm just wondering why everything always turns physical with you. It's like you think you're some kind of gladiator running around fighting the evil empire. We live in a civilized society. You know that, right?"

Adam wasn't surprised by Elliot's condemnation. He had never understood that every man had to do what he could. Adam said only, "We live in different worlds, brother. In my world, a man has to fight."

Elliot's unchanging expression hinted at just how unsatisfying the answer was. "But even if the fight was necessary, why not call the police afterward? You blew our one good lead. Tell me there was a good reason for that."

"There was a good reason." Adam tossed the thin black wallet onto Elliot's desk.

Elliot immediately opened it. As he studied the contents, his face turned ashen. "You're kidding me."

"Afraid not."

"The guy you assaulted works for the CIA?"

Adam smiled, drawing some pleasure out of his brother's discomfort. "So it would seem."

"Shit," his brother said uncharacteristically. "This can't be good, Adam." Elliot's hands were trembling.

"CIA or not, if he's the one that put the pliers to Maria, he deserved a hell of a lot more than I gave him."

"I suppose, but . . ." Elliot mumbled.

"You suppose?"

"That's not what I meant. Don't turn my words on me." His face was turning red.

"I just don't want you to forget why we're here."

"I haven't forgotten. But I can't believe that the CIA would torture Maria. Certainly not in her bathroom."

Adam shrugged. "I'll admit it leaves questions. But we don't have much else."

Elliot sat quiet for a long time before speaking. "What do we do now?" He looked like a kid who had just been sent to the principal's office.

"We could follow your suggestion and go to the police. What was that detective's name in the newspaper article—Conner, Carver, something like that?"

"Carter," Elliot answered. "Do you honestly think that will do any good now?"

Adam suddenly felt weary. Weary from having to think about why someone would torture a beautiful lady in her own bathroom. Weary from having to quibble with his brother. Weary from having to beat the hell out of a government asshole. He took another long drink and used his thumbs to slowly rub his temples.

"Probably not," he answered. "If Denver's anything like the rest of the country, each detective might have a dozen or more cases open at any one time. I doubt if a missing hooker would get his shorts in a wad, no matter what we've found. Besides, if we contact the police, we will be all but delivering the key to the CIA."

"It's our only real clue."

"Exactly."

"But can we really do this alone? We're talking about the CIA. They don't play games. If we interfere with an investigation they have underway, we'll end up in jail. If they're not the ones who grabbed Maria, then someone else is involved. Someone who's violent and dangerous."

Adam nodded. His brother seemed to understand the risks. "The bottom line is that we have to watch out for the good guys and the bad guys. Hell of a situation."

"I can't ask that of you."

Adam doubted the fresh brotherly concern and wasn't about to give Elliot an easy out. "I'm a big boy. I can take care of myself."

"It could be dangerous for you." Then, as if an afterthought, added, "For us both."

"I'd say it's likely to get rough," Adam agreed, wondering if his brother was really going to pussy out.

"The intelligent thing to do is let the authorities handle this," Elliot said, testing his retreat.

Adam shrugged, trying not to show his disgust. "Like I said, it's your call. But I think you know what will happen to Maria if we don't find her."

Elliot sighed. "I don't want to think about it."

"So, what do you say?"

After a long silence, Elliot said, "I suppose Lara had it right. I owe Maria. Besides, if I don't go through with this, it'll surely lead to more regret and guilt. Believe me, I don't need that."

Adam saw resignation in his brother's eyes. A decision had been made. "For what it's worth, I think you're doing the right thing."

Elliot nodded an appreciation. "Let's talk money," he said, changing directions entirely.

"Let's not," Adam countered. Their discussion of money always led to Elliot adopting a tone of "I have it and you don't," and he just wasn't in the mood.

"Here's the deal. I want to treat your involvement in this like I would any other business transaction."

"We're family. You don't have to pay me."

"Please don't make this difficult," Elliot pleaded. "It's been a hard day."

"Fine. What do you propose?"

"What are your normal rates when you're working a case away from home? Scratch that, it doesn't matter. I wouldn't consider that if I was hiring someone else. I'd pay what I thought it was worth. So, here's my offer. I'll give you one thousand dollars a day plus expenses. How's that sound?"

"Like a hell of a lot of money."

"Before you start bartering on the streets of Baghdad, you might consider reworking your strategy," Elliot said, grinning.

Arguing seemed pointless. "Fine," Adam said. "It's your piggy bank."

"Good. Then it's settled."

"Since you're so eager to spend money, we might as well get a few things while we're waiting for confirmation about the tooth."

"Go. What do you need?" Elliot asked, shuffling in a desk drawer and pulling out a miniature yellow legal pad.

"Let's start with a gun."

Elliot looked up alarmed. "A gun? What for? I mean, don't you already have one?" He set his pen down on the pad, refusing to even write down the questionable item on the all-important "to-do" list.

"I have several, but not with me. I didn't think that I would need one. I could have one mailed, but that would take a few days. By then, this whole thing might be over. No, I think it would be safer if I arm myself soon as possible."

"But why? Christ, Adam, do you really need a gun? I'm not comfortable with this."

"Elliot, listen to me. Maria is probably already dead. If someone's willing to kill her, they will have no qualms with killing me," then added, "or you."

"A gun," Elliot repeated, considering the implications. Reluctantly he acquiesced, saying, "I guess you're probably right. This is serious after all. It's taking time to sink in. That's all. Frankly, I'm not used to this sort of thing. Maybe I need a gun too." His eyes darted towards Adam as if he had just licked his finger and was testing a hot match.

Adam knew that Elliot was expecting him to scoff at the suggestion. After all, in both their eyes, Elliot was a levelheaded lawyer, not some gun-toting adventurer. But, then again, there was a bloody tooth, a missing girl, and a well-dressed man with a serious headache just now climbing out of a hospital bed somewhere.

Adam only replied, "Maybe you do."

Chapter 7

Teddy Johnson, or TJ, as the seedy side of town knew him, leaned forward on the display case. Large beads of sweat dropped from his forehead, splashing against the dirty glass. An old, rusty fan hummed nearby, blowing a steady breeze across his behemoth frame. Given the late hour, his store was quiet save for the fan and the sound of his breathing as it wheezed in and out like the air from a leaky tire.

"God, give me some relief," he prayed halfheartedly. TJ knew no relief was coming. His relationship with the Almighty was very likely in the shit can, and besides, his exhaustion and discomfort had taken a lifetime of gluttony and self-indulgence to create. Not only indulgence with food, but with liquor, cigarettes, and women. TJ had never been one to say "no," or even "not now" for that matter.

The food was probably to blame for his four-hundred-plus pounds, but the other vices surely took an equal toll on his body and soul. He blamed the women for several painful bouts of gonorrhea and syphilis, the cigarettes for his high blood pressure and raspy voice, and the liquor . . . ah hell, the liquor wasn't to blame for anything.

TJ smiled a big greasy smile, licking at his swollen purple lips. *People think I'm a pig, but that's okay. I know how to live, that's all. Sucking the sweet nectar out of life, that's me.* He'd learned a nifty sounding word that lent an exotic flavor to his gluttony. *Hedonism. Oh yeah, baby, that's me, TJ the hedonist.*

He recalled a particularly satisfying encounter a few nights ago when he had nailed an unusually young prostitute working Denver's west side.

Well, even he would have to admit that "nailed" was probably too strong a word. Given his girth and physical limitations, he'd only been able to lie like a beached walrus while the girl rode him. Much to his disappointment, it had taken only a minute or two until he was spent.

He consoled himself as he always did. *I screwed her, and that's all that matters. Another piece of patch to add to my collection. And a young one at that. She'll remember TJ all right.*

"How old was that cream pie?" he asked aloud. "Eighteen? Younger?" He licked at his lips again. "Yep, I just know how to live, that's all. TJ the hedonist," he whispered to himself.

He heard a car pull into the gravel parking lot in front of the store. *Probably another punk trying to fence a car stereo, or some junkie willing to hock his sister's virginity for twenty bucks.*

Come to TJ. I've got what you need. Come to TJ.

* * *

A bright blue-and-yellow neon sign flashed: TJ's GUN AND PAWN. The letter "A" in "PAWN" flickered irregularly with an occasional popping spark. Adam shut off the engine of the Ford Taurus he'd rented an hour earlier.

Elliot sat in the passenger seat picking nervously at his perfectly manicured fingernails as he stared out the window. "I was probably overreacting," he said to no one in particular.

Adam stared at him curiously. He'd witnessed a remarkable transformation during their brief drive across town. In less than fifteen miles, a confident corporate attorney had morphed into a timid teenager faced with buying condoms on prom night.

"You know, what I said about needing a gun," Elliot clarified. "It's really not necessary. I won't be involved in anything directly. Now you, you I can understand. But me . . ." He trailed off without finishing.

Adam shook his head, partly amused, partly disgusted by what he was witnessing. "Suit yourself," he said, opening the car door and stepping out.

After only a moment of hesitation, Elliot let out a resigned sigh and followed his brother into the pawnshop.

The store was as unexceptional to Adam as it was fascinating to Elliot. Typical pawnshop paraphernalia was sprawled chaotically about in every direction. To their immediate left was a large stuffed grizzly rearing up on his hind legs. It was covered in a heavy winter coat of deep brown fur, armed with an unnatural smile and wearing an oversized pair of orange fishing waders. Somewhere there was a taxidermist with way too much time on his hands.

Camouflage clothing, archery supplies, pocket knives, fishing rods, and gun accessories lay scattered about the room on short metal racks. Farther into the store was a long glass counter with dozens of shotguns and rifles hanging high on the wall behind it. The reek of human perspiration stretched from corner to corner, rivaling that of a Cuban refugee boat.

Adam led them to the gun counter, which was serviced by a balding, grossly obese man who looked to be in his early fifties. The clerk's face was flushed a splotchy bright red, and his corpulent frame spilled over in every direction from a heavy wooden stool. He rested with both elbows on the glass counter, as if his body would suddenly collapse if it were forced to support its own weight.

"The name's TJ," the shopkeeper slurred with a raspy drawl. "What can I do you out of gentlemen?"

"Just looking," Elliot immediately replied.

TJ's bloodshot eyes studied him for a moment before shifting to Adam.

"We're looking for a couple of handguns, along with some ammo," Adam said. "Preferably all new."

"Well, you boys have come to the right place. We got guns, and most everything's new or near about it," TJ said with a wave of crusty fingers that looked as if he'd just used them to pick his bulbous, blue-veined nose.

As they moved closer to the counter, Adam and Elliot saw that inside the glass case were several long shelves lined with handguns. Almost all of the firearms were out of their original boxes and had bright green sale tags tied to their trigger guards. Adam doubted if many of the handguns were in fact new, but it didn't matter much. He began looking carefully from gun to gun.

"Where y'all from?" TJ asked.

Elliot waited a moment for Adam to answer. When he didn't, Elliot said, "We're locals. I mean, pretty local. We live in the general area. But not real close."

Adam grinned at Elliot's piss poor attempt at maintaining any sort of anonymity. His brother was an awkward bird when in unfamiliar circles.

"Um-hum," TJ replied with a shit-eating grin. "Looking for anything in particular? I have some real bargains here. Take this twenty-five caliber," he said, pulling a small automatic from the case. "I can let you have this for less than you'd spend on a little hoochie down on Colfax. It's a real good—"

"How about this one?" Adam interrupted.

"Hmm?" TJ slid the wheeled stool towards Adam, never removing a huge fold of fat from the countertop.

"The Browning Hi-Power. How much?" He could see the tag hanging on it read seven hundred dollars.

"You know, I could tell right off you two knew what you were doing. Yep, right off, I could tell that. And as I'm sure you already know, Browning, they make some fine firearms. Finest in the world, some would say."

"Yeah, but how much?" Adam asked coolly. It occurred to him that it wasn't his money he was spending, and as far as Elliot was concerned, seven hundred or seventeen hundred wouldn't make much difference. But it was the principle of the matter. No way was he going to pay this slob too much for anything. Just for grins, he planned to make it a bit uncomfortable for the gelatinous huckster.

"Let you have it for six-fifty," TJ answered through squinting eyes.

"Elliot, come over and get a feel of this one," Adam directed.

Elliot moved quickly to stand beside his brother. The shopkeeper removed the pistol from the case and handed it to him butt first.

As Elliot held the firearm, Adam could see a sense of excitement coming over his brother's face. Guns had a way of doing that to people. He could only hope the same excitement wouldn't get his brother or someone close to him killed. Unfortunately, they tended to do that to people too.

"Feels like a schoolgirl's titty, don't it?" TJ prodded, picking up on Elliot's obvious satisfaction.

"Uh, yeah, it feels fine," Elliot said, nodding his head. "You know, balanced and all."

Adam suspected he would have gotten the same reaction if he'd selected the cheapest Saturday night special in the store. But in truth, the Browning was a superb firearm, so Elliot was calling it right this time.

"We'll give you five hundred, and—" Adam started.

"Whoa Nelly, five hundred won't get you jack—"

"And," Adam interjected forcefully, "we'll buy that boxed Glock forty-five behind you for an additional six hundred."

"You know that Glock goes for over seven-fifty by itself?" TJ asked, his tone betraying both his annoyance and the freshly planted hope that money was going to change hands.

"Eleven hundred for the guns, but we'll be needing a few additional things like leather holsters, a couple of fifty-round boxes of those Winchester hollow points, some travel cases, and oil to wipe them down with." Adam gestured to items behind the counter.

"Hmm, let me figure this." TJ pulled out a small tablet of paper with the insignia of a local motel. After a little scribbling, he said, "That would come to just over fourteen hundred plus tax. You got that kind of money? I don't take no checks."

Adam looked to Elliot and nodded. His brother took his cue. "No problem. One thousand four hundred."

"Plus tax," TJ added.

"Plus tax," Elliot agreed. "Is a credit card okay?"

"Plastic's fine, so long as it clears."

"It'll clear," Elliot assured him.

"And I'll have to run you both through the FBI database. Not felons are you? Even if you are, we might be able to work something out here."

"We're not felons," Adam assured him. "Gather all the stuff while we fill out the forms."

A few minutes later, Elliot and Adam left TJ's pawn shop carrying packages wrapped in brown paper. Neither of them was aware of the four men studying them from a black Lincoln Continental parked in a vacant lot across the street.

* * *

"You still remember how to handle a gun?" Adam asked. He didn't want to insult his brother but felt the conversation was warranted for both their safety.

Elliot sat on one of the business chairs in Adam's suite, holding the Browning Hi-Power with both hands. He brought it up and lined up the sights as though he were about to start shooting groundhogs hiding in the bathroom. "It's been a while, but I think I can manage." His voice had a strange John Wayne drawl to it.

Adam wasn't so sure. The last time he'd seen his brother use a firearm was when they were kids plinking cans with their father. "Just in case you aren't familiar with that particular model, it's a nine-millimeter, single-action semiautomatic."

Elliot looked up with a blank face but didn't dare betray his ignorance with words.

"To you and me, that means that each time you pull the trigger, a bullet comes out. Depending on whether there's already a bullet in the chamber, you either have to cock the hammer or pull the slide for the first shot. You got it?"

"Uh, yeah, cock the hammer, got it."

"Let's load it."

"Now?"

"We didn't buy them to scare people. We bought them to shoot people. Come on, let's do it together." Adam removed the Glock from its box. Working slowly so that Elliot could mimic his actions, he slid bullet after bullet into the magazine. After the Glock's ten-round capacity was reached, he said, "Keep going. You can put five more in yours."

"Five more? You mean this one holds fifteen bullets?"

"Yes, so load it all the way up."

Elliot did as instructed. As he finished, he said, "How come you didn't get one that holds fifteen bullets?"

It was obvious that Elliot was trying to decide if he should be proud of this special feature or if he had been somehow misled by his devious brother into buying a substandard pistol that held entirely too many bullets.

Adam understood that magazine capacity was one of the many trades that a handgun owner had to make. The more rounds it held, the heavier the firearm, but also the greater firepower that it provided. Also, legislation had come and gone that outlawed high-capacity clips like the one Elliot had, so to be compliant, manufacturers had sold their weapons with ten-round magazines.

Adam didn't tell his brother any of this. Instead, he said, "I wanted the forty-five. It has more punch than the nine-millimeter. I figured it'd been a while since you last shot, so it made more sense for you to get one that kicked a bit less." Besides, Adam knew if he ever had to shoot more than ten rounds before he could reload, he would surely already be dead.

Adam chambered a round and helped Elliot to do the same. After lowering the hammer on the Browning, he pointed out the safety switch and reminded Elliot once more about cocking the hammer for the first shot.

With the guns having been successfully loaded, Adam slipped the Glock into its holster and tossed it on the bed. Elliot put the Browning into its holster and set it in his lap like a half-eaten sack lunch.

"You know the law, Elliot, so I won't begin to tell you when you're allowed to shoot someone. But here's a final bit of advice from your little brother."

Elliot sat up straight and looked at Adam with an unusual amount of respect. This was clearly a situation in which traditional roles had been forgotten.

"If you have to shoot, don't hesitate, and don't try to wound."

"It won't come to that," Elliot said with a nervous laugh. "I mean this is a bit ridiculous if you really stop to consider the odds of—"

"Listen," Adam said with a calm but stern voice. "All I'm saying is if you know you have to pull the trigger, don't be indecisive. You shoot for center mass, and you shoot a three-round burst. Remember that, okay?"

Elliot looked away.

"Okay?" Adam repeated.

Elliot looked back to him, frustration clearly on his face. "Fine. I got it. Three rounds. Center mass."

Adam hoped that if his brother ever found himself in such a situation, he would remember the advice. A gun fight was no place for hesitation.

Suddenly the phone on the small conference room table began to ring. Both brothers looked to one another.

"Any idea who that might be?" Elliot asked.

"Only you and Lara know I'm here." Adam picked up the receiver. "Yes."

"Mr. Reece, this is Charles from the front desk." His voice was noticeably edgy.

"Hello, Charles."

"Sir, I'm sorry to bother you, but I'm afraid there's been an incident down here. Nothing that couldn't be handled, but I thought you might want to know."

"What happened?"

"A man came in about ten minutes ago asking about you," Charles answered. "He identified himself as a federal agent but didn't offer any identification. When I politely refused to give any specifics of your stay here, he became rather threatening."

"Did he hurt you?" Adam felt himself growing warm with anger.

"No. Thankfully, the hotel detective came to my aid."

Adam didn't even know hotels had detectives any more. Then again, he didn't stay at places like the Hotel Mona very often. "What happened?"

"Once my man arrived, the stranger just left without another word. I found that rather odd, considering his claim to be in law enforcement." The clerk hesitated. "Sir, are you in some sort of trouble?"

"Not that I'm aware of," Adam answered honestly. "If you see this man again, will you be sure to call me? I'd like to have a word with him."

"Absolutely."

Adam thanked him and hung up the phone.

"What was that about?" Elliot asked.

"Someone's onto us. They asked questions about me at the front desk."

"You think it's the people who grabbed Maria?"

"I don't know. None of this is making sense right now. If the CIA wanted to know something about me, they wouldn't have to play hardball with a hotel clerk."

Both men stared at the phone as if it were about to ring again. A sharp beep suddenly sounded, and Elliot recoiled.

"That's me," he chuckled nervously, reaching down to free the BlackBerry from his belt. "Shit," he whispered, staring at the glowing LCD display.

"What?"

Elliot closed his eyes and took a moment to answer. "The tooth. It was Maria's."

* * *

Lara and Adam sat opposite each other on saggy orange vinyl benches. A coffee-stained laminate table extended between them.

After Elliot had left his hotel room, Adam kept his word and called Lara to tell her about their conversation. They'd agreed to meet somewhere where they could talk inconspicuously. She'd suggested Lulu's Diner, a greasy spoon just off Colorado Boulevard, assuring Adam that the food was awful, the coffee good, and more relevantly, the customers were street people who had more important things to worry about than other people's business.

The restaurant was bustling with a rowdy evening crowd. The sound of clinking silverware and the smell of greasy sausage and cigarettes filled the diner.

"You're both committed to this? Even Elliot? I'm surprised. I figured he'd run for cover at the first sign of trouble."

"He's digging deep right now, looking for courage he didn't know he had. But I'd say he's definitely in. I think you guilted him into it."

She smiled. "The only positive outcome from our lunch from hell."

"I thought you two were going to start pulling each other's hair," Adam joked.

"I can't stand him. Sorry for that. Him being your brother and all."

"No need to apologize. I can't stand him half the time either."

She laughed. "You love him. I can see that. And I'm sure he can too. It says a lot about you."

"What can I say? I have a strong sense of family."

"I'll try not to get ugly with him," she said. "But no promises."

"I'll be happy if you can just keep from strangling him with his necktie," he laughed.

"Again, no promises," she said, smiling.

"Who knows? Before this is all over, you may end up hating me too."

She searched his face until their eyes met. "No. That won't happen."

"Don't tell me—my dashing good looks, right?" he said, grinning.

She smiled and shook her head. "No . . . something else." Before he could respond, she quickly changed the subject, "Can I see the identification you got off the joker in the mailroom?"

Adam pulled it out of his pocket and handed it to her, a bit disappointed that the moment they'd shared had passed.

"You may not know it," she said, "but I'm a bit of a kook."

"Believe me, I know it," he snickered.

"I'm serious. I've spent way too much time reading about conspiracies and government cover-ups. A hobby of mine I guess. Now it comes home to me. What are the odds?"

"We don't know there's any sort of conspiracy here."

"I suppose not, but I have this feeling. I can't shake it. We're involved in something much bigger than just my sister's disappearance."

"Elliot and I are leaning towards the idea that her disappearance is related to the map and locker key. How the CIA plays into it isn't clear yet."

"Do you think they did that to my sister?" Before he could get away without answering, she added "I'm not asking what you know. I'm asking what you think."

Adam set down his nearly full cup of coffee, the steam rising in front of his face. He'd always enjoyed the smell of the java much more than the taste. "At this point, there's no way to say for sure, but I wouldn't put it past the CIA to torture someone." He immediately regretted using the word "torture," even though it clearly fit.

"Anyway," he quickly continued, "whatever she's gotten herself into, some elements of the government obviously consider it important enough to intercept her mail and probably put surveillance on her phone and apartment."

After a moment, his words sank in. "You mean they heard everything we said inside Maria's place?" she asked. "They were listening?" She looked around suspiciously at a restaurant's patrons.

"My guess is that they were monitoring us the whole time, which means they know who we are and where we live." Adam didn't mention the anonymous visit that had been paid to the hotel clerk.

"They don't have any right to spy on us like that. They don't have the right to do any of this. Sure as hell not hurt my sister."

Adam didn't answer. He didn't know if they had the right or not, and it probably didn't matter anyway. The CIA did what they wanted. From what he understood of the organization, they worked outside the law as often as they worked inside it. That wasn't what disturbed him.

It was that the CIA was involved at all that had him concerned, and a bit puzzled. The agency usually limited itself to matters of national security and foreign intelligence gathering. Less sticky matters were often passed down to the FBI, or at times even the NSA. For the CIA to be involved in a domestic issue meant that it was something they didn't trust to anyone else. Something they never intended to become public. Their involvement was not headed for the five o'clock evening news. Clandestine was the name of their game.

"How about the key?" he asked, trying to steer the conversation in a more productive direction. "Have you come up with any ideas as to what it fits?"

"I thought of one possibility," she answered. "Maria worked out at a gym near her house called Olympia's. Maybe it unlocks her locker there."

A broad smile crossed his face. "Good work, Lara." He was convinced having her involved was their best chance of discovering what happened to Maria. Lara knew her sister, and that knowledge was critical to uncovering clues.

His smile proved contagious. "You think that could really be it? Something so simple like a gym locker?" Her voice sounded hopeful, like that of a child talking about what Santa might bring for Christmas.

"It's the best lead we have," he answered.

"First we find the map, and then we trade for my sister. That's how this works, right?"

Adam gave a halfhearted nod. "I guess so." He felt certain they both heard the unrealistic thread of optimism Lara was using to stitch the hopeful scenario together. Personally, he doubted Maria was still alive but didn't see any reason to press his pessimism on Lara. Right now, she needed hope. Hell, for all he knew, Maria might be cooped up in a secret detention facility, sucking on a teabag to stop the bleeding caused by an overzealous interrogator. Until they knew differently, he didn't see how it hurt to go on that optimistic assumption.

* * *

For the first few moments, Adam understood that he was dreaming. That awareness quickly faded. Matsumoto was standing at the front of the dojo, squat and strong, his white *gi* freshly pressed and offsetting a thick mat of unkempt salt-and-pepper hair. His class had just finished a lengthy set of stretching and falling exercises.

"To prosper, a man requires balance," Matsumoto began. Out of courtesy, he spoke slower than normal so Adam could translate from Japanese to English. "He must find this balance in all things. Suppose a man has a job that pays a fortune but does not allow him to properly raise his children. Will he prosper in life?"

Matsumoto raised one foot in the air. "No. His lack of balance will make him unstable." He rocked side to side. "Easily defeated."

Matsumoto planted both feet and steadied himself. "Judo is a reflection of life. To remain balanced, you must be connected to the earth beneath your feet. You must use your ki, your spiritual energy, to be a tree with roots that reach far below your opponent's. By doing so, you can weather any storm he commands."

He surveyed the class. "Cowboy, come to the front."

Adam stood and took his place in front of Matsumoto. A position he had taken on numerous occasions, most of which ended with him lying flat on his back.

Still looking at the class, Matsumoto said. "Is Cowboy balanced?"

Several students nodded noncommittally, most remained still.

Without warning, Matsumoto grabbed one of Adam's lapels and tugged hard. The thick cotton *gi* pulled free from his belt, and his neck jerked forward from the force. Adam felt anger beginning to swell within him.

"What about now?" Matsumoto growled. "More or less stable?"

Again, no one answered. The violence had set a mood of importance.

Matsumoto slipped his other hand behind Adam's collar and pulled the *gi* across his neck.

Instinctively, Adam reached up and grabbed Matsumoto's hand. Despite his size advantage, he could not budge the teacher's grip. With the loss of air, he felt desperation starting to take hold.

"What about now?"

Adam tried to choke out a protest.

"Do you see how easily balance is lost? How easily concentration is broken?" Matsumoto released him. "Now throw me."

"Sensei?"

"For two weeks, we have practiced a single throw, *ashi guruma*, the leg wheel. You appear proficient at it. So throw me. Show me what you've learned."

Still feeling the burn from the *gi* against his neck, Adam shot ahead. He grabbed two handfuls of uniform and drove his right hip and thigh into Matsumoto. But as he spun to pull him around for the throw, Matsumoto suddenly reversed direction and swept both Adam's feet out from under him. Surprised, he fell hard, his head thumping the mat.

Adam took a moment to shake off the dizziness before standing.

"What have you learned?" Matsumoto asked.

"That I'm too slow."

Matsumoto shook his head. "No. We go again." Without warning, he slapped Adam hard on the side of his face.

Adam felt the sting of Matsumoto's hand and immediately tasted blood. He whipped his head back to glare at his teacher. He wasn't used to letting someone hit him freely and wasn't entirely sure he would allow it to happen again. He felt his hands involuntarily tighten into fists at his sides.

"Do you feel it, Cowboy?" Matsumoto's tone was much softer than his actions had been.

"What?" Adam asked between clenched teeth.

"The energy within you. Your ki. It is so strong. I can feel it all around me like the hot waters of the *onsen*. But can *you* feel it? Or do I need to hit you again?"

"No, I can feel it all right." And on some level he did. There was a tremendous amount of something building inside him at the moment. Anger, frustration, humiliation, but something else too. An internal flame.

"Tell me what you know about your ki." Matsumoto directed.

"It makes me stronger, faster."

"Yes, this is true for styles like *kenpo*. In those martial arts, you are taught to release it for additional power. What you must also learn is to use it to balance yourself. This is the way of judo."

Adam felt the anger within him subsiding. Matsumoto's violence now seemed more instructional than sadistic. "How do I do that?" he asked.

Matsumoto placed both hands on Adam's shoulders and pressed down. "Instead of letting it rise to the surface and undercut your balance, push it down deep into the earth. Use it to hold yourself still in a world where everyone else is moving."

Matsumoto appeared to be asking him to hold it in, and that didn't feel natural. "I'm not sure I can. It . . . it wants out."

Matsumoto laughed and the class joined in. "Yes, Cowboy. This is true. But even a fool can let his ki out. It's being able to channel it from within that will set you apart."

* * *

At just past eight the next morning, Adam and Lara stood looking up at a twenty-foot, gold-painted, plaster statue standing guard in front of Olympia's Health and Fitness Center. The sculpture was of a Herculean man with an immense black barbell raised high above his head. The bodybuilding titan wore a pair of skintight bikini briefs constructed from an American flag.

"Now *that* is sexy," Lara said with a grin.

"You go girl," he coaxed, giving her a light shove.

Both of them burst out laughing.

Adam was glad to see that she was in good spirits. Standing in front of the gym that might give them some answers brought a ray of hope to him too. It felt like they were onto something.

The utterly ridiculous bikini-briefed mammoth reminded Adam of the old Azar's Big Boy restaurant mascot. If this gym was anything like most he'd been to, the hamburger-praising Big Boy might well be the more appropriate deity for many of its patrons.

After a moment, and more than a few shared laughs at the statue's expense, Adam pushed open the door to the largest gym in the Denver metropolitan area. Inside, scores of people milled about. Neat rows of Cybex and Nautilus machines lined nearly every wall. Four separate exercise rooms spawned off the main area.

A long, gold check-in counter stood just inside the door. Behind the counter stood a beefed-up surfer dude and a Baywatch bombshell. The sandy-haired "dude" was busy counting the number of purple MegaCarb beverages in an illuminated cooler beside the counter. The "bombshell" was doing everything possible to look the part of a goddess while manning a computer terminal.

"Good morning," said the busty brunette. "Are you members?"

Adam couldn't help but notice how the girl's chest swelled and then deflated with every breath she took. "No, Porsche, we're not," he answered, reading her nametag. "We're here on behalf of Maria Sativa. I believe she's a member though, right?"

"Oh my, I wouldn't know," she laughed. "There are so many Olympians these days. Let me look."

To Adam's surprise, the young lady turned to the computer console and typed with astonishing speed. He'd never seen *his* secretary's fingers move so fast. Not to mention the fact that Libby's bust didn't inflate to half the volume that Porsche's did. He made a mental note to ask Libby to improve her typing and chest inflation skills when he got back to the office.

After only a few seconds, Porsche turned back to face them. "She's an Olympian all right, but guest workouts aren't officially allowed. We're just too busy this time of the morning. Maybe if you came back a little later, like around eleven, we could make an exception." She winked at him.

"Oh no, we're not here to work out," he said with a warm smile. "You see, Maria has fallen ill, and she left some important work papers in her locker. She sent her sister and me to retrieve them."

Porsche's perfect green eyes narrowed a bit as she weighed the honesty of his words. Before she could offer a confirming wink or a disapproving frown, Lara stepped forward.

"Look, I'm her sister, and I need to get Maria's things," she said without catching the happy-go-lucky mood Adam and Porsche had been striking. "I've got identification." She held an open wallet in front of her with as much implied authority as a detective might hold up his badge.

Porsche studied the driver's license only briefly before saying, "Okay, I guess you can go ahead and get what you need. I wouldn't want her to get in trouble."

As Adam and Lara turned to leave, Porsche suddenly called out, "G47."

Surprised, they both looked back at her.

"Her locker. It's G47, but I suppose you already knew that." Her subtle smile suggested she knew all along that they weren't being entirely candid.

Adam nodded appreciatively as he and Lara advanced toward the locker rooms.

As they neared the ladies locker room entrance, Lara turned to him. "G47. That isn't the number on the key, is it?"

Adam pulled the key from his pocket, saying, "No."

"Well, give it to me anyway," she said with an extended palm. "I can at least give it a try."

Adam hated not to be there when she opened the locker, but given that it was a women's changing area, it didn't seem possible. At least not without being attacked by a throng of shrieking, towel-covered women.

"Don't go far," Lara said. With that, she disappeared into the locker room.

Adam turned and surveyed the gymnasium. It was really quite impressive and certainly didn't seem to be lacking in membership. There were at least sixty people working out in the main room alone. Most were meatheads or soccer moms, but he also noticed a group of people wearing white uniforms in a smaller room directly across from the locker area. Curiosity peaked, he moved closer.

Inside were twenty or more karate students standing rigidly at attention. To their immediate front was a barrel-chested man with an angry face and a long ponytail of frizzy, gray hair. From his loud bark, Adam could only assume the instructor was unhappy with his class.

"You're still not getting it!" the teacher shouted. "What's the problem here? Is it me? Am I asking too much? You look like a bunch of sissies, all that slapping and touching each other." He moved about in an exaggerated spastic motion.

"This isn't what I taught you," he continued. "Don't you ever tell anyone that I'm your teacher because God knows that I'll deny it. Not a one of you is worth my training, not one. It's no wonder you got your asses kicked at the *budokai* competition last month. I was ashamed of each and every one of you."

Adam rubbed his eyes, frustrated by what he was witnessing. The instructor's demeanor was no better than that of a drill sergeant on Paris Island who'd just found out the recruits had pulled an all-nighter with his teenage daughter. Unfortunately, bullies had been a part of the martial arts since they'd migrated to the States and probably long before that.

"What can I do?" the man continued unabated. "I can show you and show you, but eventually you have to do it yourself. We'll go one more time. Who wants to be my *uke*?" he asked, his tone suddenly turning soft like the touch of a coiling python. No one responded, and many of the students quickly looked to the floor.

They're terrified of him, Adam thought, shaking his head. He'd always been amazed at what people would do to learn the martial arts. In his many years of study, he'd seen countless students of all nationalities, but particularly Americans, who for some reason had come to the conclusion that if they could just master the tools of hand-to-hand fighting, they would find some supernatural meaning to life.

Some of it was surely Hollywood's fault, glamorizing to the point where impossible feats had become routine. Promising that given enough pain and dedication, anyone could defeat an army of ruthless terrorists with little more than a broomstick and a few well-chosen catchphrases.

Most Americans who studied the martial arts were in search of an inner strength. Something they incorrectly believed could be bestowed upon them with a certificate and later worn like a protective medallion. Most never realized they had only to search within to find their individual power.

Of course, there were exceptions. Adam had once witnessed a man who weighed about as much as a ten-year-old girl and had no martial arts training, take on a gang of street thugs to protect his pregnant wife. With only a brick and the lid to a trash can, he'd killed one armed man and sent two others to intensive care. For thirty seconds, that mild-mannered insurance salesman had turned from prey to predator. It was as Adam had told his own class more than once, "The outcome of a battle is rarely determined by the size of the man in the fight, but rather by the size of the fight in the man."

As Adam heard the instructor further berate his students for their reluctance, he was suddenly tempted to step into the room and volunteer. *It isn't my fight,* he told himself pragmatically. He continued watching, only subconsciously aware that his feet were slowly sliding him closer to the action.

Angry that no one volunteered for what was obviously going to be a painful lesson, the instructor screamed out, "Mr. Byrd, get up here on the double!"

A lanky young man, no older than eighteen, with a freckled face and bright red hair immediately rushed forward. He took a fighting stance in front of his teacher.

"Attack me with a roundhouse kick," the instructor directed. He held an open palm up near his head to indicate where the kick should target. Adam thought he could hear a disconcerting hint of sadistic amusement in the teacher's voice.

The young man shot up a high roundhouse kick, being careful not to make contact. The instructor shuffled slightly away and brought a sharp forearm strike to the instep of the young man's foot. He followed it with a quick flicking front kick to his groin. The combination of unrestrained strikes sent his student to the mat, curled up and moaning as he clutched both his foot and balls.

Adam had seen Japanese hard styles like this before. It was common practice for practitioners to attack the weapon coming at them, whether it be a hand, foot, or beer bottle. The technique was often quite effective and could break the small bones in the hand or foot if executed without restraint. The flicking front kick that the instructor had fired was a short, fast strike used solely to take away an opponent's kicking ability. The logic being that it wasn't very appealing to kick someone if every time you lifted your foot, they slapped you in the groin with one of their own.

"Did you see that?" the teacher asked his class. "The strikes are sharp and fast." His eyes were now lit with an unnerving and angry energy. He was paying his students back for something that had been done to him long ago. "Now get back into the ranks," he said, motioning to the teenager still reeling from the blows.

As he watched the teenager half-limp, half-crawl his way back to the line, a thought came to Adam. He recalled that, historically, martial arts instructors would drop in on other dojos either to perform courtesy demonstrations, or worse, offer a challenge in hopes of stealing away students. It seemed only natural, perhaps bordering on an obligation, that he participate. On one level, he completely understood that it was a rationalization, but he was willing to acquiesce that pragmatism was something he had yet to master.

Adam stepped into the room, now fully aware of what he was doing.

As he entered, the instructor immediately turned to face him. "No spectators!" he barked from the front of the room. "Out!" He pointed at Adam as viciously as a prosecutor might finger a serial murderer.

Adam continued to advance, first along the back wall then up along the farthest column of students. The teacher began to yell again, but seeing that it would do no good, closed his mouth and drew both arms powerfully down to his sides. Adam thought he looked like an immovable stone gargoyle, not so different from the ridiculous flag-briefed Olympian standing guard outside the gym.

As Adam approached, the instructor suddenly shot back into a deep, low karate stance. "You want some of this?" the man snarled.

Adam stood casually in front of the agitated instructor. And though he was playing it cool, he was also careful to stay just outside striking range. "Your style is solid, but your mind is clouded," he said, doing his best Bruce Lee impersonation. In his assessment, every truly competent martial artist should be capable of impersonating the famous master.

"Kiss my white ass, Chinaman" the man said, evidently not appreciating the much-practiced impression.

The class was absolutely quiet as the students looked to each other with confusion. No one knew what was going to happen next.

"I would like to see how your style works. I am therefore volunteering to be your *uke*," Adam offered with a deep exaggerated bow, still careful not to take his eyes off the man. "Would it be acceptable then if I kicked at you the way your student did? I wish to experience your defense for myself," he taunted. "It was difficult to see from the back of the room."

The instructor smiled, revealing two missing front teeth. "Whatever you send my way, I'm going to chew up and spit out," he said, inviting the attack with a quick wave of his hands.

The man was deep in his front stance. Too deep. Adam moved with such speed that the instructor barely had time to execute his shuffle and outward block. As for his flip kick, it never left the ground.

Much to the teacher's surprise, Adam did not follow the predetermined script. Instead, he fired the roundhouse kick well below the man's waist. The instructor's outward block found only air as the instep of Adam's shoe contacted him hard on the outside of his lead ankle. A sickening crack sounded through the room as the teacher's lead foot shot high in the air.

He screamed, hopping around on his good foot.

Adam didn't hesitate, immediately spinning around and sweeping the man's remaining foot off the mat.

The instructor hit the floor with about as much grace as an NFL linebacker trying his hand at tap dancing.

Adam stepped away, watching him roll around, groaning and cursing loudly. "Just as I thought, a clouded mind," he said, returning to his impersonation.

"You son of a bitch!" the teacher cried. He clutched his ankle with both hands in a manner not so different from the way the young "volunteer" had a few moments earlier. Adam knew the bully was no longer a threat. He had intentionally broken his ankle, and the swelling would prevent him from standing.

Adam stepped toward the screaming teacher, who was already covered in a heavy sweat from the pain. The man put his hands up in a pitiful defensive posture, but fear was now filling his stare. Adam reached down, tore the black belt from the man's waist, and stepped away. A flash of relief showed across the instructor's face, and he went back to nursing his ankle, cursing softer now.

Adam turned to face the murmuring class. "Can you see only the belt and not the man wearing it?" He held the heavy cotton belt dangling in front of him like a dead mamba. For a moment, everyone stared at him, wide-eyed, but one by one they began to look to the floor.

After a few moments, the young Mr. Byrd bowed, turned, and walked out of the class. Adam nodded slowly and smiled, at least one had understood. He tossed the belt back to the instructor and left the makeshift dojo. His daily work of making things right was now officially complete.

As he exited the room, he saw that Lara was standing just outside. She had a mischievous grin on her face.

"Do you mind telling me what that was all about?"

"Just practicing with a local instructor," he said. "We do that sort of thing for one another. It's a professional courtesy."

The tilt of her head and suspicious eyes told him she wasn't buying into the lame story.

"Ah, he was an asshole," he confessed. "I figured he needed to be taught a lesson."

"And what exactly did you teach him, Master Lee?" she asked in what Adam rated to be the absolutely worst Bruce Lee impersonation he had ever heard.

He stared at her. She looked expectantly at him to come up with some philosophical truth, some great wisdom that could be found only in the Far East. He thought for a moment before finally coming up with an answer that followed respected Confucian logic.

"That it hurts like hell to have your ankle broken."

* * *

Adam and Lara sat in her Volkswagen, the car parked in front of Olympia's.

"You're one of those karate types? All that moo shu, chop suey stuff," she said, moving her hands in front of her with a playful chopping motion.

Adam chuckled. "Yeah, something like that."

"A tough guy?" she taunted, punching him softly across the car.

"Hey, that hurt," he said, rubbing his arm and smiling.

"How long have you been doing it?"

"I've been involved in one style or another since I was a child," he answered. "I started at an old boxing studio when I was nine. From there, I got involved in karate and eventually judo."

"Let me see your palms," she said, holding out her hands.

Reluctantly, he laid his hands in hers. He was hoping she wasn't about to put a cigarette out on them as some Shaolin test of his dedication.

Instead, Lara rubbed her fingers gently across the calluses lining nearly ever crease of his hands. "From the story your hands tell, you must be quite skilled," she said, her face turning serious for a moment.

Feeling self-conscious, he pulled his hands back and put them in his lap. "I can hold my own," he said. Trying to get the conversation back on track, he pulled the orange plastic-topped key from his pocket and started examining it once again. "Tell me again what was in your sister's locker."

"Like I said, there wasn't much. The locker was one of those types that required an external padlock, although it was odd that hers didn't have a lock at all. Inside, I found only shorts, a jogging bra, sneakers, socks, and shampoo. That's it. I guess I could have brought them out, but I didn't think any of it was important. We can go back in and get the stuff if you like."

"Nah, I'm sure you're right." He sat silent mulling over what little they had to go on. He contrasted his growing feeling of hopelessness with Lara's unexpected sunny demeanor. He didn't want to spoil the mood, but had to ask, "I don't mean to rain on your parade, but you're sure upbeat for having found only a bra and shampoo."

Lara was quiet for a moment, and Adam immediately regretted his words as her magical smile faded. "I just like to see people get their due. I enjoyed seeing that bully get his. That's all."

Neither of them spoke for several seconds. "Besides," she continued, "I'm starting to gain confidence in you. I believe you're going to figure this out. I really do."

Adam looked at Lara and thought he now understood a small part of her nature. She was a person who respected strength and action. It was in his strength that she apparently found hope. In a sense, he thought it also helped explain her utter disgust for Elliot.

For a fleeting moment looking at the hope in her eyes, Adam too felt absolutely certain that he would find her sister. Not only would he find Maria, he would find her alive and well, and they would all laugh together until tears fell. He didn't allow himself to put words to the questionable prophetic vision.

"Well," he started slowly, "if the key doesn't fit her gym locker, what does it unlock? Any more ideas?"

"Only thing I can come up with is maybe a locker at a bus terminal or an airport. Both sound like reasonable choices if she was looking for some place safe and anonymous to hide the map."

Adam nodded. "I've had the same thought."

"My sister could be running short on time," she said. "We'll need to split up to cover more ground."

"That's going to be kind of tough, given that we have only the one key," he said, rolling it between his fingers.

"One of us can take it, and the other can just go check out the possibilities. If either of us finds lockers with the right number and matching orange plastic keys, it's a good bet we're onto something,"

"Sounds reasonable. How many bus terminals are in town?"

"At least three, and then there's Denver International, the big airport out east you flew into," she said. "I tell you what. You take the bus terminals, and I'll work the airport. Both are going to be big jobs."

"Okay. Do you want to take the key with you?" he asked, hoping she didn't want to carry it off by herself.

"You keep it. After what I saw you do to that karate instructor, I think you can take care of yourself." She winked. His spoiling of the moment had evidently been forgiven.

Adam considered their plan for a moment, and then said, "If you find anything, call Elliot at his office or cell number. I'll keep in touch with him throughout the day as well. Also, if you see anyone following you, get to airport security immediately. Then call my brother, and I'll come get you. Do not, I repeat *do not*, attempt to do anything on your own. Clear?"

Lara smiled, but Adam didn't return the affection. He wasn't convinced that any of them were in any direct danger, but he also didn't want to see Lara suffer her sister's fate.

Her smile turned down just a bit with his stern gaze. "Okay, tough guy. I'll call you if I get into trouble." Lara raised three fingers in a mock Boy Scout salute. "Promise."

Chapter 8

General Duke Livingston sat staring down at a plastic glass filled with cheap champagne. The words of a particularly annoying city mayor rang out over the public address system of the large hotel banquet room.

Livingston absolutely hated this sort of event, but he also understood its importance. A charity luncheon at the Veterans of Foreign Wars today, a biography signing tomorrow, a public debate with his three contenders next week, and a campaign trail of unending jet-setting around the country trying to lock in votes before the primaries. There was no letup in sight.

"General Duke Livingston is a bona fide military hero," the announcer boomed. "He has seen a combined total of nine years of combat during his tours in Vietnam, Grenada, Somalia, Bosnia, and Iraq. He is one of the most decorated soldiers ever to serve in the United States Army, and it is my pleasure to introduce him here to you today. Please join me in a warm round of applause for America's greatest hero and the next president of the United States."

The room erupted with enthusiastic applause. Livingston lifted his weathered but strong frame out of the chair. There wasn't a pound of fat on him, and his advisors told him that exuding such strength might just carry him in the election. Standing tall with shoulders back, head held high, he walked confidently to the stage. He wanted everyone in the room to see his strength. He was no politician. He was a soldier, just as they once had been.

As he reached the podium, Livingston shook the master of ceremonies' hand. "Thank you," he said, intentionally squeezing the mayor's hand hard enough to cause him to wince. *Remember my strength.*

General Livingston turned to the podium and carefully adjusted the microphone. He placed several blank cue cards in front of him and put on a small pair of half-moon reading glasses. In reality, the glasses and cards were worthless props. His advisors had suggested they made him seem more like a politician and less like a general, which was especially important when the cameras were rolling. Having some small weakness made him more endearing to the general public, more of a grandfather figure. And people trusted their grandfathers.

The whole intricate game of building a popular image disgusted Duke Livingston, but he played along as he knew he must. In a sense, the charade was simply a part of the political "rules of engagement."

"My fellow soldiers," he started as the crowd's applause slowly ebbed. "I come to you today to ask for your support." Livingston's voice was as gruff as the largest of the Three Billy Goats. "For the last forty years of my life, I have served this fine country of ours. Like many of you, I have crawled through the swamps of Nam, slept with scorpions in the arid deserts of Iraq, and dodged the bullets of snipers in the mountains of Bosnia. I have killed, and I have nearly been killed. I have been shot, stabbed, burned, rifle-butted, and spit on for this country. My country!"

The room exploded again with clapping and cheering. General Livingston waited, nodding to the friendly audience. These were his people. This was his easiest sell, and his advisors had recommended that he make it early in the campaign to build a solid base of support. The veterans and active military were his. It was a start, but by itself, it was not enough.

He raised both hands palms outward. "Thank you, thank you. I believe this great country of ours needs a leader. Not a politician who folds to special interest groups. Not a smooth-talking liberal who doesn't know right from wrong. A leader, I say!"

The crowd erupted again.

"I promise I will never surrender in the face of danger. I will never yield to so-called popular sentiment that goes against the moral foundation of this country. I will fight every battle with the same passion I have demonstrated throughout my entire life. In short, I will lead this country to a greatness not seen in recent years."

The veterans filled the room with thunderous applause. Waves of people, some as old as eighty, rose shakily to their feet clapping or stomping their canes wildly in support. General Livingston was their president. He would never forget them or the sacrifices they'd made.

Duke Livingston was still beaming a steel-toothed smile when the bullet silently ripped into his left eye, sliced through his brain, and finally exited by punching out the back of his skull.

* * *

"Recapping our top story straight off the AP wire . . . General and presidential nominee Duke Livingston was killed three hours ago by an assassin's bullet. The details are still sketchy, but what's been confirmed at this point is that he was shot while giving a speech at the VFW convention center in Dallas at approximately 1:00 p.m. central standard time. We have no official report on whether there were other casualties or any arrests resulting from this horrific act of violence."

Adam turned up the radio as he pulled into a parking spot at the Velvet Tiger restaurant in downtown Denver.

"No further information is available at this time, but officials have announced that the FBI will hold a press briefing within the hour. We will keep you up to date here at WTTK, home of the news and weather, twenty four hours a day."

Adam didn't know much about General Livingston other than he had been a war hero who had recently announced his candidacy. His untimely death was sure to dominate the news for some time.

He turned off the car and headed into the restaurant.

The Velvet Tiger was a classy restaurant that served authentic East Asian dishes. Adam had eaten there only once several years before, but it was his understanding that the restaurant was owned by a well-connected Thai businessman who'd made his fortune in auto parts. In the entryway were dozens of photographs of the owner shaking hands with important politicians, including the city's mayor and several of the state's previous governors.

The restaurant wasn't crowded, and Adam quickly located Elliot sitting at a finely set dinner table. He approached and took the seat opposite his brother. After giving their orders to a particularly striking Asian waitress, both men turned their attention to each other.

"Anything?" Elliot asked expectantly in a hushed voice.

"Not on my end," Adam answered. "I went from one crummy section of town to the next checking the bus terminals. I'm pretty sure that the key doesn't fit a locker at any of the Denver terminals. On the bright side, I did get to meet an interesting one-legged war veteran who uses a golf club to fend off the crack whores who work the terminal bathrooms." He took a long drink of ice water. "How about Lara? Has she been in touch with you? She was going to hit DIA today."

"She left a message a few minutes ago on my service asking for you to call her, but she didn't indicate if she'd had any luck."

Adam slowly shook his head.

"You don't look hopeful."

"Call it a hunch, but I don't think Maria was that predictable. She knew that someone might go looking for the map. Bus stations, gym lockers, and airports are all pretty obvious."

"It's quite possible she was careful enough that we may never discover what the key fits. And if we can't determine what the key goes to . . ." Elliot sighed, though it came out a bit pretentious.

"I look at it a little different. Maria understood that she might get caught. Why else send the key to Lara for safekeeping? She knew she was in danger. If I were in her shoes, I would have left a clue just in case it all went sour. Maybe Lara is forgetting something Maria said or did."

"Or perhaps *we've* overlooked an important clue," Elliot said. "Maybe we should search her apartment again, just in case the two of you missed something."

Adam set the key on the white linen tablecloth in front of him. Next, he withdrew the note from his jacket pocket and placed it beside the key. "Let's look at this together," he started. "We have a key that apparently goes to some type of commercial locker, probably a rental somewhere. The locker number is T1276. Does that identifier have any meaning?"

"Hmm. The numbers could indicate a date . . . say December of '76? That's a stretch and has no logical basis. So I guess the answer is no. The numbers don't mean anything to me."

"To me neither. She may have picked the number because it had some special significance to her and was therefore easy to remember. Whether she did or not though is probably beside the point. We know the number. It's the location we're after." He picked up the handwritten note. "Listen carefully to this." He began reading it, his voice just above a whisper.

Dear Lara,

I'm sure you're going to find this amusing, but I'm in trouble again and am sending you this key for safekeeping. Please don't ask what it goes to or why I feel the need to hide it. Just park it somewhere safe for me. I'll get it from you next week when things cool down a bit. If anyone asks whether you've heard from me, say you haven't. Whatever you do, don't mention the key to anyone. I'm onto something big, really big.

Love your sis,

Maria

"It is written a bit oddly, isn't it," Elliot commented. "The wording is sort of strange in places. Of course, it could just be the way she wrote. Without something to compare it to, it's difficult to know for sure."

"The words 'just park it somewhere' sound strange to me," Adam said. "Forced, if you will."

"Something related to a vehicle?" Elliot asked. "Perhaps a search of her car is in order. You said that you and Lara never made it to looking in her car, and the police could easily have overlooked something."

"Could be. The first few words also sound odd," Adam said. "Why would Maria assume the situation would be amusing to Lara? Unless they had some odd relationship, being in trouble shouldn't sound amusing at all. Maria was in obvious danger and should have known it would worry her sister. To say it was amusing seems inconsistent."

"I agree, and then there's the 'cool down a bit,' and 'big, really big.' The fact is any of the words could be hints or nothing at all. We're sitting here analyzing every word of her note when it might be nothing more than her particular style of writing."

The waitress interrupted their conversation by bringing a plate of prawns with mung bean noodles and another with salmon parcels. Adam picked up the key and note and placed both in his jacket pocket beside the photo he'd removed from Maria's apartment.

Something nagged at him but refused to come into focus. He relaxed and turned his attention to his meal. He'd found during his study of Eastern meditation that things often became clearer when they were allowed to roam freely in the mind for a while.

As both men began devouring the deliciously prepared meals, Elliot changed the subject entirely, saying, "Did you hear about General Livingston?"

Adam swallowed a mouthful of spicy fish. "Just a few minutes ago on the radio. What's the story? Some lunatic pop him or what?"

"That's just it, no one knows. The police don't even have a suspect from what I've heard. Livingston was apparently up on stage giving a speech when somebody shot him. One station reported that he was shot right through the eye."

"Sounds professional."

Elliot nodded. "Some of CNN's so-called experts were suggesting that same thing. Others are saying it might be a disgruntled voter tired of the sordid campaign rumors and accusations. Given the tone of this presidential race so far, that seems just as plausible to me."

"Have things grown that ugly?" Adam wasn't ashamed to admit that he didn't follow politics. He tended to expend his efforts on things close enough for him to affect, and national politics were beyond his circle of influence.

"The mudslinging is as bad as I've ever seen it. On the democratic ticket, Vice President 'Lucky' Joe Marino is trying to paint his rival, Robert Greene, as an elitist casino tycoon. Greene is responding with allegations that Lucky Joe is a mobster gone legitimate. The republican side of the isle has been no more civilized with General Livingston and Senator Dick Shoemaker trading jabs about tax policies, military spending, and countless other issues. And don't forget the independent out of Texas, William Tyler, who has rallied the black vote by highlighting racial injustices still occurring throughout our country."

"I haven't heard of Tyler," Adam admitted.

"That's not too surprising since he's never been a media favorite. From what I understand, he's a Texas oil baron who made his money selling across Europe and Asia. History has proven that a black man is electable, but it remains an uphill battle. The sad truth is that our country still has its share of rednecks and bigots who would vote for their flatulent three-legged dog before voting for a black man. Tyler's best bet is to get picked up as a vice presidential running mate by one of the primary winners."

Elliot took another small bite of steamed broccoli before continuing. "Over the past few weeks, things have grown pretty heated. Allegations of corruption, marital infidelity, tax evasion, you name it," he explained. "Frankly, I'll be embarrassed to vote for any of them."

"It's your lucky day then."

"Why's that?"

"As of this afternoon, your choices have been narrowed down by one," Adam said with a smirk.

"Morbid but true. Even though I probably wouldn't have voted for Livingston, he was touted as a military hero who'd made his share of sacrifices for our country. I can respect that. Besides, he seemed . . . noble."

Adam was surprised to hear his brother's recognition of a trait as intangible as nobility. It didn't seem to fit with what he knew of Elliot's practical, bottom-line assessment of the world.

"Who are you going to vote for then? If you don't mind my asking." With any other person, Adam would not have added the qualifier, but with Elliot, it was required.

On this occasion of tasty fish and shrimp, his brother didn't seem to mind the personal intrusion. "I'm not really sure. With the primaries only weeks away, I guess it's time to give it some serious thought. Over the years, I've voted on both sides of the aisle. But to answer your question, it's between Senator Shoemaker and Lucky Joe in my mind."

"Why do they call him that?"

"Who? Lucky Joe?"

Adam nodded.

"It either came from his time as a boxer—"

"He used to box?" Anything to do with physical combat interested Adam.

"Yes, professionally for a bit back in the seventies. I'm not sure if his nickname stemmed from that or from allegations about ties to the Italian mafia."

"Sounds like a colorful guy," Adam remarked.

"I guess so," Elliot paused for several seconds. After a moment of indecision, he finally said, "I don't know if I've ever mentioned it, but I used to know Marino's daughter."

"Really?"

"His eldest daughter Janice and I both went to Harvard at the same time. I didn't know her all that well, but we did spend some time working together on briefs and articles. I doubt that she would even remember me now."

Elliot's words were presented with as much fanfare as buttered toast, but something in his eyes told Adam that there was more to this story than his nonchalance suggested. "Impressive. My brother hobnobbed with the daughter of the vice president."

"I know a lot of people," Elliot said with a bit of bravado. "Most of them I don't like much, but being in the circles of power and money can have its advantages."

"The last poll I saw showed the four major players in a statistical dead heat. How do you think Livingston's untimely death is going to play out?"

"My guess is that most Republicans will stick to their party and migrate over to Senator Shoemaker, but the general's death won't exactly hurt

Lucky Joe either. Livingston had been an effective and outspoken critic of the vice president as of late. His death will surely serve as a windfall for Marino since the criticism has led to a steady decline in the vice president's ratings over the past few months."

Adam said. "I'll admit that I've never been one to predict the outcome of political races. Voters can be pretty fickle."

"I wholeheartedly agree. Anything is possible in politics." Elliot paused as he so often did when introducing anything personal about himself. "At times, I've even considered running for office myself."

Adam wasn't surprised at all by the revelation. In his eyes, Elliot was the most ambitious, pragmatic, and correspondingly selfish person he'd ever known. Not to mention that he loved being center stage and had suitcases full of money. He was perfect for politics.

Adam decided to pick at him. "I don't know . . . winning a seat on the city council can be rather tricky."

Elliot cast him a disparaging look. "I'm talking about Congress."

"Of course you are. Will I be calling you Representative or Senator?"

"A seat in the House is more easily won, but with elections every other year, it lacks any long-term security. So, even though it would be more difficult, I would probably try for a seat in the Senate. I still haven't decided if I even want to bother with it. It would require a great deal of time, effort, and money. One day I'll have to give it some serious thought." He raised his glass daintily and took a sip of the wine.

Again, his tone was nonchalant as if only simple dinnertime conversation were being exchanged. Adam was surprised at how naïve Elliot must believe him to be. He was not his brother's confidant, not someone whom untested ideas were sounded off of over dinner. Elliot wouldn't have mentioned his aspirations unless plans were already in motion. Undoubtedly there were already slick posters being printed, buttons being laminated, and inflated promises being handed out like political cotton candy.

* * *

Pecos Bill: Howdy, partner. I see you been busy roping.
Bulls-eye: Yes. One down.
Pecos Bill: Any luck on what you lost?
Bulls-eye: No. If your people hadn't been so careless, we might have it in hand by now.

Pecos Bill: I heard about that. I also heard she used to put her boots under your bunk. I hope it wasn't too upsetting for you.

Bulls-eye: Your people need to learn not to remove a target until all the information has been retrieved. It's part of being professional. You know that as well as anyone.

Pecos Bill: True. The lead rider was one of our more enthusiastic cowboys. He jumped the gun a bit. I heard a rival bunkhouse is out looking, too.

Bulls-eye: Yes, I've been watching. So far, they've found nothing.

Pecos Bill: They need calling out?

Bulls-eye: No. Not yet anyway. They don't know anything, and besides they are doing our work for us. Let's see what they turn up.

Pecos Bill: Are the cowboys dangerous?

A brief pause.

Bulls-eye: One may be.

* * *

Later that night, just as Adam lowered his head onto the hotel room pillow, the answer finally came to him. Not in a mad flurry of revelation or even a moment of spiritual enlightenment. Rather, it slowly congealed like strawberry Jell-O setting up in the icebox. Once set, the answer was so obvious, so undeniable, it couldn't have been any clearer if Maria had told him herself. Adam knew precisely what the key fit.

He glanced at the clock and saw it that was just past ten o'clock. Fumbling around, he finally found the switch on a bedside lamp as he nearly fell out of bed with excitement. In the nightstand drawer, he found the Denver metropolitan area yellow pages. Snatching it up, he quickly began flipping pages as he moved over and dropped down on the sofa. He passed what he was looking for twice before finally finding it: *Amusement Parks*. There were two parks listed, Twisters and Lakeshore. He hadn't heard of either one but assumed they consisted of the usual rides, games, snow cones, and more important, storage lockers.

Adam leaned over and grabbed his jacket from a nearby chair. Digging inside the pocket, he found the photo he'd removed from Maria's apartment. He studied it again. Maria stood with her head leaning on Lara's shoulder, beaming with childish joy. In her right arm, she cradled a large pink panther that had undoubtedly been the grand prize at some carnival booth.

He scanned the photo for the name of the park or anything that might suggest one park over the other. Only the blurred images of people and the colorful lights of a fantasy world filled the background. Nothing indicated which park it was. He flipped the photo over to see if anything might be written on the back. Again, nothing.

Adam leaned back against the supple leather. "Maria, I think it's time we found this mysterious map of yours."

He picked up the phone and started to dial Lara's number. She could provide an answer as to where the photo was taken, and it seemed a good bet that the careful play on words in Maria's note was referring to a place her sister was familiar with.

Adam hesitated. When they'd last spoken about their fruitless searches of the airport and bus terminals, Lara said she was exhausted and planned on getting to bed early. He hated to wake her on a hunch, even if it did feel incredibly right. Elliot then? With his brother, he'd likely get an earful about dragging him out in the middle of the night for something that could be accomplished just as well the next morning. He hung the phone back up. Tonight, for better or for worse, he was going it alone.

"Which one then?" Adam said aloud. "Twisters or Lakeshore?" He saw that both were open only when weather permitted during the months of November through March. As mild as the Colorado weather had been lately, he felt sure the parks would be open.

According to the listing, Twisters closed at 11:00 p.m. and Lakeshore at midnight. It made sense to start with the park that closed first and then try to make a last minute dash to Lakeshore if necessary.

The courtesy call from Charles at the front desk still had Adam alarmed. If government spooks were gathering information about him, it was a good bet they were watching his room, or at the very least watching the Hotel Mona.

He dialed the front desk, hoping his watchdog was still on duty.

"Hotel Mona," a familiar voice announced.

"Charles, this is Adam Reece."

"Yes, sir. How are you this evening?"

"Just fine. I've a favor to ask of you."

"Of course. What do you need, sir?" The eagerness in Charles's voice confirmed his interest in staying involved in the adventure.

Seeing no reason to hold back, Adam said, "I have the nagging feeling that the guy who inquired about me earlier is watching the hotel. I'd like to slip out this evening and sort of in a hurry. I could use your help in making that happen."

The phone was silent for a moment. Finally, Charles said, "I'm sure you understand that as a hotel representative I couldn't possibly be involved. I do know, however, that our cooks, dishwashers, and maids come in and out of a backdoor in the kitchen area. It's around the time that many of them are getting off for the evening, so it might be a rather easy way to leave unnoticed."

"That's useful," Adam said. "Thank you, Charles. I don't suppose you know of a taxi company that could be here in short order do you?"

"I'll place a call for you, Mr. Reece. A car should be here within ten minutes. Should I request they pull around back just in case you happen to be passing through the kitchen?"

Adam grinned. "That would be perfect. Thanks again."

"Just doing my job, sir. Good night."

Adam hung up the phone. Ten minutes wasn't long, and he didn't want the taxi driver pulling around front, thinking there'd been some kind of mix up. He quickly dressed, donned his shoulder holster and jacket, and headed downstairs.

Chapter 9

Twisters was a huge, antiquated amusement park filled with a wide variety of rides, all of which looked to be in need of some serious attention. Adam suspected the place was just trying to hold its own in the face of mega-parks that were quickly overtaking the industry.

The distant Ferris wheel and endless, intertwined white roller coaster tracks brought a comfortable feeling of nostalgia. Adam remembered the many summers he and Elliot had spent at parks much like Twisters, riding the Boomerang and the Whiplash. He was sure that by today's standards such rides would barely offer a thrill, but in his time, they provided the edgy rush that every generation seeks.

Adam had systematically worked his way from one locker area to another but still had yet to find the prize he sought. Nevertheless, he had noticed that many of the unused lockers held keys that looked remarkably similar to Maria's. Despite his lack of success, Adam was now quite convinced the key he held fit a locker somewhere in the park. It was just a matter of time.

Ahead of him, he saw what was, according to the park map, the second-to-last unexplored locker area. This one was inside an open-air building with a small, outdoor restaurant attached to the front of it. A bright red-and-blue sign identified the fine eating establishment as the Waffle Cone Cantina. Even at eleven thirty at night, the place was buzzing with young life.

Adam carefully pushed his way through a crowd of rowdy teenagers, many of whom had a collection of decorative rings hanging from their noses, belly buttons, and lips. The young men and women laughed and jumped about without regard to whom they bumped or banged. The source of their jubilation was rap music pounding out of a portable boom box.

Adam couldn't understand most of the lyrics as they were drowned out by a deep resonating bass, but he could clearly hear a surprisingly vulgar chorus as it rang out, "your pussy ain't worth the Ramada." He guessed that single line pretty much summed up any deep, hidden meaning the song had to offer.

Looking past punked-out heads of purple-and-orange hair, he made out several rows of lockers inside. He continued toward them until he could read the numbers: T1159, T1160, T1161. He was close.

He forced his way into the open-air structure. At knee height toward the back of the building, he finally found it, locker T1276.

He slapped his forehead with an exaggerated understanding as it finally registered that the "T" stood for Twisters. Adam was feeling very good, so good in fact he couldn't have wiped the smile off his face with a Brillo pad and a half bottle of Clorox. He'd managed to put several pieces of the puzzle together, and the payoff was finally at hand.

Out of habit, he looked left and right but saw no one watching him with any interest. The rowdy youths were busy slam-dancing and couldn't have cared if he was about to remove a nuclear warhead from the locker, so long as he didn't touch their radio. A man grinning wildly at having found a locker was about as interesting as a bottle of ketchup.

Adam knelt and faced the locker. It wasn't particularly large, just big enough to hold a few pairs of sneakers and shorts before the big water splash ride. He withdrew the key from his pocket and slowly inserted it into the lock.

Taking a deep breath, he gave it a twist. The key turned to the right, an audible clunk sounding as the locking mechanism sprang open. The key was now held in place, the locker being the type that required the user to put in additional quarters each time it was to be used.

He looked around again, this time motivated by a feeling that he was being watched. Something important was about to be revealed, and in his experience, revelations often came with conflict. Despite his uneasy feelings, the frolicking, half-naked teenagers danced on, not a single one looking in his direction. Perhaps tonight would be different.

He turned his attention back to the locker, slowly pulling the metal door open. And there it was, sitting against the far wall. The map.

He carefully removed it, letting the door slam back in place. To his surprise, the map wasn't an antique parchment stamped with some secret Masonic symbol. Instead, it was a commonplace road map that might be picked up at a gas station for navigating a cross-country trip with a car-load of kids. He read the blue lettering on the front of the map.

Rand McNally—United States of America.

"Okay, now I'm confused," he said, his words barely making it to his ears in the presence of the thumping rap melody. "Maria, what the hell were you doing hiding this?" He looked at the map, thinking of possibilities. "If it isn't the map itself, then it's something on the map."

He started to unfold it but quickly decided that Twisters wasn't the best place to study a full-sized road map. His hotel room, Elliot's office, or even Lulu's Diner would be a more suitable location. He stuffed it into his coat pocket. *Mission accomplished.*

A sudden rush of movement to Adam's left caught his attention. He whirled, his hand instinctively moving to the firearm hidden inside his jacket. Four men in dark suits were shoving their way through the crowd of teenagers.

Not waiting to see who the uninvited guests were, Adam turned and darted out the back doorway. He immediately collided with a heavy-set couple, the man and woman each carrying a large souvenir cup of soda and a funnel cake. Despite showering them with cola and powdered sugar, he didn't apologize, offer to help, or even slow his reckless advance. Instead, Adam bolted full speed through the colorful lights and chiming sounds of the amusement park.

* * *

Elliot looked a bit like Dirty Harry hosting a slumber party—dressed in red flannel pajamas, glasses off, hair still wet from the shower. In his hands, he gently cradled the loaded Browning Hi-Power handgun. He turned the barrel towards the mirror, sighting in on his reflection.

"I've got him covered, Adam," he said with mock excitement. "Don't worry, bro, I've got fifteen bullets."

Elliot chuckled at the utter foolishness. He hadn't let himself go this far out in a very long time. Maybe getting a gun hadn't been such a bad idea after all. It did give him a newfound sense of strength, even if that vigor came stapled to a stomach full of butterflies. He held in his hands the means to kill someone. Not outtalk them. Not bankrupt them. To *kill* them.

But he already knew how to kill. Knew what death looked like up close and personal. Knew the sour smell of blood. The difficulties in disposing of a body. He closed his eyes, forcing dark memories to retreat before they overwhelmed him. This was not the time for guilt. He was having fun. Living for a change, rather than wallowing in self-pity. He took a deep breath and turned his attention back to the mirror, forcing himself to smile again.

He stuck the firearm back in the holster then quickly pulled it free. "Thought you were going to get away, didn't you?" he said to his evil counterpart looking back at him from the glass. "What? You want to see that again?"

He pushed the gun back into the holster, watching his adversary for any sudden movement. "Ready . . . go!" He jerked the Browning free again. But this time, because he was still unfamiliar with its weight, the gun slipped from his fingers. It smashed into the mirror and then crashed heavily into the porcelain sink.

Elliot jumped back, his body stiffening for the impact of a bullet. The fact that the gun hadn't discharged was of little consolation. He drew in a shaky breath and stared at the now-splintered image before him. After a moment of silent reprimand, he carefully retrieved the handgun from the basin. Without another word, Elliot walked into his bedroom and put both the gun and holster in the drawer of his bedside table.

* * *

Adam was covered with sweat. For nearly twenty minutes, he'd been racing in and out of novelty shops filled with warped funhouse mirrors, long rows of Skee-Ball games, and worthless carnival souvenirs. He couldn't see his pursuers at the moment but instinctively knew that he hadn't shaken them. They were still very close.

Several times during the pursuit, he'd been tempted to get to a vantage point and initiate a fight with one or more of them. Adam had never minded a good scrape, but he suspected the four men were well prepared for any resistance he might offer.

Even in the unlikely event that their sheer numbers wouldn't be enough, they were likely carrying stun devices or other disabling tools of the trade. Of course, they could also just stab or shoot him, depending on the seriousness of their particular agenda.

Adam tended to discount the likelihood of deadly force since it seemed improbable that anyone would be willing to kill in such a public forum. He also hesitated to brandish his own weapon for the same reason. If push came to shove, though, he would draw it and see how far they were willing to play the game.

Any way he looked at it, it was a no-win situation. A shootout with four government agents, which he assumed they were, was not something he could ultimately win regardless of who walked away from the gunfight.

He wasn't sure how they'd been able to track him from the hotel. Perhaps they had a phone tap on the front desk, or maybe they were careful enough to watch the service entrance. Either way, it confirmed that they were professionals.

He told himself that if it hadn't been for the chaos of screaming children, spinning rides, and flashing lights, he would have detected them sooner. Fortunately, that same advantage now fell to Adam in his attempt to escape. He worked to stay amidst the largest crowds and the noisiest noisemakers, hoping that somewhere along the way he could slip out one of the park exits.

Regrettably, with Twisters scheduled to close within minutes, the crowds were quickly thinning. Adam understood that his luck was about to run out. If he tried to leave with the mass exodus, he would quite probably be grabbed by the goons. Unfortunately, being grabbed in a dark parking lot offered up new kinds of nasty alternatives to his captors.

As Adam spun out of a particularly noisy arcade, he spotted an opportunity. Directly ahead was Monster Mansion, a haunted house ride complete with spiderweb windows, tombstone-covered lawn, and its fair share of life-size ghoul statues out front.

With the late hour, and the ride evidently not being hip enough for the teenage crowd, there were only a few people standing in line. He ran for the entrance. As he got closer, he began vaulting his legs up and over the maze of railings used to corral the heavy midday crowds. Within seconds, he was face to face with a pimple-faced attendant. The boy's only responsibility was to administer the boarding of passengers into small floating vessels, each shaped like a coffin.

Adam showed the red ink stamp on the back of his hand, and without waiting for the young man to motion him forward, leapt into the nearest boat.

"Slow it down, mister," the boy droned without a hint of conviction.

Adam dropped to his knees between two small benches. After only a few seconds, the vessel jarred and began moving forward. He rose up slightly to see if there were any signs of his pursuers.

To his great disappointment, all four men were standing just outside the railing surrounding Monster Mansion. And they were looking his direction. The leader motioned for two of the team to enter the ride and the remaining man to follow him to the disembarking ramp.

Before Adam could formulate a plan, he was blanketed in complete darkness as the floating car bumped its way through the haunted house entrance. A gigantic green monster suddenly leapt at him with a loud pneumatic *hiss*.

Adam gasped, instinctively drawing back and putting his hands up defensively.

"Moo haa haa," the mechanical beast moaned. "Scared you, did I? Well, don't be afraid, boys and girls. I'm Gordo the Goblin, and I will be your guide through Monster Mansion. You must remember above all else to keep your feet and hands inside the coffin at all times. The water around you is filled with all kinds of things that love to eat little fingers and toes. Now sit back and enjoy the ride. I'll see you again at the end of your brief visit . . . if you make it that far. Moo haa haa."

Adam saw that Gordo was in reality nothing more than a huge plaster head. It was painted bright green and had glowing yellow eyes, although one of them remained milky and dim. Large flakes of crusty paint were peeling off the side of its massive jaw. After the creature finished the safety speech, its features darkened, and the mechanized monster slowly retreated into a small alcove in the entryway wall.

He couldn't hear the men outside but knew that two were undoubtedly getting into a vessel behind him. The ride was incredibly dark, making it impossible to see what was ahead or behind by more than just a few feet.

"Shit," Adam cursed himself. "Trapped."

Several smaller automated ghosts and ghouls sprang up from the banks along each side of the narrow channel of water. Distorted screams and laughter played overhead on hidden loudspeakers.

He scanned the channel banks for anything large enough to hide behind, whether it be a headless specter or a mummy's sarcophagus. It was then that he saw a possible way out of the dilemma. Along the far right wall was a dim red-and-yellow sign with the single stomach-soothing word, EXIT.

"Service exit," he reasoned aloud. He glanced back over his shoulder to be sure his pursuers couldn't see him. Only a thick darkness lay behind him. Knowing that this might be his only chance, Adam placed both hands on the sides of the floating vessel and carefully stepped over the side.

Surprisingly warm water soaked him to his waist. The coffin continued to pull him, and he found it difficult to stand. He leaned awkwardly forward, instinctively refusing to let go. The vessel began to drag him toward a large black door leading to the next room of the ride. Taking a chance, Adam released the coffin.

And though he could feel the steady current tugging at him, he spread his legs and managed to steady himself. He looked at the outline of the shore that was now completely inanimate and dark. Ten feet. No further than that.

Adam fought the urge to run or dive ahead. Instead, he began inching himself forward with small, deliberate steps. The walls and bottom of the water channel were slippery due to years of water polishing as well as being covered with what looked like a layer of genuine monster slime. With each passing second, his heart began to pound harder and faster. He knew that he didn't have much time.

The giant goblin suddenly sprang to life at the entrance to the chamber.

Adam plunged face first into the water. As he dropped below the surface, a wet silence as complete as anything found in the ocean's depths suddenly engulfed him. He wanted to credit his reaction to keen survival instincts, but it was little more than a panic reflex induced by the monster's sudden animation. The damn thing had scared him again.

He also knew that it had probably saved him since the contraption would only have come to life if the next boat had triggered the limit switch. His pursuers were very close.

Adam stared up through murky water and saw only a smear of yellow light. *The goblin,* he thought. To be absolutely sure that the men were out of sight, he would have to wait until it was dark above him. It would mean waiting until both the goblin and smaller creatures had finished their "moo haa haa's." He forced himself to relax.

How long can I hold my breath? he wondered. *A minute or two? Will it be long enough?* He wasn't sure.

He stared up through the water, feeling the pressure building in his chest. After what seemed like forever, Gordo's yellow glow finally dimmed. Despite the temptation, he stayed underwater.

He saw the surface glow green and yellow once again as the smaller creatures animated along the bank. A dark depression at the water's surface no more than three feet from him floated ahead at a painfully slow pace.

Adam's eyes began to burn, and he felt his heart pounding powerfully against his chest. *I will stay down until the light goes out. I will stay down. I will stay down!* He fought the growing urgency for air that was only a foot above his head. Just as he felt he could bear it no longer, the room fell dark.

He leapt up from beneath the water, sucking in deep gasps of damp air.

* * *

"Hello?" a tired voice croaked from the other end of the line.

"Elliot, it's me. I need your help," Adam said in short puffs of air.

"Adam?"

"Listen, I'm at a gas station at the corner of Thirty-Fifth and Federal. I need a ride as quick as you can get here."

Adam was still winded from his long run, and the cold night air burned his lungs. After his escape from Monster Mansion, he'd slipped out one of the smaller park exits and hurried down dark side streets until there was little risk of anyone happening upon him. From the lit silhouette of distant roller coaster tracks, he guessed that he was now about a mile from the park.

"What's happened?" Elliot asked. "What are you doing on Federal at this time of night? Adam, tell me what's going on."

"I'll tell you all about it when you get here," he said. "Can you leave now? I'm cold." Saying the words brought with them the realization of just how chilled he really was. The February Colorado wind, along with his being drenched from head to toe, raised a dense array of goose bumps over his entire body.

"It'll take me twenty or thirty minutes, but I'm leaving now. Just stay put. I'm coming."

Adam moved to the dark side of the gas station and waited. He considered going into the convenience store to warm up but decided that he couldn't chance it. With the kind of luck he was having, his pursuers stood a very real chance of happening by for a late-night cup of coffee or a Slim Jim with cheese.

Twenty-two minutes later, Elliot's black Audi A-8 pulled into the parking lot.

Adam hustled over to the car and climbed into the passenger seat. Visibly shaking from the cold, he blew on his hands trying to keep them from stiffening. The crisp leather seats felt hard and brittle through his wet clothing.

"You're freezing," Elliot said, looking at his brother with concern.

"I'm all right," he answered in a shaky voice.

"Grab my suit coat from the back seat and put it over you."

Not having the strength to argue, Adam leaned back and retrieved the coat.

Elliot adjusted one of a myriad of controls on a dashboard that resembled the cockpit of a modern jetfighter. Warm air began to circulate over Adam, and a concentrated heat spread from the seat cushion beneath him.

As weary and cold as he was, Adam couldn't help but smile when he noticed Elliot's red flannel pajamas peeking out from beneath his long gray overcoat. It was heartening to know that his brother cared enough to hurry. Adam was grateful but felt particularly pathetic as he reluctantly draped what must have been a thousand-dollar worsted wool suit coat over his chest and shoulders. He closed his eyes and finally let the world stop moving. He was safe.

The one thought that kept coming back to him was that his bright idea of going it alone might not have been so bright after all. It wasn't that he thought Lara, or even Elliot for that matter, would have offered much resistance against the four assailants. It was more a feeling that with one of them in tow, different decisions would have been made. Decisions that probably wouldn't have left him soaking wet, exhausted, and cuddling feebly behind a fancy suit coat in his brother's European luxury car.

Elliot cruised slowly down Federal and waited for Adam to warm a bit before initiating his questioning. After a couple of minutes, he couldn't hold it in any longer. "Are you going to tell me what's going on?" His words were words of frustration, but his tone was soft.

"I got the—oh shit, the map!" Adam dug his hand into the inner pocket of his wet jacket. He pulled out the folded shape of the map. It was soaked all the way through but hadn't degraded to the point of coming apart. With careful attention and a bit of luck, it looked salvageable.

"You found it?" Elliot asked, startled.

"Yeah. Unfortunately, it got a bit wet," he said, holding it up between them. "Hopefully it's still in good enough shape to answer the big question of why Maria thought it was so valuable."

"But where did you find it?"

"In the amusement park," he said, motioning towards the roller coaster tracks in the distance.

Elliot stared at the soggy, folded Rand McNally map. "She hid a road map? This is what she thought was worth a million dollars? Are you sure?"

"Best as I can figure. Perhaps by studying it back at your place we can figure out what she's gotten herself into."

"Maybe it's a treasure map of some sort," Elliot thought aloud. "You know, perhaps it shows the location of an ancient artifact or a bag of money stolen from an armored car robbery. Something like that."

Adam considered the possibility for a moment. "Could be. But if so, why wouldn't she have just gone after it herself?"

"Could be it was too difficult for her to get to alone." After he spoke, though, Elliot seemed to dismiss his own idea saying, "I don't know. It's probably something else entirely."

For an inexplicable reason, Adam found the words "something else entirely" to be a bit ominous. It was often the yet-unseen evils that proved the most terrifying. On the other hand, he wasn't willing to completely surrender to his intuition given that his brain was currently not much warmer than a banana popsicle.

The car unexpectedly lurched forward, sending both men reaching for the dash. They spun around to see the headlights of a large dark sedan dropping back after having collided with their rear bumper. With the intense shine of the high beam headlights, it was impossible to tell who or even how many people were in the vehicle.

"What the hell?" Elliot exclaimed both in fear and confusion.

After the car retreated a few feet, the engine roared and it raced forward, crashing once again into the back of the Audi. Adam's palm hit the windshield, cracking it into a star-like pattern that spread several inches across the glass.

Adam pulled the Glock from its holster, barking, "Get us out of here! Whatever you do, don't crash or let them force you off the—"

His words were cut short as the car smashed into them for a third time.

Elliot pressed the accelerator, and the Audi immediately began to pull away from the sedan. Adam wrapped his left arm around the headrest and gripped the handgun with both hands. He hesitated to fire. Even shooting at the engine of the pursuing car could accidentally kill some-one, and he just wasn't ready to up the stakes that high yet. He waited.

The Audi quickly reached eighty miles an hour as it raced down a long stretch of Federal Street. The sedan was keeping pace but unable to get close enough for another collision. Luckily the road, which was bustling with impatient drivers during the day, was now relatively deserted.

As if in answer to the optimistic assessment of the road conditions, an unaware motorist suddenly turned blindly onto the street in front of the speeding Audi.

"Hang on!" Elliot yelled, swerving briefly into the oncoming lane of traffic. The Audi started to fishtail, but he turned into the skid and brought it back under control.

The sedan used the opportunity to close in, and the cars were once again bumper-to-bumper.

Ping, ping, ping. Small metallic jolts resonated through the frame of the Audi.

"Shit!" Adam exclaimed. "They're shooting at us. Keep your head down!"

Elliot looked over at Adam, fear filling his eyes. "This is crazy," he whined. "Let's just pull over and give them the map. Throw it out the window or something. This isn't worth dying for."

The major flaw with his line of reasoning was that people who are willing to kill for a map, are just that: people willing to kill. They would need to take care of Elliot and Adam once they retrieved it. This wasn't one of those games where everyone shook hands at the end.

Ping, ping. More bullets plunked through the trunk. Adam could see a man leaning out the window of the sedan, a large pistol in his hand. Since he couldn't hear the shots, Adam assumed the weapon had some sort of silencer.

The back window suddenly exploded into thousands of tiny shards of glass. The blast sent Elliot into a high-pitched squeal.

"You okay?" Adam yelled, hoping his brother hadn't been hit.

Elliot stopped screaming but otherwise didn't answer. His eyes were now glued to the road, hands maneuvering the car nimbly across the lanes. He seemed to finally realize that he was racing for his life.

He's okay. Just scared, Adam concluded.

He looked back at the sedan. Their pursuers had upped the ante. The time for restraint had passed. He took aim, yelling over the engine and fresh rush of cold night air. "It's going to get loud in here! Just keep us moving!" He saw Elliot nod, gripping the steering wheel with all his strength.

Adam fired through the gaping back window. The report of the Glock was deafening inside the car. He fired again and then a third time. All three rounds hammered into the engine compartment of the sedan.

With the third shot, the pursuing car pitched violently to the right, the left, and then began dropping back as a steaming spray of green liquid began spilling out from under the hood.

The chase was over.

* * *

A bright red electric sign brazenly announced to all weary travelers that the Cherry Pit Motel offered free HBO and an outdoor pool four months of the year. It further proclaimed that the rooms were recently renovated, and every form of credit card was readily accepted. What it didn't proudly broadcast were the stiff, smelly mattresses long since retired from hospitals and nursing homes, toilets that ran all night long, and carpet irreversibly stained from years of traveling pooches making it their personal outhouse.

Neither Elliot nor Adam noticed the deficiencies of the less than luxurious accommodations. Both men stared down at a large map spread across the queen-sized mattress that had been incurably infested with smoke, urine, and dried semen.

After eluding their roadway attackers, they had agreed it was time to get somewhere safe. If nothing else, it would give them a chance to talk—to make sense of things before returning to a world in which they were the hunted.

In front of them was an ordinary traveler's map showing the roadways, rivers, and appropriate borders of the continental United States. The only unusual markings on the map were three small blue circles around the cities of Washington, Dallas, and Las Vegas. Beside each location were the blurred images of words. Words that were once undoubtedly clear and would have proved invaluable. Now, however, they had degraded into little much more than smudgy ghosts of blue ink.

"Shit," Adam said with a heavy sigh. "After all this trouble, it's ruined." He felt absolutely sick with disappointment. *I should have just shot those schmucks instead of hiding like some pussy.*

"Maybe not," Elliot countered with an unexpected note of optimism. "Look at this." He pointed to a smudge above Dallas. What does that look like?"

To Adam it looked to be an incomprehensible blue ball with tentacles. "If this is one of those psychiatric ink blot questions to see if I'm all screwed up, I can save you the trouble."

Elliot smiled, clearly enjoying being in a position of strength. "Look carefully. And here above the other two cities." He moved his finger from one to the next. "Notice anything?"

Adam stared intently at the blurred images. The smears were all different, each having once been a single character. Below the single characters were longer, more complex blurs indicating writing of some sort. "Sorry, nada."

"Numbers, Adam. The cities are numbered." He moved his fingers from Dallas to Las Vegas to Washington, saying, "One, two, and three."

Adam stared at the blue smudges again. It was a reach, but he thought he could make out the numbers one, two, and with a couple of shots of Irish whiskey, maybe even three. The cities did indeed seem to be numbered.

"Okay, you're hot tonight. So what does it mean?" Adam asked, already considering the implications. In his given state of depression, he couldn't immediately come up with anything. He found himself replaying a continual reminder that they wouldn't be playing this game of "smudgy ink balls" if he hadn't ruined the map in the first place.

"Of course, I don't know the specifics, but in the broadest sense, it means that there is some order to the cities. Perhaps suggesting one must travel to Dallas to get or do something, then to Vegas, and finally to Washington. I think there's a sequence of events being outlined here."

"Even if that's so, just knowing the order doesn't seem to get us much. We're back to where we were with the key. We've got the *what* but not the *why*."

Elliot started to speak but stopped himself. Finally, he said, "So it would seem."

Adam flopped back onto the nasty bed. "This sucks," he said.

Elliot remained quiet for nearly a minute as he studied the map, rotating it, looking at it from both sides, and even using his eyeglasses as a magnifying glass. After the careful examination, he said, "Aha."

Adam opened one eye. "You see something?"

"No . . . but I think I have something nonetheless."

"What?" Adam asked, sitting up.

"Let me show you rather than tell you."

Adam leaned in close.

"Maria came to me saying she'd found a map. By 'found,' I'm now pretty sure she meant stolen. You agree?"

"I've never met her, but if you think so, then that's probably the scoop."

"Yes, she most definitely stole a map. But from whom? My guess is from someone she was seeing. After all, Maria wasn't a burglar, and her boyfriends were the only people she had intimate access to. It wouldn't be too far of a reach for me to believe that she would swipe something she thought valuable from a client."

"A real give-and-take girl," Adam said.

Elliot didn't break stride. "She stole a map from her lover and hid it at the amusement park. Then things started to heat up. She realized she was in danger, which is why she sent the key to her sister for safekeeping. Just in case."

"Along with a cryptic note that offered a hint as to the map's location," Adam added. "Only neither ever arrived due to a careless mistake of being cheap with the stamps, leaving Lara completely unaware of her sister's predicament."

"Exactly. Then things went bad for Maria. Her boyfriend hurt her trying to get the map back." Elliot's voice shook just a bit as he said "hurt." "Only it wasn't just him. He called in professionals, the type who specialize in extracting information."

"Which means her boyfriend was either in the agency himself or had some important ties to them. Perhaps a politician," Adam offered. "Whatever the map is, it's important enough for the CIA to get involved in a very personal way."

"A politician . . . yes, I could see that." Elliot's eyes moved about as he considered the new idea.

"It would have to be someone with political clout."

"Not just clout," Elliot corrected, "but also actively engaged in something of national interest."

"Something worth killing for. Those boys weren't shooting dart guns."

"Are we reading too much into this? Could it just be some sort of criminal organization?" Elliot asked.

Adam recalled the four men in the theme park. "The guys who chased me sure carried themselves like agency operatives. Well coordinated, not to mention well dressed."

Elliot grinned. "Can't have our country's spies dressing like bums."

"One thing we know for sure. They want this map."

"Do they?"

Adam turned to look at his brother. "No?"

"That's what we missed. Ask yourself why they want the map." Before Adam could answer, he continued, "Remember, we're assuming it was their employer's map to begin with. He surely already knows what's written on it. So, why go to the trouble to recover it?"

Adam looked down at the map with newfound interest. "Of course. It's not about the map. It's about keeping the information contained."

Elliot nodded. "The interesting part is that they must assume that by now we've read the map, which of course we haven't. That puts us in a curious position."

"Not curious. Dangerous. There's only one good way to make sure someone doesn't reveal information."

"What's that?"

Adam made his fingers into a mock pistol and tapped the barrel against his forehead.

Elliot shuddered. "Then we need to fix this. Let them know that we're not a threat."

Adam shook his head. "I don't know how we'd ever convince them of that. Besides, being a threat is the only thing we've got going for us. If we want to have any hope of finding Maria, we have to force them to make a mistake."

Elliot thought about it for a moment before nodding. "What do you think they'll do next?"

Both men sat quietly on the flea-infested bed, considering that all-important question. After a moment Adam turned to his brother, his eyes wide with concern. "Lara. They're going to try for Lara."

Elliot looked confused. "Why Lara?"

"Think about it. She's the one person whose whereabouts are still known. If nothing else, she'll give them something to barter with. These people won't wait until morning. They're out on the road tonight and will sure as hell want something to show their superiors after screwing the pooch with us."

Adam stood up, haphazardly folding the map. "That 'something' is going to be Lara."

Chapter 10

Calling was out of the question. Adam assumed that Lara's phone was tapped and that agents were watching her every move. A warning call could lead to chloroform-wielding stiff shirts kicking in her door. Of course, that logic assumed that the bad guys hadn't already decided to grab her, in which case their impromptu rescue was going to be for nothing.

Adam pushed the thought from his mind. If Maria's treatment proved anything, it demonstrated that these creeps were not about to follow the Geneva Convention. The thought of Lara tied to a chair while they worked her over with a pair of pliers was too much even for him.

The more things unfolded, the more convinced he became that Maria had become entangled in something related to national security. The trick was to figure out what she'd become involved in without having the same fate befall the rest of them.

After leaving the Cherry Pit Motel, Elliot and Adam headed directly to Lara's apartment building. Her residence was on the thirty-seventh floor of an executive high-rise apartment building in downtown Denver—the Brookfield Towers.

When she'd given them her address at their first meeting, Lara had specifically instructed them to call before ever coming over. The complex was evidently very particular about letting guests into the building without prior permission from a tenant. In this case, however, it wouldn't matter. They weren't going to use the front door.

Elliot pulled the bullet-ridden Audi into the Brookfield Towers underground parking garage, one level below the street.

Slipping off his damp jacket, Adam drew the Glock. A quick check confirmed that he had seven rounds remaining without a reload. He slid it back in place and secured it with a tight Velcro strap.

"Park over there," he directed, motioning to an elevator housed in a thick concrete shaft.

"What exactly are we going to do?"

"Just follow my lead," Adam said, exiting the vehicle. Before Elliot could get free of his seat belt. Adam leaned his head back in. "But leave your gun."

"You brought yours," Elliot said, sounding like he'd just been told he couldn't bring his teddy bear to a sleepover.

"Trust me."

Elliot shrugged and got out of the car.

A few moments later, the two men stood inside the elevator. Elliot held the button to keep the doors open.

"Why not just ride directly up to her floor?" he asked.

Adam pointed to a sign above the panel of elevator buttons. "That's why."

WITHOUT A RESIDENT KEY, THIS ELEVATOR STOPS IN THE MAIN LOBBY.

ALL GUESTS ARE REQUIRED TO EXIT THE ELEVATOR AND CHECK WITH THE SECURITY OFFICER ON DUTY.

"Ah," Elliot said. "What's the plan?"

Adam studied a small panel in the ceiling of the elevator car. He rose on his tiptoes and pressed it upward. One edge lifted up an inch or two.

"I'm going up there to the top of the car. You ride the elevator to the lobby and start asking for someone. It doesn't matter who. Just make up a name. I'll ride up while you keep security busy."

"But the elevator will be stuck at the lobby," Elliot said, still confused.

"No, it won't, because you're going to hit the button for the thirty-seventh floor before you get off. The guards won't think anything about letting an empty elevator go up unattended. They'll think someone on an upper floor has requested it. I'll ride up with the car, drop back down just before it stops, and exit on the thirty-seventh floor. Then I'll get Lara and be right down."

Elliot weighed the plan. "What should I do when they realize the person I'm looking for doesn't live here? They might think I'm some kind of nut. After all, I'm wearing my pajamas under this coat." He flashed open his trench coat to reveal the colorful flannel.

Adam chuckled, sliding the elevator service panel aside. "That's fine if they do. Once they decide you're either a kook or just mistaken, take the elevator back down to the garage and get the car ready to roll. You never know, we may have to exit in a hurry. Oh, and one more thing," Adam said, hoisting himself up into the dark elevator shaft. "Keep a look out for anyone suspicious."

"Right, and what exactly am I supposed to do if someone suspicious does show up?" Elliot looked frustrated.

Adam poked his head back down through the ceiling. "The answer's always the same. You do whatever it takes." A moment later, he disappeared behind the panel as it dropped back in place.

* * *

Adam waited in darkness broken only by the hum of the rising elevator and thin traces of light seeping in from floors above him. Below, he heard Elliot being escorted from the elevator, quickly explaining how he was looking for a "Mr. John Smith."

Imagination was never one of his brother's strong suits. At least such a common name might keep them busy for a while. There were probably a half-dozen Smiths in the building, any one of which might have a first or middle name of John.

The elevator shuddered and resumed its climb. Adam waited a few seconds to be sure the car had left the lobby. Then he felt around the lip of the panel, feeling for a gap or protrusion with which to lift it. To his dismay, the panel was well finished, the fit as seamless as a German sports car.

"This isn't good," he said, looking up into the darkness. He imagined razor-sharp blades spinning far above him at the top of the shaft. Of course, he was much more likely to simply encounter a cold concrete ceiling, but being crushed instead of diced offered little consolation.

"Come on, big boy. Don't panic." He turned his focus back to the panel.

He rapped on it like one might knock on a door. It vibrated up and down with each strike. An idea came to him. He struck one edge sharply with his palm, and the other side lifted just enough for him to slip his fingers under it. He slid the panel aside and quickly dropped down into the car.

The elevator continued to climb without interruption until it came to a stop at the thirty-seventh floor. He exited and quietly navigated the floor until he arrived at Lara's apartment.

"I sure hope I'm at the right place or someone's about to get an interesting late-night surprise," he whispered.

He considered knocking softly to wake Lara but feared the room might be bugged. If agents were listening electronically as he suspected they were, alerting Lara might cause them to move in and cut off his escape route.

He decided on a more clandestine approach. Sneak in, gently wake her, and slip out quietly into the night without anyone ever knowing he was there. Of course, if they were monitoring the room with sensitive enough equipment, he was busted.

Adam worked his lockpicks in the deadbolt, taking no more than a minute to release the latch. He then turned his attention to the door handle mechanism. Both opened with little more than a metallic *click*. He cracked open the door and leaned his head in. The room was too dark to make anything out. He slipped into the apartment, quietly closing and locking the door behind him.

A black stillness lay before him. He stood motionless, leaning back against the door as he waited for his eyes to adjust. Objects slowly solidified . . . a couch, a sliding patio door, a small kitchenette, a partially open bedroom door.

Moving as silently as a cat, albeit an aging one with cataracts, Adam approached the bedroom door. He listened at the doorway to see if Lara had stirred. Nothing. Not the rustle of covers. Not even the sigh of deep breathing. All was quiet.

He slowly advanced into the room. The soft blue light from a bedside clock provided only a trace of illumination. Directly ahead was the bed. To his right was a mirrored dresser, and to his left, he could see a sliding closet door.

He stopped to listen again. Nothing. Adam wondered if he was too late. What if they had already grabbed her?

He moved to the bed with a new urgency. As he came up beside it, he saw that the covers had been pulled back. It was indeed empty. "No," was all Adam could mutter as he felt his heart drop through the floor.

A snakelike hiss sounded from behind him. "Who are you?"

Adam spun, reaching for his pistol. Instinct told him to steady his hand before he pulled the gun free. He was clearly at the disadvantage.

From a shadowed corner, an indiscernible dark figure emerged, holding a handgun in front of it. "Don't," a sharp whisper warned, indicating his reach for the gun.

Adam thought that he recognized the voice. "Lara, it's me. Adam." He kept his voice low hoping that she could identify him, her eyes surely better adjusted to the darkness than his.

For a moment she didn't move, the gun still trained at his head. Then she slowly lowered the weapon and moved closer.

As Lara closed to within a few feet, Adam could see that she was wearing only a pair of black cotton panties and a short black T-shirt that hung just below her breasts. He couldn't help but suck in a gasp of air.

"What the hell are you doing here?" she asked, her voice never rising above a whisper.

Adam found himself without words. Her presence so close in the darkness was completely intoxicating. He detected the sweet scent of day-old perfume mixed with a hint of perspiration and her natural pheromones.

"I asked why you're in my bedroom at . . ." she glanced at the soft blue light of the clock, "three o'clock in the morning." Her voice was still very tight.

Adam understood her apprehension. Pulling a gun on someone in the middle of the night would rattle anyone. That she had even heard him enter the apartment was impressive. He could attribute it only to her living in a heightened sense of awareness since her sister's mysterious disappearance. People rise to the occasion.

He forced himself to look up from her sensuous figure and meet her gaze. Even focusing on the dark shape of her shadowed face made it difficult to compose his thoughts. "I found the map," he managed to get out.

When she didn't speak, he continued. "It was in an amusement park locker. But when I got there, some goons tried to grab me. Later, Elliot and I were shot at and nearly run off the road. These bums mean business, and I thought they might come after you next."

Lara's shoulders slumped as she noticeably relaxed. "You came to save me?"

Adam couldn't be sure if there was a ring of gratitude or amusement in her voice. Maybe a touch of both. "Yeah, something like that," he answered.

Both of them had thus far spoken only in whispers, and Lara now moved even closer, her voice turning almost indiscernibly quiet. "What was on the map?" A hint of edginess again crept into her voice.

Adam understood that she desperately wanted to know why her sister had been kidnapped and perhaps even killed. He fought a lump in his throat. "Not much. It's a long story, but the map is illegible. We can't read anything on it other than a few numbers." Then he confessed, "It was my fault. I ruined it, Lara. I'm sorry."

Lara nodded. Then she did something that made Adam's heart pound hard against his chest. She stepped in so close that her body rested lightly against his. He could feel the heat and soft press of her thinly covered breasts. She offered no explanation for her sudden advance, and during a brief moment of insanity, Adam felt an urge to retreat.

He fought the madness, choosing instead to place one hand on the curve of her hip, just above the thin waistband of her panties. He wasn't sure what her reaction would be, but he felt a desperate need to touch her, even if just for a moment. Her skin was perfectly smooth and intensely warm against his palm and fingers.

Lara didn't withdraw from his touch. Instead, she stood motionless, inches from him, her sweet, musky breath washing softly over his face and neck.

He felt her probing gaze and returned it even though the darkness prevented him from seeing her eyes.

They stood there motionless for a long time, until Lara finally moved. She reached up and slowly took Adam's hand in her own.

He was intensely grateful she'd allowed the moment to last as long as it had. Expecting her to release his hand, their intimacy ending there, he was stunned when she gently pressed his hand directly against her covered breast. He could feel the softness of the knit T-shirt and the smooth curvature of her breast beneath.

She continued to hold his hand there as he slowly, almost unconsciously, began caressing the nipple with soft, slow circles of his fingertips. Immediately he felt her tender flesh grow hard and take shape.

Lara's other hand moved to Adam's groin. Lightly, she began to drag her palm up and down across the now swollen bulge.

Adam could think of several good reasons why they shouldn't be doing this. Elliot waiting downstairs and the threat of agents busting in the door were the two most obvious. He also understood that he didn't have a prayer of finding the willpower to stop what was happening.

He placed his other hand behind Lara's head and gently stroked her soft hair. She leaned her head back, pressing against his open palm while increasing the pressure of her massage.

Adam slowly pulled her forward and brought her lips to his. They kissed softly, their tongues occasionally sparking against each other like two electric eels. The intensity grew as she began to softly chew on his lips, her tongue probing deeper into his mouth. He met her aggression with equal fervor, sucking softly on her tongue and pulling her harder against him.

Lara's lips left his and moved greedily down his neck where she stopped to bite and lick playfully. Adam felt the world spinning as he closed his eyes, feeling only the soft golden strands of hair, the tender round nipple pressing against his fingers, and the warm, moist sensation spreading across his neck. He struggled to catch his breath as he felt her unbutton his jeans and slowly lower the zipper.

The spontaneity and complete eroticism of the encounter held him weak and unable to gain any sort of masculine control of his partner. He let her work the magic she possessed without daring to ruin the perfection of the moment with a manly blunder.

Slowly Lara lowered herself. Her breast fell away from his caress, but he made no move to follow her. He felt the warmth of her mouth against his stomach. Her tongue moved in slow circles, leaving moist traces of its passing. Gradually she moved down his abdomen.

Adam felt his pants and underwear sliding down his legs but found no shame at being exposed to her. He couldn't be sure if it was the cover of darkness that gave him this confidence or if it was just the completeness with which she now possessed him.

Slowly she took him in her mouth. The warmth and pressure were enough to make Adam gasp aloud. She took him fully with each slow rhythmic pass until he was about to erupt with pleasure. She seemed to sense this and slowly withdrew from him.

Lara brought herself up to her full height and kissed him hungrily on the mouth once again. He could smell and taste the pungent sex in her breath now.

Knowing instinctively that it was his time to act, Adam bent at the waist, slid one arm under her legs, and gently lifted her into the air. She offered no resistance or hesitation as he took two steps and lowered them both onto her already disheveled bed.

* * *

Adam and Lara lay curled against one another, naked and warm.

He replayed the events of the past half hour over and over in his mind. In a moment of understanding, he realized their lovemaking had forever changed things between them.

When it came to lovers, he felt that time could be divided into two halves: the time before their first lovemaking and the time after. He and Lara had now crossed that temporal divide. Nothing would ever be the same again.

Adam wanted to say something to her, to somehow express the importance he placed on their intimacy. Words didn't come to mind that adequately described his feelings, so instead, he gently squeezed her shoulder. In response, she turned her face toward him and kissed him lightly on the chest.

His mind was still swimming when he suddenly remembered Elliot waiting down in the garage. Everything came flooding back with a renewed sense of urgency. They were all in danger.

Adam sat up quickly. "Get some things together," he said. "We have to go."

Chapter 11

"Nice work," Lara said to Adam, pointing to the bullet holes and broken glass that used to be the rear window of the Audi.

The two of them climbed into the car, the engine already alive with a soft German hum. Adam rode shotgun, and Lara hopped in the back, tossing her gear ahead of her onto the empty seat.

"Sorry it took—" Adam stopped in mid-sentence. Elliot sat straight and stiff, his leg bouncing like a jackhammer. He was gripping the Browning tightly in his lap. The weapon was cocked and ready to fire. "Elliot, what happened?"

Elliot was unable to speak for a moment, finally blurting, "They were down here."

"Who?" Lara asked from the back seat.

"I don't know who!" He hit the steering wheel with an open palm.

Adam slowly reached over and closed his hand over the Browning. He put the flesh of his thumb and forefinger between the hammer and strike plate as he gently took the gun from his brother. "Take it slow. Tell us what happened."

Lara was now leaning forward listening intently.

"Two guys in a white minivan. They were down here in the garage. I was just getting back to the car when they rushed me. If it hadn't been for the gun . . ." Elliot's voice broke.

He swallowed hard and continued, "The pistol was here on the seat. I managed to pull it on them just as they were getting to me. The sight of the gun stopped them, but they didn't retreat. I think they were trying to decide if I really had the nerve to shoot."

"Did you?" Lara asked from over his shoulder.

"That's just it. I did. I pointed the gun at them and pulled the trigger. Can you believe they didn't even have a weapon out? I was just so damned afraid."

"You shot them?" Adam glanced out his window for any signs of blood.

"No. Nothing happened. I squeezed the trigger hard, but it wouldn't fire. That's when I remembered what you said about having to cock the hammer for the first shot. They didn't even know I was trying to shoot them. Isn't that downright hysterical? These men stood there glaring at me, completely unaware that I was trying to kill them."

Elliot seemed dangerously close to an emotional breakdown. Adam put a hand on his shoulder.

"What did you do?" Lara asked.

Elliot took a deep breath, and with it seemed to find a measure of control. "Realizing what I was doing wrong, I cocked the gun. By then, I had collected myself a little. I told them to leave us alone. I couldn't think of anything else to say. In retrospect, I realize I could have asked them where Maria was, or what they wanted, or how they'd found us, or a dozen other useful things. But at that moment, I couldn't think."

Adam squeezed his shoulder. "It's okay, bro. You're in one piece, and that's what matters. What happened next?"

"They backed away. I told them to stop, thinking I could hold them at gunpoint until you arrived. But they just kept backing up. They were looking me right in the eyes, and I didn't have the nerve to shoot anymore."

"So they left?" Adam asked, once again looking around the parking garage.

"Yes. They just climbed back in their van and drove out. I swear one of them even winked at me as they pulled away. I . . . I couldn't stop them."

"You handled it fine," Adam offered, generally meaning it.

"If the gun hadn't been within reach . . ." Elliot fell silent, staring at the cement wall in front of the car. "I might be dead right now. Dead."

"You're all right," Adam said. "Do you think you can get us out of here before Tweedle Dee and Tweedle Dum return with reinforcements?"

"Yeah, okay." Elliot's hands were trembling as he put the car in reverse. "What took you so long? I thought you might have run into trouble, too. I wasn't sure if I should come up after you or what exactly." His voice trailed off with exhaustion.

"Sorry," Adam said. "Lara needed to get a few things together." His words only hinted at the truth. It had taken a few minutes for Lara to pack a bag with fresh clothes, cosmetics, and other items she deemed important, but that definitely wasn't why they were late.

Adam felt a bit of shame come over him and glanced up into the rearview mirror to see Lara looking directly at him. He didn't see embarrassment in her eyes but perhaps a little worry. He wondered if she feared betrayal, that perhaps he would reveal their intimacy. He hoped that wasn't the case. Adam had always been able to keep a secret. If she didn't know it now, she would eventually come to appreciate it.

"Where to?" Elliot asked, sounding a bit more like the man he'd been an hour earlier.

"Get us to a hotel," Adam answered. "Preferably near a mall."

"A mall? What do you mean? Like a shopping mall?" Elliot asked.

"Yes. You and I are going to need a few changes of clothing, and we can't chance going back to either of our places."

"I do love to shop," Lara chimed in.

"What do you mean we can't go back?" Elliot asked, obviously not pleased with what he was hearing.

Adam didn't really blame him. The evening had started with a simple late-night call for help. Elliot had probably thought they would soon be sipping warm cognac in front of his fireplace while talking about their next investigative move. Unfortunately, things weren't going in the direction of an armchair investigation. Life was about to change for all of them.

Adam took a breath and tried to give his brother the straight scoop in as comforting a tone as he could manage. "Look, they were watching us. All of us. That's how they found me in the amusement park. That's how they found us in your car on Federal Street. And that's how they found you here. They know who we are, where we live, where we work, and what establishments we're likely to frequent. Hell, they probably know how many times we hit the head each day. If we go back to anything they know, we're dead or grabbed for sure. Our only reasonable move is to go underground for a bit. And that's exactly what we're going to do."

* * *

Bulls-eye: Your people are becoming a problem. Their incompetence is interfering with my work.

Pecos Bill: Well, la-dee-da.

Bulls-eye: Do you understand what I'm saying?

Pecos Bill: What I hear is that the outlaws have done wandered off the plantation with what you lost. That's what I hear.

Bulls-eye: They have yet to cause us trouble. But if your people keep pushing, this could get out in the open. We don't want that.

Pecos Bill: No . . . we don't. Maybe it'd be best all-round if they just went the way of the three-legged whippoorwill. Not saying you don't have everything under control and all.

Bulls-eye: They still have value to me. Stay away from them.

Pecos Bill: Whoa, now. Just a cowboy's take on the situation, that's all.

Bulls-eye: Is it all set up?

Pecos Bill: Of course, it is. Everything's in place just like you asked.

Bulls-eye: Good. One last warning. Keep your people out of my way, or I'll remove them.

Pecos Bill: You can count on that, partner. No one wants to be in your way.

* * *

"It's going to be a busy day," Adam said, sipping a steaming cup of hot coffee.

The three had spent what was left of the night at a motel not far from the Westland Crossing shopping mall. After a quick stop at a bustling donut shop, they stopped the Audi in an empty supermarket parking lot and began enjoying hot drinks and breakfast sweets.

Adam was pleased to see the group in good spirits, considering they'd managed to get only a few hours of sleep. "Elliot, I'd advise you to get in touch with your firm. Let them know you'll be out for a while. We don't want anyone calling the police thinking something's happened to you."

"Right. Any idea how long all this is going to take?" he asked, rifling through the open box of donuts.

"Better tell them a couple of weeks in case this thing takes on new twists. Given what little we know now, I can't imagine how it won't."

"Fine. I'm due a vacation anyway."

"Just so we know the rules," Adam said, turning to look at both Elliot and Lara. "All calls from now on should be made only from a landline in a busy location. They should be kept short, and once they're done, you should immediately leave the vicinity. Also, Elliot, we're going to need to get you to a branch of your bank for some serious cash. We won't be able to use credit cards because of traceability concerns."

"We're getting awfully cloak-and-dagger about all this," his brother remarked.

"I know. But given that I'm still fishing broken glass from my pants pockets, I'd say caution is in order."

"How much money?" Elliot asked, his voice betraying wariness in trusting anyone, even his own brother, with his wealth.

"Let's say twenty thousand," Adam said, knowing it was going to get a reaction.

Elliot looked up sharply from the donut box, a particularly large, coconut donut dangling in his fingers like from a crab's claw that wouldn't let go. "Twenty thousand dollars? You want me to get twenty thousand dollars cash?" His voice was loud to everyone in the car.

Lara turned away from them, busying herself by slurping the cream off a large cup of foaming hot cocoa.

"Yes, but don't worry, we probably won't spend even half of it. It's just this may be your only chance to get cash for a while. Better get enough."

"What are you talking about? They can't take my money."

Adam shrugged. "I wouldn't be so sure. If the bozos chasing us really are CIA, they can freeze your funds. I have no idea if they would, but they could if they wanted to. It's the government, and they can dick you just about any way they choose." Adam stopped to let his words sink in. "So, get the twenty thousand while you still have a chance. Hell, get more if you want to."

"How do you know I can still get to my accounts?" Elliot asked. "Maybe first thing this morning they're freezing my money and issuing orders for anyone trying to access the funds to be detained."

"Truth is, I don't know," Adam answered. "I'm guessing they wouldn't be able to move that fast. Everything went down late last night, and decisions would have to be made. Important people make those decisions, and important people don't generally work at three in the morning. I think you'll be okay getting the money first thing this morning. But like I said, there are no guarantees."

"A risk *I'm* going to have to take," Elliot said with a smirk. Not getting a reaction, he took a deep breath and resumed his donut scavenger hunt.

"After the bank, the three of us will need to go on a shopping spree," Adam said, looking first to Lara then to Elliot. "We're going to need several outfits—socks, underwear, belts, the whole works. Also, the car needs a new rear windshield and a little Bondo patched over the bullet holes. I can just see the state trooper's face now, should we happen to get pulled over."

"That's a lot to do," Elliot said.

"Yep," he agreed. "All this works on my assumption that you don't mind footing the bill for this adventure."

Adam had given a great deal of thought about having his brother pay for all the necessary expenses. Elliot had always treasured his treasure. His reluctance or willingness to part with it would serve as a decent measure of his dedication to finding Maria. If he balked about the expenditures, Adam was prepared to walk away from the whole affair and catch the next flight home.

Elliot never looked up from the box of donuts. "I understand my part in this. I'm providing the capital."

"Great! My very own sugar daddy." Lara exclaimed from the back seat. "I've been needing some new clothes, and maybe a Gucci handbag too!"

Elliot sighed. "I may need more than twenty thousand after all."

* * *

Elliot opened the car door but didn't step out. "What if they try to grab me? Should I run for it?"

"No," Adam said, shaking his head. "If it goes sour, just stay cool. I'll get you out. Don't ask how, because I don't know how. Maybe I'll call in a bomb scare or maybe I'll just pull guns and scare the hell out of everyone. No matter what, we won't leave without you."

Elliot studied his brother, weighing the magnitude of the promise just made.

Adam really hoped he wasn't going to get emotional, especially in front of Lara.

He nodded, saying only, "Be right back." With that, Elliot scrambled out of the car and headed toward the bank. He walked with an uncertain stiffness, like that of a bank robber approaching his first heist.

Adam watched his brother disappear into the bank and offered a silent prayer that Elliot wouldn't do anything stupid in there. Neither Lara nor Adam spoke for over a minute, both staring at the glass double doors to the bank. Since their intimacy the previous night, there had been no mention or suggestion of how either felt concerning what had happened.

He could see in his peripheral vision when Lara briefly glanced his way then turned back to stare at the bank. "About last night . . ." she started.

"I hope it goes without saying that I don't normally . . . you know what I mean, I don't . . . it's not like me. That's all I'm saying."

He turned to face her. "I would never take what happened for granted, Lara. It was the most perfect experience I've ever had with a woman."

She turned to him, her eyes searching his face for signs of insincerity. After a moment of indecision, she said, "It was nice. Since our first meeting, I . . . felt something. Then when you came to save me . . . Well, that was probably the sweetest thing anyone's ever done for me. You just don't know."

Adam smiled. "When I got up this morning, it all seemed like a dream. A really good dream, mind you," he said with a laugh. "Then when I saw you come down from your room this morning, I felt this bond between us. I know that sounds like a line, but I felt it."

"We shared a lot last night," Lara offered. "I lost myself with you for a while, and that's not like me."

He saw an undeniable intensity in the blue cover of her eyes. There was something exceptional about Lara Sativa, and he was just beginning to see how beautiful and truly unique she was.

"I'm going to show you just how much of a fool I am," Adam said. "Bare my heart and all that."

"Go for it," she said, smiling, her tone turning more playful.

"I want last night to be the start of something."

"The start of what?"

"The start of more nights like last night." It was his turn to smile.

She squinted at him, her eyes alive with fire. They looked at each other for a long time, saying nothing.

"Would it be okay if I kissed you?" he asked. "Just for a moment, I promise. I know it's a bit pathetic, but I want to consummate this, and a handshake just isn't going to do."

She answered by placing her hands on both sides of his face and pulling him to her. They kissed with the same passion and ferocity they'd shared the night before.

Finally, she pulled away. "There, sealed with a kiss."

Adam felt his heart pounding, his face becoming flushed. "There's something here between us. Something exceptional. I wonder if Elliot and Maria felt the same thing."

"Maybe," she said with unmistakable disappointment. "Or maybe they had something different."

Adam immediately realized that he'd made a terrible mistake. "I'm sorry. I hope you know that isn't what I meant. Forgive me?"

She sat quiet for a moment, staring at him. "On one condition."

"Anything." And he meant it. Whether she called for going a few rounds with Mike Tyson after he hadn't eaten in three days or scaling Mount Everest in the nude, he would gladly take up the challenge.

"Promise that you'll grant me the same forgiveness should I ever need it. I tend to do a lot of stupid things." Her voice was much softer now.

Adam kissed her on the forehead, grateful that her request didn't involve losing an ear to a cannibalistic boxer or, even more importantly, extremities to a frigid mountain. "I never give up on those I care about," he said. "All you'll ever have to do is ask."

"Okay, then you're forgiven." She leaned in and kissed him gently on the lips.

Both of them turned as they saw Elliot hurrying toward the car. They pulled away from each other but not with a sense of urgency. Adam didn't care if Elliot knew about their relationship, but he also didn't see the need to complicate things in a situation that was already complex enough.

Elliot fumbled frantically with the door handle, jerking the car door open like he was trying to start an industrial lawnmower. He stumbled into the Audi, nearly cracking his head on the doorframe. Even though it wasn't quite seventy degrees outside, he was covered in sweat.

"Got it," he said, placing a large white bank envelope on the seat beside him. He stabbed the key in the ignition and immediately started the car.

As they pulled out of the parking lot, Adam asked, "Everything go okay in there?"

"Fine," Elliot replied, rapidly tapping the steering wheel with his fingers. "I just got nervous, that's all. It's not like people don't notice when you take out that kind of cash. Trust me. They notice."

* * *

The day was filled with frenzied shopping. The three worked from store to store in Westland Crossing, one of Colorado's largest upscale shopping malls. Adam found it interesting how each had distinctive tastes, even under the immediate threat of being on the lamb.

For Adam, his new wardrobe consisted of two pairs of blue jeans, a pair of khaki Dockers, four identical knit golf shirts in various colors, a heavy gray wool sweater, matching white-and-black turtlenecks, a thin belt that could be worn with just about anything, a pair of comfortable black Timberline walking shoes, and all the necessary undergarments.

In contrast, Elliot bought several pairs of wool trousers, a full suit in navy—which he insisted needed tailoring, a handful of white pima cotton French cuff dress shirts, two belts, a pair of Bostonian dress shoes, three remarkably similar red ties, and enough underwear to last him through the next millennium.

Having brought some things from home, Lara didn't need as much. What she picked up tended to be casual, including a pair of stretch pants, a striking dark green jumpsuit, a couple cotton blouses, a sweater, a pair of lightweight running shoes, and a few undergarments.

Adam also purchased several boxes of ammunition from a sporting goods store for both his and Elliot's handguns, since they were now unable to retrieve the rounds bought earlier from the pawnshop. He didn't ask if Lara had brought the firearm she'd brandished the previous night. He suspected that she had, although she made no mention of needing to buy ammunition.

By two in the afternoon, the shopping was complete, the freshly repaired Audi stocked from floorboard to ceiling. Adam offered to take the wheel, and Elliot gratefully accepted.

Adam recalled that for many years his brother hadn't particularly enjoyed driving. He believed it stemmed from a couple of bad accidents on icy roads that Elliot had been involved in as a teenager. To this day, Adam thought he detected a bit of trepidation each time Elliot sat behind the wheel. He wasn't sure how the previous night's high-speed chase might have affected his brother's already-shaky automotive confidence.

As they pulled out of the shopping mall's parking lot, Adam saw Elliot staring blankly out the window. "You okay?"

Elliot groaned. "I'm just bemoaning our situation. We're on the run from people willing to kill us for a road map. Worse yet, we've come to think that they work for our very own government. I was just thinking that perhaps we should stop planning our next move and start thinking about how this thing is going to end."

Adam considered his words. Elliot was right. He'd been so busy working to outmaneuver the bad guys that he hadn't given much thought as to how to actually resolve the situation.

"You're right, big brother. I tell you what. I'll try to keep us out of the clutches of our enemies. You figure out how we can end this mess."

Elliot turned to him, excitement in his eyes. He'd obviously been waiting for the invitation. "I have a friend who's fairly high up in the FBI.

I could contact him. Let him know what's happened. I'm sure he'd help. At the very least, it might put us back on the right side of the law."

"Absolutely not," Lara exclaimed from the back seat. "I don't trust the FBI any more than the CIA."

"Come on. What's wrong with the FBI?" Elliot asked.

"You ever heard of Malcolm X?" she asked.

"Don't tell me," Elliot said, closing his eyes in disbelief. "The FBI killed Malcolm X?"

"Maybe. Maybe not. Either way, they sure set the stage for his untimely demise." Lara looked to see if either Adam or Elliot was interested in her claim.

"Oh, please go on," Elliot said, shaking his head.

"When Malcolm X separated from Elijah Muhammad's group, it was under less than friendly terms. He was subsequently poisoned and his house fire-bombed. The police did nothing to protect him, despite his pleas."

"More likely a sign of the racially charged times than any sort of conspiracy," Elliot muttered.

Lara never broke step. "Later when Malcolm was scheduled to speak at New York's Audubon Ballroom, every one of his guest speakers unexpectedly canceled. The normally heavy police presence was inexplicably reduced to two officers. While he was speaking, a mock scuffle broke out near the stage. When he attempted to quell the minor disturbance, he was gunned down by a total of sixteen shots from at least five different assassins."

Lara had been rattling off the information as if she was afraid they wouldn't let her finish. She paused to take a breath and then continued with a bit more control. "Malcolm's bodyguard, along with the crowd, caught two of the killers. Even though his bodyguard was later revealed to be an undercover cop, not a single officer came to his aid during the apprehension or his subsequent attempt to resuscitate Malcolm X."

"Even if what you're saying is true, the worst you've described is police complicity," Elliot said. "I don't see a tie to the FBI."

Lara held up a single finger. "Coming to that. You'd think with two of the killers in hand, the authorities would easily have broken the case wide open. The odd thing was that one of the shooters mysteriously disappeared after being mentioned only in the initial press release. The other one candidly confessed to shooting Malcolm and stated that he'd been hired by FBI agents, not rival Muslims as the agency asserted.

"Not long after that, one of Malcolm's followers claimed to possess evidence that could prove his killers were government operatives. Like so many before him, once he opened his mouth, he had to be quieted."

"Dead?" Elliot asked, playing along.

"The very next morning. Officials declared it to be an epileptic fit, even though recent medical exams had explicitly stated he was in excellent health. Probably most damning of all was the public disclosure that J. Edgar Hoover had in fact told Lyndon Johnson that the best way to get rid of Malcolm X and Martin Luther King, Jr. was to capitalize on existing conflicts between competing black nationalist organizations."

Elliot started to interrupt, but Lara held up her hand to stop him.

"Maybe the FBI didn't pull the trigger," she continued, "but from what I've read, they got all the parties together and maybe even provided a little financial incentive to get the job done."

"Really, Lara," Elliot scoffed. "To hear you tell it, our entire government is filled with unscrupulous thieves and murderers."

"You said it, not me," she countered.

"You're living in a world found only in the minds of Hollywood moviemakers or overly imaginative authors," Elliot said.

"Maybe," Lara said, "but I don't trust the government. Period."

"Look, we have to trust someone. I know this guy. He's a friend, and besides, it's becoming pretty clear we could use some help. I don't see how we have much choice."

"No FBI," Lara repeated.

He sighed, exasperated. "Fine, but when we end up in jail, you just remember I was the voice of reason."

"Don't worry," she said in a consoling tone. "We're not going to end up in jail. We might end up dissolving in a bathtub filled with hydrochloric acid, but we won't go to jail."

Elliot shook his head. "Girl, you need some professional help."

"All right, you two," Adam interjected, hoping to keep a real fight from flaring up. "Given Lara's objection to the FBI, what else do you have up your sleeve?"

"Not a freaking rabbit," Elliot said, stewing from the rejection. After a moment he said, "It comes down to one question."

"And that is?" Adam asked.

"How do we best spend our time?"

"Car bingo?" Lara said, picking at him.

Elliot emitted an exasperated snort.

"The way I see it, we have two choices," Adam said. "We can remain here in Denver and try to get the attention of those after us, or we can go to the locations on the map and see what develops."

"Staying here sounds dangerous, but going anywhere else sounds futile," Elliot said. "We don't know what we're looking for."

"Sure we do," Lara said. "We're looking for my sister."

"That much I know," he admitted. "But we don't have any specifics. What to do. Where to go. Who to talk to. Little stuff like that matters."

"You'd rather stay here then?" Adam prompted.

"No," Elliot said simply. "Even though I think it's very likely a wild goose chase, I'd still vote for leaving town. I don't like getting shot at. Plus, we can get John to handle the information gathering here. That way we'd be working this thing from both ends."

"You could have him start with auto repair shops close to the amusement park," Adam suggested. "Those boys had to fix that radiator somewhere. We might get a name out of that."

"Good idea," Elliot said.

"Then it's unanimous?" Adam asked. "We follow the map?"

"We follow the map," Elliot agreed.

They both looked to Lara. She nodded. "Road trip."

"Anyone know the quickest route to Dallas?" Adam asked.

"Quickest route?" Elliot seemed confused. "Just head east to the airport. Surely you're not suggesting we drive."

"Believe me, it's not that I like planting my butt on a car seat for countless hours," Adam said. "But the way I see it, the airport is too risky. If the CIA is looking for us, they'll be monitoring DIA flights for our names. Unfortunately, with identification requirements at the airports, we couldn't fly under aliases without lengthy preparations."

"But . . . but . . ." Elliot stammered.

"The other drawback to flying is that we couldn't ship our ammunition. They'd allow us check the handguns as long as we had locked cases and proper tags, but the ammo would have to remain behind. That could put us in jeopardy for a time in Dallas."

"I agree," Lara piped in. "We're sure to be arrested if we show up at an airport. It's much safer to stick to the road."

"Fine," Elliot acquiesced, "but Dallas is about twelve hours from here. If we're going to drive, we should at least try to make ourselves comfortable. Do me a favor and pull into the parking deck up ahead so I can run into the bookstore." He pointed to a multilevel deck across the street from the mall. "Coffee and a couple of newspapers will make the trip survivable."

"I could use another hit of caffeine too," Lara said.

"It's a miracle," Adam said, laughing.

Both looked to him, puzzled.

"The two of you agree on something. A miracle, I'd say."

Lara popped him on the back of the head.

Elliot just rolled his eyes.

Adam navigated his way through the parking deck and pulled the car into a short-term parking spot just outside the doors of the Stitch in Time bookstore. He could see from the clientele moving in and out that the store catered to a college crowd.

Thoughts of navigating the book bonanza in search of a yuppie-style coffee bar didn't excite Adam. Unlike his well-read brother, he wasn't born with an innate desire to rummage through old books in search of two-hundred-year-old chronicles of Thomas Jefferson's womanizing. The occasional Dean Koontz or Stephen King bestseller usually sufficed. Adam wouldn't admit it for fear of being labeled an uneducated bumpkin, but he'd just as soon catch a movie than spend a week plowing through a lengthy novel.

As Lara and Elliot opened their doors to get out, Adam said, "I'll wait here. That super-espresso whipped mocha java whatever the heck it was I had this morning was as much caffeine as I need for the day."

They both laughed and headed into the bookstore.

* * *

Toxin: You rang?

Pecos Bill: I've got some roping for you.

Toxin: Who's the target?

Pecos Bill: A strapping hombre, so best watch yourself on this one. There's a package at the usual drop with all the goodies inside.

Toxin: How soon is this going down?

Pecos Bill: Real soon. Take some advice from your old friend. Do this one quick and skedaddle.

Toxin: Why? What don't I know?

Pecos Bill: Bulls-eye's roping on this here rodeo, too.

Toxin: Shit and double shit.

Pecos Bill: I'd say that about sums it up.

* * *

Adam watched as Lara and Elliot exited the bookstore carrying large green cups of steaming drinks and armfuls of newspapers. As they pushed their way through the set of double doors, a teenage mother approached from the parking lot. The young woman held an infant with one hand and pulled a reluctant toddler with the other.

After Lara exited, Elliot stepped aside holding the door and motioning for the young mother to enter. She offered a thankful smile and squeezed her way through the open doorway. As they passed, the little boy suddenly tugged at his mother, causing her to accidentally bump into Elliot. The cup of hot coffee he carried was inadvertently knocked from his hand, falling directly toward the toddler.

Incredibly, as the cup fell through the air, Elliot simultaneously released the newspapers and sliced both hands downward, successfully snatching the falling cup with only a small splash spilling across his hand.

The mother didn't apologize or even notice the near disaster. Instead, she continued her haphazard march into the bookstore, dragging the most fortunate tot behind her.

When Elliot climbed back in the car, Adam said, "Wow. That was one great save."

Elliot's hands were shaking. "It's amazing what people can do when working purely on reflexes. Even a paper pusher like me."

"All I can say is that somewhere Jackie Chan is green with envy." That the catch was made at all was surprising. That it was made by a brother he'd always considered physically inept was just as he'd suggested . . . amazing.

"You sure you don't mind driving?" Elliot asked, unfolding a copy of the *Wall Street Journal.*

"Not a bit," Adam said.

Adam glanced in the rearview mirror and saw Lara sipping coffee and casually studying the front page of the only nationwide newspaper left in print, *USA Today.* She didn't seem to notice his admiring eyes.

He wondered what the future held for them. In a way, it was the not knowing that was so exciting. At this very moment, anything was possible. It was as if he were being whisked away to Neverland, his future now in the hands of hungry crocodiles and dancing faeries. There was no way a mere mortal could ever guess what magic lay ahead.

Chapter 12

Adam was steering the car onto I-25 South in Denver when Lara suddenly sat up straight in the backseat. She began flipping back and forth between two sections of the paper, her face alive with excitement. Elliot was buried in stock tables and didn't appear to notice her erratic behavior.

"What's up?" Adam asked, looking at her in the rearview mirror.

"Stop the car," she said with urgency, leaning forward over the seat.

Adam didn't ask why. He glanced around for the quickest way to pull the Audi onto the wide paved shoulder.

Elliot looked up from his pages of dividends, IPOs, and earnings reports. "What's the matter?"

"We're heading the wrong way," she exclaimed. "We have to turn around."

"What are you talking about?" Elliot asked with furrowed eyebrows. "I thought we agreed that going to Dallas was better than staying here."

Adam listened to them but chose not to jump in, focusing instead on safely negotiating the remaining two lanes of busy after-work traffic.

"I don't know how I did it, but I think I've figured it out," she said. "I understand the map."

"What?" Elliot's voice betrayed both hopeful excitement and a bit of resentment.

She didn't answer until Adam had safely brought the car to rest on the shoulder and both men were facing her. "We need to go to Vegas," she said. "Not Dallas. Dallas is already done. Look." She held out the front page of the newspaper. It showed a color photograph of an Army general, the headline reading, "Livingston's Assassin Still At Large."

"That's General Livingston," Elliot said. "He was shot yesterday while giving a speech. What does that have to do with Maria?"

"I'm not sure I follow either," Adam added.

"Listen, I think this is what the map is all about. This is the reason Dallas was circled," she stammered, tapping the front page of the paper. "This is why my sister was . . ." She didn't finish her sentence, obviously unsure of what word adequately described what had happened to Maria.

"You're not making any sense," Elliot said. "What would Maria have to do with the murder of a presidential candidate?"

"I don't know how she's involved. But look," she flipped several pages back in the paper. The story she brought forward was without a photograph but the headline read, "Billionaire Greene Hosts Krakatau-Sized Vegas Gala."

"The article goes on to say how this moneybags, Greene, is hosting a big party tomorrow night for all the overpaid broadcast egomaniacs."

"I remember reading about that," Elliot said. "So what are you suggesting? That the map indicates what . . . murder locations? First, Livingston in Dallas, and then Greene in Las Vegas?"

She pointed a confirming finger at Elliot. "Give that man a cigar."

They were the first complimentary words she'd ever sent his way, and Elliot seemed to grow a couple inches taller because of it. "That would leave the third circle for whom?" he asked.

"I don't know. How about Senator Shoemaker? Or the vice president?"

"D.C. *is* circled," Adam offered. "And I recall hearing that a big presidential debate is scheduled for a few days from now."

"That makes sense," Lara said.

"Makes sense? You're kidding, right?" Elliot looked determined to punch holes in her theory. "We've got a map with smudgy blue ink around three cities. That's it. To link that to Livingston's murder is as far away from making sense as we can possibly go."

"Once again, inside-the-box thinking," Lara chided. "We have much more than the map."

"Then enlighten me, because I don't get it," he said.

"First, there's Maria. From what Adam told me, it seems very likely that she was involved with someone of political importance."

"It could just as easily have been someone from the mob," Elliot interjected.

"How about the man in the mail room? The CIA was trying to intercept her mail. Why would they be involved if this isn't something of national importance?"

"The government does have some interest in this, but that doesn't tie Maria to General Livingston," Elliot countered again.

"What about the men who tried to run you off the road? Or the ones who came after you at my apartment? Or how about the guys who tried to grab Adam? It all adds up to a well-coordinated effort."

"Coordinated, yes. I'd even go so far as to say deadly. No argument there," Elliot agreed. "But again, there's no connection that I can make to the Livingston murder."

"Squirrels are dropping pinecones on your head, but you don't want to believe that furry little beasts are living in the trees." She was losing patience. "Don't you get it? No one's going to present this to you as a well-written legal brief. We're going to have to put it together all by ourselves and go on some hunches." Lara turned to Adam, obviously perturbed with his brother the naysayer. "What do you think?"

"I understand Elliot's hesitation, but the truth is we don't have much else," he said, trying to work both sides. It was his job to keep the peace. If matter and antimatter were ever to come into contact . . .

"Besides," he continued, "as unlikely as the scenario sounds, it does align with the facts. We have Maria, probably taken and tortured by professionals. We have a dead general in a city circled on our map. We have two major televised events involving the other presidential candidates, also in circled cities. Not to mention that all three events are in the order indicated on the map. To top it all off, we have government agents trying to cap us for what appears to be nothing more than a Rand McNally roadmap. We're sure as hell into something big."

Adam felt Lara's hand touch him softly on the arm. He had apparently passed her test of faith.

"Come on, Adam," Elliot said, shaking his head. "It's still a reach."

Adam slowly nodded. "Perhaps, but there's something else too."

"What?" Both Elliot and Lara said together.

"The way Livingston was killed . . . it was awfully public. Why not shoot him on his way in or out of an event? Much easier to arrange, I would think."

"The killer wanted an audience," Lara said, her voice chilled. "But why?"

"Maybe he gets his kicks from seeing his work on the news," Adam suggested. "It wouldn't be the first time a sniper took unnecessary risks to receive TV time. You can bet the media will be showing clips of

Livingston's last few moments for years to come. This guy was trying to leave his mark on history. If he really plans to kill the other candidates, my guess is he'll try to do it in very public forums."

"Like a big media party or a political debate," Lara said.

Adam shrugged. "Could be."

"You're both making everything fit into a nice little picture," Elliot said, "but there are countless other possibilities. I'll accept that we're onto something very dangerous. I'll even agree that the map is of some national importance. But the thread tying our predicament to the assassination is thin at best."

When no one responded, he continued with his case. "Perhaps our government is far from trustworthy, but consider another scenario. What if there's a nut on the loose, and the CIA is just trying to track him down. Maybe the map is part of his particular method of operation, and the agency is trying to retrieve it for clues. By holding onto it, we could be obstructing justice."

"Then why would the CIA be trying to kill us?" Adam countered. "Those guys weren't flashing badges and asking questions last night. They let bullets fly before we'd even had the chance to run a stop sign."

"The map isn't worth killing for unless those words mean something," Lara said, jumping in.

Elliot took a deep breath and let it out slowly. He looked to Lara first. "Look, I don't mean to obstruct you in this. I know your sister's life hangs on what we do, but we're taking a huge leap of faith on what could be simple coincidence. It's important that we head down the right path if we're to have any hope of finding her."

He turned to Adam next. "As for your assertion, we don't know that the people shooting at us were government agents. We only know that the one guy you accosted in the mail room worked for the CIA, and from the way you've told it, you picked that fight. I'll say it again, the CIA is very likely on the same side we're on."

Adam detected the stink of superiority beginning to spew from his brother. He needed to do something fast to prevent it from growing into an all-out poison gas attack. Following judo philosophy, he gave ground.

"You're right," he said. "We're not certain that the CIA is behind anything sinister. But I think we can all agree that someone out there is trying to kill us. I don't know about you, but that keeps me up at night."

"Lord knows I don't need that," Elliot said, falling silent.

Adam felt relieved. The redirection had worked, even if only tempo-rarily. "Regardless of who is right, we surely all agree that we've gotten ourselves smack dab in the middle of something nasty."

Lara looked to Elliot, and they both reluctantly nodded.

"In my eyes," Adam continued, "the question then becomes how to figure out the nature of this beast."

"The only way to know for sure is to either approach the CIA in some manner, or to continue to see what we can uncover on our own," Elliot said. "Do I really need to say that going to the authorities is usually the better way to proceed?"

"There's no way I'm turning myself into that neo-fascist, brainwash-ing agency," Lara objected. "Remember Lee Harvey Oswald—"

Elliot raised a hand, signaling for her to halt. "Desist. Another account of our treacherous government is not necessary. I surrender."

"You surrender?" Lara said, her eyes narrowing with suspicion.

"Listen, Lara," he said, his voice much softer now. "I don't agree with you. Then again, I don't have to. At the end of the day, this is your call. Your sister's life hangs on what we do, and I don't want to be responsible for the consequences of a poor choice."

Adam shook his head, partly amazed at his brother's extempora-neous skills but mostly just disgusted. Elliot was a tricky little bastard. He was trying a new approach cloaked in apparent acquiescence. He wanted Lara to question her confidence, and in turn, reconsider having him take the reins.

Lara took a deep breath before answering his challenge. "I know there's a lot resting on this decision, but I have a strong feeling about this. Call it sister's intuition."

"So, where are we going," Adam said, looking out the window at an unending line of cars streaming by. "Dallas or Vegas?"

Elliot looked to Lara expectantly.

Her voice was calm and strong when she answered. "For better or worse, we're going to Vegas."

* * *

Adam felt his eyes growing heavy. He'd been driving for a little over eight hours, the last half of which had been in the dark. The monotony of the interstate was now becoming unbearable. Still he pressed onward.

With each passing minute, they drew another mile closer to their Nevada destination.

Adam had no way of knowing if there was anything to Lara's proposed scenario of a political murder spree. If nothing else, it did provide them with a path forward. They would find Robert Greene and present their suspicions along with the map. Adam wondered how a powerful tycoon like Greene would react to such a speculative warning.

Elliot sat in the seat beside Adam, his head resting on a rolled-up newspaper braced against the passenger window. His eyes were closed, but Adam doubted he was asleep. Looking in the rearview mirror, he saw Lara lying across several bags of clothing they'd purchased earlier. She looked peaceful and quite out of it.

Adam turned on the radio, hoping to break the hypnotic trance of the dashed yellow lines. He quickly adjusted the volume so as not to disturb his sleeping companions.

"Sharpy here, back from break. For those of you just joining us, tonight's commentary is on corruption and how it relates to the upcoming presidential election." The radio announcer was smooth and confident.

Adam recognized the broadcaster's voice. It was Bob Sharp, a popular radio personality who hosted a nightly talk show focusing exclusively on politics. Sharp was conservative from head to toe and used every minute of every show to push his agenda as well as bash anything he took as even remotely "lefty liberal."

Bob Sharp wasn't a shock jock in the common use of the term, because he rarely cursed or used any sort of vulgarity. Instead, he appealed to the common sense of his audience, often using slanted interpretations to sway listeners to his way of thinking.

The few times Adam had listened to his show for more than just dial-passing seconds, the announcer was emphatically belittling callers who disagreed with him. On the whole, Adam found Sharp to be pompous and arrogant, but also equally witty and entertaining. This seemed to be one of those times when such entertainment could help pass the seemingly endless miles.

"Last hour, we discussed the implications of organized labor's endorsement of Lucky Joe Marino. Now, I'd like to turn to an exclusive story that you can say you heard first on this show. According to documents released anonymously to the *Washington Post*, our beloved vice president has been keeping some questionable company of late.

"I've been telling you to watch out for this guy for a long time now, and this latest scandal once again demonstrates that he's nothing more than a sewer rat. According to the *Post*, documents show that Lucky Joe has been working in cahoots with known gangsters to swindle the working class. It's all right here in front of me." The announcer shuffled some papers to emphasize that he held tangible evidence.

"I'm not making this stuff up, people. According to the article scheduled to be printed in tomorrow's news, Lucky Joe has been reaping profits from an insurance scam. This 'insurance company' allegedly offered premium policies to Los Angeles-area shopkeepers. Now, you ask, what did this high-priced insurance cover? Fire? Flood? Earthquake? Guess again.

"The policies were primarily directed toward ethnic establishments, including Korean, Hispanic, and African Americans, and offered, I'm quoting now . . . 'protection from catastrophic loss due to vandalism, riot, or other unforeseen mob activity.'

"I think it's especially telling how the policy includes the choice use of the word 'mob.' Maybe you missed that. But remember, people, I'm a trained broadcaster. If you're thinking something about this smells as foul as a bag lady passing gas in the elevator, you're right on target. It's pretty obvious that this ostensible insurance company was in fact just a cover for organized crime. It might not be as blatant as thugs with brass knuckles stopping by to clean out the cash registers, but it has the same end effect."

Sharp cleared his throat and began to impersonate Marlon Brando in *The Godfather*. "I'm talking fedoras, big cigars, and lots of linguine with clam sauce. The technique may be a bit outdated, but the racket is tried and true. We're talking good old-fashioned extortion."

Returning to his haughty announcer's voice, he said, "What does this all mean to you, the common voting man, you ask? Simple, it means that if the liberal, left-wing, feminist-loving, tree-humping, ozone-farting fanatics have their way, we'll have a man who's allegedly working in close collusion with the mafia as the next president of the United States.

"Now if that doesn't scare the hell out of you, I don't know what will. Today it's insurance scams. Tomorrow, who knows? Or worse yet, what promises might Lucky Joe have already made to the gangsters behind this ring? There's no easy way out of this for him. Once you're in with the family, they don't just say, 'Ah, have a great presidency, and come by for garlic bread on your days off.' No, sir. If this article is true, and I'm personally inclined to believe that it is, it should serve as a serious wake-up call."

The announcer exhaled a deep, audible sigh to accentuate his point. "Be back in a minute with more. Stay tuned."

"What an idiot," Elliot mumbled, never bothering to open his eyes.

Turning off the radio, Adam glanced over at him. "Not buying it, huh?"

"Bob Sharp could tell me that the sky was blue, and I wouldn't believe him." He adjusted the rolled-up paper in an attempt to get more comfortable. "He's one of the best liars in the business."

"And the article in tomorrow's *Washington Post*? You think he's spinning it?"

Elliot sat up, abandoning his quest for sleep. Yawning, he said, "Probably."

"You said you knew Marino's daughter in college. Ever have any reason to think her father was involved with organized crime?"

Adam actually had two reasons for the question. First, he was curious about Elliot's firsthand take on Lucky Joe. What's more, he wanted to see just how well his brother knew the vice president. From their earlier conversation, Elliot had played it off as if he knew almost nothing about the man. Adam suspected there was more than his brother had let on. Given their newfound interpretation of the map and the mission they were adopting from it, it seemed important to have a clearer understanding of the candidates. Lucky Joe was as important as any.

Elliot took too long to answer. "I wouldn't know."

"How close were you and his daughter?"

Elliot wiped the lenses of his glasses with a small handkerchief. "Like I said, we weren't close at all. We saw each other around campus a bit and worked on a few of the same projects. That sort of stuff. Nothing worth remembering."

An edgy quiver in his brother's voice told Adam that there was more to the story.

"How much farther?" Elliot asked, changing the subject.

"Not far. Maybe another two hours."

"Good. My back is killing me."

"What do you expect with these economy cars?" Adam said, barely hearing his own words. He was picking at a splinter that had worked its way into his consciousness.

Coincidence, he'd found, was usually not coincidental at all. As an investigator, he'd learned to take coincidence as unadulterated proof of something until proven otherwise. If a person's wife disappeared shortly after a large life insurance policy had been taken out, it was a sure bet the hubby had knocked her off. Such was the way of the world. There were occasions when such assumptions led to an embarrassing accusation that later proved false, but those instances were quite rare. What initially appears to be coincidence is more often than not a sure sign that two things are unmistakably tied together.

What were the odds of his brother having a girlfriend who ended up stealing a map outlining assassinations of presidential hopefuls? One in a million. Just as they would be for anyone else in the world.

Now what were the odds of that same brother actually knowing one of the candidates? Not only knowing him, but being uncomfortable enough with their relationship that he felt a need to deceive his own brother.

Adam felt the splinter of coincidence growing sore with infection. Soon it was going to need attention.

* * *

At Elliot's suggestion, the group decided to make a final pit stop about an hour outside Las Vegas in the town of Hubertville.

Adam pulled the Audi into the parking lot of a small filling station, Pappy's Basket. He'd barely brought the car to rest at an old row of gas pumps when Elliot and Lara both eagerly piled out. Everyone needed a dose of the cool night air.

"I'll top us off before we push on to Vegas," Adam said, working the nozzle into the tank.

"I'm going to find a restroom," Elliot said. He hurried with a noticeable urgency toward the small brick building that doubled as a grocery store.

Lara stretched, moving her neck from side to side and reaching high into the sky.

Adam was glad to see her animate again. The drive had been long and silent for the most part, and he'd missed her company. "We're almost there," he comforted.

"Poor thing. You must be a wreck," she said, walking up to him.

Adam felt small hands crawl up his back and come to rest on his shoulders. She began to knead the tight muscles with surprising strength.

"You've done this before," he said, enjoying the attention.

After a moment, she said, "Where else are you hurting, sweetie?"

Adam was about to ask that she move her magic fingers to his lower back when he turned to face her. "Is that what I am? Your *sweetie?*" He liked the sound of it.

She reached forward and held his hands. The expression on her face was kind but also unusually serious. "I don't know what you are, Adam.

This is new for me, and I'm struggling with it . . . trying to figure out what it means." She closed her eyes for a moment and smiled up at him.

"What?" he asked.

"Just remembering something from a long time ago, that's all."

"Tell me."

"When I was a little girl, my mother bought me this pink sweater. I remember that sweater so well. Soft . . . warm. I must have worn that thing day and night for three months. It made me feel safe. Loved, you know?"

Adam squeezed her hands gently.

"You make me feel like I'm wearing that sweater, Adam. And I like it . . . a lot. But I'm not a little girl anymore. It's harder to surrender to those feelings. I've been a loner for a long time. I wish I could explain it better."

"I think I understand. You're saying, let's give it some time. I'm cool with that."

Lara leaned forward and gave him a warm hug. Before he could reciprocate, she stepped away. "I'm going for a soda, you want something?"

He could still feel the heat from her body as it slowly left his skin. "I'm good."

"Suit yourself," she said. "See you in a minute . . . sweetie." With that, she turned and headed toward the small store.

Lara hadn't been gone but a minute when Adam realized he'd forgotten to ask Elliot to pay for the gas inside. Deciding that another opportunity to hear Lara call him "sweetie" was worth a walk to the store, he headed in.

As he entered the store, Adam scanned the many rows of candy, chips, and magazines. Lara was already at the register with a large Mountain Dew and a bag of pretzels, but the rest of the store appeared empty.

"Seen Elliot?" he asked.

"He said something about the bathroom, remember?" she said, handing the teller a couple dollar bills.

It seemed strange to Adam that his brother would remain in a convenience store bathroom for one second longer than absolutely necessary. Something didn't feel right. He looked out the storefront window, but the Audi was the only car in sight. He felt the reassuring weight of his handgun hanging in the shoulder holster under his jacket.

"I'm going to check on him."

Lara nodded as she listened to the elderly attendant counting back her change, penny by agonizing penny.

Adam saw the word TOILETS hand-lettered on a manila folder taped just above a small hallway at the back of the store. He weaved his way around racks of Wild Rider condoms, stacks of motor oil, and a fifty-gallon drum filled with icy cans of Coors.

As he neared the hallway, he heard whispering. He stopped and listened.

Elliot's voice was hushed and hurried. "No, no, that won't work. You won't be able to reach me for a while. I'll call you again when we get to Las Vegas. Just see what you can do." The pay phone made a metallic *ching* as the receiver was cradled.

Without thinking why, Adam stepped away from the hallway and turned to a glass cooler filled with an assortment of drinks. Keeping an eye on the hallway, he opened one of the glass doors and pretended to be pondering his selection.

Within seconds, Elliot emerged from the hallway. Noticing Adam, he came over.

"You get the car filled up?"

"Yeah," he replied, "but you'll have to pay the old man at the front. It's about fifty bucks." Adam rummaged through the sodas, waiting to see if his brother would reveal the nature or even the occurrence of the phone call.

To his dismay, Elliot offered only an uncharacteristic pat on the back before heading to pay the clerk.

Chapter 13

It was just before 2:00 a.m. when Adam finally pulled the Audi into the overcrowded parking lot of the Krakatau Casino.

True to its name, the front of the casino was carved into an immense, man-made volcano. A never-ending eruption of golden "lava" spewed out the top, signaling that there was enough wealth to be had by all. Surrounding the volcano was a chromatic river filled with thousands of free-floating underwater lights all swirling chaotically in the shallow depths.

Anywhere else in the world, such a sight would surely have drawn crowds of onlookers. But this was Las Vegas. It barely drew the occasional second glance.

After several minutes of circling, Adam finally found a free space and parked the sedan. He was amazed that even at this time of night the place was at near capacity.

"We're here," he said in his best *Poltergeist* imitation. "I hope one of you worked up a plan while I was driving."

Lara and Elliot were now fully awake, and though they had rested several hours, Adam thought both looked as tired and sluggish as he felt.

"I suggest we approach this thing straightforwardly," Elliot said while smoothing back a particularly buoyant Elvis hairdo caused by hours of sleeping against the car window. "We introduce ourselves to Mr. Greene. Tell him about the map. Then if he doesn't throw us out as loonies, we can try to recruit his help."

Lara shrugged. "I don't have anything better than that."

"Okay," Adam agreed. "I wish our proof was a bit more irrefutable. If we get tossed out, our trail goes cold, and this long drive was for nothing."

"Oh, don't worry about that," Lara said. "It wouldn't be cold for long."

Perhaps it was the time of night, but Adam didn't see what she was getting at. "What makes you say that?"

"Simple," she answered. "If the map is what I think it is, the assassin is coming to Greene. All we'll have to do is wait around until the bullets start to fly."

* * *

The main floor of the casino stretched immeasurably in every direction and was thick with tropical rainforest plants set directly into the floor. Ivory pillars carved with elaborate characters of some lost tribal language separated three different gaming areas. To the left were cards, to the right were slots, and directly ahead were the roulette tables.

At the very center of the casino sat an immense dark blue marble fountain inlaid with carved ivory elephants and angry voodoo gods. A fine, wet mist sprayed high above the fountain, the moisture turning to vapor and dispersing throughout the casino.

A dozen or more straw huts, serving as wet bars, were carefully placed throughout the main room so that patrons never suffered a dry throat or a full wallet. The bartenders wore woven grass skirts, their faces and chests painted with black-and-red streaks like those of village witch doctors.

As with many casinos, where owners would rather guests not worry about the time of day, there were no windows to the outdoors. The cool shadowy nature of the room, along with piped in noises of tropical birds and roaring felines, cast a convincing jungle feel.

After studying the immense room for a few moments, the group moved to one of the straw hut bars along the far wall. A well-muscled man wearing a primitive grass skirt and leather sandals immediately turned his attention to them.

"What can I get for you?" he asked while wiping out a stainless steel mixing shaker.

"I don't know about these two, but I'll take a cold beer," Adam said. "Whatever's on tap is fine."

"Make that two," Lara said.

"Three," added Elliot, holding out three fingers.

"Coming right up," the tribal bartender said. He pulled three glasses from a cooler, lined them up in front of a spigot, and began piping the foamy yellow beer into the first glass.

"Having any luck?" he asked the group as a whole.

Unsure of who should answer or what exactly to say, no one spoke for a moment.

Taking the initiative, Adam finally replied, "We're not really here to gamble. We're tired and hungry, and looking for—"

"Say no more," he interrupted. "The prime rib buffet, right?"

"Uh . . ."

"Don't sweat it. People come out of the woodwork to catch some grub here. It's all part of the Vegas charm. Trust me, we'll get it back from you before you leave." He offered an all-knowing smile.

"We're here to see Mr. Greene," Elliot suddenly blurted.

"How's that again?" the bartender asked, bringing his eyes to rest on Elliot but never stopping his mechanical filling of the three glasses.

Adam stood aside and let his brother give it a go.

Elliot tried to collect himself. "We have some urgent business to discuss with the owner of this casino. We need to speak with him right away."

"Uh-huh," the man said, putting the three beers on the counter. "That'll be seventeen-fifty."

Elliot quickly pulled a twenty from his wallet and paid for the drinks. The bartender made change, but then, without speaking, turned his attention away from the group and began washing out several wine glasses.

"Hey," Elliot said. "I'm not sure you understand. We need to speak with Mr. Greene. It's urgent. Can't you—"

"Look, mister, I serve drinks. I'd have better luck getting you a date with Madonna."

"Oh . . . okay then." Elliot stammered. He turned to Adam and Lara and shrugged.

"Let's just look around a bit," Adam said, shaking his head.

With that, they turned away from the bar and slowly moved into the noisy gaming area of the casino.

"How about we mingle a bit . . . see if we can find anyone of importance," Elliot said. "I'm sure someone around here can help us." He quickly added, "If you get lost, just meet back at that bar with the helpful witch doctor."

Everyone agreed, and the group dispersed into the crowd of late-night gamblers.

Adam didn't even know the rules to most of the games going on around him. Feeling less intimidated by levered machines than those manned by fulltime swindlers, he moved to several long rows of slot machines.

Each slot machine had a large blue light on top. A few of the lights flashed, indicating a winner of some importance, but most remained dark. He found that single image to be an uncannily accurate representation of Las Vegas as a whole. A few lucky winners found nirvana, but many more just kept reaching deeper into their wallets for the never to be realized dream of having a swirling blue light of their own.

Adam worked his way slowly up the narrow isle of slot machines, looking for anyone who stood out in the crowd. He stopped to study the rather eclectic group surrounding him.

Just ahead was a large contingency of elderly women, complete with flower print dresses and suitcase-sized handbags. They gathered around a single slot machine, graciously offering one another the honor of being the next to pull the magic handle.

To their right were a male prostitute and his client. The young gigolo wore skintight red leather pants and a thin white silk shirt that hung loosely over his smooth shoulders. His older companion was dressed in a traditional navy sport coat and was holding a large tropical drink. His free arm was draped over the youth's partially exposed shoulder as he whispered something in his ear. Both men seemed to be enjoying their evening.

Just beyond Adam's reach stood a middle-aged couple in matching Hawaiian shirts. A camera hung from the man's neck, and the woman was busy explaining her winning strategy to her husband. They both snorted with unabated excitement as they dropped dollar after dollar into the belly of the mechanical beast.

Turning to look behind him, Adam saw a businessman intently studying a slot machine as if unsure how the device operated. He had no coins out but held something in one hand, possibly a wallet or ballpoint pen.

Beyond the confused businessman sat a young Japanese couple collecting a large pile of coins. The bright blue light flashed wildly atop their machine, washing an almost hypnotic sky-colored wave over the surrounding gamblers. "Just a few more coins," the light promised seductively, "and yours will flash too. Just a few more coins . . ."

Sights and sounds spiraled around Adam, working to drive any and all thought from his mind. He felt a growing numbness to the world around him, as if everything was slowly shifting out of focus. What would normally ring of intensity now began to feel dull and quietly distant.

He hadn't been to Vegas in several years, and in one crashing moment of understanding, he remembered why. He hated everything about it— the foolish waste of money, the grossly extravagant nature of everything and everyone, and worst of all, the decadence that everyone was so ready to accept.

The entire town was an elaborate illusion as carefully crafted as a stage magician's act of pulling six doves and a silk handkerchief from a volunteer's ear. Where else could one get married by a skydiving Elvis or live out his fantasies with a ranch full of beautiful young women willing to do anything for the right price? Spontaneity, excitement, and pleasure had brought with them decadence, gluttony, and immorality.

"Man, I must be tired," he muttered, shaking his head.

But the words did little to relieve his anxiety. There was something wrong with his being in the casino. Something intangible, yet still threatening. It was as if a faceless shadow was tracking him, waiting for him to look away. Waiting for the opportunity to swallow him in darkness.

Deciding that Elliot and Lara could find their own way in this house of blue lights and witch doctor bartenders, he turned back toward the entrance. After taking only a few steps toward the door, however, he stopped.

The stop was so sudden that his foot remained suspended an inch above the floor as if he was about to step on a coiled rattlesnake. From the corner of his eye, he'd seen something. Something unnatural even for this carnival of sin. He'd caught sight of it only for an instant, but with something so strange, an instant was enough.

It was a syringe.

The businessman he'd seen studying the slot machine stood with his hand hanging loosely by his side, carefully cupping a white, plastic syringe. The man's hand worked to conceal it, but he was careful to keep the needle pointing safely away.

Why? Adam asked himself. *Could be a doper . . . but he holds himself too straight, too strong to be a druggy.*

Perhaps what disturbed him most was not that the man held a syringe but the way in which he held it. He kept it concealed but still very much at the ready, the needle's sharp point extending down beyond the tips of his fingers.

He's going to stick someone. The idea seemed absurd, but it rang true nonetheless.

Adam judged the distance between them to be at least fifteen feet, outside striking range without a serious leap. Looking around as if uncertain what area to explore next, he studied the man with each pass of his eyes.

At just over five feet tall, the man was short, but he looked to weigh about as much as a small Canadian moose. He wore a dark gray pinstripe suit, indistinguishable from dozens of other businessmen who'd stopped by to try their hand with Lady Luck. He blended in. It occurred to Adam that this probably wasn't by accident. It enabled him to easily disappear into the crowd if he needed to escape.

Having spent more than his fair share of years working the streets, Adam had known many kinds of people who lived in violence. From whores to dealers and gangbangers. Instinct told him that this man was something far worse than any of those. He was a killer.

The only thing Adam didn't know for sure was whom he was out to kill. His first thought was that the well-dressed stranger might be the assassin Lara suggested was coming to kill Mr. Greene. But that didn't make sense. If someone was gunning for Greene, a video-monitored casino floor didn't seem like a very good venue. Besides, a syringe was probably the worst weapon one could pick for the task since it would be very difficult to get close to a man like Mr. Greene. Even in the unlikely event this guy could get close enough to use the syringe, bodyguards and security would nab him two seconds after Greene yelled "ouch."

So, if it wasn't Mr. Greene, then who was the target?

Careful not to let the man out of his field of vision, Adam shifted his attention back to the people around him. Neither the grandmothers, the gigolo, the young Japanese lovers, nor the middle-aged Tropicana-garbed couple seemed likely candidates for murder by lethal injection. That left only Adam or someone who had yet to arrive on the scene. The syringe was out and ready to be used. That seemed to narrow it down to just one.

Adam saw only two real choices. One, he could get as far away as possible. Or two, he could confront the man.

Unfortunately, they had left their handguns in the car when Elliot pointed out it was a federal offense to possess a firearm in a casino. None of them felt like taking the unnecessary risk of being arrested, tossed in the slammer, and spanked by a host of angry tattooed inmates just for the comfort of having a piece. Especially since at the time, the only danger the casino posed was losing a bit of Elliot's money at the roulette wheel.

Stand or run? It should have been a simple decision, but it never was. To Adam, the answer always depended on the circumstances. A wrong decision either way could be fatal. Anyone in his profession who didn't appreciate that tended to die early in life. This seemed like a case when running would only postpone the inevitable, and the next time Adam might not be as fortunate to spot his attacker. Next time he might feel the disturbing prick of a needle. No, this was one of those occasions when he had to roll up his sleeves and kick some Canadian moose ass.

The would-be killer had yet to turn his attention from the slot machine, but Adam was certain he was watching him from the reflection off the glass. Deciding to keep it simple, he turned and began walking toward the main entrance.

The noise, lights, and ever-present hustle no longer tugged at Adam's psyche. Everything but his target had become part of the backdrop, vibrant colors changing to shades of gray, ringing bells muffled as if someone had put a damp rag over them. A pink cow could have roller-skated by, singing the "Star Spangled Banner," and Adam wouldn't have missed a single twitch of the man's body.

As Adam passed directly behind the stranger, the man turned. His motion was slow and deliberate, not fast enough to alarm anyone. Adam imagined the syringe hanging point down, the needle glistening with some deadly substance. As he continued to move past the dark-suited stranger, the muscles in Adam's body tingled nervously, ready to react in one explosive instant.

The killer continued to turn, bringing the needle slowly forward at thigh level.

Adam spun on the ball of his lead foot, stepping forward and across his body. His trailing hand shot out low in a downward parry. It struck the man's extended wrist, locking around it like a steel shackle.

Before his assailant could react, Adam was already on the move. He stomped in with his right foot, landing it hard atop the stranger's black penny loafers. His hope was that the sudden pain would bring his opponent's attention to his foot, which is exactly where it didn't need to be.

He continued his attack by shooting a fist into the man's gut. The punch landed hard, but it felt like he was hitting a heavy bag filled with sand.

The killer tried to wrench both his trapped hand and foot free while shoving Adam back. His foot came free of the pin, but Adam's hand held fast.

Adam reached up and grabbed the thumb on the hand pushing against him. With a powerful twist, he cranked it backward until it gave way with a sickening *pop*. The stranger screamed, yanking furiously in an attempt to free the hand holding the syringe.

Sensing it was the right moment to yield, Adam relaxed his control of the man's wrist. The killer detected the sudden weakness and pulled his hand back in a powerful, "let me have it" jerking motion.

Adam shuffled forward, maintaining a light grip on the man's wrist as he pulled it toward him. Then in a reversal of motion, Adam reached out with his free hand and pulled hard on the man's opposite ear. The stranger's head fell forward as the hand holding the syringe finally tore free. The two met, the moist silver needle sliding effortlessly into his beefy neck like the fangs of a pit viper.

The killer's face immediately turned a pasty white, and his body slumped as if his strength was seeping out like air from a leaky balloon. Adam held him fast, the needle buried to the hilt against his neck. The palm of the man's hand had inadvertently pressed the plunger about halfway in when it struck. The poison was in him, and there wasn't a damn thing either of them could do to change that now.

"Who are you?" Adam snarled, not sure how much time he had before the man lost consciousness.

The stranger's eyes were already glazing over, and he seemed unable to understand the simple words. Just as Adam was about to ask him again, the man spoke. His speech was slurred and muffled as if his tongue had suddenly grown to three times its original size.

"Focking bad lock," he garbled.

Then his legs buckled, and he collapsed to the floor. He lay there jerking with powerful spasms. In less time than it took to give final rites, he fell as still as a frozen winter's morning.

Adam felt no remorse for the piece of shit lying at his feet. Anyone who would poison an unsuspecting opponent was a coward. Pure and simple. Killing was one thing. Killing like a pussy was another. Overcome by a mix of disgust and adrenaline, Adam gave him one final kick in the ribs.

It was only then that he became aware of the screams and horrified gasps coming from casino patrons all around him.

* * *

Adam, Lara, and Elliot sat without speaking in a bleach white detention room. The small space was furnished with only a square stainless steel table, two matching metal chairs, and the heavy fold-down bench on which they now sat. The walls, ceiling, and floor were painted in a seamless, glossy white that might fool someone into thinking he was in God's imperial waiting room. All three stared at the heavy metal door inlaid with a small Plexiglas window, the only way in or out of the holy antechamber.

Following the brief but deadly scuffle on the casino floor, Adam had been quickly apprehended by six security officers who seemingly materialized from thin air. When Lara and Elliot had come to his aid, they too had been detained.

Each had been searched and then sequestered to small chambers where they were individually questioned as to their identities, motives, and actions. Following the initial interrogations, they had been regrouped into a secure room where, as far as they could tell, they'd been left to rot.

Adam looked at his watch. It was six fifteen in the morning. He closed his eyes and leaned against the wall. It had been a long night, and the party didn't appear to be over just yet.

The lock on the security door clanked loudly as the bolt released from the door jamb. Everyone stood, looking expectantly at the door. Four men wearing dark-blue-and-black casino security uniforms entered. All were armed with automatic handguns, but their weapons remained holstered. They positioned themselves like a protective barrier in front of the open doorway.

A middle-aged man in dark blue cotton trousers and a white Polo shirt entered. He had thin, black hair lined with intermittent traces of gray and a wiry build that suggested a dedication to fitness. He wore glasses with tiny circular lenses.

"You have no right to detain us here," Elliot immediately started. He'd been cooped up for the past several hours without even a chance to exercise his God-given right to a phone call. The injustice of it all was about to cause him to spontaneously combust.

"Yes, yes, and I'm so sorry about that," came the soft voice of Mr. Greene as he gently pushed past his security people. "I'm afraid it may well have been a simple misunderstanding." He slid a chair from the interrogation table and took a seat immediately in front them. "Please, sit down. We have much to talk about."

Greene's tone was too consolatory for anyone to do anything but what he requested. All three reluctantly returned their aching bottoms to the metal bench they'd come to loathe.

"As you may already know, I'm Robert Greene. I do sincerely apologize for the long delay." He reached forward to Elliot, then Adam, and finally Lara, shaking each hand warmly with both of his own.

"My security officers felt it best to take no further action until I arrived. Surely you can understand this since there's a . . ." he hunted for a delicate way to put it, but didn't find one. "Well, since there's a body involved."

"He died?" Adam asked, not surprised by the confirmation.

"I'm afraid so. We rushed him to a nearby hospital, but he was already gone before we got him on the gurney. Coronary arrest, they said. Was he an acquaintance of yours?" Mr. Greene studied Adam carefully.

"Like I told your Stormtroopers, I'd never met him before tonight," he answered. "I'm sure your cameras caught the whole thing. He attacked me with a syringe, and I defended myself. That's it. End of story."

"Oh, maybe just a bit more, yes?" Mr. Greene prompted as if probing an old friend to tell him more about a particularly juicy Friday night date. "After all, you either had eyes in the back of your head or were anticipating his attack. Not something that seems likely if indeed you'd never met?"

Adam couldn't help but like Mr. Greene. He came straight ahead without dancing around his questions and yet managed to keep the tone cordial—hell, even friendly. It felt as if any minute he might send for iced tea.

With an uncanny empathy, Robert Greene turned to his security team leader. "Fetch us a pot of some hot coffee, would you? I'm sure our guests are all very tired."

Adam smiled. Oh, he was good.

Mr. Greene turned back to him waiting for a reply.

"I saw the syringe before he tried to stick me," Adam answered. "But I didn't know the man."

"I see. Might I ask why you didn't simply call security and have him arrested?"

The question seemed quite reasonable, and Adam wasn't sure he could come up with an answer that wouldn't make him look like an overzealous fool. After deliberating a moment, he said, "He could have ditched the syringe. Without it, your people wouldn't have held him, and I'd have never known for sure what he was up to. Besides, if he got away, I'd have to worry about him in the future."

Mr. Greene rubbed his chin as if giving the answer its due consideration. "Hmm, I suppose what interests me the most is why you don't seem overly surprised or concerned by what happened."

Adam had known for some time that he possessed a calm indifference when it came to violence. It was something that had been with him since he was a child, like a favorite toy. He didn't share this, however, saying only, "I've met trouble before."

"You're not concerned that someone tried to kill you?"

Adam met Mr. Greene's inquisitive stare. "Everyone is concerned when someone tries to kill them. Maybe I'll have a good cry later."

Mr. Greene smiled, apparently not offended by the sarcasm. "We all cope in different ways, yes?"

Adam nodded. "Yes, we do."

"I suppose this all leads us to the most important question. The reason you're here in the first place," Mr. Greene started. "I understand the three of you were asking about me at the bar earlier. Might I ask why?" He looked from one person to the next as if challenging them to put forward their best spokesperson.

All three turned to one another, unsure of who should lead.

Adam shifted about uneasily, worrying that the washed-out road map and Lara's unsubstantiated hunch might not be enough to warrant Greene's consideration. *Just wait for the coffee*, he thought. He hated the thought of getting abandoned in that room again without something to wet his throat.

Lara shattered his hopes of stalling by blurting out, "Mr. Greene, we think your life may be in danger."

Robert Greene turned his attention to her, his green eyes alive with curiosity. "Please go on."

"This all began when my sister disappeared more than a week ago. She'd come across a map that we believe shows the locations of three political assassinations. We further believe that you, sir, are one of the targets." She spoke calmly and rationally. If her words hadn't been so absurd, she'd have been as believable as an anchor on the six o'clock news.

Adam felt sure Mr. Greene would get up and leave the room without another word, hence no coffee. Instead, he leaned forward, saying, "And who is behind these assassinations?"

"We're not sure. However, we do know that the CIA is involved," Lara replied as if it was a matter of fact.

Oh Lord, Adam thought, *if that wasn't enough to send him running, nothing would. And so close to having refreshments.*

"Why do you suspect the CIA?" Mr. Greene asked as if he was hearing nothing more surprising than Sunday's Bible sermon.

"Look, we're not sure about the CIA or much of anything for that matter," Elliot interjected.

Lara cut him down with a look that could castrate. "*He's* not sure, but I am. We had several run-ins with them already. Trust me when I tell you that there are agents hired by members of our government out there gunning for you."

"Any idea why our government would want me dead?" Mr. Greene asked.

"You'd know better than me. You're rich, powerful, and most importantly running for office. Not so different from General Livingston, and last time I checked he had an extra hole in his head."

Mr. Greene nodded. "And your sister? Is she still missing?"

A pained expression came over Lara's face. "Yes."

Mr. Greene reached out and gently placed a hand on her shoulder. "I'm sorry. I know this must be especially difficult for you."

Adam was unsure if Mr. Greene was buying into her story or just pandering to a pretty girl. Either way, it didn't matter; the man with the coffee was finally coming through the door.

After the coffee had been handed out to everyone except Greene, who politely refused, the conversation continued.

"My sister came into possession of the map and tried to sell it to Mr. Reece here," she said, gesturing with a flick of her hand toward Elliot.

"I see. And you think she's involved in this CIA conspiracy?"

"Not directly," she answered. "She's in over her head. If I'm certain of anything, it's that she's a victim in all this." Lara choked out the last painful words.

"I see. So, you're here to warn me of a threat on my life, and even more importantly to find your missing sister, yes?"

"That's it exactly," she answered triumphantly. She looked at Adam and Elliot as if to say, "See, that wasn't so hard."

"What about you?" Mr. Greene said, turning to Elliot. "You don't seem to buy into the whole CIA assertion. Surely a man of your stature wouldn't be running around the country on a wild goose chase. You have a successful law firm, and your time is valuable. Why come here at all?"

Adam smiled again. Mr. Greene had done his homework and knew exactly how to work each person. He found himself admiring Greene's careful handling of the different personalities.

When Elliot heard Mr. Greene's words, he sat up and straightened his clothes in an attempt to recover what little dignity remained after an all-night car ride. All eyes were now on him, and that was exactly the way he liked it.

"Despite what Lara believes, the truth is that we don't know what is going on. We did find a map, but it wasn't readable. We were shot at by someone, but we don't know by whom. Adam did take a CIA identification badge from a man searching her sister's mail, but we're not sure if the search was illegal. And now, my brother has indeed been attacked by a syringe-wielding psychopath, but this could also prove to be nothing but a violent coincidence.

"But to answer your question, I'm here for much the same reason as Lara. I'm searching for Maria, and as far-fetched as it sounds, this was the most credible lead we had."

"Yes, yes, I see. Well, I should tell you the man in the casino had no identification at all. Nothing to indicate he was part of any government agency," Mr. Greene said.

"The fact he had no identification is by itself an indication," Lara corrected.

Mr. Greene nodded thoughtfully. "I guess that brings me back to you, Adam. You don't mind me calling you Adam, I hope."

"You brought coffee," Adam said, holding up the cup. "Call me whatever you like."

Mr. Greene gave him a warm smile. "What exactly is your role in all this?"

"Me? Hmm. I guess I'm just trying to keep everyone alive."

Mr. Greene nodded at his words. "You are apparently good at this, yes? My men have paid you many compliments on your reactions and speedy dispatch of your adversary. You have had extensive training, yes?"

"I wrestle alligators on the weekend," Adam said, grinning.

Mr. Greene smiled. "I see. Tell me, Adam, do *you* buy into the conspiracy that Lara speaks of so confidently?"

Adam was once again impressed with Mr. Greene's ability to manipulate people. He had evidently sensed something between Lara and Adam, or perhaps had reviewed video footage that might have shown an intimate look shared between the two of them. Now, with but a single question, he'd managed to put Adam in a most defensive position. He wasn't sure Mr. Greene was necessarily even interested in the answer. It felt more like he was simply attempting to assert subtle control over a man who prided himself on being in control.

Adam felt Lara's cool blue eyes turn to him expectantly. It was once again a time to choose his words carefully.

"I'm a private investigator by profession, so I've seen my share of bizarre happenings. It wasn't that long ago that I discovered a child sitting alone in a motel room eating boiled peanuts while laughing at Darkwing Duck, all after being kidnapped by a harmless vagabond who resembled Santa Claus. Is it possible that we're caught up in a CIA plot to kill presidential candidates? I don't see why not. Besides, the guy in the casino tipped the scale in favor of believability just a bit." Adam saw a bright, and God love her, heart-warming smile beaming from Lara.

"Why do you say that?" Mr. Greene asked, seemingly more interested in the answer this time.

"Simple. He was waiting for us. If the pecker heads after the map were just lone guns, they wouldn't have had the resources to find us in Vegas so easily. The only thing that could have led them to think we were headed to Vegas is the map. In my mind, it's not too big a stretch to conclude that the map indeed indicates something is going to happen here."

"What about the possibility that you were followed. Or that one of you accidentally let slip your destination?" Mr. Greene asked.

"We've been together since we discovered the map, and no one here would make that mistake." Even as he said the words, Adam recalled Elliot's unreported phone call. Was it possible that the phone call had set in motion a chain of events that led the killers to find them?

"Do you feel certain the man in the casino had selected you as his specific target? You don't think that you were just in the wrong place at the wrong time?"

"I'm sure that wasn't the case."

"Again, might I ask how you know that?"

"The man who attacked me wasn't a nut job looking for his next victim," he said. "When I passed him, his eyes never left the slot machine. He wasn't looking for a target. He'd already found one. And, let's face it, there were easier targets within reach. Why pick a big strapping guy like me?"

Lara nudged him playfully and he grinned.

"Yes, yes, I see," Mr. Greene said.

"Will we be questioned by the police?" Elliot asked.

"I would think not," Mr. Greene answered. "The hospital doctors concluded that the man died of a massive coronary. My people let that diagnosis stand without any embellishment."

"There were a lot of witnesses," Lara interjected.

"True, but as far as the patrons are concerned, it was a simple scuffle. Two men arguing over money—or at least that's the rumor being disseminated. A reasonable story along with a handful of chips for their inconvenience, and the conflict is easily contained."

"Then I guess we owe you some thanks," Adam said.

"Perhaps, but it was you who came to warn me." Mr. Greene turned to the group as a whole once more. "Who has the map now?"

All eyes turned to Adam. "I do," he said.

"Would you mind too much if I had a look?"

Adam withdrew the map from the inside pocket of his jacket and moved to the table where he unfolded it for all to see. Even the four security personnel looked on with interest.

Mr. Greene examined the map slowly, moving his finger across the smudged words just above each of the three locations. "Not very read-able is it?" he remarked.

"No, but if you look carefully, you will see the three locations are numbered. You are number two," Lara said.

"Yes, those could be numbers all right," he agreed. Turning to Adam, he said, "Too bad the rest is so washed out. It looks like there was some writing beside each location that might have shed light on the meaning of the map. Would you mind if I had my people take a look at it?"

Adam hesitated, unsure how to respond. He glanced at Lara who flashed back a look of serious reservation. He didn't want to give up the map he'd worked so hard to retrieve either. On the other hand, closer examination might give additional information. Perhaps some high-tech optical tricks could recover the lost writing. In the end, however, it was really Lara's decision, and he suspected she wouldn't have any trouble refusing.

Before he could answer, Mr. Greene said, "That was unfair of me. We have yet to fully establish our trust. You hang onto it for now. Then, as we become better acquainted, perhaps you will feel comfortable releasing it into my charge."

Looking away from the map, he turned back to the group. "I'll be frank with you. I really have no way of knowing if what you are suggesting has any merit. It's impossible to doubt Lara's conviction, but I can't be certain that the conviction is well-founded. On the other hand, someone wanting me dead is not something I find outside the realm of possibility. Besides, one can never be too careful with one's life, yes?"

Adam and Lara nodded. Elliot yawned.

"Here's what we'll do. You three came here at least in part to warn me, and for that, I am grateful. To return the favor, I would like you to be my guests for a few days. At least until we get a better feel for this whole matter. Would that be acceptable to each of you?"

"Fine by me. I just need a shower and a nap," replied Adam.

"Sounds good," said Lara.

"As long as we're free to come and go as we wish," Elliot added.

"You'll be free to go anywhere you wish," Mr. Greene answered. "You are my guests, not my prisoners."

"What about your party tonight?" Lara asked. "Are you going to cancel it?"

Mr. Greene thought for a moment before answering. "I see. You think the assassin may make his presence felt at the party. That would of course be the most logical opportunity."

He took a long pause before continuing. "No, I don't believe that canceling the party would be the right thing to do. Just as Adam didn't think calling security would put his fears to rest, I too want to know if someone wants me dead. We will, of course, take special precautions."

"Would you mind if we came?" she asked. "We could help keep a look out."

Without hesitation Mr. Greene answered, "I wouldn't have it any other way."

Chapter 14

The VIP suites of the Krakatau Casino Hotel were five-star all the way. Deluxe crystal bars, huge feather beds, Jacuzzi tubs, antique mirrors, coordinated cherry furniture, and gorgeous views overlooking the decadent city below. As nice as the Hotel Mona had been, the casino suite made it look about as plush as a Bangkok whorehouse.

Adam pushed blindly through the room, barely noticing the furnishings or incredible view of the strip below. His only interest was a soft place to lay his head. Glancing at his watch, he saw that it was just past eight in the morning. Twelve hours until the big hoedown at Mr. Greene's ranch. Just enough time for some shut-eye.

He took a running leap toward the mammoth white-canopied bed, easily large enough to comfortably sleep a fully grown Cyclops. The incredibly soft mattress swallowed him whole. In that moment of being comforted by billows of down feathers, life was good. The last thing he noticed was the handful of fresh rose petals spread delicately across the Egyptian cotton pillowcase.

* * *

The boutique-style restaurant located on the ground level of the train station was famous for serving the best cow tongue in all of Sendai. Their specialty consisted of a large bowl of sticky rice and red beans, some miso soup, hot tea, pickled cucumbers, and several thin slices of expertly seasoned beef tongue. Despite an initial hesitation to try the delicacy, Adam was surprised to find it particularly delicious.

The entire judo class was in attendance, taking up nearly every available seat. The night was to be a celebration to honor those who had been promoted. Adam felt especially proud since he'd been awarded his brown belt, and with such was now recognized as one of the school's senior students.

There was much laughter and even more sake working its way around the table. Matsumoto moved from student to student, congratulating each on his accomplishment. Rather than offer congratulations to Adam, however, he leaned in close and said, "I would speak with you tonight."

As the night wore on, students slowly excused themselves—some to get home to wives and children, others to search for a late-night karaoke bar. In the end, only Matsumoto and Adam remained. They sat opposite each other, kneeling at a small table.

Adam sipped a cup of hot tea, waiting for Matsumoto to choose his words. The importance of patience was among the many things he'd learned since arriving in Japan.

After a time of enjoying the newfound silence, Matsumoto said, "In America, when a wife becomes angry, will she shout at her husband?"

Adam was surprised by the question. His teacher was not one for making idle conversation. "Probably," he answered. "American women tend to be pretty strong willed. Not to mention vocal."

"How will the husband react?"

"Different in every case. Some might apologize. Others might try to reason with her. Probably most would simply yell back."

"I see," Matsumoto said, nodding.

"And in Japan?" Adam asked.

"Again, different in every case. A good husband would first try to overlook the outburst. Then if it continued or grew worse, he would pull his wife close. Holding her tight until the loss of control had passed. When she finally collected herself, she would be grateful to him."

"Interesting," Adam said, imagining how the same sequence might end very differently in his country.

Matsumoto took a long sip of tea. "Do you remember our first meeting here at the train station?"

"Yes." Since his arrival, they had never spoken of the three young men Matsumoto had turned on him.

"Do you know why I asked them to challenge you?"

Adam shrugged. "I can only guess it was to see if I was worthy of your training. Yet, when I defeated them . . ."

"Yes?"

"When I defeated them, you told me that I had failed."

"You still do not understand why?"

"No."

"I had little doubt that you were skilled in *kenpo*. The men were never meant to test you physically." Matsumoto studied Adam for a reaction.

"But they attacked me."

"Hardly a challenge for you."

Adam looked down at his empty plate, feeling embarrassed. "I suppose not."

"Yet with all your strength, you had no wisdom."

"When I learned *kenpo*, the philosophy was simple. You beat your enemy until your hands fall off. That was all I knew, and that is what I brought with me to Japan."

"And now? Like the husband faced with an angry wife, do you understand that other choices are available to you?"

Adam smiled. The lesson was now clear. "*Hai, wakarimasu.* I understand."

"Tell me."

"I have learned that aggression can often be redirected. Such is the way of judo."

"If you had to face the same young men tonight, how would you handle it differently?"

Adam rubbed at his chin thoughtfully. "I'm not sure. Perhaps I could redirect their aggression toward one another. Or maybe I could diffuse the situation by simply appearing more humble."

"And if all your attempts failed?"

Adam paused for a moment. "Then I'd beat them till my hands fell off."

Matsumoto smiled and nodded his head. "It is good you have come to this understanding. It will forever be your way in this world."

* * *

Somewhere a phone rang. It sounded far away and wasn't particularly welcome. Adam ignored it. The ringing became more persistent, sounding closer this time. The third ring sounded directly beside his head. Blindly groping around, he found the telephone handset and pulled it to his ear.

"Unh?" he announced with every bit of intelligence he had at the moment.

"Want to get a bite to eat?" It was Elliot's voice. His brother sounded much more alive than Adam felt.

"What time is it?" he croaked. It felt as if he'd just climbed into bed, and he was definitely not interested in getting breakfast.

"It's four in the afternoon. We're heading out to Greene's ranch in a couple of hours. I thought you might want to grab a bite before we left. Lara said she was up for it. I think she's planning to pick you up on her way down."

Four in the afternoon? Adam was stunned. Hadn't it been eight in the morning just a moment ago? Adam felt groggy, thoroughly exhausted. A distinctly sour smell confirmed his need for a shower.

"Give me half an hour. I'm going to grab a quick shower. Where are we meeting?"

"First floor, down in the Lava Lounge. I'll see you there in a bit."

Adam hung up the phone, took a deep breath, and began his slow descent from Mount Feather Bed.

* * *

The water was hot, the lights in the bathroom uncomfortably bright. Adam felt as if he had the world's worst hangover even though he knew the few ounces of beer he'd consumed couldn't be to blame.

A fine, strong mist sprayed across his chest. He lowered his head and let the water wet his shoulders and back. The heat slowly massaged life into his sluggish limbs. He rolled his head in a slow circle, the water spraying across his face like dozens of small bee stings.

"Anyone in there?" a soft voice announced from just outside the shower.

Adam slid the frosted glass shower door open enough to peek out. Lara stood leaning nonchalantly against the frame of the bathroom door.

"How did you get in here?" He asked, trying to hide his absolute delight in seeing her.

"You'd be surprised what a smile and a wink will do for a girl these days," she said with a playful grin.

"Give me a minute. I'll be right out."

"No hurry," she said, unbuttoning the top of her bright yellow silk blouse. "Actually, I haven't had a chance to get a shower myself. Do you think there's any way I could squeeze into yours?"

Adam raised his eyebrows but said nothing. Things like this didn't happen to mortal men.

She unbuttoned two more buttons, and he could see the lace of a white bra peeking out from underneath. "That is, if you don't mind," she said, approaching slowly.

"You do look dirty," he said with a grin. In truth, she looked perfect, and he seriously doubted her claim about not having taken a shower. But when a beautiful woman feels the need to stretch the truth in order to strip naked and climb into his shower stall, Adam was capable of being the bigger person and overlooking her deceit.

Lara slid the blouse down off her shoulders and dropped it to the floor. With a quick flick of her fingers, the bra sprang open in the front. Placing one arm to cover her breasts, she let the bra fall to the floor as well.

"Don't look," she said, her face flushing. "You make me nervous."

Adam shook his head. "You've got to be kidding. My God, Lara, you're gorgeous."

"Oh great. Now I really feel self-conscious. Remember, the last time we were together it was dark."

"Okay, I won't peek." He ducked back into the shower but left the sliding door ajar. Adam couldn't help but listen intently through the sound of rushing water for Lara undressing. There was something wonderfully voyeuristic about her exposing herself through the soap-covered shower glass.

Lara stepped into the shower behind him and slid the door closed. Adam turned to face her, letting the water splash against his back.

Lara no longer held her hands in front of her protectively. Instead, she presented herself like a freshly unwrapped present.

Adam studied her, taking the time to notice every gorgeous detail. Lara's shoulder-length, blonde hair hung straight, pulled to one side of her smooth face. Slender, muscular shoulders sloped softly downward. Her small, firm breasts pointed toward him with a supple fullness. Their points were a dark pink and not yet fully protruding. His eyes went down to the distinct ridges of her flat stomach, and then to her slim hips and a light golden patch of soft pubic hair. Long, smooth legs and the colorful contrast of bright red polished toenails completed the beautiful portrait before him.

Lara stood motionless, studying his face for a reaction. "Well?"

As his answer, he stepped forward and put both his hands on her trim hips. She leaned forward until her nipples barely touched his chest. Then she began rocking from side to side, dragging them softly across him. He watched in manly fascination as her nipples became full and pointed.

He brought his mouth to hers. She responded by wrapping both arms around his neck and returning his passionate kiss. He slid his hands to her buttocks, pulling her tight against him. They kissed that way for a very long time, neither one surrendering ground. Finally, Lara retreated.

"No fair," she said. "You're already clean. I guess you're just going to have to wash me."

Adam released her and moved slightly to the side where she could get into the stream of spraying water. She stepped forward and turned her back to him. He reached for a bar of white moisturizing soap, and quickly lathered it into thick foam.

Lara leaned forward, placing both hands on the shower wall like a prisoner about to be frisked. He started with her shoulders, smoothing the soap across her soft skin. Then he gently kneaded the well-defined muscles in her back and arms. He spread the lather gently under her arms, using the tips of his fingers to tickle the tender flesh, and even though the water was refreshingly hot, he saw her body shiver from his touch.

His hands worked farther around to the front, finding her firm, round breasts. He gently massaged them, carefully scrubbing his palms across her tender nipples. He felt her buttocks press lightly backward against him. He reached down, stroking the ridges of her well-defined stomach. Sliding further, he felt the wet mound of pubic hair under his foamy fingers. His hands smoothed inside both legs, sliding in large circular motions. With each circle, the backs of his thumbs came into contact with the creases of her delicate flesh.

Adam leaned in close and nibbled softly on her ear. Lara's hand snaked up backward and held tightly to the back of his head.

"Take me," she whispered. "Take me like this."

Lara bent sharply at the waist pressing her buttocks hard against him now. He entered her slowly, sliding up and forward until he was about halfway in. A tight pressure squeezed against him as she constricted tiny muscles deep within her.

Lara moaned and drove back against him hard. Together, they moved in perfect unison, grinding side to side, rocking forward and back, finding and exploring every possible way they could press their intimate flesh together. The combination of hot streams of water and the intense motion of their bodies soon sent waves of sexual warmth tingling through their loins.

"Now, Adam," she begged. "Do it now."

He felt tight, involuntary contractions coming from deep within her. The sensations proved too much for him. Adam closed his eyes and surrendered to the wet ecstasy surrounding him.

* * *

The Lava Lounge was an exclusive dining area that sat atop a large circular platform overlooking a pool of crimson water. It was surrounded on all sides by a man-made volcanic reef. A waterfall spilled from underneath a small diving platform and fell forty feet to the pool below. Two professional divers were working their way up a long rope ladder dangling from the coral cliff.

Lara and Adam followed the hostess up a winding, cast-iron staircase.

As Adam reached the top of the staircase, he was surprised to see Mr. Greene sitting with Elliot at a large round table. The table was made from tightly woven bamboo shoots and sat beneath a huge tropical straw canopy. The six identical tables on the platform remained empty even though the restaurant was at near capacity. Two of the casino's security guards were stationed near the staircase landing.

As soon as Mr. Greene saw Adam and Lara, he stood and motioned to them. Moving around the table, he slid a heavy bamboo chair out for Lara. She sat, thanking him for the pleasantry.

Adam took a seat between his brother and Lara. Despite the interesting ambiance of the restaurant, his thoughts remained in part back in that steamy shower stall.

Lara on the other hand seemed quite engaged in the moment, simultaneously flipping open both the oversized menu and a leather-bound wine list. "Mexican," she said in a particularly jovial voice.

"If you're thinking of having some wine, try the house Cabernet," Elliot offered, pointing to an already-open bottle on the table.

Adam noticed that Elliot had nearly emptied his own glass, but Mr. Greene had chosen to refrain. Recalling his refusal of the coffee earlier, Adam wondered if Mr. Greene abstained from all caffeinated or alcoholic beverages. He'd read somewhere that extremely wealthy people often became obsessed with their health. Living longer when rich evidently has its appeal.

"Love some," Lara replied, never taking her eyes from the menu of smothered enchiladas and cinnamon sopapillas.

"Hungry, huh?" Adam asked, smiling with chest-thumping bravado. The smile quickly turned to a grimace, however, when Lara reached under the table and pinched him hard on the inside of his thigh.

Elliot leaned over the table and poured Lara a glass of the rich red wine. As he moved to pour his brother a glass, Adam placed his hand over the top and shook his head. He was still feeling a bit sluggish from the drive, but more than that he wanted to have his wits about him at Mr. Greene's party.

"You're missing out," Elliot said, placing the bottle back on the table.

Adam ignored him and began to explore the menu for himself. He'd never particularly appreciated his brother's insistence that people eat or drink what he deemed worthy. He'd once spent an entire afternoon arguing with Elliot about which was better: a Coney dog with an ice cold Heineken or a filet mignon with a glass of 1933 Cheval Blanc. In the end, Adam overruled Elliot by pointing out that a Coney dog could be enjoyed with another of man's greatest culinary inventions. Cheese fries.

* * *

Enormous synthetic "lava rock" plates of half-eaten burritos, tamales, and chile rellenos sat before the gluttonous group. With Lara having drained two glasses of wine along with a tall bottle of imported cerveza, conversation at the table had turned to a very unusual topic.

"I'm telling you, UFOs are for real," she said, wiping her mouth with a large red napkin.

Everyone looked at Lara without speaking. For the past several minutes she'd been moving from one alleged government cover-up to the next. Somehow, she'd now arrived on the scene of alien spacecrafts.

"Okay, let me give you a relevant example," she said, obviously seeing doubt in her dinner partners' eyes. "Did you ever hear of a guy by the name of Robert Lazar?"

Elliot laughed. "You're kidding, right? Lazar was that physicist nut who claimed to be studying flying saucers for our government."

"He was a lot of things, but he wasn't a nut. I'm surprised a pencil neck like you has even heard of him." The wine had evidently loosened Lara's tongue even more than usual.

"Robert Lazar," Mr. Greene said, rubbing his chin. "Yes, yes, I remember him. At the time, people around here had a strong opinion one way or the other about him. After all, his story first came out on a Las Vegas talk show."

"Okay, clue me in," Adam said, feeling left out. True, it was a conversation about alien spaceships, but still, being left out was never any fun. "Who's this Lazar fellow?"

"Back in the late eighties, he claimed that he'd been working on a secret government project to reverse-engineer flying saucers that had crash-landed on Earth," Elliot said. Then with a rotating finger beside his temple, he added, "Whacko."

"There were some around here who thought he was an honest scientist turned victim of a government cover-up," Mr. Greene said. Adam wasn't sure if he was defending the subject or just the pretty girl who'd introduced it.

Elliot sniffed loudly and rolled his eyes.

"While working at Los Alamos, he was recruited by Edward Teller—the father of the hydrogen bomb," Lara said. "At Teller's insistence, he went to work for a government contractor called EG&G. Once there, he claimed to have been given some ultra super-secret security clearance, which he referred to as 'majestic clearance.' Supposedly even presidents don't have that level of clearance."

"Come on," Elliot moaned. "Surely you don't buy into all that." He wasn't speaking to anyone in particular, just appealing to the general sanity of fellow burrito eaters.

"Please continue," Mr. Greene said, momentarily touching Lara's arm.

Adam smiled. If there was one thing Elliot had yet to learn, it was that beauty always trumps reason when introduced to a table full of men.

Lara glared triumphantly at Elliot. "Anyway, Lazar's clearance allowed him to work with things most people only dream of. He worked at Area 51, the restricted zone outside Nevada's Nellis Air Force Base."

"Even I've heard of Area 51," Adam said. "Didn't the government claim they were simply conducting weather experiments there?"

"Typical cover story," Lara answered. "Several high-level military officials later admitted that they'd been involved in extensive research of advanced aircrafts. Lazar went even further, claiming that he'd worked with a total of nine different flying saucers. He claimed funding for the black project came from the Strategic Defense Initiative program."

"Last time I checked, SDI was the big military defense program designed to defeat incoming Soviet nuclear missiles," Elliot countered.

"Lazar argued it was just as much for defeating incoming flying saucers as it was for shooting down missiles," she said. "He said President

Reagan knew all about it, and that was the reason he backed the SDI program so aggressively. Keep in mind that during his administration Reagan did make several unusual comments about extraterrestrial life."

"The man had Alzheimer's," Elliot said. "Plus his wife . . . oh, don't get me started."

Lara ignored him. "Lazar was later caught up in some bogus scandal relating to writing computer programs for a brothel. He was convicted of pandering and sentenced to three years probation. Obviously, he'd made a few enemies and needed discrediting."

"Did he ever offer any proof?" Adam asked.

"Nothing that would stand up in court or even in a rational person's mind," Elliot quickly interjected.

Lara cut threatening eyes at him. "He was given four different lie-detector tests. Two of the experts said he was telling the truth. The other two said the results were inconclusive. He also produced a W-2 tax form showing his clearance level and an internal phone record for Los Alamos that clearly showed he worked there at one time. After the scandal broke, though, the government took the plausible deniability route and said they'd never heard—"

Lara suddenly broke off, her face twisted in obvious discomfort. "I'm sorry," she said, clutching her abdomen. "My stomach . . . it's not feeling well."

"You all right?" Adam asked, resting his hand on hers.

"I . . . I don't know. If you don't mind, I think I'm going to lie down for a while."

Both Mr. Greene and Adam helped her to her feet. Even Elliot looked concerned.

"Come on, I'll take you up to your room," Adam offered.

"No, that's okay," she said. "I'll be fine. Ring me when you get ready to go to the party, and I'll come down. I just need a few minutes to rest. All those enchiladas and Mexican beer must be taking their toll."

With that, Lara excused herself and left the restaurant.

* * *

Adam listened as the phone rang for a fifth time. He was just about to hang up the lobby's courtesy phone and go check on Lara when she finally answered.

"Hi, Adam," she said with a shaky voice.

"Hey, girl, you still sick?"

"Sick isn't the word," she replied. "Whatever was in those enchiladas is doing a number on me."

"Can I get you something?"

Adam had found there are two kinds of people: those who like to be pampered when ill and those who don't want another human being anywhere within two hundred miles. He personally threw himself into the first group but wasn't sure where Lara fit.

"No, that's okay," she answered. "I sent the bellboy for some of the pink stuff earlier. I should be better in a while. I hate to even say it, but I think you guys are going to have to go on without me tonight."

He could hear the disappointment in Lara's voice. "Are you sure? I don't mind waiting for you." Adam meant what he said, but he also wanted to get to the banquet as early as possible while things were being set up.

"I don't think I'm going to be over this anytime soon. Go on without me. Just promise me one thing."

"What's that?"

"Promise me that you'll be careful."

"I'm always careful," he lied.

"I mean it. Whoever this guy is, he's good. If he's gunning for Mr. Greene, he wouldn't think twice about shooting you or anyone else who gets in the way. That's the way they have to be. Just stay out of his line of fire. Okay?"

"I'll try," he said.

Adam hung up the phone wondering how he could possibly keep that promise.

Chapter 15

Adam watched as a long line of black limousines idled patiently at the guard booth. One vehicle after another was systematically searched and then let through to Robert Greene's desert getaway. The spread was immense even by the Who's Who of the Rich and Famous standards, spanning well over a half-mile from edge to edge. That didn't account for the hundreds or perhaps thousands of acres of surrounding desert land that Mr. Greene undoubtedly owned.

A dozen or more beautiful white-and-brown Palmetto horses were barely visible in the quickly extinguishing light as they roamed freely over the western third of the ranch.

At the center of the spread was a mansion designed with a very modern, eco-friendly persona. The finish was white stucco that must have required daily scrubbing given the dry, dusty environment. Massive arrays of solar panels lined one side of the roof, and a large white-bladed windmill spun not far behind the residence. The home also had banks of enormous glass windows lining all four sides.

To either side of the residence were large single-story structures. A contingent of servants lived in one of the buildings, with the other being used to house a collection of Ferraris, Porsches, and Bentleys. Of the two buildings, the one that held the automobiles had the larger air conditioning unit.

The gardens were expansive and immaculate. Lush green grass and the passionate colors of exotic flowers brought the illusion of life to the desert. Adam thought the ranch was like a mirage—a small pool of moist, cool life in the middle of tall dunes of hot, arid sand. It didn't belong here, and time would eventually dry it up just as it had every other living thing that tried to make the desert its home.

By the time Adam and Elliot had arrived, many of the guests were already in the main gardens milling about, sipping champagne, and eating an assortment of cheeses and petits fours. Dress for the occasion was uniform and without creative expression, simple black ties and black dresses respectively. Evidently this was not the occasion at which to make an Oscar-style fashion statement. Both Adam and Elliot were thankful for the tuxedos provided courtesy of Mr. Greene.

In characteristic hobnobbing style, Elliot opted to stay near Mr. Greene himself, offering the rather lame excuse that he would "help keep an eye on him." Adam suspected his brother was much more interested in establishing connections with some of the high-profile media stars. Who better to make introductions than the host of the extravaganza himself?

As packed full of ego-pumping fun as the party promised to be, Adam was more interested in the security. Mr. Greene had given him full license to check the grounds and general security setup but understandably had not advanced any authority to make changes. That was fine by Adam. He didn't want the responsibility for Mr. Greene's safekeeping.

There were several layers of security. As expected, the banquet area itself was covered with undercover personnel. Even though the men were dressed in tuxedos, noticeably wary eyes and the occasional squawk of radios betrayed their presence.

Beyond the main area, numerous two-man teams with German shepherds patrolled the grounds. These men were definitely not meant to be covert, brazenly carrying Uzi submachine guns. The perimeter of the ranch was encircled by a ten-foot stone wall with serious hemorrhoid-causing spikes lining the top. Going over it was possible, but going over it quickly was not.

Cameras were everywhere—on top of the buildings, along the wall, at the guard booth, and even in the trees. An electronically controlled iron gate that was as stout as any medieval portcullis served as the only entrance to the ranch. Adam counted an even dozen of heavily armed security personnel guarding the gate. Without exception, every car entering was thoroughly checked, dogs smelling both the car and visitors for the slightest hint of explosives. State-of-the-art facial recognition software was also used to ensure that each guest was who he or she claimed to be.

The stage area where Mr. Greene would be speaking from was relatively exposed, but the podium itself was protected by a clear face shield made of thick bulletproof Lexan. Three men in long, black coats stood guard on the stage. Adam had seen such garments before. They were made of woven Kevlar fibers and would stop an incoming bullet with little more than a memorable bruise. These men were bodyguards in the literal sense of the word. If they saw anything threatening, they would toss Mr. Greene to the ground and cover his body with their own.

The more he studied the security, the more impressed Adam became. Mr. Greene's team certainly seemed to have things well in hand. This was of no surprise given that he had resources rivaling that of an Arabian prince.

Adam felt certain the assassin would have to operate as an intruder. The guests and staff were just too well screened. If he were an intruder, where could he hide? There weren't many viable options.

"How would I kill him?" he asked himself, being careful not to speak loud enough for anyone to overhear. "Of course I could always use poison or explosives. In which case, I wouldn't have to be here at all."

But his gut told him death by remote control wasn't this guy's style. This killer wanted to witness his handiwork. Adam couldn't justify the assessment since he based it solely on a single prior crime. Still, it felt right.

Instinctively, his eyes turned to the rooftop of the mansion.

"If I could get up there somehow, I could do it." He shook his head. "But how?" The walls of the building were in plain sight and would take even a skilled climber several minutes to maneuver up. The inside of the building was even more carefully guarded, which ruled out sneaking up some internal staircase under the guise of being a servant. "What's more, even if I did somehow manage to get up there, it would be impossible to get away afterward."

Somebody had once said that an assassin was impossible to stop if he was willing to trade his life for that of another. Adam suspected in most cases that was probably true. However, he also suspected that this particular assassin wasn't willing to make such a final exchange. If the map was really a schedule of kills, he had more work to do.

"Okay, so there's the roof. How else?" He rubbed his chin, searching the compound for vulnerabilities. "Where else could I shoot from? I'd have to have a line of sight to the stage. And it would have to be from the side, behind, or at a steep vertical angle to get around that plastic shield."

The only other elevated structure in the ranch was the wall that surrounded it. What if the assassin climbed the wall and shot from the top?

Was that even physically possible? The space atop the wall was only a few inches wide, not enough to act as a stable base on which to make the shot. Even if he could get on the wall, it would have to be one hell of a shot given that it was a good four hundred yards from the nearest wall to the stage. A sniper on the wall would have lighting to his advantage, but still the range and nearly impossible balancing act would make it a very difficult shot. And yet, was it possible?

Adam saw Ken Stalker standing a few feet away holding a gadget of some type. Earlier in the evening, Mr. Greene had introduced Stalker as the head of his security team. From their brief exchange, Adam had come away with the feeling that Mr. Greene had already spoken with Stalker about their little rescue group from Colorado. Such was to be expected, just as it was expected that dedicated security personnel had surely been assigned to watch the would-be rescuers.

Adam approached Stalker and saw that he was looking at a small handheld LCD monitor. "Mind if I ask what you've got there?"

Stalker looked up. Having been introduced as a retired Navy SEAL, he looked the part—mid-fifties, athletic build, hair still trimmed in the characteristic military crew cut. "It's the receiver for a FLIR we have scanning the dark areas of the compound," he answered.

Only an ex-military grunt would call the exquisite ranch a "compound." Adam leaned in closer to take a look. "FLIR? You're talking infrared?"

"That's right," Stalker confirmed. "This thing is state of the art." He turned the screen to face Adam but didn't hand it over. "The camera is equipped with an RF transmitter so that I can pick up the image standing here or anywhere else on the compound. I can also pan and tilt a dozen cameras as I see fit. If anything unusual shows up, we move on it immediately."

Adam had seen IR cameras before, but the image displayed on the small monitor was extremely sharp and clear. The screen showed a group of partygoers enjoying drinks as they huddled together gossiping. The camera was fine enough to show the temperature gradients across their faces as they consumed the cool drinks. Probably more interesting still were the distinct thermal footprints they left behind as they slowly meandered around the buffet. Even the most skilled ninja would have a hard time evading the ever-seeing eyes of Stalker's IR cameras.

"What about outside the wall?" Adam asked. "I was thinking that someone might be able to climb it and make a precarious shot from the top. They would have elevation." It was a reach, and Adam found himself hoping an obvious expert like Stalker wouldn't ridicule the idea.

"Thought about that," he said. "We've got three roaming patrols on motorcycles just outside the compound. Their sole duty is to hug the walls and shoot anything bigger than a grapevine."

Another thought came to Adam. "Any chance of someone shooting from the air?"

"I've got a high-speed helicopter circling the outermost perimeter. If anything comes in our airspace, we'll see it before they can get off a shot."

"Pretty tight."

Ken Stalker looked up at him. He looked strong, but there was an undeniable air of nervousness about him.

"Yet you're still worried."

"Always," Stalker answered before turning and walking away.

* * *

The night grew colder as darkness took hold. The crowd drew in close, the laughter and chatter mixing to create an incessant buzz. Adam felt his stomach twist like a sour dishrag as the stage underwent the final preparations for Mr. Greene's address.

It occurred to him that he had no idea what the billionaire was going to say. In truth, it didn't really matter. Political speeches always boiled down to the same two things: vague statements about the candidate's position on timely issues and promises to do favors for the listening audience.

Whether it came from Mr. Greene or someone else, it was still just political babble. Nevertheless, Adam didn't hold the lack of substance against politicians. He fully understood that they operated in a world in which evasion and duplicity were the only practical tools to please diametrically opposing sides. Such was politics.

Adam surveyed the area once again to see if he could come up with some last minute, life-saving revelation. Security was everywhere . . . on the ground, in the air, outside the compound, and within. Short of calling in the National Guard, there wasn't much else that could be done.

He looked about the considerable crowd. Mr. Greene stood several yards away with two close associates, undoubtedly discussing specifics of the speech. Elliot was no longer at his side. Adam shook his head. No doubt his brother had found a friendly ear in the media willing to listen to his upcoming political plans.

At precisely eight o'clock, presidential candidate Robert Greene took the stage. He moved quickly but without panic to stand behind the clear plastic shield. Silence slowly rippled through the crowd of high-profile guests as they realized things were officially getting under way. All eyes were now on Mr. Greene.

"Let me begin by saying to all my guests . . . welcome." His words were even and resonated with control. He swung both arms open in an inviting gesture.

Pop! A sharp sound shot out from the audience. Mr. Greene instinctively ducked, and his three bodyguards rushed forward. The crowd voiced a collective gasp. For a moment everyone stood motionless, waiting to see if Greene would suddenly fall from an assassin's bullet.

He didn't.

Adam whipped his head in the direction of the sound. A portly middle-aged woman stood alone in front of a small stone fountain. At her feet lay the remnants of a broken champagne glass. She looked absolutely mortified as everyone fixated on her. Adam saw her silently mouthing an apology to Mr. Greene.

As it became clear that the threat wasn't anything more than flying shards of glass, a quiet laughter began to move through the crowd. Even Mr. Greene, who had now regained his composure at the podium, chuckled lightly.

"I'd say that took a good year off my life," he said. The crowd shifted from a chuckle to a full laugh followed by a round of applause. Mr. Greene smiled, allowing the joke to run its course.

As the laughter and applause began to ebb, he continued. "Now, where was I? Ah yes, I was just about to say that I hope to have the opportunity to talk with each and every one of you before the night is through. With the exception, of course, of Mrs. Douglas, who will never be invited to another party."

More laughter.

"Kidding, of course," he said, smiling and waving to her. "Tina's a dear friend, as are many of you. I sincerely appreciate each and every one of you coming tonight. I'm sure most of you came for the free food, but you're going to have to suffer through my boring speech before dessert is served."

The crowd gave him another laugh, this one more obligatory.

"I think most of you know why I asked you here tonight. I wanted to have the opportunity to share a message with friends. A message of opportunity. A message of hope. With the primaries just around the corner, it would seem that many of the candidates are running on empty promises of reform. Now who here has ever heard of politicians doing such a thing?"

Another round of supportive laughter and applause.

"Those of you who know me," he continued, "understand that I'm not the sort of person to offer that type of rhetoric. I'm a man of action. A man of business. A man of compassion. But most important, a man of vision."

Adam saw several people in the audience nod in agreement. Mr. Greene seemed genuinely well-liked by the uppity liberal crowd.

"I have a host of topics to cover in this speech, so I hope you'll bear with me. Given your profession, I promise to field questions immediately afterward. Now let us begin—"

Adam stood in stunned horror as a huge explosion of dark red ink suddenly splashed across the inside of the podium's plastic shield. Mr. Greene immediately toppled sideways to the plywood stage floor. A few seconds later, the crack of a gunshot sounded far to the west.

Adam was already running toward the stage before most of the audience fully understood the horrible violence they'd just witnessed. By the time he neared the stairs, complete pandemonium had engulfed the crowd. Most were trying desperately to get away from the stage, away from the horror, away from the blood. Not necessarily sure where they wanted to go, just pushing with mob panic to escape. A few of the more hardened reporters rushed toward Mr. Greene in hopes of an up close and personal story.

Adam shoved onlookers aside and forced his way up the platform stairs. As he fought to get within a few feet of Mr. Greene, he saw Ken Stalker standing close by, barking orders into a handheld radio.

"To the west! Outside to the west!" He pointed wildly that direction. "Go! Go! Go!" Immediately following his command, loud motorcycle engines could be heard racing away from the ranch. A few seconds later, a small black helicopter buzzed over the top of the house as it also raced westward.

Adam's eyes turned to Mr. Greene. An old man knelt beside him, digging frantically in a large medical bag. A heavy gauze bandage was packed against the side of Greene's head. The bandage was already nearly soaked through, and a large pool of blood spread outward on the stage. Adam didn't need to be trained at Johns Hopkins to know that the billionaire was way beyond bandages and a bit of antibiotic cream.

"Shit!" he cried, looking off in the direction of the shot. With the help of bright security lights, he could now see all the way to the far wall. Only startled horses danced about under the glare of the lights.

Adam was confused. Where the hell was the shooter? "How?" he mumbled to himself.

Stalker stood listening to the silence of his radio. He shook his head. "I'll be damned."

"How?" Adam asked.

"Long range. Like a mile or more."

"No one can make that kind of shot." Adam considered himself a decent marksman, but five hundred yards was near maximal range. After that, the bullet trajectory drops off, not to mention that any slight bit of wind pushes the bullet off course. He'd never met anyone who could come close to hitting a man in the head at a mile.

"Probably a tripod system under computerized control. There are all kinds of high-precision computerized mounts on the international arms market these days. I just can't figure out how he had time to set the damn thing up."

"What do you mean?" Computerized targeting was well outside Adam's expertise.

"Those things take hours to set up, not to mention requiring several test shots for calibration. There's no way this shooter had that kind of prep time, and he sure as hell didn't get any free test shots. We were just out in the desert on patrol twenty minutes ago." Stalker rubbed at his eyes. "There's really no other way it could be done. Unless . . ."

"Unless what?"

"Unless he didn't use a targeting system at all."

Adam stared at him confused. "Is that even possible?"

"An hour ago, I'd have said no. Now, I'm not sure. He'd have to be a world-class marksman. The likes of which I've never seen. Not in the SEALs and not in the private sector. This guy would have to be one in a million."

* * *

Sometimes, life just shits all over you. And tonight is surely one of those bowel-moving moments. Such were Adam's thoughts as he walked slowly down the hotel corridor toward Lara's room.

He dreaded telling her what had happened. She and Mr. Greene had established a respectful, almost-friendly relationship, and he felt certain that she'd be upset with the news of his untimely death.

Hell, he was upset. As billionaires go, Robert Greene seemed like a decent enough guy. He'd been courteous enough to listen to their ideas even when they were stretched as far as Lara's tended to be. Yeah, he was a stand-up sort of guy. Too bad there was a gaping hole in the side of his head.

To make bad worse, Adam knew that they were all sure to be interrogated by federal investigators when it became known why they'd come to Vegas. Questions about the group's motives and possible broader involvement would undoubtedly arise. He feared that a washed-out map and Lara's conspiracy theory wouldn't be enough to escape the sights of a federal prosecutor.

He sighed. That was a worry for tomorrow. Right now, he had to break the news to Lara. He tapped softly on the door, hoping that she was awake. Leaning in close, he listened for footsteps. There were none. He knocked a little harder. Still nothing.

He checked his watch. It was half past eleven. Mr. Greene had been shot over three hours ago. He'd waited around to see if Stalker's men were going to find the shooter. They hadn't.

Having thought it rather inappropriate to ask for a ride back in the limousine, Adam had taken a forty-minute taxi ride back to the casino. To top it all off, he'd been unable to locate Elliot after the shooting. He wasn't particularly worried, though. His brother had probably hitched a ride from one of his newfound media friends and was undoubtedly having nightmares in his own bed by now.

Adam knocked on the door again, this time hard enough to disturb the dead.

Still no response. She was probably passed out on the bed, or worse, praying to the porcelain god. Even if she didn't want to be disturbed, he felt a duty to give her the bad news. After all, Greene's death confirmed what had previously been ridiculed as a far-fetched idea. Two cities circled and two presidential candidates murdered. Her theory had proven to be deadly accurate.

Adam tried the doorknob. It turned with little effort. He felt his heartbeat pick up the pace. Lara was not the type of person to leave her door unlocked, regardless of how sick she was.

He pushed the door open a couple feet and leaned inside. Only the bathroom was lit, and from it, he heard a soft trickle of water. The rest of the room was dark and deathly still.

"Lara, you in there?" She had already proven herself to be a very light sleeper. Yet, there was no rustle of covers. No flushing of the commode. No turning off of the water. Nothing.

Adam stepped carefully into the room. With his back pressed against the wall, he slid into the suite a few more feet until he could see the entire bathroom. The sink spilled over into a large pool on the tile floor. He also saw a string of red letters scrawled across the bathroom mirror.

Adam closed his eyes, letting the horror fill his very soul. He knew what was on the mirror. Blood. Following the handbook of psycho clichés, the killer had scrawled a message in his victim's blood. Lara's blood.

He felt himself growing nauseated and suddenly had trouble getting enough air. Clenching his teeth, he forced back the terror and hit the nearest light switch. He surveyed the suite. Covers were scattered about the room, chairs overturned, wine glasses broken, lamps kicked across the floor. Everywhere he looked were remnants of one hell of a fight.

Adam felt as if he might vomit.

He turned his attention back to the bathroom, moving to the doorway and scanning the room to confirm that it was empty. He half expected to find Lara lying dead in the Jacuzzi, her body broken and battered, but the elegant powder room was empty.

He saw words written on the mirror only a few feet from him but had yet to turn his eyes to them. Fear clawed at him. Whatever they said, the message was the same. Lara was now in the same kind of trouble as her sister.

Adam swallowed hard and turned to the mirror. Large red, wet letters were smeared over its surface.

Stay out of this.

Adam put his hand to his face but did not cry. He was too horrified, too afraid for Lara to cry. He wanted only to kill. Whoever had spilled her blood would die a horrible death.

After a moment, he looked back at the words. He didn't want to touch the letters, but he had to know for sure. He reached out and ran his fingers over one of them. It smeared across the smooth mirrored glass.

He stood for a long time staring at his fingers and the glossy red streak. Then he began to laugh. It began as a soft chuckle but didn't stop until tears were streaming down his face.

Lipstick. Thank God. It was only lipstick.

* * *

Elliot had been drinking; that much was clear. His hair was a mess, his eyes bloodshot, and his breath as foul as roadkill.

Adam pushed his way into his brother's room, nearly knocking him to the floor in the process.

"What do you want?" Elliot slurred. He didn't wait for an answer. "Some big adventure we're having here, Adam. I'm surprised Cupcake isn't down here right now gloating about the novelty of this conspiracy we've uncovered."

Elliot turned away from the door and flopped onto an oversized chair. An open bottle of Jack Daniels, a crumpled brown paper bag, and a crystal water glass sat before him.

Adam gave serious consideration to going over and beating the shit out of his brother. "She's gone, you dick."

Elliot looked up, his face twisted as if he was trying to hear an instant replay of what Adam had just said. "What are you talking about? Gone where?"

Adam paced the room, calming himself. Yes, his brother was a smart ass. But no, he wasn't in any way to blame for what happened to Lara. Beating him senseless probably wasn't in order, even if it would feel great for the five seconds that it lasted. "She's been taken. Just like Maria."

Elliot tried to stand, wavered a moment, and then sat back down. "Taken? By whom? What's going on here, Adam? What have we gotten ourselves into? We're both going to end up in jail . . . or worse, like Mr. Greene."

Good old Elliot. Even in a drunken stupor, he was still capable of thinking only of himself. "You know what?" Adam said. "You're probably right. Why don't you just climb your scrawny ass into bed and pull the covers over your head."

Elliot looked at him with hate in his eyes.

"It's not about you," Adam said. "Don't you get that?"

"Fuck you," Elliot spit out.

"I'm going after Lara."

A silence fell over the room, and for a moment, Adam thought his brother had fallen asleep. When Elliot finally spoke, his voice was a little too loud for the suite. "I'm going with you."

Once more he stood, but this time, he stumbled into the small table, knocking the whiskey over. Elliot made no move to pick it up. Instead he watched in fascination as it spilled out onto the immaculate white carpeted floor.

After a moment, he let loose a short emotional outburst. "I'm sorry, Adam. I'm sorry about Lara. I'm sorry I ever brought you into this. I'm sorry about being such a selfish bastard. I'm sorry about everything." Then, as an afterthought, he said, "And I'm drunk."

Adam felt his anger melt away. Seeing Greene's murder was more than Elliot's sheltered soul could handle, soberly anyway.

He moved to his brother, slid one arm around his shoulder, and helped him to the bed. "Come on, big brother. You better get some rest. Tomorrow's going to be another rough day, I'm afraid."

*   *   *

Morning brought with it a renewed understanding of what had to be done. Adam and Elliot sat in the lobby of the Krakatau Casino Hotel, their luggage resting at their feet. It wasn't quite seven in the morning, and both had agreed they needed to leave Mr. Greene's property post-haste. A Filipino cleaning lady pushed a large mop nearby while humming softly to herself.

"We should go to the authorities," Elliot said. "They'll be out looking for us. We should initiate the contact so they won't think we have something to hide. If we don't, we're likely to be charged as coconspirators in all this."

Adam sat leaning forward, elbows resting across his knees. "Listen, I'm not like Lara. I don't have anything against the police, FBI, or anyone else in positions of authority."

"Then why are you hesitating?"

"We've got people dead, friends missing, and nothing but confusion as to who's behind this mess. Bringing in the authorities makes sense. The problem is that the debate is scheduled for tomorrow. If we go to the authorities now, they'll hold us for sure. We'll never make it to D.C. in time. That's the last stop, the last chance to catch him. If we don't stop him there, we'll never see either Lara or Maria again."

"Two candidates have been killed in less than a week. The debate will surely be called off," Elliot said definitively.

"No, it's still on," Adam said with equal confidence. "The news had a big piece on it this morning. Marino, Shoemaker, and Tyler all came out publicly to express their outrage. They also made it a point to say these acts of terrorism wouldn't send them cowering. They confirmed that the debate is still on."

"Utter foolishness," Elliot huffed, apparently not appreciating being upstaged. He took a long sip of coffee.

"The debate is on, and we have to be there," Adam summarized.

"Why?" Elliot asked, latching onto a new weakness. "Really, Adam, why do we need to be there? What exactly are we going to do? What good did we do here?"

Adam leaned in close, his voice low and hard. "Maybe you're right. We couldn't stop Greene's murder, and maybe we won't stop the killer in D.C. either. But we have to try, Elliot. Don't you get that? Sometimes you have to fight the fight even if you get your ass kicked."

Elliot's answer was a condescending stare.

Adam felt himself growing angry, the conversation feeling like a rehash of the previous night. "I'm going to D.C. to catch this guy. You can come along, or you can go back to your shoe shines and fancy meals. I don't give a shit either way."

Elliot's face grew red, and he met Adam's glare. "Don't talk to me like that. I've lost just as much as you in all this."

"Maybe, but there's a difference between us. You've already given up."

"I'm just a realist."

"Is that your two-dollar word for quitter?"

Elliot sighed. "Fine, you win. We'll go to the debate, but you better be right about catching this guy. If we're present at another assassination, we'll never be able to keep ourselves out of a federal penitentiary, and I, for one, don't want to spend my life in prison."

Chapter 16

Following Mr. Greene's death and Lara's abduction, caution had to be abandoned in favor of expediency. Elliot and Adam checked their firearms as luggage, bought two first-class tickets to Washington, D.C., and rolled the dice of chance. To their surprise, no government agents were waiting for them at the airport, and they were allowed to board without so much as a suspicious stare.

Despite the soft and spacious seating in first class, Adam fidgeted from side to side. Elliot looked no more comfortable sitting beside him as he talked quietly into the onboard telephone. After a moment, he returned the phone to its cradle.

"It's all lined up," he said. "We're officially on the A-list of invited guests to tomorrow's debate. At five thousand dollars a ticket, though, I'd have to say that 'invited' is a bit of an exaggeration."

Adam barely heard him. Money had less meaning now than ever. Only one thing mattered. Finding Lara. It all came down to the debate. It would be the final opportunity to get the jump on the killer. If they blew it, or if the killer didn't show up, it was over for the Sativa sisters.

What if the worst happened? What if the debate came and went and they were no closer to a solution? Lara would die. Maria would die. Another politician would die. Adam closed his eyes trying to keep despair at arm's length. His chest felt constricted as if he were being embraced by a three-hundred-pound gorilla. He knew what it was. He'd felt it many times before. *Responsibility.* Responsibility for Lara. Responsibility for Greene. Responsibility for the whole goddamn world. It was stupid and irrational. Just as Atlas had agreed to the burden of holding up the world, somewhere along the way, Adam had adopted his role as protector of the weak.

He sucked in a deep breath, recalling the popular cartoon of a frog being swallowed by a large stork. Defiant to the end, the frog reaches out of the bird's mouth to strangle his feathered foe. *Defiant to the end.* He drew strength from the words.

The conflict ahead was not so different from a judo contest. He and his opponent were facing off for one final match. Both aware of one another's skills. Both prepared for the imminent struggle. He told himself that this was one battle he was not allowed to lose.

He began to play back everything that had happened, hoping for additional insight. It began with Maria stealing a map she believed uniquely valuable from a client who, unbeknownst to her, was either himself a killer or, at the very least, had some questionable acquaintances. Once Maria discovered she didn't have the gold mine she'd hoped for, she mailed it to her sister for safekeeping. Then things took a turn for the worse, and she found herself cornered by her client along with some of his handy helpers.

With the kind of torture Maria had endured, she would've spilled what she had done with the map. But if that were the case, Lara would have been paid a late-night visit long before last night. So, for whatever reason, the killers must have made a mistake and accidentally killed Maria prematurely, before they found out about Lara.

Knowing they'd screwed up, the killers had taken all the normal precautions, including intercepting Maria's mail and watching her residence. Along came Adam, Lara, and Elliot, poking their noses into her disappearance.

With Adam's behavior at the amusement park and the group's arrival in Las Vegas, the killers became convinced that they had the map and thus were capable of affecting the planned assassinations.

An attempt was made to kill the most threatening of the three but failed. Adam still couldn't explain how syringe-man got on the scene so fast. Perhaps he was originally scheduled to be there for backup, in case the shooter couldn't get Mr. Greene.

Following the first bungled attempt, the killers decided to take a different approach to nullify the threat. They kidnapped Lara when she could barely hold her head up, let alone offer a real fight. Perhaps they'd even somehow orchestrated her sickness.

But who exactly was the enemy? And why were they killing candidates? Could they really be connected to the CIA? Or was the agency simply conducting an investigation, as Elliot had suggested? Could it be a misdirection of some sort?

His reasoning was interrupted by Elliot's hand on his shoulder. Adam waited for meaningless words of encouragement. Surprisingly, none came. His brother apparently knew him well enough not to offer empty promises of how everything would turn out just fine. Neither of them had any idea what would happen next.

He closed his eyes and saw Lara's beautiful face, her mysterious blue eyes. *She's alive,* he assured himself. *But if she's not,* he added, *I'm going to kill someone.*

* * *

Elliot dialed the number carefully.

It was answered on the first ring. "Walker."

"It's me."

"Listen, you need to end this thing and come in."

"I can't. Not yet. Not until after the debate."

"That doesn't sound smart. We both agreed if things went bad, you'd call this off. The only reason your name hasn't floated to the top is that I've been shielding you. That and the fact that the Bureau is having to track down so many leads from the party. But, trust me, this won't last. Pretty soon they're going to realize that you're knee-deep in this."

"I know. But I have to do this. There's only one more to go."

"You're playing a very dangerous game. You know that, don't you?"

"Believe me, I know. Just have your people there, okay?"

"Don't worry. We'll be there."

* * *

The debates were scheduled to start at seven thirty at the Hall of Stars, a retrofitted coliseum originally built to support semipro basketball and hockey leagues. Unfortunately, the coliseum had never drawn a large enough audience to keep the lights on. A local entrepreneur eventually bought the building and rented it out as a convention center for various activities, including technology shows, business conferences, and motivational seminars.

Adam and Elliot arrived at the Hall of Stars at just past six in the evening. The VIP dinner was to be served at six thirty. Elliot had opted to dress in the conventional three-piece navy suit he'd picked up earlier. Adam wore a pair of blue jeans and a white button-up shirt.

Adam would have felt better with a pistol stuffed in his waistband. Unfortunately, with the plethora of metal detectors and residue-sniffing canines, there was no way to enter with a firearm. He drew little consolation from the massive security presence, given the killer's demonstrated ability to outwit Mr. Greene's extensive precautions.

Elliot and Adam had discussed the possibility of approaching authorities at the debate and explaining their assassination theory. After talking through the likely flow of events, both agreed they would surely end up in some detention room and interrogated for endless hours. This scenario wouldn't help whoever was scheduled to be executed tonight nor would it advance the long-term careers of a corporate lawyer or private investigator. That left them to their own devices, at least until it became clear who was behind the murders.

A petite woman in a red dress escorted Elliot and Adam past the main bleacher area and onto the floor of the coliseum where forty or more tables had been set up near a makeshift stage. She showed them to one of the many tables set with fine linens and expensive silverware. Most of the tables were already at least partially occupied.

An elderly couple was seated at their table, and there were place settings for six other guests. Forty tables, eight people to a table, five thousand a head, Adam didn't need to do the math. There was a lot of money being made at this event. And that wasn't counting the few thousand second-class bleacher seats that probably had some kind of money tied to them.

A heavyset lady sitting at the table smiled at both brothers as they took their designated seats. As if the three seconds of momentary silence were killing her, she suddenly stood and leaned halfway over the table with a hand extended. Her large bosom nearly knocked over several glasses of water.

"Hello," she said. "I'm Barbara Dodson, and this is my husband, Charlie. Introduce yourself, Charlie."

Charlie, a gaunt man with bleached, wrinkled skin and a toothpick hanging out of his mouth, nodded an almost imperceptible nod.

"Hello," Elliot said as his hand bounced up and down vigorously under the woman's control.

"We're from Buffalo," she said, shifting her hand over to Adam. "Well, not Buffalo proper, closer to Orchard Park, really. But no one knows where that is, so I just say Buffalo. Don't you just hate it when people tell you they're from some tiny little town? Like you would have any idea where it might be in the first place. That's why I just say we're from Buffalo."

Elliot started to speak but was quickly cut off.

"We're so excited about being here tonight," she continued. "Aren't you excited too? Of course you are. Who wouldn't be? It's truly an historical event."

"We're just here to pick up chicks," Adam said with a grin.

For a moment she looked at him confused, but then bellowed out a huge laugh. "You . . . you had me going there. You're a cad, you are!" She laughed again as if to emphasize the magnitude of his wit.

The table fell awkwardly silent as her laughter trailed off. Fearing that the table would grow cold, she quickly said, "So, who are you rooting for?" Before anyone could answer, she continued, "We like Senator Shoemaker. Good, honest man. Marino on the other hand has always seemed a little shady. Not that you couldn't like the vice president. No, no, we'd understand if you did. He's just not to our liking, that's all I'm saying. I'm not saying we dislike him. I mean, we're patriots and all, and of course we like and support our country's elected leadership. As for Tyler, well, he's just not our type, if you know what I mean. I'm not saying that because he's black. We're not bigots. Oh, heavens no. My hairdresser is black. Where are you from anyway? Have you been to this sort of thing before?" Her words rattled out in a seemingly endless procession.

Adam glanced at Elliot who looked equally mortified. Life at this table was going to be excruciating by anyone's measure. Only one thing to do. "I live in Knoxville, and my brother here is from Denver," Adam said, gesturing to Elliot. "He goes to these sorts of things all the time. I believe he's even met the vice president. Haven't you, Elliot?"

Elliot turned to his brother with a look of disgust.

"Oh really?" the old woman exclaimed, clapping her hands together while bouncing up and down. "You must tell me all about it. When was it? Was he already the vice president, or was it during his time as a senator? What did you think of him? Is there anything to the awful rumors about his involvement in organized crime? Oh please, tell, tell."

"If you'll excuse me, nature calls," Adam said. "But you just continue on without me. I know my brother loves talking politics." He stood, patting his brother on the back.

Elliot looked up with pleading eyes. "Adam, you can't—"

"Oh, but I must," he said, turning and quickly parading away from the table. He could hear Mrs. Dodson already starting in on his most unfortunate brother.

* * *

From the back of the large coliseum, Adam now had a decent position from which to survey the setup. The area closest to the stage was reserved for the most important guests: fellow politicians, financial backers, outspoken Hollywood media types, and friends and family. Just beyond the exclusive tables were a few dozen more set up for the generous supporters like Mrs. Dodson and her husband.

Guests who didn't feel the need to pay thousands of dollars for a single meal had to sit in the bleachers. The distant seats to the far left, right, and rear of the stage had been roped off and were inaccessible. That kept the riffraff corralled into a manageable area where the Secret Service could keep a better eye on them.

Even if Mrs. Dodson were to suddenly choke on a chicken bone and the table became peacefully quiet, Adam doubted he would be partaking of the meal tonight. He was here for one reason only, to find the shooter before he could sight in on his next target. It was only through apprehending the killer that he had any chance of rescuing Lara.

Though all three candidates would gather on stage, he guessed the killer had only a single target. Short of using a rocket launcher, killing more than one seemed utterly impossible.

Given Stalker's comment about the shooter likely being a world-class marksman, Adam believed the killer would once again opt for a long-range rifle shot. Of the three candidates, his gut told him that Vice President Marino or Senator Shoemaker were the most likely victims. The assassin had an order to his madness. To kill an independent like Bill Tyler who had virtually no chance of winning the presidential election was like passing on the flame-broiled rib eye to eat a hamburger.

It didn't really matter anyway. All the candidates would be within a few yards of one another during the debate. Regardless of the target, the shooter needed a vantage point from which to get off a clean shot and still get away afterward.

In some ways, the debate was to be the killer's easiest challenge yet. Unlike Mr. Greene's desert hideaway, where every guest was checked and double-checked, the debate had onlookers from every walk of life. Anyone willing to pay the hefty privilege tax was allowed to sit at tables within a hundred yards of the stage.

Still, it seemed unlikely that the shooter would be willing to undergo the extensive background check required for sitting at the VIP tables. That meant he would either work his way into the remote bleachers or, more likely, try to slip in unnoticed altogether.

If the assassin was successful in getting off a shot, the situation would quickly become uncontrollable for the Secret Service. With several thousand spectators, the Hall of Stars would become a massive stampede.

Once again, Adam felt intense pressure to have some kind of breakthrough, something that would give him a leg up on the killer. He took a deep breath and continued his careful assessment of the coliseum. He didn't care how it happened . . . brilliant insight or simple dumb luck. This time things had to be different.

* * *

By a little after seven in the evening, the Hall of Stars was packed with the usual suspects: wealthy donors, lobbyists, and politicians. Adam also noticed that a sizable area in the bleacher's nosebleed section had been set aside for the un-paying "common man." It was predominantly filled with middle-class supporters but also had a large contingency of high school students who had been bussed in as part of a select Civics class field trip. Politicians could never forget about public relations.

At precisely seven thirty, Vice President Marino, Senator Shoemaker, and William Tyler walked in procession onto the stage. Large red, white, and blue streamers draped down from the ceiling, and hundreds of helium flag balloons were tied in small clusters across the stage. A huge banner spanned the back of the platform that read, "Honor the Fallen."

Each of the three men waved to the audience as they stood beside one another, sending an obvious message of political solidarity. Adam doubted that such solidarity would hold up during the night. The race was really down to two men, neither of whom had ever shown anything but pure acrimony toward the other.

The announcer, a media personality that Adam recognized from Greene's fatal bash, introduced the three candidates. At his introduction, each of the three men drew loud applause from the audience. Adam was surprised that even Tyler appeared to have his fair share of supporters. Or maybe there was just a large assembly of people who shared Adam's preference to always root for the underdog.

After the brief introduction, the announcer asked for a moment of silence in memory of General Duke Livingston and Robert Greene. The crowd became quiet, many people lowering their heads in respect for the two men. The overhead lights were dimmed, with only the stage remaining well lit.

As the announcer quietly extolled the virtues of the "fallen heroes," Adam saw a small flicker of light shine momentarily from high above the bleachers. It glimmered from behind a large dark window that overlooked the entire coliseum.

Quick inspection revealed that there were four such windows around the top of the auditorium. From their distributed placement and obvious vantage points, he guessed they were light and sound control rooms. That made sense since the Hall of Stars would have required areas for the scorekeepers and sports announcers.

If the light had remained on, it wouldn't have bothered Adam. But it didn't. Instead, it flashed only briefly before going dark. He guessed it must have come from a small secondary source rather than an overhead light since it didn't illuminate much of the window. More like a small flashlight or a lighter. If it hadn't been for the temporary dimming of the main coliseum floor, he would never have seen it at all.

He studied the other three control room windows. One was brightly lit, the other two dark. None gave off a flicker of light like what he'd just witnessed. Someone was in that control room. Someone who didn't want to be seen.

Adam wheeled around and ran toward the exit of the main coliseum floor. He had already determined that the stairwells and elevators resided in the outer ring of the building. As he darted out the exit, he entered into a long hallway that curved around the coliseum. Not far ahead were two elevators with a Secret Service agent standing guard. In the hope of not alarming the man, he slowed to a walk.

As he neared the elevators, he saw that signs hung on gold chains blocking both sets of doors, proclaiming them OUT OF ORDER. The Secret Service agent immediately turned and studied him as he approached. Adam was surprised to see that the man looked barely old enough to drive.

"Bathroom?" Adam asked with an urgent smile.

"The public bathrooms are back the way you came. Just inside the main entrance." The agent pointed behind Adam. The young man's eyes were alert with obvious suspicion.

"You're kidding, right? Don't tell me that's the only one. The toilets are spilling all over the floor. I'm talking ankle deep. There must be some kind of backup in the sewage system 'cause all the commodes are running over at once." Adam clutched his stomach. "Man, I'm about to bust here. Can you call someone to get in there and fix it?"

The agent looked him up and down carefully before replying. "My superiors wouldn't like it if I used my comm link to call for that. I'm afraid you'll have to wait for maintenance to fix the toilets."

Adam grimaced. "Look, I'm going to have to find someplace fast. Isn't there another john up around this hallway that I can use?" He clutched at his stomach and stared with pleading eyes. *I'm going to get by you one way or another. Take this opportunity to make it the easy way.* The thought of bashing an innocent young man's head into the elevator doors didn't appeal to Adam, but if that's what it took to save Lara's life, he was ready and willing.

The agent bit nervously at his lower lip. "You're not supposed to go back there." He sounded more like a teenager talking to an adult now.

"Hey, how about you come with me? I've really got to go. It'll take just a minute. Jesus, you can hold the toilet paper if you need to." Adam's voice had reached a squeal.

"I can't come with you. I can't leave my post."

Of course you can't. He looked at the young agent with as much "about to lose it in my britches" desperation as he could muster. *This is your last chance. Take it.*

"Go on," the young man said. "Just hurry up. If you're not back here in three minutes, I'm calling for someone to go in and get you. And if that happens, you'll spend the rest of the night locked in a cell."

"Thanks, man. Thanks a lot. I swear I'll be back in just a minute."

Not waiting for the inexperienced agent to recoup better judgment, Adam shuffled ahead. Once out of the agent's sight, he went right past the bathroom doors and pushed through a heavy metal fire door marked STAIRS.

* * *

Bart Valin spoke into the small, sleeve-mounted microphone. "Clear at seven."

"Roger, seven clear," replied a female voice into his earpiece. "Stay sharp."

Agent Valin shook his head in utter amazement. "Now what the hell does that cherry know about staying sharp?" he grumbled to himself in a tone more amused than bitter. "Fifteen years in the Secret Service, and I'm guarding a door."

He stood with his back just a few inches from the door marked C-3, inside of which was one of the four arena control rooms. Having searched the room an hour earlier, he was now serving as sentry to ensure that no one entered.

One of the first steps when dealing with a shooter was to secure all vantage points. He understood that. It wasn't that he disagreed with someone maintaining security at this position, especially given the recent assassinations. It was logical and necessary.

Just not me, he thought. *I've got too much experience that could help down on the floor. I'm better than this, and they should know that. She should know that. I need to be on the floor. I might catch something, maybe the fear in someone's eyes or the twitch of nervous fingers. Even more important, if the shit does start to fly, I could keep my head. The rookies down there will be lucky not to wet themselves.*

He was sure his being stationed outside a relatively inaccessible control room was Parson's doing. Karen Parson, the know-it-all Ivy League graduate. Karen Parson, the hotshot agent who got lucky a year ago and bagged the pimple-faced teenager gunning for the governor of North Carolina. Karen Parson, the shake-my-ass-and-watch-how-high-you-jump bitch.

What in the hell did she know about security anyway? Real security, not that textbook bullshit she'd studied between keg parties and blow jobs in college. Parson didn't know dick. If she did, she wouldn't have a senior agent like him standing sentry at some piss-ass location like this. And yet, the white shirts somehow felt she was supervisor material. Yeah, that made a hell of a lot of sense. It was amazing what a nice set of tits could get a woman.

However it had been decided, placing Parson in charge of a critical security detail like this was a mistake. One that might well cost a man his life.

Agent Valin rubbed his eyes. It was going to be a long night. He consoled himself that if everything went to shit, Parson's day in the sun would soon come to an end.

* * *

Adam shoved the door open to the emergency stairwell. Two signs were on the opposite wall. One indicated that Control Room C-3 was to the left; the other pointed to the right for C-4.

"Which one?" he asked through labored breathing. He'd lost his bearings coming up the stairs and was no longer sure of direction.

No time to play eeny, meeny, miney, mo. He turned left and ran down the corridor. After a fifty-foot hallway, he took a sharp left and almost ran headfirst into another Secret Service agent, this one much older than the one guarding the elevators.

"Whoa," Agent Valin said, one hand pressing forward in a stopping motion, the other going to the butt of his holstered automatic pistol. "Where do you think you're going?"

Still winded, Adam bent at the waist replying through deep gulps of air, "I'm glad . . . I found you. There's someone in the . . . control room. We've got to get in there."

Agent Valin squinted at Adam, sizing him up. "No one is in the control room." His voice was cool and controlled. "How about you show me some identification?"

Adam slowed his breathing and stood erect. He met the man's wary stare with the soft assurance of a weaning puppy. "Listen, there's no time for this. Open the door and see for yourself. There *is* someone in there. I saw a light from down below." He tried to sound convincing. This man had to believe him. It had taken entirely too long to get up here, and there wasn't any more time.

The Secret Service agent unsnapped the retaining strap on his holster. "I said I needed to see identification. Better yet, put both your hands on the wall beside you, and do it slowly." His mannerisms were sure and confident.

Shit! Adam thought. He had to get into the room, and it had to be sooner rather than later. *How sure am I? It was just a flash . . . could I be wrong? There's no going back once I commit to getting in there.*

"Listen, you can arrest me in a minute. But open the door first and see for yourself. Please, man, this is important," he pleaded. "You can't afford to be wrong."

Maintaining a grip on the butt of his handgun, Valin brought one sleeve to his mouth. "Seven needs assistance with a code fourteen." His voice was calm and measured.

Adam now saw the small helical coil of a receiver wire behind the agent's ear. If he was ever going to get into the room, it was now or never. In a couple minutes, agents would be crawling all over the area. Unfortunately, he suspected their arrival would be way too late for at least one of the three people on the stage floor, and that would mean too late for Lara.

Adam stepped in close, intending to wrestle away the handgun and make quick work of his adversary. To his surprise, Agent Valin side-stepped and managed to draw the firearm in a fluent practiced motion. Before he could bring it to bear, though, Adam spun his back into him, grabbing the agent's gun arm with both hands. He squatted and brought the elbow down sharply against his shoulder.

Valin spit out a painful curse but didn't release the gun. Adam tried to slam it down again, this time hard enough to break his arm. As it came down, the agent twisted his shoulder slightly, and the blow lost much of its effectiveness. It was, however, enough to cause Valin to release his grip, sending the handgun thudding heavily to the floor.

Agent Valin quickly adapted, driving a knee into Adam's back. When he'd gained a little distance between them, Valin pulled his arm free and struggled to get a solid choke hold from behind.

Adam winced from the pain as he felt his body bending awkwardly backward. Not having enough balance to throw, he stomped backward. The heel of his shoe scraped the flesh from Agent Valin's shin and smashed down against the instep of his foot. Feeling a slight weakening in the grip holding him, Adam repeated the attack several times. On the last of three powerful stomps, Valin cried out and shoved him away.

Adam spun to face him. Both men eyed the gun lying between them, but neither moved for it. This was to be settled in hand-to-hand combat. Adam considered renewing his argument for entering the room but decided against it. The time for talk had clearly passed. The only way into the room was through this guy. Unfortunately, he now suspected the agent had been in a scrape or two in his time.

Agent Valin crouched slightly at the waist much as a wrestler might. He didn't advance. *No need to,* Adam thought. *He knows reinforcements are on the way. Everything is working in his favor.*

Adam shuffled in with a low, fast sidekick. Valin blocked it away by raising and twisting his lead leg. He grabbed Adam's shoulder from the side and tried to execute a foot sweep. To counter the takedown, Adam stepped around and drove his shoulder into the man's chest. Together, they crashed into the corridor wall, smashing a large hole into the plaster.

Valin suddenly dropped down with a tremendous elbow strike. It landed hard on Adam's shoulder, and he felt his legs buckle momentarily. The agent brought another strike down, and again it hit with full force. Adam felt himself grow light-headed, his strength draining away.

Desperate to stop the attack, he lunged forward, smashing the crown of his head directly into the agent's face. The blow hit with a tooth-loosening *crack*. Valin became disoriented, and Adam immediately brought a knee up into his ribs. The knee hit a bit low, striking his bladder, and the agent's trousers immediately darkened as urine spilled out.

The agent's eyes were now glazed and distant. Blood oozed from a split lip. Adam moved to finish him. He struck out horizontally with both an elbow smash and an open palm strike, sandwiching the man's head between the two. The blow hit hard, and with one last *umph*, Agent Valin collapsed.

Unsure if it might be a ruse, Adam quickly snatched up the handgun—a Smith and Wesson ten-millimeter. He pulled the slide back just enough to see that a round was already chambered. He quickly turned it toward his opponent. The agent remained still, and his breathing was already slowing. This fight was over.

Adam turned his attention to the door. No time to search for a key. He slammed his foot into the door with everything he had. All three hinges tore away from the frame as the door smashed flat into the room.

Pistol in hand, Adam leapt into the darkness.

* * *

The room was long in shadows, but what Adam could see was no more comforting than a tribe of hungry cannibals. Directly ahead stood a dark figure, his gun inches away from Adam's face. Knowing it was too late, but unsure what else to do, Adam slowly raised his own firearm to the ready position in front of him.

For a reason Adam didn't understand, the assassin didn't fire, and because of that hesitation, the killer's advantage was lost. Both now stood only a few feet apart, guns fully extended away from their bodies. A few pounds of pressure would cause someone to die. It was as simple as that.

Adam paused, assessing his situation. Dark computer consoles sat quietly about the control room. The far wall was a huge observation window overlooking the mass of people below. A small circle had been cut in the glass, and a M40A3 sniper rifle lay near the opening.

The killer was dressed in a dark jumpsuit, black gloves, and a black neoprene face mask. An assortment of Batman-style gadgets hung from a small black nylon utility belt around his waist.

Am I too late? Adam wondered. Had the assassin already taken the shot? He realized a part of him didn't even care.

"All I want is the girl," he said in a steeled voice.

The assassin's gun seemed to waiver for a moment as if his resolve was shaken.

Suddenly, Adam felt a hot slap against his right shoulder blade. He fell forward, just as the assassin adjusted his point of aim and fired three quick rounds past Adam's head into the hallway behind him.

Adam tucked and rolled, landing under an announcer's chair that was bolted to the floor. Unable to easily free himself from the tangle of the chair, he instinctively swung his gun toward the hallway. He felt a warm wetness of blood spreading across his chest and back.

"Don't shoot!" he yelled.

A spray of bullets ripped into the console above him. Sparks and small pieces of metal fell over his face.

He saw three dark silhouettes enter the room. They wore tactical jumpsuits and carried MP5 automatic assault rifles with long round silencers. Thin red laser beams projected away from the weapons as they sliced into the darkness of the room. Even in the chaos of the moment, Adam wondered why Secret Service agents would use silenced weapons.

The assassin dove behind a console just before a dozen bullets riddled the glass observation window behind him. A huge curtain of shattered glass splashed out to the auditorium floor fifty feet below.

More bullets tore into the console just a few inches above Adam. One of the men advanced his direction, gun bearing down on him.

"I'm a bystander, don't shoot!" he yelled.

As if in response, he saw the pinpoint of red light settle on his chest.

Seeing no other choice, Adam fired his own weapon, aiming for center mass. The man jerked backward but surprisingly didn't drop. The laser began moving back toward him. Adam let the firearm belch again, and then a third time. The man shuddered and took two steps back but still didn't fall.

Vests, he thought. *They're wearing vests.*

Not waiting for the man to recover from his last shot, Adam brought his aim up and squeezed off another round. The man's head popped backward as if hit with a ball-peen hammer. He immediately spun around and toppled lifelessly to the floor.

Adam felt his gut seize. *Did I just murder a federal agent?* He consoled himself with the fact that he'd be the one dead if he hadn't pulled the trigger.

"Behind the console," one man whispered. "The shooter's behind the right console. The other one's on the floor. He's hit."

They knew he wasn't the "shooter," and yet they were still out to kill him. What in the hell was going on? A fourth man entered the room and immediately turned toward him. Before Adam could take aim, he ducked behind the edge of the nearest console.

Adam watched from the floor as the other two men split up, one going right, the other left around the large console the assassin had hidden behind. They moved cautiously but with practiced coordination. These men were professionals. Four men . . . were they the same men who chased him in the amusement park?

Bullets tore up the floor in front of Adam as a red laser dot moved across it. From where the fourth man now knelt behind the edge of the console, he couldn't quite get a clean line on Adam.

Adam scrunched his legs in tight and started to wriggle toward the end of the console. If he could just get around the corner, he would have better cover. As he slid forward, he saw the dark-slimy trail of blood his body was leaving behind.

The assassin suddenly popped up from the far side of a distant console. He fired his pistol with a soundless flash, and the closest man's head exploded in a shadowy spray. The dead man's partner spun, firing a long, moving burst, but the bullets found only walls and bright sparks from electronic CRT screens. The assassin had already vanished. This time Adam couldn't be sure which way he'd moved.

The sudden demise of his teammate must have caused the agent targeting Adam to rethink his position because the random floor shooting stopped. Adam crawled faster. He had to make the corner.

As he reached the edge of the console, Adam felt his breathing turn raspy with a wet gurgling. He swallowed and tasted blood. *Lung shot.* The realization hit home. *I'm dead in a couple minutes without medical attention. I'll suffocate in my own blood. A hell of a way to go.*

Surprised at how much strength he still had when so close to death, Adam pulled himself around the corner. Suddenly the agent who'd been targeting him just a moment earlier shuffled around the opposite corner in a deep crouch.

There was no time to aim. Adam squeezed the trigger, the gun jumping wildly in his hand. The bullet sliced through the man's neck, severing his right carotid artery. A huge pulsing spray of warm blood shot high into the air before raining down on them.

Demonstrating incredible grit, the man slapped one hand over his wound while using his other hand to bring the rifle to the ready.

Adam lunged forward, catching the MP5 and shoving it up and away. Bullets whistled by with sharp puffs of air, and Adam felt a sting as one tore through the tip of his ear. Frantic to stop the firing, he smashed the pistol into the man's face . . . once, twice, three times. There was a soft crunching as his nose and cheekbone collapsed. The gunfire stopped, and the man fell back from the brutal pistol whipping.

Adam pounced upon him, striking again, this time driving the barrel deep into his neck. Incredibly, the man was still conscious and trying to work a knife from his boot. Seeing little choice, Adam squeezed the trigger. The man's body jumped as if being hit by electric shock and then lay still. Unwilling to taking any chances, Adam braced his forearm against the man's partially destroyed throat. He held it there until the flow of blood slowed and finally stopped altogether.

Another bright flash lit the control room, but Adam could no longer see what was happening on the other side of the console. He crawled to the nearest wall and propped himself against it. He held the handgun weakly in front of him, its weight now feeling uncomfortably heavy in his hands. He waited, unsure of who he would see next. Unsure if it even mattered.

His eyes closed and were slow to open. When they finally did, the dark form of the assassin was kneeling close to him. The firearm Adam had held a moment earlier was now lying several feet away. He could hear only the soft rasp of his breathing and a strange *hiss* that sounded like the air leaking from a bicycle tire. He felt woozy and weak. Death was on his white horse and galloping fast.

The assassin was doing something to him. What was it?

Adam felt himself rolled onto his right side. A hand reached around and pulled out his wallet. Confusion set in. What was happening? The killer pulled two plastic credit cards from his wallet and then tossed the wallet to the side.

"Don't . . . go over . . . my limit," he choked out in a bloody pink spray. He'd forever promised himself that, if at all possible, he was going to go out with a joke. Given the circumstances, it was the best he could do.

With a flick of his wrist, the assassin flipped open a butterfly knife and sliced Adam's shirt in front and back. He then pressed the credit cards over the entry and exit holes in his back and chest. Adam noticed that the hissing sound abruptly stopped. He closed his eyes for another instant.

When he opened them again, the figure was across the room holding the sniper rifle in one of the dead men's hands. He assisted the corpse in firing the gun into a nearby wall.

Adam suddenly realized that he too was holding a firearm in one hand. It wasn't the Smith and Wesson he'd used earlier. The silencer had been removed, but he felt sure it was the Beretta that the assassin had used to kill the other two men in the room. Adam lay there clutching the weapon, confused, exhausted, and barely able to maintain consciousness.

The assassin looked back over at him.

That's it, Adam thought. *My turn to die.* He didn't even bother to try to bring the Beretta up since it was surely unloaded.

Instead of killing him, though, the assassin gestured with a quick three-finger salute. He then lowered himself into a large hole in the floor and disappeared as he slid a removable panel back into place. The room immediately fell silent except for the rasp of Adam's labored breath and the occasional spark of a shattered computer monitor.

Chapter 17

Adam swept a stiff broom across the worn canvas mat. The dojo was empty save for himself and Matsumoto who knelt in one corner meditating. Since his very first day, Adam had been assigned the chore of cleaning the studio each night after practice. It was not a punishment, simply a duty that befell the foreigner. He didn't mind staying after class. He had no family to hurry home to, and the chore allowed him never to feel pressured to leave. Instead, he used the quiet time to reflect on what he'd learned. He suspected that this was Matsumoto's motivation, though they had not discussed it. It was the way of the Japanese to leave much unspoken.

Most evenings while Adam cleaned, Matsumoto would retire to a corner of the dojo and begin a lengthy meditation exercise. When Adam finished cleaning, they would exit the dojo together with hardly a word spoken—both respectful of the other's time of reflection. Tonight was different, however.

As Adam put up the broom, Matsumoto said, "May we talk?"

He approached Matsumoto and knelt facing him. "Of course."

"Tell me, Cowboy, how do you feel you are doing in your study of judo?"

Adam hesitated. Humility was very important to the Japanese, so he chose his words carefully. "I'm improving, but I still have much to learn."

Matsumoto snorted softly. "Surely, you know that you are one of my strongest students. Since your arrival, you have taken to judo better than I could have imagined."

"Thank you, sensei." He had not known until now that Matsumoto recognized his progress.

"Your strength is found in your determination. The other students claim you are *fumetsu*, unbreakable. They hold you in great esteem."

Adam shifted, a bit uncomfortable at the praise. He said nothing.

"You and I have a bond. Have you felt it?"

"Yes," Adam answered. Since their first meeting he had felt uniquely connected to Matsumoto. He could not, however, put it into words.

"Just as that of a river to the mountains. Each must accommodate the other."

Adam bowed in respect.

Matsumoto closed his eyes, brought in a deep breath through his nose and let it out through his mouth. "Close your eyes, Cowboy. I wish to teach you."

Adam did as instructed.

"Take a moment to relax yourself. Let your emotions leave your body. Instead, think only of your inner self. Feel every beat of your heart, every breath of air in your lungs."

Adam began by first tightening and then relaxing each muscle in his body. He then cleared his mind of distractions and worries. Having practiced *kenpo* for many years, meditation was not new to him, and he quickly found himself rested and at peace.

When he saw that Adam was ready, Matsumoto continued, "The world is connected by an infinite set of strings, everything bound to everything else. To understand this, you must allow your ki to travel beyond your own self."

Adam was surprised by the reflective tone of Matsumoto's voice. It was as if he were relaying the meaning of an ancient Japanese artifact.

"Concentrate on extending your ki throughout the dojo just as we do in rooting ourselves during judo," Matsumoto continued. "Allow your energy to travel along the floor, to snake up the walls, even to flow through me."

Adam slowly released his ki into the room, his internal energy flowing out and away like soft billows of smoke. With the extension, he began to envision the room in great detail . . . the stained floor mat, the heavy oak door with cracked blue paint, the weathered Japanese flag hanging from the ceiling. Sounds and smells also came to him, the musky odor left by men who had struggled against one another, the chirp of a cricket sitting in the windowsill, the air passing in and out of Matsumoto's body.

"I am imagining the room," he said. "Many details, many sounds and smells."

"Good. But do not only imagine. See and feel the dojo in your mind's eye. Everything is there for you. You have only to reach out to it. Extend from a point just below your navel. This is the nexus for all your ki."

"I'll try." Adam slowed his breathing and continued releasing his thoughts, emotions, and very soul into the room. Slowly over several minutes, new details came to him. Things he had never consciously noticed before. The silent rhythm of the air as it pulsed from the air duct high overhead. The split in one of the large wood beams supporting the ceiling. The halo of moonlight that passed through the window and fell on the very spot where Matsumoto knelt each night during meditation.

"The dojo is like an animal, alive and breathing," Matsumoto said. "Can you feel it?"

"Yes. I'm like a blind man finding sight. How is this possible, sensei?"

"I can tell you only what I know. If you learn to channel your ki, you will be able to travel across the cobwebs that bind this world together. You will see the clouds dance in the sky, hear the heartbeat of a hummingbird, and feel the cool depth of the sea. Such extension can bring about both knowledge and healing."

And though others might have taken Matsumoto's words as an abstract lesson, Adam accepted them as metaphysical truth.

"Such extension is only possible for those possessing great ki," Matsumoto continued. "You were blessed, as was I, with such power. Mastery requires a lifetime, but tonight you have begun your journey. This knowledge is passed to you alone. Please respect its importance."

Adam felt powerful emotions stirring within him. He could say only, "I am honored."

Matsumoto fell silent. Together the two men sat, both extending their energy into the small studio. After several minutes, Matsumoto roused and brought his hands together with two sharp claps.

The door to the dojo opened and Adam heard the soft footsteps of someone entering behind him. He remained completely motionless, still trying to unravel the newfound mysteries of the small room.

"Answer me this question," Matsumoto said in barely a whisper. "Who stands inside the door?"

At first, logic tried to intervene, telling Adam that this was a puzzle that could be solved by deduction. The heaviness of the stranger's steps or perhaps the rhythm of his breathing might provide an answer.

He forced such reason from his mind, and instead allowed his ki to once again fill the dojo. In his mind's eye, an image slowly material-ized. A young man, balding before his years. Thick muscular forearms and hunched shoulders. Before he could second-guess the image, Adam said, "Aida-san."

"And how do you know this?"

"I . . . I can feel him. I can sense his disturbance of the ground, of the air. I can detect his odor as it spins its way through the room. More than anything, I can feel his ki."

"Open your eyes and see for yourself."

Adam opened his eyes and turned to look at the door.

Fumio Aida stood looking at the two of them, hesitated a moment, and then offered a deep bow.

* * *

Adam extended himself farther than ever before. First came a small room, lights and tones splitting the sterile darkness. Beyond was the hos-pital, white coats and the smell of sickness everywhere. Outside its walls was a city. People raced through cold citadels of steel and glass, unaware that he'd settled over them like a smoky phantom.

Still he went farther. Out across the water. The waves rising and fall-ing as they danced to the moon's midnight orchestra. The business of life beneath continued despite his ghostly intrusion. Then across the land filled with trees and birds, cars and farmhouses.

Adam didn't know how far he now reached. Distance could no longer be fully measured by simple metrics of miles or feet. He now moved in another plane of existence. A dimension where time and space were only semblances of truth.

The energy of the life he'd encompassed was more powerful than any force he'd ever imagined. It was on the sprawling web that connected all life together that he finally rested. And with his rest, healing began.

* * *

The first round of consciousness came two days later, and for an instant, Adam wondered if he had died. An unlikely angel stared down at him, but in place of wings and halo were a split lip, bruised cheekbone, and swollen eye.

Adam blinked several times, trying to shake the delirium. The hospital room came into focus, and he began to understand where he was. He tried to sit up. Plastic intravenous tubes, an oxygen mask, and wires from electronic monitoring equipment all resisted him.

"Whoa, pal, take it easy," Agent Valin said, pushing him gently back to the bed. "You took one through the lung. It's going to take some time before you're ready to play football. How you survived at all is a goddamn miracle. Even the doctors say so."

Adam was confused. This was the man he'd fought in the corridor. The same man he'd smashed in the head, kicked in the bladder, and otherwise inflicted with great pain. Why was he acting as if they had just returned from a round of barhopping together?

Adam moved the breathing mask down to his chin. "Hey, man, sorry . . . about the . . ." His throat was too sore to continue. Evidently, whatever medical attention he'd received included the dragging of long strips of fine grit sandpaper up and down his windpipe.

"The name's Bart Valin, and don't sweat the bruises. You did what you had to. I haven't had my ass kicked in a good twenty years. It's nice to know someone can still humble a guy like me."

Adam only blinked trying to make sense of his words.

"Besides, you did it," Agent Valin continued. "You saved him. You saved Senator Shoemaker. You're a bona fide national hero."

"Hero?" Adam repeated hoarsely. He emitted a short but painfully wet cough. Tears leaked out the corners of both eyes.

"In fact, we're both heroes," the agent said as he carefully replaced the oxygen mask.

Adam looked up at him with wrinkled brows, now even more bewildered.

"I know . . . I know," the Secret Service agent said in a hushed voice. He looked around the otherwise empty room, as if to be certain he was still alone. "Just so you know. I gave it to them straight about what went down, but they didn't want to hear it. They concocted a bullshit story about us fighting side by side in a big shootout with four international terrorists. When I told them they were full of shit, they gave me direct orders to keep my mouth shut. Hell, I was even promoted to section chief. I know it's a bribe, but do you know how big a jump that is? I'm a chief. No more cherry assignments. No more Karen Parson."

Adam closed his eyes, trying desperately to comprehend what he was saying. Who was Karen Parson? Who concocted the story, and why? What terrorists? Why hadn't he mentioned the assassin?

"Hey, you can still spoil this thing. Personally, I don't think it's a good idea, but it's your call. I take my hat off to you. I don't know how you took all four out on your own, and I think you're due some major badass credit for it. But I guess I'm hoping you wouldn't mind sharing the spotlight. You'll have a friend for life. But, like I said, you call it as you need to. I'll back you either way. Orders be damned." The man squeezed Adam's shoulder.

Adam once again pulled his oxygen mask down. "Who gave the orders?" he choked.

"Huh?"

"Who told you to play along?" Adam's voice was barely a whisper, and even at that, each word caused him to wince.

Agent Valin again looked around the room. Leaning in close, he said, "Deputy director of the Secret Service. Do you understand what I'm telling you? The order came directly from him to me. No one in between. I've been reassigned to a new section. A fresh start. A thorough cover-up. You get what I'm saying?"

Adam waited for more. Things still didn't make sense.

After a moment of consideration, Agent Valin continued, "Look, I'm going to shoot straight with you. Follow my lead on this one. Keep your mouth shut, and take the credit they're willing to dish out. The alternative isn't pretty for either of us."

Adam stared into the agent's eyes, and for the first time he thought he saw a healthy dose of fear hidden in them.

* * *

The next time Adam woke, the room was dark. Agent Valin was gone, and only the beeping heart monitor now kept him company. He wasn't sure how many days it had been. All he knew for sure was that the wall clock read four, and the darkness outside his window indicated that it was nighttime.

He discovered a small paper cup of water beside his bed. He sat up and carefully drank several swallows. The water hurt going down, but it was bearable. He took several slow deep breaths. The urge for spastic coughing was gone. Overall, he was feeling better. With another day's rest, he thought he might be able to get up and walk around a bit.

The silence and darkness of the hospital room helped to clear his mind. Such moments of silence were rare, and he thought it a good time to consider the situation.

How did I come to be here? he wondered. No, that wasn't the right path. Starting from the beginning would likely lead him down a frustrating path of unknowns. He had to be more cautious in his reflection if there was any hope of drawing conclusions.

Where to start? he wondered. *Facts first. Then let those facts spill to conjecture. All right then, what are the facts?*

He'd been right about the assassin in the control room. The carefully cut hole in the glass, the rifle, and Agent Valin's comment about Shoemaker being unharmed, all confirmed the shooter was there to kill the senator. *Fine, so that much is known.*

There'd been a shoot-out with four men. Their identities were still unclear, but he understood their assignment. They were unquestionably there to kill the assassin. Since no one could have known Adam would be in the control room, he had to conclude he was just in the wrong place at the wrong time. Given their weapons and indiscriminate use of force, he didn't think they were FBI or Secret Service.

Who then? Agent Valin had referred to them as "international terrorists." Could that really be true? He doubted it. Killing political assassins didn't exactly fit with a terrorist agenda. Besides, he didn't see how four heavily armed terrorists could have gained access to a controlled area.

The authorities were denying any connection to the men, and that meant they fell under Adam's "if you shoot me, I shoot you," rule. No harm, no foul at having killed two of them.

The official denial didn't prove they weren't part of some agency, just that they'd become a liability. Trumped up charges of terrorism and four dead bodies could do wonders for the reputed competency of a law enforcement agency, especially in light of the recent assassinations. Terrorists were easy for the public to understand because the term collectively lumped together any and all bad guys willing to do extreme things to hurt the country and its citizens. In being so labeled, they could then be blamed both for the public assassinations and anything else that required a patsy.

But if the terrorist claim was untrue, it suggested that, for whatever reason, the men had been allowed access. That pointed to government involvement, whether it be a corrupt individual or an entire government organization. Once again, Lara's far-fetched assertions of conspiracies didn't seem so outlandish.

The bigger question is how could they have hoped to pull off the deception? It would require the cooperation of the investigating agencies. Admittedly, with a little doctoring, most of the evidence could be made to support it. The guns were there. A Beretta found in Adam's hand had killed two of the terrorists, and the Secret Service agent's gun had killed the others.

Also, there were no witnesses who could betray the truth other than Adam and Agent Valin. That meant the conspirators had to get both a private investigator and a Secret Service agent to go along with a charade.

Agent Valin had been given the proverbial carrot-and-stick, bribed with a promotion while simultaneously threatened with unspoken professional and perhaps personal harm. As for Adam, the same approach was basically in play. Go along with the concoction, and he would be made a hero. Go against it, and people would suffer. Agent Valin hadn't said the words, but he'd delivered the message loud and clear. Just as he had been supposed to do.

Why the cover-up? Agent Valin said he'd attempted to tell his superiors the truth, but they wouldn't hear it. So, either he was lying, or more likely, that the truth was irrelevant.

If the four men were government operatives, as Adam suspected they were, why had their agency disavowed them? The answers to both seemed to be the same. People in power wanted the general public to believe that the recent assassinations were the work of the four evildoers now lying dead.

The biggest problem with this scenario was that the real assassin hadn't been caught. What happened when another politician got his brains blown out at the next campaign stop?

But that wasn't going to happen, was it? Somehow the four "terrorists" were tied to the assassin. They knew where he would be. They knew when to show up. They were there to finish him just before, during, or possibly after the heinous act. And if they were there to finish him, it meant the assassin's job was complete.

Adam suspected that if the men had been successful in killing the assassin, along with a nosy private investigator with possible ties to terrorist organizations, they would have been hailed as patriotic agents of the U.S. government.

Two all-important facts floated to the surface. First was that the assassin and those sent to neutralize him were somehow connected. And second was that whoever handed the orders down to Agent Valin understood the threat to be over despite the missing sniper. To Adam, this led to only one logical conclusion. The deputy director of the Secret Service, the assassin, and the four terrorists were all sleeping in the same blood-stained bed. How else could it be explained?

That anyone had yet to question Adam about what happened in the control room was further proof of government involvement. In any other situation, a dozen Secret Service agents would be holding a pajama party in Adam's room, waiting for him to regain consciousness—perhaps even administering some smelling salts to speed the process.

In this case, however, the agency had sent only a single man, Agent Valin. His courtesy visit was only to allow Adam the opportunity to rediscover the truth. The implied message was that people who make noise during cover-ups conveniently disappear or die. A bullet wound through the lung could lead to complications . . .

Adam now came to the most puzzling question of them all. Why had the assassin not only spared but gone so far as to save his life? Only one possibility came to mind. The killer, or someone directing him, had a reason to want Adam alive. That led to one of two answers. Either Adam was to play an integral part in the conspiracy, or his life was spared for some personal reason.

Adam spent a great deal of the early morning hours weighing both possibilities. In the end, it wasn't the realization that he was entangled in a dangerous cover-up that disturbed him the most. It was the single final conclusion that he'd arrived at.

I know the assassin's identity.

* * *

Adam held lightly to Elliot's arm as he lowered himself into the wheelchair beside his bed. Having been hospitalized for nearly two weeks, he was desperate to get away from beeping machines, fluorescent lights, and crabby women in chalky white uniforms.

"I don't need this thing," he grumbled. "I'm fine."

"Hospital policy. You don't have a choice in the matter," Elliot said. "Everyone leaving the hospital has to be in a wheelchair. Liability reasons. If you think the gunfight was bad, try walking out of here under your own power."

Adam saw that one of Elliot's hands was wrapped in a thin white gauze bandage.

"What happened to you?"

Elliot looked at the bandage. "You weren't the only one wounded in battle. Can you believe that Dodson lady accidentally stabbed me with a steak knife when all the shooting broke out? I'm just glad she missed my heart." He chuckled.

Without further argument, Adam lifted his feet and placed them onto two metal flip-down footrests. As Elliot moved behind the wheelchair, the hospital room door unexpectedly swung open.

An elderly man in a dark suit and tan wool overcoat entered. Two male assistants followed closely behind.

Adam immediately recognized him as Senator Dick Shoemaker. Standing well over six feet and having broad shoulders and thick tree trunk legs, Shoemaker looked like a retired linebacker. His head was covered in a thick matting of combed gray hair that hadn't been entirely tamed.

"The men of the hour," the senator bellowed, extending a giant intensely warm hand first to Adam and then to Elliot. "How are you, Adam? You look fit enough to go out and save the world. Again." He smiled a jolly man's smile.

"I'm feeling much better, sir," Adam answered. Even though he wasn't sure he'd be ready for a round of *randori* with his Kenju class anytime soon, he did feel markedly better.

"I came here to personally thank you both," Shoemaker said. "Most especially you, Adam, for the injuries you received on my behalf. When a man willingly suffers for another, it forever sets him apart. I can't begin to describe just how much I appreciate what you've done."

"You're welcome," Adam said. He thought for a moment but found that he didn't really have anything else to say. He'd never met the senator and knew very little about him. He may have saved his life, but it was really the life of a complete stranger. "Thanks" and "you're welcome" seemed oddly sufficient.

Senator Shoemaker, however, had more to say. "I've been briefed on all that you and Agent Valin did, and I'm inspired by your courage and skill."

Then almost as an afterthought, said "Of course thanks are due to you too, Elliot. If it wasn't for the two of you working so hard to find these killers, I would surely be dead right now. As it was, the bullet only missed me by this much." The senator held up two fingers separated by a few inches. "Way too close for an old fool like me."

Adam had seen the television reports of the near miss a hundred times. Apparently his struggle with Agent Valin had been enough to cause the shooter to flinch. The bullet meant for Shoemaker had hit the podium only inches from his heart.

"My brother and I were glad to do it," Elliot said. "I've personally followed your career for quite some time, and I think this country would have suffered a terrible loss if anything had happened to you."

"Thank you for saying that. I'm glad to hear that I have at least one supporter. A man of connections no less." Much like Mr. Greene before him, the senator had apparently gathered background information before their meeting.

"I know a few people. On occasion, I've even thought of tossing my own hat into the political ring."

"Just don't say into the presidential race. I'm finally starting to see a rally in my numbers, and I'd hate to lose that newfound momentum to one of the men who saved my life." The senator was speaking with a friendly smile, and even his feigned concern came out as a compliment.

"Oh no, nothing that bold," Elliot said. "I was thinking of going for a position in the Senate."

"Wonderful," Shoemaker said, clapping his meaty palms together with a *pop* that caused patients in an adjacent room to jump. "You and I need to sit down and talk shop. There are lots of things to know, and lots of people to get to know. Who better to show you the ropes?"

Elliot's couldn't hide his excitement. "Really? I know you're a very busy man with the election coming up."

"I owe you and your brother a great deal, and this would be one small way to repay my debt. Please, I insist. One of my assistants will get in touch with you over the next week or so."

"Fantastic. I really appreciate it." Elliot beamed with an unshakable schoolboy's smile.

"What about you, Adam? What favor could I possibly do for you to show my appreciation? Name it. Anything at all."

Adam thought the senator spoke like the Wizard of Oz, offering to grant a single magical wish to all who came before him. In a sense, he might just be the Wizard. Senator Shoemaker was after all a powerful man with many connections. A man who could make unlikely things happen.

"All right," Adam answered, figuring he would put the almighty Wizard to the test. "Lara and Maria Sativa."

"Excuse me?" the senator said.

"A friend of ours was kidnapped while we were trying to stop the killers. Her name is Lara Sativa. She's from Denver but disappeared while we were in Las Vegas. I don't know if the terrorists grabbed her or if it was someone else." Given his suspicions, Adam couldn't take anything for granted. "Maria Sativa is her sister. She went missing a couple of weeks earlier in Denver. We believe both of the disappearances are related to the attempt on your life."

"I see," Senator Shoemaker said, turning to an aide. "Did you get all that?"

"Yes, sir. Lara Sativa, from Denver, disappeared in Las Vegas. Maria Sativa, sister, disappeared in Denver two weeks prior. Both related to this matter."

The senator turned back to Adam and knelt so that they were at the same level. Dick Shoemaker's face had become the face of a comforting, gray-haired grandfather. His eyes were as warm as his hands had been, and his expression showed a level of heartfelt compassion Adam had rarely seen.

"Listen to me, young man. I will do everything in my power to find these two young ladies. I will call in favors from people in the FBI, NSA, and CIA. If they're on this planet, we'll find them. I give you my word on that."

Adam nodded, a bit shaken up by the man's unexpected sincerity. He extended his hand. The senator engulfed it with his own huge paw.

"Thank you, sir. I need to find her," Adam said, not bothering to clarify which of the two missing girls was "her."

The senator placed his other hand on Adam's shoulder. "Believe me. They're as good as found."

* * *

"You going back to Denver with me or heading home?" Elliot asked as he settled into a reading chair and unfolded a newspaper. "I know you've been away longer than you originally anticipated. With your injury, I'll understand it if you want to go back home for some rest. Makes sense, really."

Adam sat on the bed in the hotel room, slowly unpacking a large, black duffel bag. When he came to the Glock and Browning firearms, he stopped unpacking and set both on his lap.

"We haven't accomplished anything," Adam said, his voice dry with bitterness.

Elliot looked up. "Come on, Adam," he said, clearly annoyed. "We tracked down a band of assassins and prevented the murder of a man who will likely be the next president of the United States. Not a bad week's work if you look at it that way. Besides that, our faces are being flashed across every media station from coast to coast. We're heroes, Adam. Imagine what that will do for us."

Elliot was on top of the world right now. The adventure had been had, his reward received. Oddly, in his basking, he seemed to have forgotten about those who had been lost along the journey.

"What about Maria? And Lara?" Adam asked, slowly unloading the bullets from the Glock.

Elliot shot a hurt look over at him. "Senator Shoemaker said he'd find them. I believe him. He certainly has a better chance than we do. I'm just praying they're all right. At this point, I don't see what else we can do for them."

"But they're not going to be okay. Are they, Elliot?" Adam didn't look at his brother. His eyes never left the handgun as he slowly worked the bullets from the top of the magazine. He didn't want a loaded gun in the room right now.

Elliot turned his full attention to him. "What does that mean?"

Adam finished with the Glock, tossed it aside on the bed, and began unloading the Browning.

"It was you in the control room. Wasn't it, Elliot?" Adam's voice was cold and soft, like freshly fallen snow.

"What are you talking about?"

"It was you the whole time. You were in the control room. You helped me kill those four men." Adam paused. "You are the assassin we've been chasing."

Elliot stood up, dropping the business paper he'd just opened. "Have you lost your mind?" He was growing angrier with each word.

The sharp tone didn't begin to shake Adam's resolve. He finished with the Browning, set it aside, and stood up.

Elliot looked at him with obvious hostility, but the anger soon turned to fear. "What's with you, Adam? This doesn't make sense."

"There are holes, I'll admit. Things I don't understand. But it basically adds up. You took care of Maria but needed my help finding the map." Adam began walking slowly toward Elliot.

"No . . . that's not true. I loved Maria."

"You were conveniently never around when the assassinations occurred. First with General Livingston, then with Greene, and finally with Shoemaker. Always MIA."

"Adam . . . no. You're wrong about this. Listen to me . . ." Elliot began to take small steps back.

"You made suspicious phone calls to keep your accomplices informed of where we'd be. That's how the guy with the syringe found me in Vegas. Were you really willing to have me killed, Elliot? Your own brother?"

Elliot's face went flush. "I did make a phone call, but it wasn't what—"

"You told me that you had friends in the FBI. Friends who would do anything for you. Friends who could cover things up."

Elliot opened his mouth to answer, but nothing came out.

"You have ties with the vice president, too. Ties that you lie about." He continued to advance, hands hanging loosely at his sides.

"Please, Adam. This is nuts."

"Strangely, only three of the four candidates had attempts on their lives. Guess who didn't? Your friend and coconspirator, Lucky Joe Marino. What was the plan, Elliot? Kill off his competition, leaving only one unelectable independent candidate and a few token replacements? And for what? A guaranteed seat in the Senate, perhaps?"

Elliot had reached the far wall and could retreat no farther. When he realized that he was trapped, he snatched up a small brass lamp and held it threateningly in front of him. "Stay away from me," he warned, his voice shaking.

"Things went a bit sour. You missed the target. But hey, don't worry about it. Everything's going to work out. You've positioned yourself in good with the very man you were trying to kill. It's all going to work out for you isn't it, big brother?"

"Stop it, Adam. Stop it!"

"What really happened to your hand? Did you take a grazing bullet?"

"Grazing . . ." Elliot could barely get the words out.

Adam moved to within striking distance, but neither man lashed out.

"I only want to know one thing," Adam said.

"What?" Elliot was white with fear.

"Where is she? Where's Lara? And so help me, if you've killed her, brother or not, I'll finish you right here."

Elliot started to cry. Not bawl, just weep the soft cry of a terrified child. "I don't know what you're talking about. God help me. I don't."

"You poisoned her, didn't you?" Adam said. "The wine in the casino lounge. You had it waiting for us. She was the only one to drink from the bottle. You wanted to take us out of the picture so we wouldn't get in the way of killing Greene. Then you came back ahead of me and grabbed her at the hotel. Or maybe some of your thugs were involved in the abduction. Was it Big John?"

"Listen," Elliot pleaded. "I swear to you. I don't know where Lara is. I don't know anything about the assassinations or any poisonous wine. I swear. Do you hear me?" He was shrieking now. "I don't know!"

Adam hesitated, his fists balled tightly. "I'm going to give you one chance. Come clean with me now, or so help me . . ."

Elliot bit nervously at his lower lip, and his tears abruptly stopped flowing. He swallowed hard.

"It's not anything like what you think," he said. "It's not."

"Fine. Then tell me what it is."

Chapter 18

October—Fifteen Years Earlier—Cambridge, MA

Elliot Reece turned the faded blue AMC Gremlin onto Paddington Avenue. He held up one hand and saw that it was trembling. Even his hands implicitly knew that tonight was going to be one of the greatest nights of his life.

It's too good to be true, he told himself. *Janice Marino and me. Just too good to be true.* But it was true, wasn't it? Hadn't he found the courage to ask her out only a few hours earlier? Unbelievably, hadn't she responded with a "sure" and a blue ribbon smile? Three long months of being "just friends" were about to end.

She's going on a date with me. Just a first date, sure . . . but I know we're going to hit it off. The daughter of a senator going out with an ordinary guy like me. I can't believe it! Janice and me . . . how perfect is that?

He pulled the car in front of Sewell Hall, one of the four female dorms that were part of a housing complex known on campus as "The Quad." Elliot turned off the engine and waited glassy-eyed for his new life to begin. His fingers tapped nervously against the vinyl-wrapped steering wheel as he stared intently at a rusty, white door lit only by a single street lamp out front. The door remained quiet and closed. He waited, only occasionally affording himself the luxury of a blink.

After what seemed like an eternity, Elliot used the glow of the dash to study his watch. The dial read 7:15. She was late.

"Where is she?" he asked, his voice tight with fear. Maybe she'd called her father to let him know she was going out with him. "Yeah, I bet that's it. She'll be out in a minute." His fingers began tapping faster.

By twenty-five past the hour, Elliot was nearly hyperventilating. His face was flushed red with embarrassment, and he was breathing in short, irregular spasms.

She's going to stand me up. Some big joke. Janice and her high-society friends are probably looking out the window right now laughing at me, the loser. He felt the tears beginning to well up as he scanned the long rows of windows for a parade of giggling girls in pajamas.

The white door suddenly swung open. Janice came rushing out, jacket and knapsack in hand.

Elliot choked out a loud, emotion-filled laugh. Quickly, he wiped both eyes, sucked in a huge breath of air, and tried to get his head back in the game. He watched Janice with utter joy as she ran up to his car.

She pulled at the door to the Gremlin, but it was locked and held fast.

"Oh no," he cried out. He'd carefully planned out how he was going to be a gentleman and open the door for her but had forgotten his manners in the tension of the moment. He leaned over and tore frantically at the lock. It released, and Janice Marino, complete with freshly rolled golden curls, glossy red lips, beautiful hazel eyes, and a short denim skirt, dropped into the car.

Elliot had to look away for a moment, her beauty and sweet smell simply too intimidating.

"I'm so sorry," she pleaded in a voice filled with sweet sincerity.

"Don't worry about it. I just got here a minute ago anyway," Elliot lied with a coolness that sounded like a disturbing mix of James Dean crossed with the Fonz.

"My father was on the phone and just wouldn't let me go. I finally had to pretend that I had to pee just to hang up. He made me promise to take his new cellular phone gadget with me," she said, patting the backpack. "Parents are such a pain sometimes."

On the phone with her dad . . . I knew it. Nothing to worry about. "Yeah, I know what you mean," Elliot replied, not sure he'd heard anything she'd just said. "I made us reservations at Tarte's Bistro, but we may be a bit late for it now. If they won't take us, we'll just find another place." He said it much more calmly than he felt. In reality, Elliot had no idea of another restaurant that would impress a girl like Janice. It had to be Tarte's. There was simply no alternative. He would beg. He would plead. He would get them into Tarte's.

Janice bit her lip for a moment then leaned toward Elliot. Her sweet, musky perfume immediately brought a tingling to his loins. "Would you mind if we skipped the restaurant? I'm not overly hungry, and besides, we're so late now."

Oh my God, she's canceling. She just came out here to call this off. Elliot felt a lump as large as a pregnant bullfrog swell in his throat. "No, that's cool," he croaked. "What, you want to go out another night then?" He was sure the answer was going to be some lame promise about how they'd go out and paint the town red.

"No way," she quickly answered. "Tonight is *our* night, Elliot. I wouldn't miss it for the world. I was just thinking maybe we could do something a bit more . . . romantic." She looked at him for a reaction.

Elliot swallowed the frog and nodded vigorously.

* * *

"I've got Schnapps," Janice said, pulling a small amber bottle from her knapsack.

Elliot glanced over at her as he turned onto Rural Route 17. Janice grinned at him mischievously and tore the seal on the unopened bottle. She twisted the cap off and took a long sip.

"It's peppermint. Try it," she said, offering him the bottle.

At this point, Janice could have offered him an old shoe to taste, and Elliot would gladly have begun chomping on the leather sole. He took the bottle and turned it up for a swig. The Schnapps burned a crisp peppermint taste down his throat.

"Not bad," he said. Like most college students, Elliot had done his fair share of drinking, although this was the first Schnapps he'd tasted. Usually, it was just beer or the occasional rum and coke. The Schnapps was sweeter than what he was used to.

Janice tossed her jacket into the back of the Gremlin and slid her denim-covered bottom around on the passenger seat. "Pretty comfortable," she said, winking at Elliot.

Elliot felt his heart flutter. *What does she mean by that? Is she suggesting something? Like maybe she wants us to make out in the car.*

Janice had been giving Elliot driving directions for the past twenty minutes, and they were now several miles from mainstream civilization. When he asked where they were headed, she would just say, "You'll see."

Janice took another long drink of the Schnapps before passing it back to Elliot. He swallowed deeply, the liquid burning like molten peppermint gold. She slid closer to him. He afforded himself a quick glance, the smell of her perfume swirling around him like some airborne aphrodisiac.

Unwilling to wait for Elliot to make a move, Janice gently pulled one of his hands from the steering wheel and placed it against her exposed thigh.

Oh God. Oh God. Oh God. He licked at his lips with the expectation one feels when about to eat a delicious slice of pie. Janice's leg was as smooth as creamy cocoa butter. Elliot's hand rested inside her upper thigh. He was too afraid to move it, too afraid to do something wrong. He let his fingers soak up her feminine softness.

Janice leaned close, her small breasts pressing into his shoulder. Then she brought her mouth next to his ear and breathed softly. "Like I said, tonight's our night."

Finding a manly courage that he never knew existed, Elliot moved his fingers. It was only a few millimeters, but still they stroked her tender flesh. She leaned her head against his shoulder and slid slightly forward in her seat, spreading her legs a little. His heart felt as if it might explode. *That's my luck,* he thought, *I'm going to die before I can touch her . . . there.*

He inhaled a deep breath then forced it out. Feeling some of the nervous tension pass, his fingers stroked further. Janice offered no protest. Instead, she opened her legs an inch or two further. He felt his fingers brush against the soft silk of her panties.

Fear now having been replaced by raw lust, he continued his advance. The tips of his finger now rested firmly against her panties. Stroking ever so gently, he felt the soft, silk-covered pubic hairs underneath. She inched her legs open further, still not saying anything, just leaning against him.

His heart pounding like a three-year-old with his first drum set, Elliot slid his fingers down the outside of her panties. The thin silk had become wet and slippery. The lust was so intense that Elliot could barely see the dark country road ahead of him. No traffic passed in either direction. It was just the two of them.

He pressed and stroked against her wet panties. Janice moaned softly. Elliot stopped his motion for a moment but dared not move his hand.

He glanced down at Janice in pure fascination. Her eyes were closed, her mouth slightly open. This was his doing.

"Don't stop," she whispered.

Even in his wildest dreams, he could never have imagined what was happening. Janice Marino had just said "don't stop." She wanted him.

He pressed and slid with renewed vigor like a chef working up some fantastic dessert. Up and down, round and round. Janice moaned again, pressing her pelvis against his probing fingers. Elliot felt the panties growing wetter as she soaked the sheer fabric. He could barely breathe. He smiled and closed his eyes, imagining what he knew was coming next.

The windshield violently blasted inward, the glass becoming a blanket of a thousand sparkling splinters. Janice began to scream.

Elliot opened his eyes, confused and delirious with heated pleasure. A bloody face stared at him through the shattered windshield.

"Aagh!" he yelled, stomping the brakes. The body slid forward off the hood, rolling twenty feet in front of the car.

"What was that?" Janice screamed, sitting upright. Seeing the crumpled figure in the road ahead, she covered her mouth, saying, "Elliot . . . Elliot, we hit someone."

Hit someone? What? What is she talking about? We were touching. She felt so nice. What's happening? Elliot's body suddenly jerked with a strange involuntary spasm.

"I was just driving. The road was empty," he said with a trembling voice. He held wet fingers out in front of him, not sure of what to do with them.

"We hit someone," she repeated, her voice just as shaky as his.

"I didn't see him," he offered weakly, still putting together the horrific puzzle.

Janice squeezed his arm tightly, as if trying to communicate something she couldn't put to words.

When Elliot looked at her, he realized she was even more terrified than he was. Strangely, that gave him strength. He opened the car door and cool night air rushed in. He hadn't realized how hot the car had been, and now the night felt damp and cold.

"Don't go out there," she pleaded, refusing to let go of his arm.

"I have to," he said, gently pulling away. "He might be hurt." *That's it. He's hurt. We can get him to a hospital, and everything will be okay. Accidents happen. Everything can still work out. Janice and I can still go somewhere and . . . finish.*

Elliot stepped out of the car but left the door standing open. The small road was shadowed by a canopy of tall trees on both sides. He could barely make out the lump lying ahead in the road. It was buckled back on itself and didn't look human at all. The image of a snarling, bloody-fanged werewolf came to mind. Elliot felt fear crawl over him. He clenched his teeth and pressed ahead.

As Elliot got closer, he could see that the body was that of a young man. He was wearing a red-and-white reflective jogging suit and had a small safety light attached to his ankle. The youth's legs were twisted awkwardly underneath him, and his face was turned into to the pavement.

Elliot was afraid to move any closer. He waited, rubbing a hand across his forehead that was now damp with sweat. He watched the body, hoping to see something that might indicate he was still alive. But there was no cry for help, no agonizing squirm to right itself.

"I have to do this," he said to himself as convincingly as he could.

Elliot moved up closer and knelt beside him. He reached out with a wavering hand, paused a moment, then touched the young man's shoulder.

"Hey, you okay?" he asked.

No response.

In one brave motion, Elliot reached out and rolled him over.

He was a young Asian man about Elliot's age. His only noticeable wounds were a hideous black bruise on his forehead and one bulbous eye with a small line of blood trickling out the side. Both eyes were open, staring blankly at the salvation of the night sky. Elliot understood immediately that he was dead.

Part of him screamed to get up and run, run as fast and as far as he could. Get away from this horror. Get away from Janice. Get away from it all. Get home to where he could crawl into bed and pull the blanket tightly over his head. But Elliot's legs refused to move. Instead they held him there, forcing him to stare numbly at the face of the dead boy.

After what must have been a long time, Elliot said, "I'm so sorry." *The booze . . . Janice . . . what we were doing . . . it was my fault. It was my fault.*

"Elliot!" Janice called from behind him in a harsh whisper. "Elliot!"

He turned to see her ghostly outline standing just in front of the bright headlights. She looked like a bodiless wraith, watching from a distance, waiting to move in and claim its prize.

"I called my father. He's sending someone to help." Her voice turned softer. "Come back here, please. I'm cold."

He sighed, blinked away pressing tears and returned to the car.

* * *

Thirty minutes later, a white Cadillac pulled up behind Elliot's Gremlin on the deserted county road. The headlights flicked off, but the orange parking lights remained lit.

Elliot and Janice looked through the wide, flat back window of the Gremlin as a single figure emerged from the sedan. Both exchanged nervous glances, but neither of them spoke as he slowly approached their car.

Tap, tap. The man rapped his ring on the driver's side window. Elliot saw a large, but impeccably dressed, middle-aged black man staring in at him. Unsure of what else to do, he rolled down the window.

The man quietly surveyed the two of them, finally focusing on Janice.

"Are you okay, young lady?" he asked in a voice deep enough to sing bass in a prison yard quartet.

"Yes . . . yes, I'm fine," she stammered. "Did my father send you?"

Elliot noticed that her entire body was shaking.

"He did," he answered, but offered no more as he studied the inside of the car. "The two of you been drinking?" He stared down at the half-empty liquor bottle lying between them on the seat.

Feeling he should come to Janice's aid, Elliot said, "It was my fault. I should have—"

The man raised a single enormous finger to his lips in a hushing motion.

Elliot immediately closed his mouth.

"I asked if you've been drinking, young lady."

Janice swallowed hard, and her eyes began to water. "Yes, sir."

The man closed his eyes for a minute, and Elliot suddenly became inexplicably afraid. Afraid for his very life. After a moment of consideration, the black man reopened his enormous white eyes. His stare was so intimidating that both Janice and Elliot looked to their laps.

"Hand it here," his voice resonated.

Not waiting for Janice to react, Elliot snatched up the bottle and passed it through the open window. The man stuck the bottle inside his jacket pocket.

"Is that it?" the dark stranger asked.

Unsure if he was allowed to speak yet, Elliot remained silent.

"Yes, sir. That's all," she answered without looking up.

The man nodded. "Get out of the car, boy."

Elliot's eyes grew wide, and his heart began pounding violently in his chest. *He's going to kill me.* He felt his eyes tear up, this time with pure concentrated fear.

"You made this mess, and you're going to help clean it up," the man added as he turned away and walked back to his car.

Help clean it up? What kind of help can he possibly want from me? Elliot was engulfed in a strange mix of terror and confusion. He looked to Janice, who only shrugged in matching frightened uncertainty.

Elliot opened the car door, and this time, Janice didn't try to stop him. If he was going to get killed, she had apparently surrendered to letting him face his fate alone. It had come down to every adolescent for him or herself.

Elliot began walking toward the stranger's car. Before he reached the Cadillac, however, the man was already returning his direction. He carried a huge rolled-up shape draped long ways over one shoulder. In the darkness, Elliot couldn't tell what it was.

As they neared each other, he was able to discern that it was a large rolled-up carpet. Without having to ask, he suddenly understood what was happening.

The man gestured with a hand now covered in a yellow surgical glove. Elliot followed silently as they moved toward the body lying in the center of the road.

The stranger tossed the carpet to the ground a few feet from the dead boy. He moved close to the boy and squatted beside him. After a moment of inspection, the man stood and kicked the carpet. It rolled lazily open. Elliot wasn't sure in the glow of the headlights, but he thought he could make out large splotchy bloodstains covering the inside of the carpet. As impossible as it seemed, the stranger had done this sort of cleanup before.

"Grab his feet," the man directed.

"Listen, sir, I . . . I don't think I can do this," Elliot pleaded.

The dark stranger looked directly at him, and Elliot felt his legs buckle. Tears welled up in his eyes and slowly began to drip down his flushed face.

"Grab his feet," he repeated.

It occurred to Elliot this was the last time he would ask. Elliot nodded and moved to the boy's feet.

The black man grabbed the young boy under his shoulders and hoisted his upper torso into the air. Taking his cue, Elliot fumbled with the feet until they too were off the ground. Together they shuffled the young man over to the carpet and dropped him indignantly. The sound of his body plopping onto the carpet brought vomit into Elliot's throat. He swallowed it back. Tears still flowed freely down his face.

The stranger moved to one end of the carpet and began rolling up the young man inside. He didn't ask for help, and Elliot didn't have the stomach to volunteer. Within a few seconds, the young man had become nothing more than a bulge in an old stained rug.

"Give me a hand with this," he directed.

Not making the man ask twice, Elliot moved to one end of the carpet, grabbed the heavy corded trim with both hands, and lifted. He was surprised at how heavy the boy and carpet combination had become.

Hanging on with all his strength, Elliot shuffled ahead as they carried it to the man's waiting car. Elliot saw that the trunk was still open. The man tossed one end of the carpet deep into the trunk. Then with one solid push, he shoved the remaining rug in. He didn't, however, close the lid.

Elliot turned to head back toward his own vehicle when he suddenly felt a soft tug at his shirtsleeve. The man's grip was gentle, like that of a woman holding her lover's hand.

He froze, turning only his head to look at the stranger's face. Huge white eyes with tiny black pupils bore into him. For a moment, Elliot thought he might wet himself. This man was deciding his fate. It wasn't Elliot's imagination. Death was close at hand.

After a moment, the man rumbled, "My wife and I were out for dinner. It's our anniversary tonight. Twenty-four long, happy years."

"I'm . . . I'm sorry," Elliot said, glancing into the car. Inside, he saw a beautiful middle-aged black woman looking into a small vanity mirror as she touched up her makeup.

The stranger nodded his head. "You know, I believe you are." He released Elliot and slid a long white silk scarf from his shoulders. As he spoke, he used the scarf to slowly wipe a few drops of blood off the surgical gloves covering his hands.

"We had a nice dinner planned. I was even going to take her to a play. Me, I don't care much for that sort of thing. But my wife, she loves a good play."

The man began winding the now-bloodstained scarf tightly around one hand.

"In my experience," he continued, "there are really only two kinds of people in this world. Those who learn from their mistakes, and those who don't. The question is, which one are you?"

Elliot's eyes never left the bloody scarf. "I . . . uh . . . I'm sorry." It had worked a moment ago, and it was all he could come up with.

"If I ever see you again, it will mean that you're one of those people who can't stop making mistakes." He paused for a moment to tug at the scarf, checking to see how well it was wrapped around his hand. "You know that you don't want to see me again. You do know that, don't you?"

"Yes, sir. I know that." And he did with all his heart.

"Despite my better judgment, I'm going to give you a chance to prove yourself. If you're a smart young man, you'll go home and forget this ever happened. If you're not, well . . ." He didn't need to finish his sentence. Elliot understood the message loud and clear.

The man slowly unwrapped the scarf from his hand. "Here's what you do. Drive Miss Marino back to her dorm. Don't so much as go over the speed limit. Then turn right around and get yourself home. No stops along the way. When you get home, don't call your mother, your friends, or anyone else. This is your mess, so deal with it. You understand?"

"Yes, sir. No stops. No phone calls. My mess." Elliot turned to leave.

"One more thing."

"Sir?" Elliot reluctantly turned back to face him again.

The man moved closer, and for a moment, Elliot was sure he was going to get slugged, or worse. Instead of striking him, though, the stranger reached up and draped the white, bloodstained scarf around Elliot's neck.

"Take this with you."

"Sir?" Elliot couldn't fathom a reason for the morbid gift.

"Just in case you ever need to be reminded of what I said tonight."

Elliot nodded, now understanding that the scarf was not a gift. It was a threat.

Waiting only a moment to be sure the man was finished, Elliot turned and walked briskly to the Gremlin. He dropped himself onto the cold vinyl seat, his face stained with tears, his heart pounding, the bloody silk scarf dangling from his neck.

"Is it over?" Janice's voice was shaking.

He stared ahead into the darkness, saying nothing.

"Elliot?" She touched his arm.

He looked at her. "Yeah," he lied. "It's going to be okay."

* * *

Elliot woke the next morning with an aching pain in the center of his chest. He pressed hard against his sternum. For a brief moment, he couldn't remember why he felt so terrible. Then, in a flood, the terrible images of the previous night washed over him. A familiar numbing sadness returned, but he found that he no longer had tears to shed. An unshakable, all-encompassing feeling of dread filled his soul.

I killed him. Then . . . then rolled him in a carpet to be disposed of . . . like a piece of garbage. He closed his eyes tightly.

It all seemed like a terrible nightmare, and for one brief moment of insanity, Elliot thought that if he believed hard enough, it could actually become a dream. He opened his eyes to see if it would hold. Reality was not to be escaped. It was no dream. Methodically, he began to retrace every detail of the previous night, hoping that with his dissection he could find some relief.

The phone rang.

He sat up quickly and stared at the phone beside his bed. His heart began racing. *Who was it? Was it related to the accident? Was it the police?* Fear ripped at him like the talons of a giant bird of prey.

A second ring.

Then, in a moment of uncanny premonition, he knew exactly who it was. He picked up the phone and put it to his ear.

"Hello, Janice."

"Elliot . . . uh, yeah, it's me. Hey, we have to talk. My father wants to sit down with us both. He flew in this morning just for this. Can you meet us?" Her voice was forced, but in it, he heard a kind of pleading. She wanted this to go away just as much as he did.

"Sure. Where and when?" The thought of meeting a powerful senator like Joe Marino brought new tension to Elliot. The image of what he and Janice were doing last night was enough to stir up a new swarm of angry butterflies. *What if he knows about my touching her? Would Janice have told him? Did the big black man tell him what he suspected? What will Marino do if he does know?*

"Great. We'll come by and pick you up. Say in about forty-five minutes?"

Elliot looked at the clock. To his surprise, he saw that it was a few minutes past noon.

"Yeah, that's fine," he said. "Hey, Janice . . ."

"Yes, Elliot?"

"I'm really sorry about all this."

"Yeah, me too. It was as much my fault as yours." Her voice was strained with embarrassment.

Elliot felt a profound respect for Janice. She could easily have pointed the finger while hiding behind her daddy.

"I love you." Elliot did a double take after the words came out of his mouth. *Where did that come from? Why did I say it? Is it even true?*

She didn't answer.

Maybe she didn't hear it. Maybe I didn't even say it. He fought frantically to deal with what he'd just done.

"Sorry about that," he offered. "I'm just a bit shaken up, that's all. My nerves are shot."

"I know. Mine too," she said. "See you in a little while then?"

"Sure. I'll wait for you out front."

Elliot hung up the phone still baffled by what he'd just done.

* * *

The limousine pulled up to the curb looking like a yacht easing into its slip. With his head hung low, Elliot climbed aboard the huge black vessel.

Inside, were two long bench seats facing one another. Janice and her father sat on one side. Elliot took his designated position opposite them, his back against a thick soundproof window separating passengers from driver.

Senator Marino was a striking man one did not forget meeting. His head was cleanly shaven, and he sported a thick black mustache. As if chiseled in granite, his features exuded an air of rugged permanence.

The senator extended a hand. Elliot felt thick calluses lining the man's palm as he shook it.

"Good to meet you," Marino said. "I'm sorry it has to be under such difficult circumstances."

Elliot was stunned. Why was Senator Marino apologizing? Elliot hadn't known what to expect, but he had been sure it would be somewhere between the worst—an immediate punch in the stomach—and the best—a berating lecture on responsibility. To have Janice's father apologize to him after he'd killed a young jogger while fondling his daughter fell in the realm of drug-induced fantasy. Elliot was more than happy to walk among purple dragons for as long as they circled overhead.

"Nice to meet you too, sir," he said in a voice squeakier than he would have liked. The senator seemed like a man's man, and Elliot had always felt a bit insecure about his masculinity. He squeezed the senator's hand with as much juice as he could muster.

"My daughter told me all about you this morning." Marino brushed his hand gently against the back of Janice's golden hair. "She thinks the world of you, young man."

Elliot looked to Janice who was smiling at him. She wanted him to be comfortable with her father, and for that, he was grateful. His inexplicable declaration of love returned to overshadow any comfort her eyes offered.

"She says you're probably the smartest student at Harvard," Marino continued.

"That's not true," Elliot said, flushing. "I . . . I mean I hold my own with the top students, but there are lots of talented people here. I do okay."

"I'm sure you do. Well, son, you know why I'm here." The senator waited for a reaction from him.

"Yes, sir."

"And I imagine you didn't sleep too well last night. Lots of worry, perhaps a healthy dose of regret and guilt."

Actually Elliot had slept as if he'd been tossed in a grave, but the senator's point was still valid. He nodded his head.

"Now I want you to listen very carefully to me," Senator Marino said.

Elliot looked to his lap, knowing admonishment was finally coming. When the senator didn't continue, he looked up confused.

Senator Marino pointed with spread fingers to his own eyes. "Look here. It's important we communicate man to man on this."

He stared at the senator's eyes, forcing himself not to look away.

Marino's bushy mustache turned up in a satisfied smile. "What happened last night was an accident, pure and simple. Two young people out for an innocent drive in the country, not meaning anyone any harm. You could never have suspected someone would be irresponsible enough to be out in the dark like that, running in the middle of the road. Hell, it was as much his fault as anyone's. If it hadn't been you, it would have been someone else. The young man's carelessness led to this tragic accident. Not anything you or my daughter did."

Elliot thought of the reflective strips on the young man's jogging suit, the flashlight on his ankle. He mentioned neither.

"There is no reason something like this should ruin a promising young man. There's a lot in store for you, Elliot Reece. I can feel it in my bones. Don't let this little thing set you back. You understand me, son?"

"Yes, sir. I just feel terrible about what happened." Elliot felt his voice begin to crack but held it in check. He wasn't about to lose it in front of Janice and her father. No way.

The senator leaned forward and grabbed Elliot by the shoulder. He squeezed hard enough for it to hurt. "I know you do. Hell, anyone would. All I'm saying is this ends right here, right now. To take it any further would just hurt you and my little girl. You don't want to hurt my daughter, do you?"

Elliot shook his head. He understood what the senator was mandating. For both his and Janice's sake, this was a secret that could never be revealed. It was clear the senator wanted to be absolutely certain that Elliot understood what was expected of him.

"I understand. I won't ever speak of it to anyone," Elliot said. "You have my word."

Senator Marino sat back in his seat. "Your word is all I came for, Elliot. Now I see why my daughter thinks so much of you. You are a very bright young man."

* * *

Two days later, as part of Elliot's Monday morning ritual, he grabbed the school newspaper, the *Harvard Gazette*, and settled onto one of the many wooden study benches in Langdell Hall. He saw from his watch that he had fifteen minutes until class started.

I have to return to normal. Read the paper, study for classes, go about my life. It will all get better soon. I just have to . . . forget.

He looked about the hall and began to actually believe what he'd been repeating to himself for the past couple of days. The brick floor had recently been swept and mopped, and in that, Elliot found a twisted ray of hope. Life was continuing. Floors were being cleaned. People were going about their duties, and that was exactly what he was going to do as well.

Elliot unfolded the newspaper and immediately understood that life would never be the same. He stared with disbelief at the front page of the *Gazette*. There it was in black and white, his sin.

Gifted Asian Student Takes Own Life

Harvard Law School mourns the loss of one of its most promising new students, 21-year-old Jiro Tanaka. Mr. Tanaka committed suicide at around 1:00 a.m., Saturday morning. An unnamed witness reported seeing him acting very strangely just prior to going up to the catwalk at the top of the student center. A few minutes later, several people say they saw him plunge to his death. Campus police report that illegal substances were found on Tanaka's body, but a full autopsy has not been allowed due to the family's religious beliefs. Jiro Tanaka is survived by his parents as well as his younger sister, Saori, all of whom reside in Japan.

Elliot didn't want to read the article, but he forced himself to slowly chew one agonizing word after another. As he finished, the extent of his evil had become clear to him. Not only had he negligently killed an innocent young man in the prime of his life, but he'd been part of a cover-up that would forever scar the lives of the boy's entire family.

Elliot crumpled the paper. His face burned as he struggled for a breath of fresh air—something pure enough to stifle the evil bubbling within him. He stood, looking to the doors leading outside. He knew he wasn't going to make it. Not knowing what else to do, he held out his hands trying to catch the warm vomit as it spilled out onto the freshly cleaned brick floor.

Chapter 19

"That's it?" Adam asked with disbelief.

"My God, isn't that enough? I killed someone. No, I did worse than kill him. I . . . I . . ." Elliot stopped to take in a couple of deep breaths.

"What about your phone call from the gas station on the way to Vegas?"

"That was to Fred Walker," he choked out. "The friend I told you about in the FBI. I contacted him before we'd even left Denver. Once Mr. Greene was killed, he wanted us to come in. I was keeping him involved despite Lara's objection."

The words came out too quickly to be lies.

Despite Adam's fresh revulsion for his brother, he felt an overwhelming sense of relief. Given enough leeway, Elliot would surely mutate into a selfish, egocentric despot, but he would never become a murderer. The incident that happened on that dark county road near Harvard confirmed as much. Elliot just didn't have the stomach for death.

Yes, his brother was a manipulating jerk, but no, he wasn't a cold-blooded killer. And when it came to family, Adam had always believed you take what you can get.

He reached forward and gently took the lamp from Elliot, placing it on the table. "Come on, bro, let's talk."

Holding onto his brother's arm, Adam led Elliot to a pair of nearby chairs as one might lead an elderly parent to the toilet. Elliot was near tears but seemed to be keeping it in check. It was time for Adam to do a bit of fence-mending. His brother had revealed a secret he'd held inside for a very long time, and it seemed an ideal opportunity to help free him of the burden once and for all.

"What happened after Senator Marino came to see you?" Adam asked. "Did you and Janice continue to see each other?"

"No. I saw her around school, but we never went out again. I don't know why exactly. I just couldn't bring myself to call her. Every time I was around her, it brought back that terrible night. It was too much for me to handle. I never spoke with her about it, but I think she felt the same way."

"That's why you defend the senator? You somehow feel indebted to him for what he did?"

"Wouldn't you? I mean, I know what he did was terrible, but he also saved me that night. I might have ended up in prison. Even if not, my life would surely have been ruined."

"Not complete and full of joy like it is now," said Adam.

Elliot sighed, unable to offer a fight.

Adam took a seat opposite him. "I have something to tell you, and it's going to be hard to hear."

Elliot looked up interested. "What? I'm not the assassin if that is what you're thinking. You're just wrong. You can do whatever you want, but you're just wrong."

"I know that now, and I'm sorry. Circumstantial things . . . ah hell, it doesn't matter. No, this is about what happened that night. You want to hear it?"

"Of course."

"Okay, here goes. Lucky Joe played you, big brother."

"What the hell does that mean?" Elliot snapped.

"Hear me out. Marino didn't give a damn what happened to some young punk fingering his daughter. He just didn't want himself or his precious little princess implicated in the mess. He couldn't afford for you to create a scandal. Remember, it wasn't too many years after that when he ran for vice president. So he threw you a few compliments along with a few threats."

Elliot seemed distant in thought. "It's not like I had any choice anyway." His words held no conviction.

"I'm not going to sugarcoat it because I think you need to hear it straight. You killed that boy. No one else. You. Any way you slice it, you'll forever be responsible for his death."

"Thanks. I feel better now."

"There's more. What you did by going along with the suicide was far worse than the accident. You ruined the memory of that boy. To a Japanese family, suicide means disgrace. Such dishonor is not something you or I can fully understand. Honor of a family's name is as sacred as the most holy religious belief a Westerner might have. Do you understand what I'm saying?"

Elliot was looking at his hands, nervously twisting his fingers. "Unfortunately, I do."

"Maybe you already knew this, and that's why it's ruined you the way it has."

"Ruined me? What are you talking about?" Elliot said, his voice hard. "I'm a partner in a multimillion-dollar law firm. I draw over seven figures a year. I wouldn't call that ruined." His eyes flared angrily but quickly lost their fire.

"Whether you can see it or not, you're a broken man," Adam said. "You have been for years now. I never knew why. To be honest, I figured you'd just turned into a rich asshole. Now I know it's more than that."

Both men sat silent.

Finally, Elliot spoke. "It does haunt me you know. When I sleep, I see his face. That bloody face peering at me through the windshield. Sometimes his mouth is moving like if he's trying to tell me something." Elliot's voice broke with his words. "I don't think I'll ever be free of him."

Adam put his hand on Elliot's shoulder. "There's an old Chinese saying. It translates into something like 'You can't escape your shadow.' The curse from that night is *your* shadow. It's with you today, and it will be with you tomorrow. It's about time to make nice with it, don't you think?"

Adam was confident Elliot would belittle the wisdom, but to his surprise, he didn't. Instead, his brother nodded. "Past time."

"I don't know how you're going to come to terms with this. That's something you'll have to work out yourself. What I do know is that you need to do something. If you let this memory continue to haunt you, I'm afraid you'll die a miserable man. I don't want that to happen to my only brother."

"Believe me. I've asked myself a thousand times how I can fix this. Each time, I come up blank. The boy is dead. His memory disgraced. It can't be undone."

"It's true his death can't be undone, but perhaps the real sin can be."

Elliot looked at Adam confused. Then his eyes suddenly came alive as he finally understood what he must do. Before he could put words to his realization, his cell phone chirped loudly.

They looked at each other with an irrational nervousness. The call could be from any number of people, but as if experiencing a shared premonition, both men seemed to know it was something important. Elliot clicked on the phone and put it to his ear.

"Hello." After a few seconds of listening, he said, "Yes, yes, I have it. Thank you."

He hung up the phone and turned back to Adam, his face betraying his excitement.

"What?" Adam asked.

"It was Senator Shoemaker. He's found them."

* * *

Pecos Bill: Howdy, partner. Long time, no see.

Bulls-eye: I didn't appreciate the little stunt your hired guns tried to pull.

Pecos Bill: I heard about the bandits who tried to spoil your rodeo. Wasn't my doing, though.

Bulls-eye: They were yours, all right. I could smell your cowboy stink on them. I'm just wondering if I should be expecting another visit now that the job is finished.

Pecos Bill: I think we're done roping here, except for maybe that mean hombre that helped you out.

Bulls-eye: No. Stay away from him.

Pecos Bill: Aren't you just the top ranch hand today.

Bulls-eye: Don't do it. I'm asking nice.

Pecos Bill: I can understand why that fellow's important to you, but he could make trouble for old Pecos Bill.

Bulls-eye: He won't. Besides, he's still an asset. He can put the final nail in the coffin.

Pecos Bill: I get your meaning, partner, but who's going be sure he puts the nail in the right coffin?

Bulls-eye: Yours truly.

Pecos Bill: Fine. You get your way this time. Just don't worry this old cowhand. You get me?

Bulls-eye: I get you.

Pecos Bill: Is there more?

Bulls-eye: After this, I'm out for awhile. I need some R&R.

Pecos Bill: Good idea. Take some time to get your legs back under you. Just remember there's always another rodeo 'round the corner. Don't disappear on me now. I'd hate to have to send a posse out after you . . . or that fellow.

* * *

"Them?" Adam was astonished. Despite possessing what he considered an optimistic soul by nature, he had lost all hope that Maria could still be alive. Lara maybe, but Maria, that just didn't seem possible.

"That's what the senator said. You remember that detective listed in the Denver newspaper article? Shoemaker said we should contact him. Evidently Detective Carter has the two women or at least knows where they're at."

Adam shook his head, confused. "Why wouldn't Lara have contacted me? Or Maria, you? There's something not right about this."

A smile slowly crept over Elliot's face. "Right or not, he found them. Both of them. Just like he promised."

Adam couldn't share in the enthusiasm. Things didn't add up. "So he says."

"Look, I've got the detective's number," Elliot said, showing him the piece of paper he'd scribbled it on. "Do you want the honor or shall I?"

"Would you mind if I made the call?" Adam wanted to hear it for himself.

"Not at all." Elliot handed him the cell phone.

Adam clicked on the phone and dialed the one man who could resolve everything, Detective Carter of the Denver Police Department.

* * *

Detective Charles Carter massaged his temples. His head was pounding with the unrelenting cadence of a high school marching band. It was what he called a "perp headache."

"Let me get this right, Ms. . . . . Tiffany Duboise," he said, searching her rap sheet for a name. "You stabbed your long-time friend to death because you think she might have stolen your lighter. Do I have that much right?"

A black woman in her early twenties wearing a leopard print spandex leotard and a red tube top that barely covered her enormous cleavage shifted in the metal interrogation chair. A pack of opened cigarettes, a tinfoil ashtray, and a Styrofoam cup of lukewarm water sat in front of her.

At the end of a long drag, she said, "I don't *think* she stole it. I *know* that bitch stole it." As she spoke, white smoke billowed out of her mouth and nose like the belch of a fire-breathing dragon. Her words seemed to take shape in the puffs of thick smoke.

"You stabbed her fourteen times with a steak knife for taking your lighter?" Detective Carter glanced at the recording machine to be sure it was still on.

"I don't know how many times I stabbed that whore. She quit moving after a couple pokes." Tiffany crushed out the cigarette and immediately pulled another from the pack. Might as well enjoy the free smokes.

Detective Carter didn't want to know the answer but had to ask it anyway. "Then why did you continue stabbing her? If she was already dead, why keep on?"

"Simple," Tiffany snapped. "Respect. You know, like Aretha sings." She started to belt out the familiar chorus, her head bobbing left and right as she found her groove.

The detective raised his eyebrows in a mixture of surprise and disgust. "Would you mind explaining that to a dumb flatfoot like me?"

Tiffany tugged one strap of her bra, and then used a long gold-painted fingernail to pull what looked like a pubic hair from between her teeth. "You've never lived on the streets, have you Mr. Policeman?"

Carter didn't answer.

"Didn't think so. See, if you had, you'd know you can't let someone disrespect you. If you let one person dis you, everyone else feels like they can fuck you, too. Before long, bitches are moving in on your turf, johns are trying for freebies, and your pimp is beating the shit out of you just for fun. The street's about respect. If they learn you don't take no shit, they watch their step around you."

Tiffany took another long drag on the fresh cigarette and blew a long puff in the detective's direction. She smiled a big yellow-toothed smile. "This showed people they have to respect Ms. Tiffany."

Carter shook his head and glanced at his wristwatch. After a moment, he looked over to a large one-way mirror on one wall of the interrogation room. "I think we have enough. Can I get the hell out of here?"

Within seconds, the door to the interrogation room opened. A man wearing freshly pressed slacks, a white shirt, and a black tie nodded to Carter. "You're done, Detective. Appreciate it, Charlie. John will come up and take her back down to holding."

Charlie Carter left the interrogation room and headed directly for the sanctity of his office. Seeing the piles of folders, photographs, and an assortment of snack-food wrappers burying his desk immediately raised his spirits. *Home, sweet home.* He plopped down in his wooden swivel chair just as the phone rang.

He snatched up the receiver. "Carter."

An unfamiliar man's voice said, "Yes, hi, my name's Adam Reece. I was told you might have some information regarding Lara and Maria Sativa."

Detective Carter's faced turned up in a cynical smile. Whoever this guy was, he had pull. Real make-or-break-your-career kind of pull. Earlier in the day, Carter had received a call from the mayor himself. For some reason, the mayor of this fine smog-covered city was inquiring about the disappearance of a couple high-class hookers.

Carter had sure gotten the "atta boys" when he'd told the mayor he'd found both Maria and her sister just the day before. The mayor was in such a hurry he hadn't even bothered asking how or where he'd found them. And since the mayor hadn't asked, Carter hadn't bothered to volunteer. No reason to spoil his moment in the spotlight. Who knows, the mayor might even write a letter of commendation or some other such nonsense.

"That's right. I found them," he said.

"Do you mind if I ask when?" The voice sounded unsure, as if he thought there might be some case of mistaken identity.

"Don't mind a bit. It was yesterday evening. Found them on an anonymous tip. And if you're thinking I might be mistaken about who they are, you're wrong. It's them all right."

"I see. Do you think you could give me a number or some way to contact them?"

"Hmm. That probably wouldn't work."

"I know it's not standard procedure to give out personal information like that, but this is important. I'm a close friend of Lara's, and I really need to find her. If you know how I can reach either one of them, please tell me."

Carter sensed urgency in the man's voice. This guy cared about these girls. Really cared. He felt a long sour burrito burp come up from his belly. Being the bearer of bad news never sat well with his digestive system.

"All I'm saying is that a phone number won't do you any good. I hate to be the one to break it to you, mister, but they're dead."

"No," the man whispered.

"Afraid so," Carter confirmed. "Hey look, I didn't mean to pull your chain on this. I didn't realize it was personal or I would've just told you outright."

"Dead? Both of them? You're sure?"

"Yep. Deader than Elvis."

* * *

Adam Reece held open the door to the county morgue located just south of downtown Denver. Elliot entered first, his face as white as a virgin's wedding dress.

During the brief phone call with Detective Carter the previous day, it had been agreed that the best way to resolve the matter was for Adam and Elliot to come to the morgue for positive identification of both bodies. Fingerprints and photographs had provided tentative identifications, but it never hurt to have a firsthand visual confirmation. Up to this point, no relatives had been located.

Just inside the lobby was a small waiting area. A heavyset man sat squeezed into a chair that looked as though it had been brought in from a local kindergarten. He held a large pastrami sandwich wrapped in wax paper. He'd just taken a huge bite when the two men entered. Upon seeing them, he immediately stood. The chair initially refused to let him go, but with a sharp strike of his hand, he was free.

Adam stepped forward to meet him. Elliot stayed a few paces back, not hiding his wariness of the setting. "Detective Carter, I presume."

The detective was dressed in worn gray trousers and a wrinkled white button-up shirt. He held his hand up in a waiting gesture as he chewed furiously on the mouthful of food. After a moment, he gulped down the mother lode and said, "That'd be me. You're Adam?"

"Yes, and this is my brother Elliot," Adam said, gesturing behind him. "We both appreciate your taking time to meet us like this."

"Hey, no problem. I feel bad about the big telephone surprise yesterday. Figured, what the hell, least I could do. I hate giving people bad news. Always have, always will. And believe me, I give my fair share of it."

"We just want to put it to rest," Elliot said in a shaky voice.

Adam turned to his brother, studying him. Ever since being told the girls were dead, he'd retreated within himself. Adam didn't believe that it was because Elliot necessarily felt a tremendous personal loss from the death of Lara, or perhaps even Maria. Rather, he'd lost faith in the eternal system of justice. Despite promising words from all involved, things hadn't turned out the way they were supposed to.

"Believe me, I understand," Carter said. "I asked the doc to meet us in the examining room at noon." He checked his watch.

Adam was surprised to see a red-and-white Mickey Mouse faceplate on the watch.

When the detective saw the look, he said, "My kid gave it to me. Kind of funny, really, it sort of keeps the evil at bay if you know what I mean. Lots of cops have their talismans. This is mine."

Adam nodded.

"Ah, I'm a pussy. But we all got our ways of dealing, you know? Mickey here helps me remember that none of it means dick to me. I go home to my family at the end of the night, and the rest of the world can go to hell." The detective took a bite of his sandwich. "Come on," he garbled through a mouthful of pastrami, "the doc's waiting."

* * *

Doctor Chandi stood hunched over an illuminated microscope as the three men entered the examining room. Without looking up, she said, "Be with you gentlemen in a minute." Her voice held a thick, high-pitched Indian accent.

Adam saw that the room was divided into three primary work areas. The far wall was covered with rows of square stainless steel doors. He'd watched enough reruns of *Quincy* to know what was stored in the long horizontal chambers behind each door. Cadavers, corpses, stiffs. However one said it, they were still dead bodies, and being in a room full of them was enough to unnerve just about anyone.

The right side of the room had several tables, microscopes, weights and measures, Bunsen burners, and tall racks stacked with a collection of pots, some standing as tall as a man's waist. Adam didn't want to think of what the doctor boiled in those pots.

To the left was the autopsy area. A heavy-duty scale hung over a table covered in white butcher's paper. To both sides of the table were wheeled carts topped with instruments that would have fit perfectly in the most gruesome medieval torture chamber. Pliers, hooks, knives, clamps, drills, and saws . . . anything the "doc" might need.

Adam looked at Elliot to see how he was holding up. From the pasty white expression on his brother's face, he assumed not so well. Detective

Carter tore off another large bite of the mayonnaise-soaked sandwich. Evidently Mickey was doing his stuff. To Carter, visiting the house of the dead was about as disturbing as a trip to the barber.

After a few quiet moments of hearing nothing but the detective enjoy his lunch, the doctor finally stood up and turned off the microscope.

"Thank you for waiting so patiently." She approached them, removing bloody yellow rubber gloves. Her face and hands showed a dark Middle Eastern skin, and her frame was so slender she appeared to be little more than bones.

"I'm Doctor Vaneeta Chandi," she said, extending what was now a bare hand to Elliot.

His eyes grew wide, and his face became pained. Elliot appeared frozen in place. He stared directly at the hand she offered as if it were contaminated with some as of yet-undiagnosed plague. He was undoubtedly considering the possibilities of what she'd just finished doing with that hand. The doctor waited patiently for a moment. Then, looking confused, moved on to Adam.

Adam shook her hand, which he found to be as bony as a skeleton's but warmer than most undead. "Nice to meet you, Doctor. I'm Adam Reece."

The doctor turned to Detective Carter, but instead of shaking his hand, she patted him affectionately on the side of his arm. "Good to see you again, big man. Hope the family is well."

"Yeah, Doc, everyone's doing fine. The missus says you should come over for dinner soon."

"Sounds wonderful." She turned back to face Adam and Elliot. "The detective tells me you can provide visual identification of the Sativa sisters."

"Yes, we can. My brother knew Maria, and we both knew Lara." Adam's voice echoed in his ears as if someone far away were speaking. In preparation for seeing Lara's lifeless body, part of him had temporarily checked out to return on a sunnier day.

"He also told me you were friends of the deceased." Her face took on a comforting smile. "I'm genuinely sorry for your loss. I know this must be difficult."

The well-known "frogs in throat" syndrome kept Adam from replying.

"Well then, let's just get it over with," the doctor said, clapping her hands together softly. "They're in A23 and A24." She turned and moved toward the end of a long row of chambers.

A23 and A24, Adam thought. *Ending up as a number on a refrigerated lockbox. A hell of a way to be remembered.*

The group followed Doctor Chandi to the wall of stainless steel doors. Without hesitation or a drum roll, the doctor pulled one of the handles. A gust of cold sanitized "dead body" air puffed over them with a *hiss*. Elliot gasped loudly. Everyone looked to him for an instant then returned their attention to the dark refrigeration chamber. The doctor grabbed a molded plastic handle on one end of the tray and pulled.

Adam was grateful for Elliot's sake that most of the body was covered in a thin paper sheet. Only the face remained exposed. Adam knew immediately, both from seeing the shape of the swollen blue face and from hearing Elliot hit the hard tile floor behind him, that they'd finally found Maria.

Doctor Chandi and Detective Carter immediately turned their attention to Elliot who groaned softly as he struggled to get back to his feet. Adam didn't offer a helping hand. Instead, he studied the lifeless girl.

"I'm so sorry," he heard Elliot babbling through slurred speech.

The apology was quickly followed by an assurance from the doctor that this sort of thing happens all the time. Just to take it easy for a few minutes and he would be fine. While Elliot sat in a nearby chair trying to recover both his dignity and his sea legs, Doctor Chandi and Detective Carter returned to Adam.

"He'll be fine," she assured him.

Adam nodded.

"What happened to her? I mean, how did she die?"

"The official cause of death was cardiac arrest. But, as you can see, she suffered a great deal of trauma before that." Dr. Chandi pointed to several large black bruises on the girl's once truly beautiful face. "Multiple contusions and abrasions."

"Someone sure beat the hell out of her," Carter said, adding his policeman's addendum to the diagnosis.

"What about the missing teeth and fingernails?" Adam asked, gesturing to the swollen hands and a nearly toothless protruding jaw line.

"Yes, I'm very sorry. Like I said, there was a great deal of trauma."

"How long has she been dead?" Adam asked.

"Can't say exactly. Both of them were kept cold, so it's tough to determine an exact time of death. My best medical guess is three weeks, give or take a day."

"What do you mean both?" Adam asked.

"Both girls were found in a local meatpacking plant. The cold affects the rate of decomposition. But factoring that in, my examination suggests it's been three weeks from time of death."

Three weeks was impossible in Lara's case. Even with his time in the hospital, it had only been two weeks since she'd disappeared.

"Have you seen enough?" the doctor asked.

"More than enough," Adam replied. Despite the horror of what he was seeing, his heart was alive with hope. Things were again not adding up, and he was clinging to the inconsistency.

The doctor pushed in the long metal tray and closed the refrigerator door. She moved down a single row and popped the hatch. The air hissed again as it pushed its way out of the chamber.

"You ready?" the doctor asked, obviously afraid she might have a repeat performance.

"Ready as I'll ever be."

The doctor pulled out the tray.

Adam looked at the girl's swollen face and dark eyes and nodded solemnly. Everything had just become perfectly clear.

"I'm sorry," the doctor repeated. "She is your friend?"

"No," he replied softly. "She's not."

Chapter 20

"Holy cow," Elliot said, turning slowly in place.

The two men stood in the center of an empty living room in what used to be Lara's apartment in the Brookfield Towers. The hardwood floor, walls, and windows were bare. Just as with Maria's apartment, this place had been "cleaned."

Adam walked into the bedroom, the room he'd entered under the cover of darkness . . . the room where he and Lara had first made love. As he stared at the empty, lifeless room, he was filled with a strange mix of guilt and loss.

"When we first talked about this case, you said you'd heard Maria mention her sister in the past, right?" Adam asked.

"That's right. And I think I recall her name being Lara, although in retrospect, I can't be certain of that. We've been surrounded by the other Lara for so long, it's difficult to sort out old memories."

"But you never met her sister or saw a photo?"

"Not that I can recall," Elliot answered.

"When I first met Lara, or rather the woman who called herself Lara, she said she was adopted. Did Maria ever mention her sister being adopted?"

"No, but Maria kept personal stuff like that to herself. Her life wasn't anyone's business but her own. She had a weird sense of privacy."

Adam shook his head. "It appears we've been conned, big brother. The girl we thought was Lara was obviously an imposter. She knew enough about Maria and the real Lara to pull it off without making us suspicious."

"Agreed," Elliot said, nodding. "The question is who was she? And what could possibly have been her motivation for the elaborate charade?"

Adam looked around the empty room. "We'll probably never know who she was, but I think I at least know what she was."

"Okay, let me in on it," Elliot said.

Adam looked solemnly at Elliot, waiting for his brother to appreciate his quiet assertion.

"No way," he said. "You're telling me you honestly believe that petite girl was the assassin we've been chasing. You're kidding, right?"

"How else do you explain what's happened?"

"I'm sure I could come up with a dozen explanations more plausible than that one."

"I tell you what. Let's walk back through it. I'll lay out my reasons. At the end of it, you give me your best alternate explanation," Adam said. "Fair enough?"

Elliot rubbed his hands together. Once again, the game was afoot. "Okay, take it from the beginning."

"She showed up at your door, claiming to be your ex-girlfriend's sister. She was able to offer all kinds of specifics, down to minutiae like Maria's workout studio and dentist. Given that you're loaded, it's tempting to think this was some money con, but let's face it, she never asked you for anything. What was her motivation?"

"I'll agree it wasn't for money. Hell, she wasn't even nice to me. But that doesn't prove she's the killer. Besides, at one point, you showed me a photo of Maria and Lara. How do you explain that? Photographic trickery?"

"Hmm, good point," Adam conceded. "I'm not completely clear about the photo. I doubt someone would go to the trouble of doctoring up a photo in the unlikely event we would happen upon it. It seems more likely that she knew Maria. And from the look of the photo, they appeared to be friends."

"Okay, go on. I want to hear how all this translates into her being the mysterious gunman."

"Consider the three shootings. The day General Livingston was shot, Lara went to the airport alone to look for the elusive map. That would have given her a prime opportunity to hop a flight to Dallas, do the deed, and get back before drawing our suspicions."

"Possible but still pretty circumstantial."

Adam continued. "I have more. When Greene was killed, Lara conveniently got sick. That left her free to leave the hotel shortly after us and head to the desert outside Greene's residence. After killing him, she mysteriously disappeared, making it look like she'd been abducted."

Elliot started to speak, but Adam held up a hand. "Then comes the Senator Shoemaker incident," he continued. "When I was in the control room, I had the distinct feeling the shooter knew me. He or she not only spared my life but actually saved it. The only conclusion I can come to is that the killer had a personal reason to keep me alive."

"It could have been simple gratitude for your helping with the four terrorists," Elliot countered.

"I saw this woman's body. And though she was quite beautiful, she could easily have competed in the Miss Fitness pageant. That sort of physique requires extensive physical training. Also, when I broke into this place to get her out that night, she stepped out of the shadows with a pistol at my head. If she had wanted me dead, I'd be six feet under right now. Sort of out of character for a paralegal, don't you think?"

Elliot nodded reluctantly, still less than convinced. "I didn't get the privilege of seeing her naked, but it does paint an unusual picture. Still, though, it begs the question, why? If she was in fact the killer, why would she look me up? Moreover, why would she continue to travel around with us? Other than to let you see her naked body, that is."

Adam grinned. Smart-ass comments from his brother made him feel like things might actually get back to normal one day. He couldn't remember the last time they had picked at each other without condescension. Maybe the discussion about Elliot's past was going to make a real difference in his life.

"Consider this scenario," Adam began. "What if Maria stole the map? Lara, or whatever the hell her real name is, then came to you, thinking that you might have it or at least know what she did with it. Pretending to be Maria's sister ensured that you'd feel obligated to help. Then, before she had time to pull out, we found a real link to the map."

"The locker key."

"Exactly. So she stuck around hoping we might luck out on the map."

"Which is exactly what we did. But why hang around after it was found?" Elliot asked. "After all, it wasn't even readable. She could have taken it and disappeared at any time."

"Good question," Adam admitted. Then he quickly came up with an answer. "Maybe we served as a good cover to get close to the targets.

Remember, it was Lara who suggested what the map meant in the first place. Who better to know its significance than the killer?"

"It did seem like a very unlikely conclusion. I just thought it figured into her whole conspiracy phobia."

"You're assuming that was even real. Probably just a trait she adopted for the role," Adam said, moving to the bedroom window. Down below, he could see cars swerving in and out of busy streams of traffic, but the room was impressively silent.

Both men stood quietly reflecting on what they knew and what they didn't.

Finally, Elliot said, "If you're right, it means a killer was in our midst the whole time. Chilling."

"Cold as hell is what I was thinking."

"Who knows, you might be right," Elliot surrendered. "It would help to explain a few oddities about her. Unfortunately, now that she's done the disappearing act, we'll never know for sure."

As if in timely contradiction to his statement, Elliot's cell phone suddenly sounded. With a distinct feeling of déjà vu, both men looked expectantly at the small handset.

"What are the odds?" Elliot asked.

Adam shook his head. At this point, he'd come to believe anything was possible.

"Hello," Elliot said into the phone. After only an instant, he pulled it away from his ear and held it out for Adam. "Showtime."

Adam took the phone, saying, "Yes?"

"Meet me at Babbett's Café at three today if you want to talk." The phone clicked dead.

"What did she want?" Elliot was clearly astonished.

"She wants to meet."

"Where? When? Let's go."

"No, Elliot. This isn't meant for you. This is something I have to do alone." Adam said it slowly and with compassion. His brother had been through a lot recently, and this wasn't the time to make him feel like an outsider.

"But . . ." he started, but then changed his mind. "No, I suppose you're right. She never really liked me anyway, and you two were obviously much more than just friends. But if you go alone, you should be careful."

"Don't worry about me getting hurt."

"Why?" Elliot asked. "I know you think you're bulletproof, but this girl's capable of indiscriminate murder."

"Maybe so, but you're forgetting something."

"What's that?"

"If she'd have wanted either of us dead, we'd already be laying in chambers A25 and A26."

* * *

Adam stopped the black Audi sedan in front of Babbett's Café. A dozen outdoor tables with large red-and-white sun umbrellas were scattered to the front and side of the restaurant's main entrance. Most of the outdoor tables were already taken by patrons enjoying the unusually warm Colorado winter.

A young valet approached Adam as he stepped from the car.

"Nice ride," the boy said, handing him a small red ticket stub. Adam took the parking receipt and reluctantly surrendered the keys to the young man. He considered telling him to be careful. Then figured what the hell, it was his brother's car.

As Adam walked away, the tires suddenly barked as they spun uncontrolled for a moment. The car quickly took hold, and the young man whipped a sharp right turn onto the main thoroughfare. Adam shook his head. By the time the valet was finished, the patched bullet holes might be the least of the damage.

He approached a waiter standing just outside the tinted glass doors. The man wore black slacks and a matching black shirt and carried a handful of large plastic menus with white rope tassels.

Before Adam could speak, the waiter said, "Yes, sir, this way please." With that, he turned and led him around to the side of the outdoor café.

As soon as they turned the corner, Adam saw her. She was faultlessly coordinated with the restaurant's color scheme, wearing a beautiful red dress with large white polka dots, her hair tucked under a white sun hat. Her tan, stocking-free legs stretched out in front, as welcoming as any red carpet.

"Thanks for coming," she said, glancing behind him to be sure he'd come alone.

The waiter pulled out a chair for Adam and placed a menu on the table. "Might I get you something from the bar, sir?"

"A cold beer," Adam replied, sliding his chair in behind him. He couldn't take his eyes off her. Memories of their time together filled his mind.

"What type, sir?"

"Huh?" he asked, looking up.

"What type of beer, sir?"

"Cold."

"Yes, sir." The man quickly moved away.

"I've missed you, Adam," she said, smiling.

Adam's mind was racing, and he didn't know where to begin. He started with the obvious. "Who are you?"

"Does it matter?" Without waiting for an answer, she continued. "To be honest, I don't even have a real name anymore. Some know me as Bulls-eye, but the important thing is you've figured out who I'm not."

"You're obviously not Lara. She's dead, but I guess you already know that."

"Yes, she's dead," she replied simply. "As is my friend Maria."

"Your friend?"

She hesitated a moment, then said, "You might as well know. Maria and I were lovers." Adam must have looked shocked because she quickly added, "I'm sorry if that upsets you. She was a beautiful woman who could seduce anyone, even another woman. We were lovers for a time, nothing more . . . nothing less."

Adam was indeed surprised, but strangely not repulsed. The revelation of Lara's sexual interest in another woman only confirmed that he knew nothing about the woman before him. "Lovers, like you and me," he said, not able to hide his feeling of loss.

"No, not like us." She leaned in close, and Adam could smell her perfume. "You and I are something different. Something special. I mean that, really."

"I need to know," he said. "Did you do it? Did you kill them?"

"Who?" she asked, leaning back casually into the chair. The topic of death was apparently one that could be discussed with nonchalance.

The waiter approached with a tall, frosty glass of dark lager. Both Lara and Adam fell silent. He quietly placed the beer and disappeared with little more than a nod.

Adam continued where he'd left off. "Lara and Maria. Did you kill them?"

"No," she answered. "Not directly anyway. But I might as well have. Maria stole the map, and I called for help retrieving it. The agency handled it in their usual screwed-up manner. If it's any consolation, you and I took retribution on the bastards who killed the Sativa sisters."

Adam wasn't sure what to believe. He continued on, just trying to get answers, even if they were lies. "What was written on the map?" Adam

---

offered himself a quick guilty reminder that he'd already know the answer if it hadn't been for his late-night amusement park swim.

"Just details about the targets. Nothing that matters anymore," she said. "Information is often passed in mundane ways like a road map, newspaper advertisement, that sort of thing. I once had a target's name passed in a crossword puzzle, of all things. Microfiche and computer disks draw unnecessary attention."

"A crossword puzzle?"

"Go figure. Anyway, Maria stopped by uninvited one evening and took notice of me quickly putting the map away. To her, I was a wealthy importer. She must have figured it was valuable. Later, when I wasn't looking, she swiped it. I'm sure she was shocked as hell to find it contained only cryptic notes about the politicians. Even if she didn't understand it, she was smart enough to realize that she was in trouble. It's hard for me to feel too sorry for her, though, since it was pure greed that led to her undoing."

"So they tortured her to find out about the map. But why'd they kill Lara? I mean the real Lara. Why did she have to die?" Adam grew nauseated at the thought of the two girls lying cold and naked in the morgue. He took a long sip of the icy beer. It was bitter and had a strong malt aftertaste. It pulled him away from the disfigured bodies, and for that, he was grateful.

"That was already done before I knew about it," she answered. "They knew the map was in the amusement park. Maria told them that much. She couldn't remember the locker number but did reveal that she'd sent the key to her sister. The operatives grabbed Lara to get the key. Of course, she didn't have it and denied any knowledge of it. They killed her trying to extract information that she didn't even possess."

"Because the key had been routing around in the mail system."

"Exactly."

"So you just conveniently took the dead girl's place."

"Correct again. The agency knew it screwed up, and I convinced them to back off and let me look around a bit. Playing Maria's concerned sister seemed like an ideal method. She was between jobs, had no close friends, and her only nearby relative was already dead."

"All this because you needed to retrieve the map?" he asked.

"It wasn't that I needed the map. We just couldn't afford for it to turn up later. Too many questions were possible. A conspiracy whacko like me would have a field day."

"I assumed that was part of the act."

"What, my believing in government conspiracies?" she asked. "Sweetie, think about what we're involved in here. Besides, with as much as I've seen, I don't discount any idea, no matter how bizarre. If someone told me the government was about to let loose a horde of stomach-ripping aliens, I'd get Sigourney Weaver on the phone pronto. Believe me. Adam, nothing is too farfetched for these government black project spooks."

"Black project spooks, but not CIA," Adam said, already knowing what her answer would be.

She grinned. "Oh, you're good. The identification you found on the guy at Maria's was obviously a plant. Our operatives often carry false identification like that. Hell, people will believe anything of the CIA."

He nodded. "I don't suppose you're going to tell me what agency you do work for."

She tilted her head sideways, smiling at him. "What purpose would that serve other than endanger us both?"

"I like to know my enemies."

"I'm not your enemy. If I were, you'd be dead." Her eyes turned hard.

Adam met her stare.

After a moment, she cracked a smile. "Man, that sounded good, and you didn't even flinch."

Adam shook his head. "More games?"

Her smile quickly disappeared. "Sorry, I'm just so glad to see you. But I see you need a sign of good faith. That's it, isn't it?"

"I just want the truth."

She leaned in close, lowering her voice. "They call themselves the Diadem, and their symbol is a small gold crown. There, I just told you enough to get us both killed. Good enough?"

The name meant nothing to Adam. "Who's involved?"

"That's not such an easy question. I tend to think of them as a well-made soup. A little of this, a little of that. I know for a fact that they reach into major intelligence services all over the world."

"Is this group supported by our government?" Adam wasn't sure he really wanted to know the answer.

She didn't hesitate. "Not directly, no. But believe me, these are bad people in powerful places."

There didn't seem to be any point in inquiring further about the specifics of the Diadem. He didn't possess the ability to stop such a powerful organization, and the more he heard, the more he wanted to try.

After a moment of consideration and another taste of beer, Adam said, "One thing doesn't make any sense."

"Only one?" She seemed entirely too happy talking of murder and secret societies.

"If you knew the map was in the amusement park, and you knew the number on the key, why not just tell them which locker it was in? Even if you couldn't get the key from me without raising suspicion, someone could have jimmied the lock."

She beamed at him with a smile that proved contagious. Despite his frustration and utter disgust, Adam found himself charmed by the cold-blooded killer.

"Even though you won't admit it, you're smart, Adam. Attention to detail, that's one of your strong suits. I so like that. In answer to your question, yes, I could have retrieved the map. Why didn't I? Who knows. Maybe I wanted to see if you would figure it out. Maybe I just wanted your company a bit longer."

Adam felt utterly disturbed. He wanted to hate her. He did hate her. Yet, she was still the girl he had come to know so well. She was Lara to him. Her deception should have changed that, but it didn't.

"What about the others? General Livingston and Greene. Were they yours?"

She sat back and studied him, sipping a glass of iced tea. She took time before answering, "Yes, they were mine."

"And it was you in the control room?" He asked, already knowing the answer. "You saved my life."

"Yes to both. And you probably saved mine as well by helping me dispose of those double-crossing bastards."

"They were there to kill you?"

"Me, you, whoever else might be around. I was to be the Oswald that the government was going to get lots of good publicity over killing."

"Then why did you fix up the scene?" he asked. "You covered for them."

"It was the only way to save myself, and you for that matter. The killing was over, and they needed a fall guy. Fortunately, with a bit of ingenuity, I managed to find one nearby. I see you kept your mouth shut, too. Why is that, I wonder? You could have spoiled the whole thing. Tell me it wasn't just because you liked being made out as a hero."

Adam shook his head. "I went along with it for several reasons. First, whoever was there not only spared my life, but also saved it. As weird as it sounds, I felt I owed the killer something. Not to mention that, at the time, I honestly thought that Elliot was the assassin. I guess I wasn't quite ready to set the hounds loose on him."

"Elliot a killer?"

"We all have our off days."

She laughed. "Go on."

"I'd be lying if I didn't admit that simple survival instincts told me to keep my mouth shut. It didn't seem like a good idea to go blabbing about a missing assassin to government agents who might have been involved in the cover-up."

"Wise move on your part. You'd have been dead before you could make morning coffee."

"What about Senator Shoemaker? He gets off without a second try?" he asked, still confused about the underlying reasons behind everything.

"Something like that," she replied. "I'm officially off the case." She wiped her hands together in an exaggerated gesture.

"But why'd they do this? Why kill these people?"

"Now you'd never respect yourself in the morning if I told you that. Besides, I've said too much already. If anyone found out about this meeting, I'd probably be killed. And there'd be no probably for you."

He felt himself growing frustrated, partly from the lack of answers and partly from more personal feelings that he hadn't yet sorted out. "I need to understand this, and I'm not going to give up until I do."

"I know that, and I have confidence that you'll eventually work it all out. You just have to look beyond the obvious."

"What is that? Some kind of riddle?"

"Sure, if you want it to be," she answered. "If you really want to know the truth, ask yourself who stood to gain by what happened."

Adam rubbed his chin, considering her words. She wanted him to know but just didn't want to be the one to tell him. "The vice president. He was the only one not targeted. If everyone else had been killed, he would have been a shoo-in."

She stared at him without saying anything.

Adam nodded. "I see."

He sat silent for a moment then asked, "What about you? Aren't they going to try to kill you, or are you somehow back in good graces now?"

She grinned. "It is in fact as ridiculous as you make it sound. The best kind of assassin is one who is dead at the end of the day. In this case, however, since they have the necessary bodies, I can just disappear for a while."

"What now? Do you head into the office for your day job and wait on the next call to kill some innocent sap?" He couldn't help but feel repulsed.

"It's not like that," she said, pausing to decide how much to say. "I'm what they call a rogue. I work for them, but not with them. Sort of a freelancer. Now that this mess is all over, I'm going to take some time off. Enjoy the money this profession rewards. I know you're going to think I'm crazy for asking, but I want you to come away with me."

"You're kidding, of course," he said in disbelief.

"No, I'm very serious." She leaned in and took his hand in hers. "You and I have chemistry together. It's not just the sex. There's something special here. I know you feel it. We could be in Paris by morning. I have more money than you would believe." Her face was alive with childish hope. "Why not? We could make it work. One thing I could definitely promise is that life with me wouldn't be boring."

Adam turned away, unwilling to fall under the spell of her glittering blue eyes. He slowly pulled his hand free. "Things like this can't work out."

"Why? Why can't they, Adam? Just this one time. Can't we break the rules of this world and make it work? I . . . I need you."

He shook his head. His voice was soft but clear. "I came here for two reasons. One was to discover the truth. Most of which I have now." He stopped for a moment, letting her think about what was coming.

"And the other?" Her voice was shaking.

"To bring you to justice."

She laughed. It started as a small giggle but before long had evolved into a belly-holding, eyes-watering extravaganza.

Adam stared at her in utter bewilderment. "I mean it," he said firmly, trying to stop the uproar.

She bit her lip, and for a moment appeared to get herself under control, only to lose it once again to another hysterical fit of laughter. People from nearby tables began looking over at her.

"Just give me a minute," she giggled. "I'm sorry. I really am," she continued in gasps. "I know you're serious, and I don't mean it that way." She patted his hand like one might pat a confused child. After a moment, she finally reined in her amusement.

"You done?" he asked in a voice meant to sound threatening but came out with an embedded chuckle of his own.

She held up both hands. "I'm okay . . . I'm okay now."

"Why do you find that so funny? You don't think I'm up to it?" Even as he asked the question, he recalled she'd already been in a position to kill him on two occasions.

"Don't get me wrong, sweetie. I don't mean it that way at all. Your strength and confidence are what makes you so attractive." She sucked in a breath and dabbed at a few tears, finally more or less composed.

"No, it isn't anything like that. I'm just not used to receiving threats, that's all. You probably don't fully appreciate my situation, so you may not see the humor of it all."

Adam looked at her with interest. "Help me understand it."

"To start with, I'm not some two-bit hoodlum they pulled off the streets. To get where I am, one has to be . . . how shall I put it . . . exceptional. Did you know I was recruited while preparing for the Olympics?"

He shook his head, unsure if she was telling the truth.

"Honest. I was training to compete in marksmanship and had a damn good chance of winning the gold. I'm that good. I don't miss. Ever. I don't pull the trigger unless I know where the bullet is going to land. Maybe you don't know how rare that is. I have hit targets at over a mile. Can you imagine a mile? Maybe a handful of people in the world can do that."

She paused for a moment, giving him a chance to express doubt. Adam remained silent.

She continued. "I've been trained in all sorts of combat techniques and can kill with weapons as commonplace as a ballpoint pen or a glass of iced tea," she said, tapping the side of her glass with her fingernail. "I speak seven languages, can run a mile in under five minutes, and have as close to a photographic memory as I would ever want."

"Not a bad kisser either," he smarted.

A mischievous smile came over her. "Even that came through training. Nothing can be left to chance in my profession. Don't get me wrong. I'm not suggesting that I'm some kind of Superman. But ever since becoming accomplished, people of all statures are wary of me. I have the ability to kill just about anyone, and people who hire me know that. I'm the monster that they've created. One that sometimes they think they can't live with, and other times they think they can't live without.

"I still don't see the humor in it."

She gave him a sad smile. "It just struck me as ironic that the one man I have ever loved not only doesn't fear me but casually threatens to beat the hell out of me and drag me to the police. There's some humor in that, don't you think?"

"Loved?" The word stuck in his throat like a dry cotton ball.

She quickly turned her eyes down to stare at the tablecloth. For a long time she said nothing, just tracing the checkered pattern with her fingers. Without looking up, she finally said, "Yes. I love you, Adam. With everything I am. And please don't say you love me too, or I will probably lose my lunch."

Adam stared at the now-humble creature in front of him. Maybe she wasn't Lara, but she was everything he'd come to know. In a sense, she was Lara. His Lara. As horrible as many would find it, he realized that he loved her without hesitation or shame.

"I love you too," he said, taking in her entire beauty once again. "Nothing could ever change that."

She looked up meeting his gaze, her eyes filling with large wet tears. Then she choked out another laugh, this one much quieter than before. "God, I was hoping you'd say that."

Chapter 21

"Pinnacle Investigations." The young woman's voice was strong but happy.

"Libby, it's Adam."

"Adam!" she exclaimed. "You're alive! Do you realize you scared the bejesus out of me? Why haven't you called?"

"Sorry, I've been . . ." he hunted for the right word, "busy."

"I saw your picture all over the news. You went off and became some big hero."

"That's what they tell me."

"Seriously, you okay? I heard you'd been shot." Without waiting for him to answer, she said. "I would have sent flowers, or even come out there to see you, but I didn't know where you were. It was all kept very hush-hush."

"I'm fine now. How are you doing holding down the fort? Any problems?"

"Oh man, you wouldn't believe it. Every Tom, Dick, and Harry is now convinced you're a combination of Dick Tracy and Rambo. I've been swamped with more calls than I can count. Everything from missing persons, to suspicious deaths, to some pirate who wants you to find his lost parrot. If this keeps up, you're going to have to give me a raise."

Adam was pleasantly surprised to hear about the surge in business. Up to this point he hadn't really considered the potential benefits of his fifteen minutes of fame.

"Plus," she continued, "the media keeps calling. I'm talking every major network. They all want to hear what happened in the control room. You could turn out to be a real celebrity over this. You definitely need to milk it for what it's worth. I can't believe you haven't already done a prime-time interview with Barbara Walters."

"You know that's not my style."

"Maybe not, but you need to do something."

The truth was he'd been avoiding the media. Adam understood that in any interview, he would have to lie to have his story match what investigators had already released. It was going to require doing some homework on his part not to introduce discrepancies. Sooner or later, though, he knew he'd have to give an interview. A damn convincing one at that. It was the only way to protect himself, Agent Valin, and the beautiful murderer he'd fallen in love with.

The more he'd considered it, the more convinced Adam had become that an interview was also the only way to ensure justice was done. The imposter hadn't come out and said it directly, but with a bit of reading between the lines, it was clear she was suggesting that the vice president was involved in the conspiracy. Given the story Elliot had relayed about the young Asian boy, Adam didn't put anything past Lucky Joe.

Adam now believed that to some degree he'd figured out the general plot. The vice president was working with a secret renegade society to ensure his election. Promises of favors or maybe piles of cold hard cash had been exchanged for a few well-placed shots at the competition. Just a couple of weeks before, there had been four leading contenders for the position of president. Now only two remained. If it hadn't been for Adam, there would be only one. Replacements would have been found, but this late in the race, it would have been an easy downhill run for the vice president.

Fortunately, it hadn't worked out the way they'd planned. Senator Shoemaker was still in the picture, and according to the imposter, he seemed safe for now. That meant he would give the vice president a run for the White House. Adam intended to ensure that things went as sour as possible for Marino before the primaries. He would still win his party's nomination, but if events unfolded as Adam wanted, a dark cloud of doubt would hang over Lucky Joe. If handled correctly, that cloud could cost him the election.

After a moment of consideration, he said to Libby, "I want you to set something up for me."

"All right!" she exclaimed. "Who should I call? I think you can take your pick of just about anyone."

"I know exactly who I want."

"Who?"

"Bob Sharp."

"Bob Sharp? Who is—no way! You've got to be kidding. Isn't Bob Sharp that ultra conservative weenie on the radio? You can do much better than that loser. Come on, Adam, think big time."

"He's the one I want. He has a weekly nighttime television show. That'll give me a couple days to get ready. Also, tell him that the interview has to be live."

"But why Sharp?" Libby asked. "This doesn't make sense."

"It's complicated," he said, not wanting to get into all of it over the phone.

"I get it. Too complicated for your dumb receptionist, right?" She sounded hurt.

He sighed. "I would think by now that you'd know you're the CFO of my empire. So quit referring to yourself as my receptionist. Besides, I didn't mean it that way. The reason I want Sharp is because he has an axe to grind with the vice president. I plan to provide him with some additional fuel for the fire. By being live, I know I won't get filtered."

"You're gunning for the vice president?"

"Both barrels."

There was an awkward silence.

"What?" he asked.

"Have you thought this through? He's getting bad press as it is, and if you go on national television to make him look worse, this thing could get away from you. Are you sure about this?"

"Maybe, maybe not. But it's the best I can come up with. I can't explain it all right now. And no, it's not because you're a dumb receptionist. It's because I don't want to put you in jeopardy. You understand that, right?"

The phone was silent for a moment. "Sure. It's cool. Sorry for being a bitch. It's just that I've missed you."

He smiled. Good old Libby. Honest, blunt, caring, and a mediocre typist with minimal cleavage.

"Don't sweat it," he said. "Just make the arrangements for me. Also, call the other networks and let them know Bob Sharp is interviewing me. I bet they'll try to air his program too."

"Will do. Ring me later for the details."

"Thanks, Libby."

"Love ya."

"Love ya back." Adam hung up the phone not entirely sure of what he was doing.

* * *

Adam sat across from Elliot in Three Tops, a small downtown delicatessen that specialized in homemade sandwiches and a city-renowned six-bean chili. The place was filled to capacity with white-collar professionals from nearby banks and law firms. Adam and Elliot had managed to get a small table along one wall, and with the lunchtime racket, it was impossible for anyone to overhear them.

"You realize that I can't be a part of this," Elliot said, neatly cutting in half his turkey breast and bean sprout sandwich.

"I'm not asking you to. I just thought the least I could do was keep you in the loop. I know you and Marino have a history, and I didn't want to blindside you." Adam chomped down on a sweet vinegar potato chip he'd pulled from a large basket at the center of the table.

"How are you planning to do it? If you go on Bob Sharp's show and start ranting and raving about the ill-doings of the vice president, you'll discredit yourself very quickly. People will naturally think you're a conservative zealot, or worse that you've been bought by a wealthy special interest group. That's not the kind of publicity that's going to help your cause."

Adam was pleased to hear his brother thinking constructively for him. Even though Elliot didn't agree with him, he apparently respected his decision enough to offer sound advice.

"Of course you're right," Adam agreed. "It's going to have to be much more subtle than a direct assault. Sharp is going to have to draw it out of me. That way it will look like I am a victim of his devious wit, while the facts still come out all the same."

"You mention the facts as if they're irrefutable, but I think you're a long way from having a smoking gun." Elliot was clearly frustrated by what he considered poor decision making. "What do you really have other than a hunch?"

"First and foremost is that Marino was the only candidate not targeted. That by itself isn't damning since the 'assassins' were killed. One could argue that he was next on their hitlist."

"Or that he was simply more difficult to get to. Or that they supported his cause without his knowledge. Or a half-a-dozen other reasonable explanations."

Adam nodded, unable to refute his brother's argument.

"But you're still convinced he's behind this?" Elliot said, taking a small bite of his sandwich and immediately wiping his mouth with a napkin.

"It was what Lara said. She told me to look at who had to gain from the shootings. When I said the vice president, she just looked at me, neither confirming nor denying my accusation. I think she wanted me to come to that conclusion."

"And you trust her?" Elliot asked. "Not to insult your relationship with this girl, but she could be misleading you. It wouldn't be the first time."

Adam nodded again. "You won't get an argument from me on that. I don't trust her, but I do get a sense that she cares about me." He paused for a moment. "We love each other. Those feelings have to count for something."

Elliot started to speak then closed his mouth tightly.

"What?" Adam asked. "Don't hold back on me now."

"It's just . . . I don't get this. How could you love her? You know what she does." He leaned in close. "She's a murderer. There's no good way to paint that. She kills people for money. Have you forgotten how she blew Mr. Greene's brains all over that stage just a few weeks ago? Doesn't that register with you?" Elliot had stopped eating his lunch, and his cheeks were growing red with frustration.

Adam reached across the table and put a hand on his brother's shoulder. "Elliot, I'm not fooling myself about this. Believe me, I'll never forget that night at Greene's ranch."

His brother's touch seemed to calm Elliot. "Yet you still say you love her." His voice was more even now.

Adam took a deep breath. He'd spent more than enough hours considering the insanity of their relationship. Elliot was right, of course. Lara was a murderer. Maybe she'd glamorized it by arguing that she was a rogue assassin that killed only because she was trained in that capacity. Sugarcoat it or not, at the end of the day, people were dead. However implausible it sounded, he had come to accept the truth.

"A long time ago, I had a teacher," Adam began. "A tremendously powerful man who managed somehow never to forget the value of love and friendship."

Elliot remained quiet, not sure where he was going.

"He believed that sometimes people are bound together. That together they serve the will of the universe. For him, such bonds were irresistible forces that tied destinies together."

"What are you saying? That you feel this bond with Lara?"

"Since I first laid eyes on her."

"There's a word for someone like you."

"A hopeless romantic?"

"A sap."

They both laughed.

"But who am I to judge," Elliot continued. "If I'd followed that line of thinking, I'd probably be a happier man today."

"Janice?"

He shrugged. "Who knows? She might have been my soul mate, if there is such a thing. And I just let her walk away."

"That's something I don't think I can do."

"Don't let a little thing like her being a contract killer get in the way."

Adam shrugged. "You know me, I'm all about forgiveness."

"Okay, enough said. You're willing to take the bad with the good. I get it. Talk about unconditional love. This goes right up there with Romeo and Juliet. Let's just hope there's a better ending."

"Amen."

"Love aside, it still doesn't mean the vice president is behind any of this," Elliot said.

"No, it doesn't. But if not Lucky Joe, then who? From the cover-up, we know that government agencies are involved. It would make sense that they would align with whoever they believed would soon be in power. That points to him again."

"Not necessarily. Marino was doing well in the polls initially, but lately he's gotten a round of bad press. Most of it relates to whispers of his involvement in organized crime. The murder of two of his challengers has people talking. Your future host, Sharp, is as much to blame for the rumors as anyone."

"Okay, but of the four candidates, two are dead, and one was barely missed. I doubt a candidate would sign up to being killed as part of the plot. I just don't see any other—" Adam suddenly stopped.

"What is it?"

His eyes darted from side to side as he thought it through. "I never miss."

"What?" Elliot asked. "What are you talking about?"

"Something Lara said. She said that she never misses. Yet, she did miss, didn't she?"

"By this much," Elliot said, holding up his fingers imitating Shoemaker's motion. "I've seen it replayed on the news a dozen times. It tore a hole in the podium just an inch or two from him. He's lucky to be alive."

"But she never misses. That's what she said. Why would she say that?"

Both men sat silent, their half-eaten lunches now sitting undisturbed.

"Are you thinking what I'm thinking?" Elliot asked, his eyes wide with a mix of excitement and terror.

"She didn't miss."

"She hit exactly where she was aiming."

"Senator Shoemaker wasn't supposed to die."

Adam felt his heart beating against his chest. For the first time, this felt right. "The anonymous call," he said, thinking out loud. "Detective Carter said he'd found the two bodies on an anonymous tip. That would have been about the time we spoke with the senator."

Elliot said, "He promised you that he would find them, and you're thinking he delivered."

"I think he saw it as a good time to tie up loose ends . . . get us off the trail. With the girls dead, and our discovery that we'd been betrayed by the imposter, he concluded that we'd stand down."

"Makes sense. Why continue to risk our lives when we no longer had a personal stake in it?"

"Exactly."

"Let me see if I've got this. Senator Shoemaker decided he wanted to be president. He knew the competition was especially fierce this election. So he approached, or maybe was approached by, a particularly ruthless organization that offered to help. The plan was simple. Two of the candidates would be killed. A false attempt would then be made on his life to eliminate him from suspicion. That would leave all the damning speculation to fall on—"

They spoke in unison. "The vice president."

* * *

How does one go about nailing a powerful senator protected by operatives willing to kill you for looking at him cross-eyed? Adam had replayed that question for the past twenty-four hours. With less than six hours until showtime, he had yet to formulate a clear solution.

Standing inside a retail electronics store, he watched a huge bank of televisions simultaneously playing the evening news. The top story would have been the same even if the televisions hadn't all been tuned to the same station. It began with a rehash of all that was publicly known about the assassinations of General Livingston and Robert Greene and concluded with the fateful Washington debates.

It showed the now-famous replay of the assassin's bullet smashing into Shoemaker's podium and the chaos that ensued. A video camera frantically scanned the area, finally resting on the control room window just seconds before it shattered from a spray of bullets. The story concluded with a still photo of Bob Sharp and beside him, an amateur photographer's snapshot of tonight's most honored guest on *Sharpy Speaks Out*, Adam Reece.

Adam marveled at just how quickly things had changed. Just a day earlier, he'd been working on a plan to discredit the vice president. Working to that end, he'd arranged to be interviewed by a conservative talk show host with a clear agenda against Marino. Now, with Shoemaker in his sights, Bob Sharp seemed like the exact opposite of what he needed. Sharp had been pushing Shoemaker's agenda for several months, acting as both spokesman and loyal attack dog. Getting Sharp to go along with any kind of assault on Shoemaker would be harder than getting Simon Wiesenthal to join the Nazi party. Sharp would fight him with witty one-liners, exasperated sighs, and as many disparaging suggestions as he could muster. Hell, he'd probably blow spitballs at Adam if the network would allow it.

On the other hand, what better way to discredit the senator than to get one of his most devout followers to turn on him in a very public forum? The interview was the key to it all. Adam was certain of it. Now, if he could just figure out how to get conservative guru Bob Sharp to roast one of his own. But how?

Proof. Adam needed proof.

Chapter 22

Watching him inconspicuously from across the studio, Adam quickly understood that Bob Sharp was as intimidating in person as he was on the radio. Though he had a soft, slightly overweight physique, Sharp held himself with utter composure. Dressed in an expensive black Armani suit and wearing a tie from his own professional line, this was a man sure of himself. One couldn't help but feel privileged to talk with Sharp. He sat in his special chair, behind his special desk, poised in front of his special microphone as a true swami among men.

Even though Adam felt the man's presence, he also understood they were to be mortal adversaries for a brief time. Much as in a judo contest, Adam saw it as a matter of correctly positioning himself. Ninety percent of any match is the simple jockeying for a position of advantage. Only then does one execute an attack. If done correctly, the opponent is caught unaware of the aggression until his feet are lifted from the mat.

Adam now had a general idea of how he must position Sharp for the throw. But he also knew that, in this arena, this man was a true master. Sharp would adapt, shift, and attack as viciously as a barracuda with a toothache. To execute the throw effectively would require patience, precision, and most important, surprise.

Adam took a deep breath, the breath before combat. He'd discovered long ago that determination was best found before the battle. When he felt that his ki was properly under control, he stepped forward onto the studio floor.

Sharp immediately noticed him, leaping to his feet. "Mr. Reece. Mr. Adam Reece. We finally meet," he said, advancing with his hand already outstretched.

Adam shook his hand, finding it warm and strong. He positioned his own hand to convey a sense of insecurity. Both men understood the importance of the initial handshake. It set the stage of who would lead and who would follow. It was a skill that successful businessmen hone to perfection.

"Mr. Sharp, a pleasure meeting you. I try to listen whenever I can," Adam lied.

"Wonderful. But please call me Sharpy. Everyone else does."

"Okay, Sharpy, will do," he replied. "And Adam is fine with me."

"Great, Adam, just great. I have so much to ask you. Everyone, and I mean *everyone*, wants to hear your story. We're going to have one hell of a night here." Sharp was beaming with enthusiasm. And why shouldn't he be? He'd just been handed an opportunity of a lifetime. This might well turn out to be one of the top five interviews of the decade.

"You're the only one I trust with this, Sharpy. Those in the liberal media can't hold a candle to you. There was never a doubt that you were the man to get my story. I only hope that I don't let you down." Adam was laying it on thick.

Bob Sharp had yet to let go of his hand. "You, sir, are the reason I stay in this business. Let me say it is a privilege, no hell, it's an honor to be here with you tonight. I want you to know that when the night is over, you'll be seen as the biggest American hero since Abe Lincoln," Sharp said, winking as he had undoubtedly done with a hundred cons before.

Sharp finally released Adam's hand, but his arm immediately went around his shoulder, guiding him towards the interview area. A dozen or more cameras circled a small sitting area that consisted of his famous white granite-topped desk, two side chairs, a small loveseat, and a table for drinks and other props.

"Boy, there are a lot of cameras. Is this normal?" Adam asked.

"Not on your life. This is a big night. Big, big night for both of us. Everyone is in on this, and believe me, I have the major networks paying big bucks, as well as kissing a little Sharpy ass to be here tonight. You should be proud of yourself. We got them good."

Adam nodded. This was the way he wanted it. Sharp couldn't afford to come off looking bad with all this press. It would finish him professionally if he did. "Is it going to be live as I requested?"

"You bet. Personally, I was thrilled to hear you wanted to go live. We're typically only a few hours delayed anyway, but live is even better.

The major networks balked a bit, but hey, we didn't give them a choice. It was live or they weren't invited to the party. Don't get nervous when I tell you this, Adam, but it's been estimated that tonight you're going to be seen or heard by over seventy million people."

Playing with dynamite in front of seventy million people . . . yeah, nothing to get nervous about. The stage was perfectly set. Now all Adam had to do was pull it off. Not an easy stunt considering the high-wire act he was about to attempt.

* * *

"Welcome, ladies and gentlemen, to a very special edition of *Sharpy Speaks Out*. Tonight is a night few of us will soon forget. It is my privilege to be the first journalist to interview a man we've been hearing a lot about lately. A man who is credited with saving the life of who I believe will be the next president of the United States." Sharp folded his hands in front of him and became completely still as he stared into the camera.

"Let me introduce our most honored guest for the evening, Mr. Adam Reece." With that, Bob Sharp stood and gave Adam a standing ovation, clapping briskly and staring down at him with an almost-tearful smile.

Adam sat looking into a dozen cameras all of which had just turned his way. And though embarrassed by Sharp's ridiculous display, he was surprised at how calm he felt. Being on television simply didn't feel the way he thought it would. Camera crews worked all around him, but without the immediate feedback of seeing himself on screen, Adam felt as if he was simply sitting alone with one man. A very annoying, egotistical, pompous idiot of a man, but still just one man.

"Glad to be here, Sharpy," Adam said, sounding as silly as he felt.

The two opponents moved in close, gripping the other's gi. *The match had begun.*

Bob Sharp stepped from behind his desk. He extended a hand to Adam who sat in the "man of the hour" chair. They shook warmly like long lost friends.

"Ladies and gentlemen, when you hear this man's story, you'll know why I felt the need to shake his hand. You're looking at a true American hero." Sharp let the image of him shaking Adam's hand last for a few moments before releasing it and returning to his self-made shrine.

"There are so many things I want to talk about tonight, but let's start with what everyone wants to know. What happened that night, Adam?

Tell us everything. We want to hear it all." Sharp leaned forward over his desk as if fearful he might miss a single word.

Adam kept an upright posture, trying to appear confident and alert, the way an "American hero" should appear. "Well, I guess the best place to start is just as the debate was about to begin."

"If I understand it correctly," Sharp interrupted, "you were at the debate doing a bit of investigative work. You and your brother had been following the trail of these killers. And this led you to the convention center, correct?" Sharp was starting off the interview by making it clear he was not a passive bystander. He was an active participant in control of his interview and would not be lost in the limelight of his "heroic" guest.

Adam felt the firm initial tug on his lapel.

The story that had been released to the media by investigative authorities made no mention of Lara or Maria, and Adam had no intention of bringing that to light now. "Yes, that's right," he said. "My brother and I had been investigating the assassinations, and we went to the debate to see if we could help prevent any further bloodshed. When I saw a flash of light from one of the control rooms, I thought I better go check it out. After running up several flights of stairs, I managed to navigate my way to the control room. I was a bit winded, I might add. That's where I met Agent Valin—"

"That's Secret Service Agent Bart Valin you're referring to?"

"Correct. When I met Agent Valin and explained that I'd seen something in the control room, he immediately acted." So far the truth and the story he related were directly in line with each other. Unfortunately, the two would now have to take different roads to the same destination.

"They must have jammed the lock or something, though," he continued, "because his key wouldn't work. Between the two of us, we managed to kick in the door."

"So there you were, exhausted from running up countless flights of stairs, standing side by side with a Secret Service agent. It must have been terrifying kicking in that door. A door you felt certain might well have one or more killers lurking behind it. Please, please go on. I don't know about the rest of the audience, but I am literally on the edge of my seat." Sharp squirmed his butt around on an oversized office recliner to emphasize his point. This was a man used to radio where sounds were important to creating images.

The two men circled each other.

Adam smiled the obligatory "heroic" smile. "As soon as the door fell, Agent Valin and I rushed into the room. We didn't know what to expect, so we both had weapons drawn."

Sharp cleared his throat, turning the attention back to him. "My audience may not know about your background. Let me interject here. You carry a handgun because you're a private investigator, and you're licensed to do this, correct?"

Adam knew the assertion that he was carrying a handgun was risky since there would undoubtedly be questions about the metal detectors and convention center security. Not to mention the fact that carrying a handgun in D.C. was illegal. But given the evidence, it seemed like the only viable solution. He would have to leave it to his coconspirators to cover the discrepancy.

"That's right. At the time, I carried a Beretta nine-millimeter. In my line of work, one has to be ready for those who will do you harm."

"The 'great equalizer,' as Colonel Colt put it, yes?"

"Indeed," Adam chuckled, acknowledging Sharp's wit. "Anyway, we entered the room not knowing what to expect. It was dark and very crowded with broadcasting equipment. To our surprise, there wasn't just one shooter, but four. All four had already turned on us by the time we knew what was happening. I felt a bullet hit my right shoulder blade. Agent Valin was a bit faster and managed to get behind cover to avoid being cut down."

"You say you were hit in the shoulder blade. If I remember the details correctly, a bullet actually punctured your lung."

"That's right. It passed through my entire body, piercing my right lung front and back."

"You see, folks," Sharp said, turning back to the camera. "What did I tell you about him being a hero?" He turned back to Adam. "Please go on."

"When we came under fire, Bart went one direction, and I went the other. The men fired short automatic bursts at us, making it very difficult to gain any sort of control of the room. Their plan was to pin us down while they maneuvered for the kill."

"My Lord, I can only imagine how terrifying that must have been."

Adam knew the "heroic answer" and followed that line. "It's a strange thing. Normally, I'd agree that something like that sounds truly terrifying. But what I found was that when you come under fire, bullets pinging all around you, it quickly becomes a matter of survival. Your mind works much faster than usual; your reflexes become more acute. Fear is deep within you, but to survive, you keep it at bay." *Bullshit, bullshit, and more bullshit.*

Adam appreciated that anyone who had ever been in combat would attest that surviving was as much about luck and panic reactions as

anything else. Bullets randomly kill your buddy but spare your life. Hero-
ism or acute reflexes didn't generally make the tiniest bit of difference in
who went home to their wife and kids.

Sharp pointed to Adam and nodded at the camera, almost as if to say,
"See, I told you . . . an American Hero."

"Even though the shooters were highly trained and well equipped,
Agent Valin used some stealthy maneuvering to quickly reduce the odds
by taking out one of the aggressors."

"Taking him out, you mean killing him?" Sharp rubbed his hands
together in anticipation. Adam was finally getting to the good part. Kicking in doors was one thing, but killing people, now that was what the
bloodthirsty audience was after.

"Yes, I believe he initially fired a few shots at the man's torso. When
he didn't immediately fall, we knew they were wearing bulletproof vests.
Agent Valin quickly adapted by targeting the head. Wounding the men
was simply not an option given the severity of the situation."

"We understand completely," Sharp said with the kind of reassurance
a father might offer a son who'd picked up a rock during a scrap with the
schoolyard bully. "You both did what had to be done. I don't think any
red-blooded American would question that."

"After he took out one of them, I found myself again under fire.
With the bullets ricocheting all around me, I had to just about shoot
blind. My first round went past him into the hallway, but the second shot
stopped him."

"It's amazing that you were able to perform so well when taking that
kind of fire, not to mention choking on your own blood. I've never met
anyone so determined."

"I'd like to say I'm a pretty good shot, but it was mostly dumb luck."
Adam was being careful to demonstrate a high degree of humility. He
wanted to appear as the reluctant hero, something that might endear
him to the audience.

"All I can say is that I don't want to be across from you at the shooting
range," Sharp joked.

Adam looked to his hands, appearing uncomfortable with the flattery.
He stumbled, giving his opponent confidence in his attack.

After a moment, Adam continued. "After my opponent dropped,
Bart and I again came under some heavy automatic fire. The control
room window, terminals, and walls were all pretty torn up."

Sharp turned to face the camera, saying, "Though actual photos of
the crime scene have not been released, I've been privileged enough to

see computer-generated recreations of the control room. That place was in absolute shambles. Bullet holes in the floor, across the walls, and even in the ceiling." Sharp's words served to remind the audience of how he was in the know. He turned back to Adam. "It was a miracle how either of you survived the onslaught of bullets."

"It was a mess," Adam confirmed.

"How were you faring through all this? You'd just been shot, after all. The blood loss, the pain, the difficulty breathing . . . it all had to be taking a toll on you."

"I was definitely beginning to feel it. My lung was filling with blood, and I was getting light-headed from the lack of oxygen."

"But you hung in there. You kept fighting."

"Absolutely," Adam choked, his voice cracking slightly. "I was fighting for my life. Giving up was never an option." He was hoping that by now the audience was exclaiming a loud *hoorah*. He would need their devotion later.

Bob Sharp nodded somberly, his face rich with choreographed compassion.

"That's when I heard Agent Valin begin to struggle with one of the men. I would have tried to help, but I had one gunning for me, too. By the time I managed to eliminate my second opponent, Agent Valin had pulled out of hand-to-hand combat and managed to shoot the man through the neck. That left four dead assassins, Agent Valin a bit battered, and me leaning against the wall gasping for my next breath."

"It's a miracle you're here with us today. I don't see how you survived. Surely medical attention couldn't have arrived that quickly. My sources say the assassins had disabled the elevators and even blocked the doors. It must have taken several minutes for backup to arrive on the scene."

"You're right, of course," Adam said. "The truth is that Agent Valin saved my life. He used an old trick taught to infantry soldiers. By placing credit cards over the entry and exit wounds, he sealed the sucking chest wound and literally prevented me from drowning in my own blood."

"Are you saying that you owe your life to Agent Bart Valin?"

"Yes, sir, I am." Adam saw no harm in presenting Agent Valin as the man clearly in command of the control room shootout. It made the story more credible and hopefully earned him an ally.

"All I can say is, *wow*. What a story we have here. Folks, we have to take a quick break, but stay tuned, we'll be right back."

With Sharp's parting words, makeup and set managers immediately stepped into the picture to adjust his tie, add a fresh puff of powder to his forehead, and adjust a chair that had been moved when he'd shaken Adam's hand.

Sharp leaned around the microphone and smiled at Adam. "You're doing great. Just great. This show is going to be talked about for years to come. Just keep the momentum going."

Adam nodded. Momentum was not going to be a problem.

After a short break, the cameraman started counting down. "Live in five . . . four . . . three . . . two . . . one . . ." He pointed toward them with a flicking gesture of his forefinger.

"Hello, everyone, we're back once again with my guest, Adam Reece," Sharp began. "Before the break, he walked us through the brutal scenario that played out the night he foiled the assassination attempt on Senator Shoemaker. We're now going to push ahead a bit and talk about how a man as close to the scene as Mr. Reece might see other ramifications of that fateful evening." Sharp turned his eyes to Adam.

"Adam, do you consider yourself to be politically savvy? You know, keeping up on the daily ebb and flow of the ongoing presidential race."

"I wouldn't say that at all. Of course, I do listen to your show, so I know a bit about the candidates, but I'm not an expert like you." Though Adam was still pandering to Sharp's ego, the compliment was given in earnest. Bob Sharp was in fact quite informed on political happenings. He was definitely a "Washington insider," one who was respected in many political circles.

"Perhaps you know then that we spend a great deal of time on this show analyzing the people who want to lead our great country. Call it a public service if you will."

"We have to hold our leaders accountable," Adam added, trying to strike the right tone of support.

Sharp turned back to face the camera. "I'm confident this brutal assassination plot will have lasting ramifications on the presidential race. Since the attempt was thwarted, Senator's Shoemaker's ratings have jumped over fifteen points. Even Bill Tyler's numbers are up to a respectable level. All the while, Vice President Lucky Joe's ratings have fallen through the floor." Speech made, he turned back to Adam. "What's your take on all this?"

Adam let the opponent guide his movement.

Bob Sharp was taking a bit of a gamble. This was, after all, unrehearsed and live, and for all he knew, Adam might have differing opinions. On the other hand, Sharp surely felt confident in Adam's conservative nature. Why else would he have specifically picked Bob Sharp as his sole interviewer?

"It's funny that you ask that, Sharpy. I've done a lot of thinking lately, and I do have an opinion about what happened that night and how it might relate to the upcoming presidential race. But I don't want to bore your audience." Adam sat up straight, presenting himself as uncomfortable, a gentile on holy ground.

A shift in body position. A subtle step guiding the two's momentum.

"I know I can speak for my audience when I say, if you have an opinion, we'd like to hear it. Isn't that right?" he asked, looking into the camera and clapping with some imagined studio audience.

"All right, but it's just my personal take on things." Adam paused to allow everything that had been said previously to fade away.

Sharp once again leaned in close, giving the impression that he expected Adam's opinion to come as a soft whisper.

Such was not the case. It was now time to redirect the interview. Adam spoke with a newfound certainty and precision. "After a bit of investigating, I've come to conclude that the men in that control room were very likely part of a complex political conspiracy." *The first sound bite of the evening,* he thought.

Sharp's eyes grew wide with a mix of surprise and delight. He couldn't have asked for a better opening.

"Uh-huh, just as I've been quietly suggesting. This was no random act of terrorist violence. Hypothetically then, just for grins, if you had to put your finger on who and why anyone would be behind such a despicable act, what would be your guess?" Bob Sharp clearly had an agenda but wasn't quite bold enough to publicly suggest what was being whispered in liberal-bashing circles. The suggestion that the vice president's friends in organized crime were somehow connected to the assassinations of two, and almost three, presidential adversaries.

"I'm willing to go out on a limb if you're willing to indulge me."

A soft pull of the gi.

"Please," Sharpy mumbled, covering his face to hide a grin. Things were about to turn golden. His most-esteemed guest was going to put to words something he'd wanted to say for weeks.

"Being a private investigator, I've been trained to look for clues. They can be all sorts of things. Anything from lipstick marks on a cigarette butt, to the outline of an address pressed into the blank page of a notepad."

"Fascinating," Sharp said with a tone that sounded very pretentious.

"In this case, however, the clues were anomalies."

"Anomalies? Help those of us not as familiar with the field. What do you mean by anomalies?" The pretense was now gone. "Anomaly" was not a word Bob Sharp had expected to hear this evening.

The opponent's footing had become unsure.

"Okay, let me give you an example. An interesting anomaly was the image I saw when I entered the control room that evening."

"Yes, yes, you described the chaotic scene for us a moment ago. You said you saw four men all armed to the teeth. That's right, isn't it?"

"True, but that isn't what bothers me. No, it was that I saw four men preparing to leave the scene of a crime that bothers me. They were clearly on their way out, having retreated away from the main window. Sort of odd, don't you think?"

Bob Sharp turned his head from side to side obviously puzzled. "I'm sorry, Adam, but I still don't follow. I would expect the men to beat feet after trying to kill the senator. Surely they wouldn't stick around to get caught."

"No, you see that's just it. They hadn't completed their mission. Senator Shoemaker was still alive, and yet the men were preparing to vacate the room. I now wonder why."

"You and Agent Valin must have disturbed them during the shooting. The assassins knew their number was up and were trying to flee." Bob Sharp began to look warm, his face slowly growing ripe. He didn't need this kind of distraction.

"No, that wasn't it," Adam said, casually brushing aside the assertion. "I'm sure Agent Valin will agree that when we arrived in the room, the men had already begun to pack up to leave. I find it very puzzling that they didn't take a second shot."

"Hmm," Sharp said, trying to keep a positive note in his voice. "I guess that's something we can all think about."

"Yeah, and there was something else."

Adam did not allow his opponent an opportunity to regain balance.

Bob Sharp's face grew long and concerned. He didn't want "something else."

"Oh?" was all he could manage.

"The other thing that really bugs me is that they missed at all. I saw the shot. It was just over a hundred yards, under excellent lighting, and offered the advantage of elevation. All very desirable for a sniper."

"Still, though, these men were under tremendous pressure." Sharp was nearly stammering.

"I thought about that too," Adam said with a smile. "After all, pressure can make any man's finger twitch at the wrong time."

"Exactly, and—"

"But then," Adam interrupted, "I considered the other two shots that the same men had done previously. In both cases, the shots were significantly more difficult. One was at greater range without elevation, and the other at night under extreme range and with moderate wind. There's no doubt about it. This was by far the easiest shot. Just sort of sticks with me how they could have missed, that's all."

A red light flashed to one side of the interview area. It was time to go to commercial.

"Well, I see my staff indicating we need to take a brief intermission. We'll continue with what's turning out to be an interesting interview with Mr. Adam Reece in just a moment. Stay tuned."

As soon as the cameras went dark, Sharp shoved the microphone from in front of him and turned on Adam.

"What are you doing?" he asked barely able to hide his frustration.

"You asked my opinion."

"Well, yes, but this is getting way offtrack. The viewers don't want to hear this conjecture. You're almost suggesting that these assassins weren't even trying to kill Senator Shoemaker. If you think you're going to use my show to further your—"

"Bob," Adam interrupted. "Listen to me very carefully." His words were calm but firm.

Bob Sharp closed his mouth. There wasn't time to get in a pissing contest. He had to know where his guest was headed, and he had to know it before they went back on the air.

"Tonight is monumentally important for you. I don't think it's a stretch to say that your very career rests on the performance you give tonight. There are two ways this evening can go. One is that you look like an unprepared jackass, in which case, you'll be mocked by every major media outlet for the rest of your life. Get ready to do live-at-five helicopter traffic reports."

"You mother—"

"The other is that you shake off that pompous, arrogant attitude for a minute, and step up to the plate to do some real journalism. This story is going to come out. Hell, enough has already been said to get people thinking and questioning. Whether you like it or not, it will come out on your show. You have an opportunity not unlike that of Woodward and Bernstein. You have a chance to take down a man who would be president."

Sharp said nothing, but his eyes had lost their uncontrolled anger. He was nibbling on the hook. Woodward, Bernstein, and Sharp . . . hmm, that had a ring to it.

"This is a chance to redefine yourself," Adam continued. "If the story gets told in its entirety tonight, everyone in America will be talking about Bob Sharp's interview. How you handle yourself during it is up to you."

Adam settled into the cushion of his seat pleased with his execution thus far. It was up to his opponent now.

Bob Sharp looked like a man performing an impossibly complex internal computation. His eyes darted around wildly, his teeth bit nervously at the inside of his lips.

The cameraman's voice rang out. "Live in five . . . four . . . three . . . two . . . one . . ." Again, the man gestured by pointing to the host.

Bob Sharp really was an amazing man. Adam would tell that to anyone who ever asked for years to come. As the camera came alive, so did Sharp. As if somehow electrically connected to that little red light, his face immediately changed from concern and indecision to complete confidence. In a word, Bob Sharp had *showmanship*.

Centering the microphone in front of him, Sharp faced the camera. "When we went to break, Mr. Reece was sharing his observations about what he called 'anomalies' he witnessed in the control room. It would be easy for any one of us to discount Mr. Reece's theories as unsubstantiated speculation, but we need to keep one thing in mind people."

He leaned in very close to the microphone, and his voice became very deep. "Why are we here? One word. *Truth*. We're here for the truth. To get to the truth, one must often go to very unlikely places.

"I know Senator Shoemaker personally. We've met many times over finger foods at exclusive parties. I take him to be an honest American trying to keep this country moving forward. I think as a gesture of friendship toward him as much as anything, we should discuss these anomalies a bit further. Keep in mind that I for one am not about to change my opinion of the senator solely on speculation, no matter who might put them forward. Though I have yet to hear Mr. Reece offer any direct criticism of the senator, I don't like the hidden implications. Mr. Reece, how do you respond to this?"

Adam understood that Sharp was pulling and shoving but unwilling to execute a full attack. Not so different from what Jim Hatchet had done during the Kenju class weeks before. As with Jim, the match could not be won by control alone.

"I respect such caution," Adam said, knowing full well that insulting the host wouldn't serve him. "I don't necessarily expect you or your audience to agree with me. I was asked my opinion and simply voiced a few concerns that were bothering me."

"Please outline those questions once more." Sharp was being careful. It was clear he was straddling the fence at this point. If no additional evidence was presented, he would fall on the senator's side. If something damning came forward, he had the option to come down on the side of "truth."

"As I mentioned, the first issue was that the assassins didn't appear interested in really killing Senator Shoemaker."

"And again for our viewers just tuning in, how did you come to this conclusion?"

"I believe this for two reasons. First, they never took a second shot, although they clearly had the opportunity. And second, is the unlikely occurrence that they missed the shot at all."

"But, sir, even you must admit this unfounded speculation puts forward a suggestion that the senator was intentionally spared."

Adam found it amusing that he had now become a "sir," and a "Mr. Reece," rather than "Adam". He nodded. "That is precisely what it suggests."

Bob Sharp didn't lose a step. He was determined to gain control of this contest. "Okay, going clearly on what is now only speculation, let's see where it takes us. What do you believe the motivation would be behind a false assassination attempt on Senator Shoemaker?"

"Sharpy, you and I think just alike. That was exactly the question I sought to answer."

Adam kept his opponent close. Distancing was not to be allowed.

"After some investigation and a bit of that luck I like to talk about," Adam said, "I think I came up with the answer."

Bob Sharp's eyes grew wide. He was very curious but also clearly terrified. Dare he let his guest further disparage a man whose favor would surely benefit him? A man who at the moment was the champion of many of his regular viewers.

"The truth, that's what we're after," Sharp said, taking the plunge into an icy cold lake of unknown. "Please, go ahead."

Adam understood that Sharp was now maneuvering. By calling Adam's bluff, he was hoping to expose some far-fetched idea that would enable him to discredit the guest and regain control.

"Let me start by repeating that this is, of course, only my opinion. I don't intend to slander the senator, only to open a forum for debate. With that said, let's go forward."

Adam asserted pressure, choosing to be the aggressor now.

"I asked myself why in the world would four known terrorists risk their lives to intentionally botch an assassination attempt. After all, it's clear from the evidence these were the same individuals who killed the other two presidential candidates. Why miss the third?" Adam paused for effect.

"My conclusion is it all came down to a process of elimination." Without waiting for Sharp to regain his footing, he continued. "Let's assume you were a candidate in a very close four-man race. How could you remove the competition before a possible debilitating loss in the primaries? If one was truly an unscrupulous man capable of anything, you might simply follow a process of elimination. Have the other candidates killed. Effective in removing one's opponents, yes, but also so obvious that it also raises the specter of your involvement. After all, if each of your competitors is mysteriously killed off, someone's bound to start asking questions about your potential connection.

"If you were really clever, however, you might take another approach. Let's say you killed two of the competitors and then faked an attempt on yourself. That does several things for you. First, it removes two candidates who might have interfered with your primary and eventual presidential win. By being targeted yourself, it also removes any suspicion of your possible involvement. Finally, if I can borrow my own words, by another process of elimination, it brings the critical public eye to fall on your remaining adversary.

"After all, he would be the only one left unscathed by the whole insidious affair. Given that Vice President Marino has historically been plagued by suggestions of involvement in organized crime, this critical eye would be given additional credibility and likely finish his bid for the White House. In the end, you would go on to a landslide victory as a brave man willing to put his life on the line to become president."

Bob Sharp leaned forward to rest his elbows on the desk in front of him. He looked absolutely mortified.

"Do you know what you've just suggested? Do you even know?" He was visibly upset. "You're saying you believe Senator Shoemaker was directly behind the assassinations of two presidential candidates. Add to that an attempt to frame the vice president for the murders."

"It is rather hard to believe, isn't it?" Adam said, rubbing his chin.

He positioned himself for the throw.

"Hard to believe? Hard to believe? Are you kidding me? It's outrageous. It's preposterous. Bordering on the insane. I don't suppose you have any proof whatsoever of this alleged conspiracy between the senator and the killers?" Sharp was getting ready to go on the offensive, making one last valiant effort to regain command of his show. "This sort of wild, unsubstantiated—"

Driving into his opponent, Adam executed the attack.

"Yes, I do." Adam's voice was quiet and calm, and at first Sharp didn't register what was said.

". . . speculation has no place in—. What . . . What did you just say?"

"I said that I have proof."

Bob Sharp licked his lips. The set was now painfully quiet. "You have proof?" His voice was just above a whisper, and his eyes started to water. "Proof?"

"Yes."

Sharp was stunned. "What kind of proof? Is it real or some more of your unfounded speculation?" There was no control in his words. He was struggling for air.

"No, it's quite real."

Flabbergasted, Sharp sat back heavily in his seat, shaking his head. "All I can say is show it to us. Show us the proof."

Adam reached inside his jacket pocket and removed a DVD. He placed it gingerly on the desk in front of Bob Sharp.

Sharp stared at the un-labeled black plastic case as if it were something the devil himself had spun from hell. He didn't move to pick it up.

"What's this?"

"Your proof."

"I gather that, but what is it?"

"See for yourself."

Now the pressure was really on. Things had gone from bad to worse to way the hell out of control. Sharp rubbed his hand over his face, which was now gleaming with sweat that had soaked through several layers of stage makeup. After a moment, he picked up the disk. Playing it presented terrible risks, but not playing it presented at least as many. If he didn't play the disk, his career was finished. And if he did, it was probably still finished.

Adam knew all this when he'd handed over the disk. Whether Bob Sharp played the DVD or not, the story was out, and others would find the evidence too.

"I don't think anyone would forgive me if I didn't play it." He gestured for the nearest cameraman who immediately stepped inside the set. Sharp handed him the DVD.

Sharp turned back to the camera. "We're going to take a very brief commercial break while we set up for viewing this. I don't think I have to tell anyone to stay tuned." Without waiting for the camera to turn off, he closed his eyes and took a very deep breath.

* * *

The large LCD monitor sat just to the left of the host. It measured a mere thirty-two inches across, but given its importance, it now seemed gargantuan.

"I hope for your sake that you have something here," Sharp said without ever turning his eyes from the dark screen.

Adam didn't reply.

The familiar voice called out. "Live in five . . . four . . . three . . . two . . . one . . ." They were back on the air.

"Welcome back to a very special edition of *Sharpy Speaks Out*. When we last went to commercial break, Mr. Reece promised to show proof of an alleged conspiracy relating to the assassination attempt on Senator Shoemaker. Is it fair to say that you've even suggested the senator may well have been involved in this plot?" He turned an accusing eye to Adam.

"Yes, sir, I believe that's fair. Although again, remember this is just one man's opinion. Let's allow the audience to decide for themselves, shall we?"

Bob Sharp shook his head in continued disbelief. "On that note, let's play the disk." He motioned to someone off camera.

The television screen rolled briefly with flickering horizontal frames before settling to a steady picture. The scene was of Senator Shoemaker during the presidential debate. Bob Sharp, Adam, and more than a dozen cameramen from various affiliates stared at the monitor with as much awe-inspiring fear as Moses had when looking at the burning bush.

The scene played out. . . .

"We are entering a new era," Senator Shoemaker began. "An era in which global awareness will be critical. My opponent would have you believe that the existing policies of isolationism are simply sound fiscal policies in which our tax dollars are not being wasted. After all, why worry about the affairs of what he recently referred to as 'insignificant little countries.'"

"I said no such thing!" Vice President Marino shouted.

"Yet you have supported abandoning intelligence gathering from third world countries, yes?"

"The administration feels that the value of such intelligence is—"

"Yes, yes, I know. Such intelligence gathering is not viewed as strategically important given the state of peace and stability abroad. Yada, yada, yada, ad nauseam. I have heard your arguments, Mr. Vice President, and frankly I find them rather lacking." The senator leaned heavily on the podium as if weary of the dialogue.

"In my twenty-four years in public office, I have never encountered a group of individuals with their heads buried so deeply in the sand. All around us we see acts of terrorism, scientific espionage, and government corruption. Does it not bother you personally that what is arguably the second-most powerful country on the planet is currently ruled by the equivalent of our mafia?"

Just then, the left side of the podium suddenly exploded into flying splinters of wood. The last image was of Senator Shoemaker being pushed to the ground by a mob of Secret Service agents.

Bob Sharp looked from the now-dark screen to Adam and back to the screen.

"Did I miss something?" he asked.

"Probably," Adam said in a calm voice.

"Then please tell me, because what I just saw has been run on every news show for over a week. Please tell me that little blurb is not your evidence." Sharp was clearly getting ready to go back on the offensive. This time nothing would stop him.

"Watch it again, but this time let me point something out."

"We will do no such thing," Sharp replied, turning the set off in disgust.

Adam leaned towards Sharp, whispering, "It will come out here or on someone else's watch. Remember, live-at-five."

Sharp stared viciously at Adam then clicked back on the television set. "I think to satisfy my audience, perhaps I should play it once again. That way there will be no doubt in the viewers' minds."

"I appreciate your indulgence," Adam said, this time loud enough for the microphone to pick up.

Within moments, the disk was playing again. As it neared the end, Adam said "Okay, slow it down here."

The frames began scrolling by with the senator's mouth moving in slow motion.

"Slower," Adam said to the unidentified man offscreen controlling the image. The screen slowed so that individual frames could be seen clicking by. When the image of the podium exploding first appeared, Adam said, "Okay, back it up to just a few frames."

The image moved in reverse with small incremental clicking steps.

"Okay, forward once again. Pay careful attention."

That was when Sharp saw it, and despite showmanship, grace, or just plain old boisterous arrogance, he brought his hand to his mouth in horror.

His opponent's legs were swept high into the air. The only thing that remained was the thud of his body striking the ground.

There it was . . . a simple involuntary flinch. Nothing remarkable by itself. Just the clenching of teeth, the sudden squinting of eyes, the gripping of the podium. It was indisputable. It was unexplainable. And unfortunately for Senator Shoemaker, it was too early.

An instant before the bullet tore through the podium, Shoemaker flinched. With that flinch, came the single undeniable conclusion . . . the senator knew exactly when the shot was coming.

Adam saw Sharp's realization, and nodded.

The match was officially over.

Chapter 23

The intercom on Betty Halloway's desk buzzed softly.

"Sir?" she said, pressing the small, red transmit button. It was uncommon for Mr. Reece to call for her. Typically, he would task her with things when he passed by on his way to meetings or when coming in or out of the office for the day.

"Betty, could you come in here for a minute?"

"On my way." Three clicks of her heels later, she stood before Mr. Reece's enormous alder wood desk.

Betty had always hated the desk personally. It seemed old-fashioned, not like Mr. Reece at all. He needed something more sleek and efficient. Of course, she'd kept her opinion to herself. They were excellent acquaintances, maybe even what some would call confidants, but definitely not venturing into the friendship realm. Succinctly put, Christmas presents were exchanged, but there were no quick pecks under the mistletoe.

"I need you to do something for me, actually two things," he said. "Both need to be kept it in confidence."

"Always, sir." Her interest was now piqued. It was not uncommon for her to handle company-sensitive paperwork or financial disclosures, but she'd never been asked explicitly to keep something in confidence. She could only assume the matter was personal in nature, and that was very uncharacteristic of Mr. Reece.

"The first is to find an old friend."

"His name, sir?"

"*Her* name is Janice Marino."

"The . . ." She wasn't sure how to ask without appearing nosey.

"Yes, that's right, the vice president's daughter. We went to school together. See if you can find her. Get me a number, and I'll handle it from there."

"Yes, sir. Is it okay if I say it's you who's looking for her?"

He considered the question. "That will be fine."

"I'll get right on it. And the other thing, sir?"

Mr. Reece sat back in his chair, his thoughts somewhere far away from the office. Betty waited without interrupting. After a few moments, his eyes cleared, and he sat forward. He had a strange sense of confidence and determination that she'd rarely seen in him. He had always possessed a strong professional drive, but this was something different. This was *purpose*.

"About twelve years ago, a young man was killed at Harvard. It was in October and shouldn't be too difficult to find in the papers. It was ruled a suicide by authorities. His name was Jiro Tanaka."

"Yes, sir, Jiro Tanaka. I have it." Betty scribbled the name down on her pad. "You would like me to bring you the newspaper clippings and police report detailing his death?" If it hadn't been for his earlier remarks about keeping things in confidence, she would've assumed this was simply some initial research into a wrongful death lawsuit. But he *had* used the words. Betty didn't think this was even remotely related to the law firm.

"No," he replied softly. "No newspapers. I need you to find his family."

Betty knew better than to probe into something that obviously troubled Mr. Reece. "Yes, sir," she said, turning to leave.

"Betty?"

She spun back around, alarmed by the sudden pain in his voice.

"Sir?"

He pulled an old white scarf draped over a small bronze statue on his desk. "Take this," he said.

Betty was confused. "What should I do with it?"

"Burn it."

* * *

The airport was alive with activity, passengers filing past the large tinted window in an endless procession. Elliot sat on a long blue sofa in the

Admiral's Lounge, a meeting area reserved for distinguished people or those who simply traveled too much. He glanced down at a slip of paper before checking the flight information monitor once more. It hadn't changed in the past two minutes. United Flight 1170 from Tokyo was arriving at this very moment.

"They'll be here in a minute," he said to the woman sitting beside him.

She had thick, curly blonde hair, a slender body, and a lightly creased but otherwise beautiful face. She sat with an inflexible stiffness, her hands clasped tightly in her lap, the thumbs working rapidly against each other.

"What are we going to say?" Janice Marino asked. Without waiting for a reply, she said, "I don't know if I can go through with this."

"I'm not sure what we're going to say, but we have to do this." Elliot's tone was deliberate but also compassionate.

She nodded. They'd been through it all several times before, each time arriving at the same conclusion. It was time to right the wrong they had committed so many years before.

"I'm afraid," she confessed. Then she reached out and grabbed his hand tightly in her own. Without warning, long streams of tears began to run down her face. "Terrified, really."

"Hey, hey," he said, leaning over and holding her. Elliot was surprised at how comfortable he was holding her in his arms after all this time. "It's going to be okay. I don't know what's going to happen, but it's going to be okay."

"How do you know that? We . . . we killed their boy. We killed him, Elliot. Then we . . . we . . ." She couldn't finish. "How can it ever be okay?" She was sobbing against his shoulder, clutching him closely now. "We have no right to ask for their forgiveness."

Elliot closed his eyes and for an instant was back at that fateful night sitting with Janice in the front seat of his Gremlin. It was cold and dark. And there was still pain, yes. But there was also something else. A chance to replace the sin with something that could be lived with . . . *sorrow*.

Not quite certain if he was acting in the present or simply in a memory of the past, he leaned close to her and kissed her on the temple. She laid her head against his shoulder, grateful for the closeness.

"Someone once told me that I was carrying this with me like a shadow," he said. "That I couldn't escape it. I don't think you can either, Janice."

She looked up, the flow of tears slowing. "A shadow?" she croaked out with confusion. Long black streaks of mascara scarred her otherwise flawless complexion.

Elliot smiled before breaking into a light laugh. "That was my reaction, too. He's a bit of a strange character."

She smiled, her eyes coming alive. She squeezed his hand, pulled her lips together tightly and nodded.

"Come on," Elliot said, standing. "Our guests have arrived."

* * *

Cold rain drizzled over Randall Walker's dark, chiseled features. His powerful lungs forced damp air in and out with the rhythm of a locomotive steam engine, his pulse throbbing with a soft cadence against the side of his neck. The gray sweatshirt he wore slowly grew darker as large patches of sweat welcomed the fresh rain.

Glancing up at the clouds, he saw a smoky mass of thick rolling thunderheads moving his way. He picked up the pace, hoping to beat the worst of the rain. It was a pace most couldn't follow. But Randall wasn't even beginning to run at his potential. No, he would save that for the track meet next week. This was just one of the many training runs to help keep his body limber and accustomed to the pain that only dedicated runners learn to endure.

Rural Route 17 was a desolate place. The road was riddled with patches of wildflowers and weeds poking through thick cracks in the pavement. The shoulders were overgrown with an almost impenetrable collage of briars, bushes, and ominous trees. Randall felt no discomfort at being so alone. It was the solitude that he enjoyed most. Route 17 was his place. A forgotten five-mile stretch that at one time had ended in a lover's lookout. Now it was slowly being taken back by nature, becoming a refuge for squirrels and deer.

As Randall came around a sharp bend in the road, he was surprised to see more people than he'd ever encountered on the path before. During his many runs down the peaceful roadway, he'd seen other people only twice. The first of which had been another single runner, and on the other occasion, it had been a small group of Boy Scouts out for a day hike.

Now before him were four people and a dark sedan that looked as out of place on this forgotten road as an alien spacecraft. Randall had always suspected that with a bit of careful navigation to avoid potholes and fallen trees, the road was still physically passable. The real question was why. Why would anyone move the large rusted sign that proclaimed the road closed and bump and bang their way two miles up an old deserted route?

The group was still fifty or more yards in front of him, but he saw that there were two couples. One pair was Caucasian, looking to be in their mid-thirties. The man's white button-up shirt and the lady's pressed slacks and blouse marked them as at least upper middle-class. The other two were significantly older, perhaps in their sixties. Their olive skin and dark black hair announced their Asian heritage even at a distance. All stood without umbrellas, evidently willing to endure the soft drizzle.

As Randall drew nearer, the four moved away from the sedan and into the center of the road. The entire group seemed oblivious to him. The younger well-dressed man was speaking, although with the noise of light rain, Randall couldn't quite make out the words. The man's wife stood quietly by his side with a single hand resting lightly on his arm as if for support. The Asian couple both stared at the gentleman with great intensity. Every few seconds, the older man would bow his head slightly, acknowledging what was being said. The old woman remained stiff.

Passing just a few yards from the group, Randall heard only a single sentence that the Caucasian man spoke. The words caused him to look to the face of the Asian woman, their eyes meeting for only an instant. In her stare, he found a disturbing blend of emotions, horror . . . sadness . . . hatred. Randall knew immediately that he'd unfairly intruded on her privacy. To see such raw pain mixed with indescribable anger brought a fresh urgency to his steps.

Randall's feet moved faster and faster, until he found himself hurling down the trail at a full run. But the pain in the old woman's eyes chased him like a relentless Nazgul. Chased him all the way home and into his shower. Chased him even into his dreams that night. And in those dreams, he heard the man's words played over and over.

"This is where we killed your son."

Chapter 24

Six Years Earlier—Sendai, Japan

The ground moved beneath Adam's feet. It was as if someone had suddenly turned on a tremendous washing machine buried deep in the earth. Having been in Japan for over three years, he'd grown accustomed to minor earthquakes. They are as much a part of Japan as the beautiful *sakura*, cherry blossoms. Fortunately, they usually lasted only a few seconds and caused little damage. He, along with the other judo students, steadied himself, waiting for the tremors to pass.

Pictures of honored guests and political leaders lining the dojo walls began to rattle. One by one they popped themselves free of their supports and crashed to the floor. The crossbeam timber ceiling began to creak as if the Greek Titan Cronus were testing his weight on it. Students began to look to one another, their faces betraying concern. Never before had they heard such noises.

The trembling escalated to a more violent shaking, sending people stumbling to every corner of the studio as they searched for support at the walls. A loud moan rose up from the floor as an uncontrolled force slowly built, like a huge pressure cooker preparing to release its steam.

Adam reached out to steady an older man standing near him who had fallen to one knee. The man forced a smile and mouthed a word of thanks, "*Domo.*"

A tremendous *crack* sounded as one of the overhead beams split from unimaginable torque. Students in its path dove to the side avoiding the huge splinters of wood and plaster that crashed to the padded floor.

With a tone of desperation, Matsumoto yelled, "Out! To the street, go!"

Everyone stumbled toward a small door, the only way in or out of Matsumoto's one room dojo. Struggling for balance himself, Adam helped those around him as they tripped and fell, fighting their way to the exit.

As Adam reached the door, another deafening crash sounded, this time coming up from below. The center of the room had split open, ripping the canvas mat, the floor, and even the joists beneath. Matsumoto had been thrown to the far side of the gulf along with three students.

With the structure now compromised, chunks of the ceiling and walls began to fall, each thundering violently to the floor. With each collapse, huge plumes of white Sheetrock dust puffed high into the air. Matsumoto and the other three disappeared in the cloud of dust and debris.

"Sensei!" Adam yelled. He could barely hear his own words through the roar of the room.

Adam quickly shoved the final two students out the door then turned back and reentered the dojo. Struggling to keep his footing, he made his way to within a few feet of the chasm that had opened in the floor. He could see the dark, wet soil spreading out before him as Mother Earth opened her womb. To his left, the entire floor had collapsed, and to his right, only a small bridge remained.

"Matsumoto-sensei!" he shouted again.

"*Hai!*" came Matsumoto's voice.

"Move to the north, and follow the wall across!"

"*Hai!*"

Careful not to get too close to the huge breach, Adam shuffled to the small unbroken section of floor that still joined them. The walls continued to bend and crack, spitting pockets of dust and splinters into the room. With every explosion, small pieces pelted him like the sting of angry hornets.

Adam placed one hand on the wall and felt it shudder beneath his palm. There was little doubt that the entire building would collapse soon. He braced himself and reached with his other hand into the cloud of dust.

"Reach out and grab my hand!" he cried.

Almost immediately he felt fingers groping at his hand and wrist. He got a solid grip of *gi* and exposed skin and pulled hard. The youngest of the students emerged from the dust as Adam half tossed him into the room.

"Go!" he shouted.

Half running, half crawling, the young man scrambled to the door.

"Now another!" he yelled, reaching into the powdery mist again.

As Adam grabbed for the hand of the second student, a large overhead light suddenly broke free from the ceiling. It smashed into the back of his neck, sending him to his knees, teetering on the brink of the chasm.

He screamed, tears spilling out as he fought to deal with the terrible pain. The halogen bulb burned against his neck, blistering the skin like bubbling caramel. He stood, hurling the lamp off his back.

Once again, he reached along the wall and found a student's outstretched hand. Before he could secure his grip, the student panicked and began to claw his way across. Adam was afraid they would both lose their balance and fall into the earthy pit only a few feet away. He turned away from the wall and encircled the student in a powerful bear hug. Before the student could react, Adam dove forward, sending them both sprawling into the room.

As soon as they came to rest, the student pulled free and began crawling to the door.

Adam quickly returned to reach once again into the dust-filled cloud. A hand was already waiting, but as he fumbled to get a grip, the ground between them suddenly collapsed. Adam felt the student fall, his entire weight suddenly dangling from his grip.

Adam fought to keep hold, first dropping to a knee, and then lying prone with his upper body dangling into the muddy rift that had opened. An audible *pop* was followed by a terrible burning pain as his shoulder dislocated. He closed his eyes and squeezed even harder, refusing to let go.

Understanding that there was no way Adam could pull him up, the student started to climb his arm like a dangling rope. With each tug, Adam screamed in pain. Eventually, the student was able to reach the edge of the floor and pull himself up into the room. He patted Adam affectionately on the back before scrambling away.

Adam didn't look back to see if he'd made it to the door. His only concern now was rescuing Matsumoto. He could no longer see a way to reach across, and even if there were, he wasn't sure he could pull Matsumoto across with his shoulder dislocated. Out of fear and desperation, he turned and smashed his shoulder into the wall. He cried out in agony as the shoulder forced itself back into the socket.

"The floor has collapsed!" he shouted, the rumbling of the room so deafening he wasn't sure Matsumoto could still hear him.

He heard a shout. "Move! I'm coming across!"

Adam backed up several feet and stood ready. He understood that Matsumoto's only choice was to try to leap across the divide. It didn't seem possible, but both now recognized that there was no other way.

From the dusty cloud came a figure hurtling through the air like a ghostly apparition. He dove head first, clearing the chasm by about a foot. As he hit the floor, he tucked and rolled forward, eventually stopping himself with a powerful slap. Beautifully executed, even for a judo master.

Adam stumbled forward and helped him to his feet. Leaning on each other for support, both men stumbled toward the door. The floor and walls continued to crack all around them with increasing fury.

Suddenly Adam felt Matsumoto's grip weaken and then drop away. He turned back thinking that perhaps he'd tripped. What he saw was horrifying. A long metal electrical conduit had separated from the ceiling and speared Matsumoto. The twisted tube of aluminum, still connected at one end to the ceiling, now completely penetrated his chest.

A dark, wet patch began spreading across Matsumoto's white *gi* as blood seeped out.

"No," Adam cried, dropping down beside him.

Matsumoto brought fingers to his chest and gently felt the conduit where it met his skin. He closed his eyes and said, "I am honored to have you with me."

"Save your strength," Adam said. "I'll get you out of here." He studied the terrible puncture wound to see how he might free Matsumoto without killing him in the process. There had to be a way. There was always a way. He believed that with all his heart.

As if reading his mind, Matsumoto said, "No." He coughed, and a spray of blood sprinkled his lips. "This is my karma, as it is yours."

"Sensei, please no. Don't do this."

"Such things are not to be denied." Matsumoto's face grew pained as the color slowly drained from him.

"What can I do, teacher? I want to help you. Please tell me how."

Matsumoto stared into Adam's eyes. "There are two things you can do for me." His voice was uneven and raspy.

"Anything."

"First, remember that in this world, there is good, and there is evil. Of this, I am sure. Promise me that you will never forget your place in this struggle."

Adam swallowed hard, feeling tears welling at the corner of his eyes. "I promise."

Matsumoto smiled and closed his eyes. For a moment, Adam thought he had passed away, but then Matsumoto's body shuddered, and he looked at him once more.

"The other thing you can do is to help me . . ." Matsumoto began, but broke off coughing suddenly. This time he spit out a mouthful of blood. His eyes were only half open when he finally continued. "I want you to help me die . . . die like my samurai ancestors."

Adam didn't understand what Matsumoto was suggesting. "How?"

"Adam-*san*, to enter the afterlife as a warrior, I must die at the hand of another man." He coughed again, blood spraying out in a fine mist.

In all the time he'd known him, this was the first time Matsumoto had ever used his real name. Until now, he had always been "Cowboy." Now as he looked at Matsumoto, Adam felt the tremendous friendship that had developed between them. Grief threatened to overwhelm him.

"Will you honor me in this way?" Matsumoto choked.

Not knowing what else to do, Adam simply nodded.

Matsumoto smiled, and tears came to his eyes. He slowly reached up and grabbed the lapel of Adam's *gi*. He pulled weakly as if the two were entering combat. In a very soft voice, he said, "I will look for a way through the darkness to find you again. Until then, goodbye, *tomodachi*, friend."

Not fully aware of what he was doing, Adam crossed his hands and reached down to grab just inside the collar of his teacher's *gi*. Then with a gentle scissoring action, he slowly drew the fabric tight, cutting off Matsumoto's breathing.

Matsumoto took one last look at Adam before closing his eyes.

In just a few seconds, Adam felt Matsumoto's heartbeat briefly falter and finally stop. He lowered his teacher gently to the ground. It was only then that he realized that the room had grown still. The ceiling no longer fell. The ground no longer shook. It was as if the earthquake had come for Matsumoto. Both had passed together.

Rain began to fall. Large drops splashed their way through the exposed ceiling to fall on Adam's face.

Chapter 25

Adam walked briskly through the airport. His pace wasn't motivated by being late for anything, just that airports make people walk fast. He carried a thick canvas bag with enough clothing for several days. Other than his trademark black duffel, little else about him was now recognizable.

Contrary to the wigs, bushy mustaches, and putty scars usually associated with Inspector Clouseau-style disguises, he'd found that going unnoticed usually required only a few simple alterations. People generally distinguish one another using physical characteristics . . . the color of a person's eyes, the style of their hair, the shape of their mouth and nose. That along with simple mannerisms like the way they walk or hold their shoulders. To alter how people saw him, Adam knew he had to change just a few of the most identifiable characteristics.

He now swaggered confidently down the long airport walkway wearing a black Stetson cowboy hat, a tight pair of Wrangler jeans, a bolo tie with a turquoise clasp, and a pair of black cowboy boots. His chin was covered with the trace of a thin goatee.

As he neared gate B14, he slowed, and then stopped. He could see a hundred or more people milling about the international terminal. For a brief moment, he considered turning around and leaving the airport, but his feet wouldn't listen to reason. The time for taking the road well traveled had passed. He resumed his walk.

As soon as he entered the gate area, he saw her. She sat straight and tall, hands resting on a newspaper in her lap. She wore a pair of faded blue jeans and an oversized gray Colorado University sweatshirt. Adam stood slightly to one side, and with the crowd of people at the gate, she hadn't yet seen him. He stood there for nearly a minute, studying her like a particularly beautiful sunrise.

As if sensing the admiring eyes, her head slowly turned as she surveyed her surroundings. Despite the disguise, she found him effortlessly. Their eyes met, but neither one moved. After a final moment of deliberation, he smiled and walked toward her. Her face lit up with indescribable happiness, and it warmed his heart to know he could give that to anyone.

As he approached, she stood and tossed the paper onto the seat behind her. Without saying a word, they embraced.

"I didn't think you'd come," she whispered in his ear.

"It was touch and go."

She leaned back to look at his face but didn't pull away. "So, why did you?" Her words were not unkind, only curious.

"I already told you."

"Tell me again," she said with an impish grin.

He looked deep into her eyes. "Because I love you with all my heart. All my soul. You are yin; I am yang. Only when we're together do I feel whole."

Her eyes began to well with tears, and she smiled from ear to ear. "Oh, you're good."

"I am, aren't I," he flirted.

"And it rhymed to boot," she giggled.

"That's me, the poet who didn't know it."

"You know that thing about yin and yang. It's quite fitting."

"How so?"

"Think about it. I'm the dark. A villain serving only the reaper. You're the light. A paladin for just causes. Complete opposites."

"Yet a piece of each lies within the other," Adam said, seeing where she was heading.

"If we can just maintain the delicate balance, we'll stay in harmony."

"And if not?"

She looked away, pretending to be interested in an overhead flight monitor. "Then I'll probably have to kill you," she whispered.

Adam felt the weight of worry she carried. It was heavy enough for them both to take turns. "There's been enough death. Let's fill our lives with happy things."

"Like sex?" she grinned, returning to their moment.

"I love that you're so frisky," he said, pinching her lightly on the bottom. "But I was talking about love, honesty, compassion, romance . . . pure things."

She seemed taken back for a moment until she saw the traces of a grin on his face. "Liar," she said, smirking.

He chuckled. "All right, you got me. It was sex from the get-go."

She bumped his hat up slightly. "I'm hoping this new look is a passing fad."

"You don't like it?"

"Sweetie, you could have come in a burlap sack and Roman sandals. It wouldn't have made a bit of difference. Showing up was all I was looking for."

"Burlap chafes my thighs."

She punched him softly in the arm. "You caused quite a mess last night," she said, gesturing to the paper behind her.

"It's in the papers already?" Adam asked, knowing it had to be.

"I think it's a safe bet that it's the headline of every major newspaper in the country," she said, retrieving the paper. The headline read: *Talk Show Guest Exposes Shoemaker's Duplicity.*

He took a quick look at the paper then tossed it back onto the seat.

"Just what you needed," she said, "more publicity."

"I do have a way with people. The crowd of media sharks mobbing the hotel this morning convinced me that I needed to go incognito for a bit."

"You weren't the only one to find fame last night. Poor old Senator Shoemaker. I bet you're not on his Christmas list anymore."

"I guess not," Adam agreed. "I suppose he's denying everything."

"Of course, but I'm afraid his toast is buttered."

"Can you tell me how this is going to end?"

She smiled a sad smile but didn't answer.

"Is he going to end up wearing cement overshoes at the bottom of the Potomac?"

"If I said probably, would it bother you?"

He thought about her words. Adam felt certain that Senator Shoemaker was at least partially to blame for the deaths of General Livingston, Robert Greene, and the Sativa sisters. It wasn't completely clear just how high up he was in the decision making, but he sure as hell had made the decision to benefit from their murders.

"Not really," he answered. "I just wonder about the other people involved. The people pulling his strings. Will they ever see the inside of a courtroom over this?"

"Sweetie, no one will ever see the inside of a courtroom. People will disappear in the dead of night or choke on poached eggs at breakfast. It will never go to trial. Some things are outside the law."

Adam nodded. He didn't like it, but he also understood that he had to accept it. As Bob Sharp had put it, it was "truth."

"What about you?" he asked. "Aren't you in hot water for the way things went down? I take it you were supposed to steer me toward Marino."

"That's true," she replied. "But it's all spilled milk now, so retribution seems unlikely. Besides, I'm not convinced your actions were completely unexpected."

Adam didn't like the sound of that at all. "What do you mean?"

She only shrugged.

"Shoemaker was behind the assassinations." Adam paused. "He was, wasn't he?"

She shrugged again.

That simple action troubled him more than words ever could have. A few moments earlier, he'd had everything figured out. Now he wasn't sure of anything.

"It all fits," he argued. "He had to be behind it. He clearly knew they were going to shoot at him. He was the one who 'found' the Sativa sisters. He was the one benefiting from the entire affair."

"He was involved," she said, patting Adam's hand like she would a soft puppy. "No question that he was working to discredit the vice president and in turn win the White House."

"But . . ."

"But nothing. At this point, I don't know much more than you do. I think you have it pretty much right, but remember, I've seen a lot of things. All I'm saying is that sometimes all the players are involved in one way or another."

He thought about her words. "You think Marino and Shoemaker might both have been involved?"

She shrugged a final time. "I've seen cases where both sides were being played just in case things went the wrong direction. Whoever ends up winning is placed in a position where he feels indebted. It just depends on how many moves ahead everyone was playing."

"No one could have known how things were going to go down," he asserted. "They couldn't have predicted that I'd expose Shoemaker."

"Maybe not, but these people adapt. They have fallback plans. And fallbacks for those fallbacks."

"But they couldn't have known what I'd do. Hell, I didn't even know what I was going to do until the last minute."

"You're probably right," she said with a thin smile.

Adam wasn't convinced. The seed of doubt had been planted in fertile soil.

"How about we just let it go," she offered. "If you completely foiled the bad guys, that's great. If there's still a tiny bit of deception left undiscovered, let's just leave it that way. As a friend of mine used to say, the sun will rise again tomorrow."

"Hmph," he muttered.

"Either way, it won't hurt for us to get out of the country for a while," she said, waving two airline tickets lightly in front of him.

Adam nodded, still uncomfortable with her suggestions. He looked down into her beautiful eyes and realized she was right. It really didn't matter at this point. No one could possibly right all the wrongs of the world. He'd have to settle for correcting the few that pissed him off the most. He shook it off.

"Before I take another step, I need to know something."

"What?" she asked.

"I need a name," he answered. "It sort of lacks the desired effect to say, 'I love you, *blank.*'"

She grinned. "You know my name, silly."

"Oh?"

"I'm Lara."

Adam furrowed his eyebrows in confusion. "Come again."

She held up her ticket for him to inspect. The name on its face was Lara Turner. "I thought it would be easier if I just adopted the name you're used to. Men are so simpleminded." She winked.

"You know you'll probably go to hell for taking that poor girl's name."

"Sweetie, if there's any justice in the world, the devil already has box office seats reserved for me."

"He better be ready for a fight."

She looked into his eyes. "What a thing to say. I'm touched, really."

"I'm as loyal as a golden retriever. You know that."

She leaned in close, laying her head against his chest. "Yes, that I do."

Their tenderness was interrupted by the grainy mechanical voice of the overhead speaker. *Delta Airlines now invites all first-class and platinum members to board at this time through gate B14 for nonstop service to Paris.*

"That's us," she said, pulling away from him and grabbing up a small carry-on bag.

Adam extended an arm to her. "Shall we?"

Lara beamed like a schoolgirl as she slid her arm into his. "I can't believe it," she said, as they walked toward the ticket checkpoint.

"What's that?"

"I've finally found my very own hero." To emphasize the point, she cuddled up against his side.

He shook his head. "Lara, I know enough to understand that you can take care of yourself."

"True," she answered. "But a girl still wants to be with a man who will occasionally walk against the wind for her."

"Well said."

They showed their tickets and moved passed a stocky blue-suited stewardess standing guard at the doorway.

As he walked down the jetway, Adam recalled the promise that he had made to Matsumoto-sensei. He had sworn never to forget his place in the struggle between good and evil. Walking arm in arm with a known killer certainly seemed to put that promise into question. But he consoled himself that Matsumoto also understood that love was to be cherished above all else. There would certainly be consequences of his decision. A battle between good and evil would ultimately arrive; sides would have to be chosen. Adam was confident that in the end he would fight on the side of justice, even if it pitted him against the woman he loved.

As for Lara, she was bouncing with excitement, seemingly unaware of Adam's reflection. "Who would have thought things would have ended this way," she giggled. "I'm going to show you such a good time, you'll never want to get rid of me."

"Never is a long time. What makes you think you'll still want me around?"

"My love runs deep, Adam," she said playfully. "It lasts forever."

Adam considered her words. To him, and maybe even to her, love had transcended right and wrong. There was no turning back now for either of them, and he hoped that their love would indeed prove as timeless as the ancient pyramids.

"So does mine, Lara," he whispered. "So does mine." Adam said the words so softly that he didn't see how she could possibly have heard them. But as he felt the grip tighten on his arm, he suspected that maybe, just maybe, she had.

Chapter 26

The hot dogs were just about ready. Bill Tyler liked his dogs with the lambskins blistered and brown, but definitely not burnt. He reached down with long metal tongs and carefully rolled the franks over one by one. Then he flipped several large black-pepper crusted porterhouse steaks. Tyler stood shamelessly wearing a knee-length smock, a white chef's hat, a pair of snakeskin boots, some old blue jeans, and a T-shirt proclaiming "Fat Texan Inside." It was all in good fun.

His two dozen guests were gathered comfortably around the large pool, chatting about the insidious place Washington had become as of late. It was all anyone seemed to talk about these days.

"Phone, dear," his wife, Karisha, called from the kitchen. She held a bowl of homemade potato salad in one hand and waved a cordless handset with the other.

Tyler looked to his oldest son, Lamar, who was playing chess with a cute girl just beginning to show signs of puberty. He gave his son a quick nod. Lamar, having recently turned eleven, was quick to pick up on his father's gestures.

"Ah, for my dad," he said, excusing himself from the game and moving to retrieve the phone from his mother. A few seconds later, he passed the handset to his father.

Before his son could get away, Tyler reached out and gently grabbed his shoulder. "I didn't know you liked chess, Lamar."

Lamar turned so his back was to the girl and grinned. "She's creaming me," he whispered, "but I'm beginning to see why people like this game."

"That's my boy," he laughed, rubbing his son's head.

Lamar returned to his game, and Tyler turned his attention to the phone.

"Hello," he said, still carefully monitoring the delicate hot dogs.

"Bill, this is Joe Marino. How the hell are you?"

"Hello Mr. Vice President. I'm very well, thank you. Having a little party over here. We've got hot dogs, steaks, and all the fixings if you care to stop by." Tyler's home in Texas was understandably a place Marino had never found the occasion to visit.

"Now that does sound delicious. Once things slow down, I may take you up on that. As you know, ever since that little talk show revelation, this place has been turned upside down. Congress is calling for an inquiry; the FBI is probing into every dark orifice; and I'm afraid it's going to get worse before it gets better. Worst of all, I think Dick is in real trouble."

Tyler smiled. He knew where this was going but was polite enough to play along. "I'd have to agree with you on that. If half of what they're saying is true, Senator Shoemaker is likely to be in jail long after my kids are old and gray."

"You and Dick were fairly close, weren't you?" Marino probed.

Not at all surprised by the question, Tyler answered, "We've shared ideas on a few occasions."

"Rumor has it he even asked you to be his running mate. Anything to that?"

"We discussed joining forces," Tyler answered. "He said we'd have the election in the bag. After what happened, I'm glad I hesitated to accept the offer."

"I would imagine so." The phone sat silent as Marino hunted for the right words. Finally, he said, "Bill, you know why I'm calling."

"Something more than a Sunday afternoon chat?" He began to remove the hot dogs and steaks from the grill, placing them on a large serving platter. His guests were hungry, so he'd have to wrap this up with the vice president. Life was all about priorities.

Marino laughed. "All right then. You're going to make me say it. I want you to be the next vice president of the United States. My right-hand guy. How does that sit with you?"

"I'm flattered, Mr. Vice President. Really, I am." Tyler was careful not to answer the question. No matter how well scripted things were, it was best not to appear too eager. Reluctance always led to sweeter deals.

"Don't be flattered; be a part of my team. With your strong independent base and the mainstream vote heading my way now that

Dick's . . . retired, there's no stopping us. Think about it, Bill. The two of us could be running the country before the year is through." Then as an afterthought, he added, "We could do a lot of good."

"It is tempting, but you and I . . . we've always had different agendas. You know that."

"Then we'll work through them," Marino countered quickly. "I know what causes you champion, and I'll give you leeway to make those things happen. You have my word on it."

Tyler pulled the last steak from the barbeque. "I'm going to hold you to that, Mr. Vice President."

"You'll do it then?" Marino's voice had grown excited.

"Why don't we finalize this thing in the morning? We can call a press conference to announce our plans. What do you say?"

"I say, hell yes! I'll get my people to work the details. Now go enjoy your hot dogs."

Tyler leaned down and took a deep whiff of his handiwork. "Oh, I will."

* * *

Bill Tyler sat sipping from a glass of warm brandy, his feet propped up on his desk. Today had been quite a day, the result of a great deal of hard work.

There came a soft knock on the door to his study. He rose slowly, moved to the door, and unlocked it. Karisha stood holding their youngest daughter.

"Sorry to bother you, but the kids are waiting for you to tuck them in."

Tyler smiled and gave his wife a kiss. "I'll be there in a minute to give out good-night sugars. I've one final thing to do."

"Okay, but come to bed before long," she said, giving him a wink they both understood.

"I will," he promised.

Tyler closed and relocked the door before returning to his desk. Before him lay an open laptop computer already signed onto the Internet. He turned his attention to the screen.

Pecos Bill: You out there, Doc?
The Doctor: I'm here. How can I help you, sir?
Pecos Bill: I've got a little roping for you.
The Doctor: I thought you might.

Pecos Bill: You know that fellow getting all the bad publicity?

The Doctor: Yes.

Pecos Bill: I hear he has a weak ticker. Be a doggone shame if it just gave out on him.

The Doctor: I could see that happening with all the stress he's under.

Pecos Bill: Well, how about you just see that it does.

The Doctor: Consider it done.

Pecos Bill: That's what I've always liked about working with cowboys like you. Things like this, they just get done.

Tyler closed the chat room, logged off the Internet, and powered down his computer. With Senator Shoemaker all but taken care of, things could move ahead without risk. The senator didn't know enough to unravel recent events, but he could still cause problems.

The trade he'd originally been approached with was quite simple. Shoemaker was to begin making public statements supporting Tyler and eventually recruit him as his vice presidential running mate. In exchange, powerful, unnamed people would ensure that they received the Republican Party nomination.

Once he'd agreed to the deal, additional demands were slowly added. This included ducking a well-placed bullet on the night of the debate. The arrangement was of course now null and void, and since everything had been done through third parties, there was no evidence to directly tie Tyler to the deal. Still, the potential introduction of his name into the scandal was dangerous. Besides, he'd always believed it best to tidy things up.

Leaning back into his favorite chair, Tyler took in the musky aroma of humidors filled with Cuban cigars. On a wall across the study hung an artist's rendition of the mythical cowboy, Pecos Bill, riding atop a powerful cyclone. Texas children still shared stories of the larger-than-life folk hero. A man who'd been raised by coyotes, taught gophers to dig postholes, and killed rattlesnakes by feeding them mothballs soaked in red pepper and nitroglycerin, Pecos Bill was a giant of a man, someone who could overcome any obstacle, no matter how impossible it might seem. Equally at home bagging buffalo in the southwestern wild as he was planning a cross-country railroad in a stuffy boardroom.

In many ways, Tyler considered himself the modern day equivalent of Pecos Bill. He too had been given a nearly impossible task with little more than red peppers and a bottle of nitroglycerin with which to accomplish it. There had been a few rattlesnakes along the way, but in the end, everything had fallen into place.

Before the year was through, he would be the nation's next vice president. At this point in the game, that was all his constituents in the Diadem had been after. The organization understood that it required patience and careful maneuvering to ultimately place one of their own in the Oval Office. With the events of the past month, that maneuvering had now begun.

It was as Tyler had said many times, "The presidency can't be bought. It has to be earned."